Bears and Eagles

R.P. Wollbaum

Jessy

For all the hard owd most
excellent work with the
i kids For all those many
years

Aug 6/ 2015

Copyright 2013 by R.P. Wollbaum

ISBN: 978 0 9940249 1 6

First Published by the Author in Canada 2013

www.bearsandeagles.com

Contents

Chapter One

"What have we here?" the raider asked his comrade as they slowly rode around the corner from the village they had just left in smoking ruins.

"Seven farmers with puny bayonets on their rifles; look, some of them are trembling," his comrade replied, wiping the blood spattered from his last victim off his sword wrist. "Look, their buddies have taken their horses too far to the rear. When they run, it will be easy pickings for us. Come on, line up; we'll hit them after they fire and run them over like usual. Stupid farm kids, these Russians never learn, all brawn no brain."

Andreas, at the right side of his little line, watched the twenty blood-soaked horses and riders assemble into two lines of ten, knee to knee. With large smiles on their faces, they began to ride toward Andreas, lances coming down, so that it looked like each one was pointed straight at him alone.

Not saying a word, Andreas turned a half turn to the right and brought his rifle to his shoulder, and his six troopers followed his lead. They might have time for a second shot; after that, they would kneel down, propping rifle butts on the ground, bayonets slanted at horses' chests and hope like hell they would survive.

"They will charge after the first volley; load fast, shoot again, then go to a knee," Andreas said, barely able to keep the bile from coming into his mouth.

"Wait!" Andreas said as the raiders spurred to a trot, horse hooves vibrating the ground, the sound of hooves and the jangle of bits and swords and lances beginning to overwhelm the senses. He felt the sweat running down his back and could hear one of his troopers lose his breakfast as his vision became full of fast-approaching horses and riders.

"Wait!" he said again, noticing one of the troopers shifting his feet. "If you run, they will kill us all."

A bead of sweat ran down his forehead and trickled down to the end of his nose. His hands began to tremble slightly and he began to see the blood smeared on the raiders' faces and along the horses' sides. The blood of villagers, innocent farmers just trying to make a life for themselves and their families, and his heart went cold and still as he sighted on the center of his man's chest.

"Ready, fire!" he yelled.

The seven rifles spit out their little volley and seven saddles emptied, bodies flung to the rear of saddles as .50 caliber bullets tore through them. The rest of the raiders spurred to a gallop; Andreas grabbed a cartridge from his chest loop and fumbled with the bolt, slamming it open and shoving the cartridge in the breach, then slapped the bolt shut.

Shit, this is going to be close, he thought, leveling his rifle on the next rider and hearing a trooper curse as he dropped a cartridge through nervous fingers to the ground. Blocking everything out but the sight of the next horse riding down on him at full gallop, the rider's blood-streaked arm holding a lance at Andreas's chest, he pulled the trigger and went to one knee, jamming the rifle butt into the ground as hard as he could, holding the rifle with both hands, the bayonet at a forty-five degree angle to the ground. The horse he had just shot drove its chest into the ground five yards in front of him, cart-wheeling its rider to land on his head in front of Andreas, breaking his neck. Looking wildly around, the next rider, with sword upraised, was thundering down on him and he began to pray, when his ears heard the bark of rifles firing from the trees bordering the trail he was blocking. This rider, as had his comrades before him, was blasted from the saddle as a bullet caught him under the upraised sword arm.

In seconds, it was all over. Andreas sunk down to his heels in the dust allowing his head to drop onto the forearms still holding the rifle, butt rammed into the ground. The smell of gunpowder in his nostrils and the sound of his heart drumming, almost drowning out the screams of wounded horses and men and the smell of blood. The stories never tell you of this, he thought, trying to still the shaking of his hands and the urge to vomit.

"Jesus Christ, Andy," said Johann, walking from the trees, his bayonet tipped rifle pointed at the fallen raiders. "You left that almost too late."

Hearing more hooves approaching, Andreas stood up looking around and fumbled for another cartridge, fearing more raiders were approaching to catch them all in the open. But it was the mounted troopers he had left to pursue or attack any of the raiders that made it out of the ambush.

"Take a section and put the wounded horses out of their misery, Johann," he said. "And have that mounted squadron head to the village to see if there is anything we can do."

6

"What about the wounded raiders?" Johann asked.

"Any of them that are minor, bring to me; the others, don't waste bullets on them, we don't have that many to waste," Andreas said, walking up to a screaming raider holding his intestines in his hands. He quickly jammed his bayonet in the man's neck, twisted it sideways and withdrew it, walking away as the man choked on the blood from the wound.

The horse handlers came up and Andreas collected his mount, Bartholomew, mounted, and, slinging his rifle on his back, bayonet still attached, collected five troopers and trotted toward the village.

"Looks like they herded them all into the church and set it on fire, Sergeant," the corporal of the troopers in the village said in Russian. "We haven't spotted any survivors, and I have just sent a few troopers in pairs to search the immediate area for any."

Christ! Bloody animals, Andreas thought, they killed everything chickens, dogs, cows, pigs.

"Oh my God," he said, slipping into his native German. A young mother was sprawled on the ground, legs spread eagled, skirt ripped open, and her throat cut; her young baby, head caved in, lying beside her.

"That's not all," the trooper said, pointing at the village priest crucified to a house door with kitchen knives through his wrists and ankles, his genitals stuck in his mouth.

"Alright," Andreas said, switching to Russian. "Gather up all the bodies you can find, put them in that barn over there, and set it on fire; we don't have time to

7

bury them. Get another group together and grab any food you can find."

"Right, Brother, we have three prisoners for you and six decent horses to add to the remounts," Johann said in German as he and the rest of the squadron rode up from the ambush site. "Christ, what a mess; oh shit, Karl! Get off the damn horse before you puke next time; you never seen a slaughter house before?"

"Easy, Johann," Andreas said. "I'm having trouble myself. Send three troopers to Vacilly to report on all this and another five to track the rest of the raiders; hopefully, we can catch the main group before they disappear on us."

The three prisoners were roughly dumped in front of Andreas who crossed his arms and stared down at them.

"What you think?" one of them said in heavily accented Russian. "You Russians no do same to us?"

"Russian troops maybe; my Cossacks, no," Andreas said. "I will give you one chance, and one chance only, to tell me who you are and where you come from. If you do, I will treat your wounds and let you go. Tell your friends that."

Andreas took his rifle from his back, reached for a cartridge from a chest loop, and loaded it as the prisoner translated what Andreas had said.

One of the prisoners spat between Andreas's feet and yelled something in his own language, and Andreas slowly sighted on the man's forehead and pulled the trigger, putting a round hole in his forehead and spraying the other two prisoners with the blood and brains that blew out of the back of the man's head as the bullet exited.

"I don't have time to question you properly as you did with the priest," he said, calmly loading another round into the rifle. "You can tell me what I want to know and I will let you go, or not. I will find the rest of your group anyway."

"I tell them you were different, not to do this. We from Turkey," the prisoner said, his companion babbling beside him eyes wide. "We camp ten miles that way, bottom of ravine, small river runs through bottom, good camps spot."

"How many troopers?" Andreas asked.

"Two hundreds, maybe two hundreds fifty, we leave for home soon," the prisoner said. "I say, no do this; we have enough, we go home. Big shot greedy, no listen. Have twenty, thirty Russian womans for take to sell in camp."

"Johann!" Andreas said in German, "Give these two a horse, the worse one we have; no tack, only a bridle and no weapons, and let them loose."

"I give you four hours," Andreas said to the two men mounted bareback on the horse. "We catch you again, you die."

"You know those two are going to head straight for their camp?" Johann said.

"I'm counting on it," Andreas said. "Spread the food we gathered among the men, and let's get out of here. The smell is beginning to bother me."

9

Six hours later, the scouts returned verifying what the prisoners had told them, but that there were four hundred invaders, not two.

"Too late in the day to do anything now," Andreas said. "Make camp; I want to hit them at first light. Everyone care for weapons, and I will make a plan tonight. How high is the ravine and is it at their backs?" He asked as he removed his saddle, bedroll, and saddle bags from his horse and started brushing him down.

"It's about thirty feet high; they don't have any sentries posted on it, and we can get up the back easy," the scout said. "They are over confident, have big campfires burning; we should see them for miles. Tents are pitched around the campfires, horse lines are far away from camp, and what few sentries they have stay close to the fires. The river is shallow; you can walk across easy and it's about three hundred yards from camp."

"Alright, it's a full moon tonight and not cloudy," Andreas said. "Take seventy-five around midnight and curve around the back. I want you on top of that ravine by daybreak but do nothing until I do. Understand?"

"Sure, what are you going to do, and how will we know when to start?" the scout asked.

"I'm going to draw them to me and out into the open for you guys," Andreas said. "Get some grub and sleep; we start in four hours."

"Look at you, all high-and-mighty Sergeant," Johann said, handing over a tin plate with a steaming sausage and potato, with a tin cup of hot tea on it to Andreas. "No cooking or making horse lines or sentry duty for you. No, there you sit calmly cleaning your rifle thinking of the girl back home, I bet."

"As if, there is no way Mother will even let us look at a girl she hasn't chosen for us, and you know it," Andreas said.

"Maybe you, brother dear, you will be the landowner. I, on the other hand, am a free spirit," Johann said.

"I'll think about that when we get home, Johann, I just want to survive the next few weeks."

"He says, as he plans to attack four hundred well-armed Turks with a hundred young, dumb, half-trained Cossacks," Johann joked.

"We will let them see what they expect to see," Andreas said. "Then, we will hit them in the ass with our longer range and more accurate weapons. There is no way I am not going to try and do something to them for what they have done to all those poor farmers. Now, finish eating and get some sleep."

Andreas and Johann were positioned in front of the other twenty-three troopers stretched out in a single line across the river from the Turks' camp.

"Nice plan, Andy, bloody sun's going to be in our eyes," Johann said.

"Wake 'em up, bugler," Andreas said. "The sun will not be in our other guy's eyes, just the way I planned. Look, the sentry has finally spotted us. Dismount, form skirmish line, horses to the rear."

"Be careful of this one," the ex-prisoner said to his commander. "He is not like the other Russians and those rifles fire farther and faster than ours do."

"We will lose a few, but then we will be among them," the commander said. "They are only twenty-five, we are four hundred. Look, they lose twenty-five percent of their men taking horses to the rear, fools. Mount up, we attack now!"

"Let them mass together for their charge," Andreas said. "We fire the first volley at two hundred yards. We should get off three shots before they get near us."

"Look at them, they couldn't make it much easier for us," Johann said. "I don't even have to aim, just point the rifle into the middle of that mass; I'm going to hit something."

"Ya, probably hit two or three with one shot at this range," another trooper said as they all went down on one knee, loading the rifles and waiting for Andreas's word.

"That's it, you just keep coming, buddy," Andreas said, slamming the bolt shut on his rifle and bringing it to his shoulder.

I hope the other guys are in position or we are dead, he thought.

"Right, boys, nothing fancy," Andres said. "Point in the middle of the group and pull the trigger. One massed volley and then fire as fast as you can after. Ready, fire!"

The little volley emptied saddles, and horses went down as the .50 caliber bullets tore through flesh, horse and human; in some cases, hitting the soldier behind. The enemy was not prepared to be hit at that distance and began to mill about, finding ways around fallen animals and forming lines again when they were hit again by the reloaded line in front of them.

"Charge!" The Turkish commander said, sensing disaster, too late.

Seventy-five bullets hit their rear, as the Cossacks on the hill opened fire and horses and men fell screaming to the ground to be trampled by their comrades. A few Turks abandoned the charge, dismounted, and tried to return fire with dated muskets to no effect other than to spread more panic among their comrades, who now tried desperately to escape.

"One shot, one kill!" Andreas yelled out as the targets started to disperse, making it necessary to aim at individual riders. "Shit!" he said, reaching for another cartridge only to find his six chest loops empty.

"Bugler, ammo to the front!" As the bugle made the call, Andreas fumbled with the cartridge case on his belt, pulling another six-bullet package out and placing them on the ground in front of him, and began to shoot again.

Andreas later surmised that the mounted troopers coming at the gallop with the ammunition spooked the Turks into thinking they were being charged by more cavalry as they split and scattered, riding for their lives in every direction but the front or the rear. Few got away as the long range of the rifles and the terrain made it easy for the dismounted Cossacks to shoot fleeing Turks down.

That's enough, Andreas thought, as he loaded his last bullet into the rifle. Taking another packet of six bullets from his cartridge case, he stuck them into the bullet loops sewn into his tunic and slung the rifle over his back.

"You want to chase them?" Johann asked, as he, like the other troopers, stood and stopped firing.

"No, let them be," Andreas said. "They won't stop until they are across the border. Take four troopers and release those women from that pen over there; you three come with me and the rest round up the loose horses. If you must, use your lance or sword to put something out of its pain; we are running low of bullets." Accepting his reins from his horse handler, Andreas mounted Bartholomew and with his three troopers in tow, rode slowly to the enemy camp.

"Keep those Turkish women away," Andreas said, pointing to the hijab-covered women standing wringing their hands in a small group in front of a large tent. There were three blonde, naked women staked facedown in front of the tent in the dirt. They had been hard used, blood and bruising all over their bodies.

Andreas dismounted, letting his long reins hang on the ground, pulled out his sword, and cut the first woman loose; as she stood, he removed his tunic and placed it on her shoulders, waving to the other troopers to do the same.

The woman, about twenty-five, her face and breasts a mass of bruises and cuts, said nothing, just walked over to Bartholomew and yanked the lance out of the scabbard on his flank. The other two women saw her and grabbed the swords out of the troopers' hands and, without closing the tunics about themselves, advanced on the Turkish women

14

sticking them in the bellies with the weapons in fury, over and over again, before the astonished troopers could do anything.

The three were soon joined by their sisters, who, having been freed from the pen, came charging, screaming their rage out to the field, grabbing any weapon they could find. There were soon no live enemies in the field.

Jesus! Andreas thought, turning his back to the carnage the women were wreaking on wounded and dead Turks.

"Andy, you're not going to let them do this, are you?" Johann said.

"Are you going to try and stop them?" Andreas asked. "Tell everyone to stay out of their way; they might be mistaken for Turks. Set up a perimeter in case some fools think to come back, and let's round up the rest of the stray horses; we need the money. After things settle down, we'll check out the camp."

Andreas walked toward the main tent not noticing the Turk lying face down taking a tight grip on his sword as he passed. Waiting until Andreas passed, the man sprang up and swung the sword in a clumsy sideswipe that, somehow, Andreas sensed and ducked back from, tripping on a body and falling to the ground, yanking his dagger out of his belt in desperation, as the sword descended toward his face.

A scream of rage, just before Bartholomew's front hooves smashed open the Turk's head, caused the stroke to miss, almost, as Andreas rolled away, catching the blade across his rib cage. Shit, that was close, he thought,

15

dragging the dagger across the man's throat to make sure he stayed dead.

"I suppose you'll want more feed now?" Andreas said, wrapping his arms around Bartholomew's neck and hugging him, man and horse standing quiet.

"My lord? You are bleeding, my lord," a female voice said. "A Cossack and his horse are more than one weapon."

Andreas took her soft hand away from his side and looked down at the gash in his shirt, it was the woman he had given his tunic to. The tunic, now buttoned, came down to mid-thigh on her, and she was clutching some clothing she had taken off of a corpse.

"Take off that shirt, my lord," she said. "If it please my lord, we will see what damage there is."

"Oh, I am far from being a lord, my lady," Andreas said. "I am but a younger son of a poor farmer and only a lowly sergeant."

Another woman, with a bucket of water, joined her, and they began to wash the gash along his ribs the sword had made. In minutes, Andreas was surrounded by women as they washed the blood and wound clean linen around his ribs. Someone had gone into the big tent and found a clean shirt, and the women fussed over placing it just so around him. Many of them just came and touched his cheek or ran their hand along his shoulders; some just smiled shyly at him.

"Isn't that always the way," Johann said. "The troopers get all the crap while the sergeants get all the girls."

16

"Where were you when your sergeant was attacked and defenseless?" the woman Andreas had saved said in German, handing him back his tunic. "Can you not see he is wounded?"

"Oh shit!" Johann said. "Is it bad?"

"No, just a flesh wound," Andreas said. "I have more luck than brains. Is anyone else injured?"

"Not a scratch," Johann said. "Oh, I lied. Kurt jammed his thumb on the bolt of his rifle, but he will live."

"Alright," Andreas said. "Tell no one I am hurt. See if these ladies need any help, would you? My lady, you are German? From which village? We will see that you get home."

"My home is gone, sir," she said. "My husband and children killed along with the rest of my village. I am asking for refuge. I am young and strong and can still bear many babies as can my sisters here." The last she had said in Russian.

"We have heard of the generosity of the hosts," another woman said in Russian, "we are all asking for refuge."

"I can only ask my leader," Andreas said. "I am but a mere sergeant and only first-generation Cossack. Johann, pick twenty men to escort the ladies and the extra horses back to Vacilly. Ladies, you will be escorted back to our main camp. It is only fair that you be given a horse each for what you have suffered, and I will recommend in my report that you all be taken into the host."

My God, the sun is just at midday, Andreas thought.

"It is only six hours to the camp," he said. "If you leave soon, you will make it while there is still light. Call assembly, bugler."

"You have all done well," Andreas said to his troop. "We have defeated a large group of enemy and liberated Mother Russia's citizens from captivity."

"And four hundred horses!" a voice at the back said.

"In the name of the Father, the Son, and the Holy Ghost," Andreas said, making the sign of the cross, some of his troopers and most of the women making the sign in the orthodox fashion, opposite to the Roman Catholic way.

"Our Lord in Heaven, we thank you for your generous gift and the victory of today. We thank you for allowing us to experience no harm and to release these, our sisters, from their captivity. We ask you to help heal them of their wounds to mind and body and to forgive us in the taking of your children's lives, as we had no other choice. We ask this in Your Son Jesus's name. In the name of the Father, the Son, and the Holy Ghost, amen."

"Alright, mount up and head out. Karl, tell Vacilly we are heading for the border crossing by the river and that we could use some more ammunition. Here, take my report with you."

Each woman made a point of walking by Andreas and kissing him on both cheeks as they rode by. The last one, the blonde German girl he had given his tunic to.

"Thank you, my lord, I will never forget what you have done for us, my lord Bekenbaum," she said.

"Again, I am no lord, madam," Andreas said.

18

"You are to me," she said. "God keep you and look out for you, Andreas."

"Hey, what's your name?" Johann said as she rode away.

"Irene, why?" she answered.

"Well, Irene," Johann said, "I intend on finding you when we get home; don't try and hide from me now."

She smiled a sad smile and turned away, digging her heels into her horse's side to trot up with the rest of the women, who began to poke her and giggle.

"Brother, really," Andreas said, putting Bartholomew into motion in the opposite direction.

"Hey, she's cute," Johann said. "Has great legs and owns a horse, what else could a guy ask for?"

"Uh, can she cook, for instance?" Andreas asked.

"Well, I can see she knows how to sew," he said, poking Andreas in the ribs.

"Ya, ya, thanks for the reminder; that hurts, you idiot," Andreas said.

"Ow, shit, can you kick the other side next time, that hurts," Andreas said, clutching his side and rolling out of the bed roll. "Sorry, sir, I didn't know it was you, Captain, sir."

"Your brother told me you had guard duty all night, sleepy head," Vacilly said. "Come on, I caught some fish while you were having your beauty sleep and they are ready to eat, and we have some fresh tea brewed."

Now the smell of fresh fish frying in a pan caught Andreas's nose as he stood and looked around, seeing the sun breaking over the treetops and troopers, rifles on shoulders, heading into the tree line. Horse handlers were taking horses out of sight around the corner of the trail.

"Scouts just came in," Vacilly said. "There's a big bunch of Austrians headed this way."

Not looking behind him, Andreas picked up his tin plate and cup and sat on his stump by the cook fire.

"That was nice work you did," Vacilly said, ladling a fish and a potato into Andreas's plate. "I have sent a report to headquarters, and the captives are on their way back to my town along with my share of the loot. We will adopt them into the host as is our way. You and your lads have seen a lot this year. More than the rest of us have seen in the last five years. Your weapons and tactics are better than ours; we are still in the old days where the lance and the sword were king. You have grasped the new reality and fight more as infantry than cavalry. This is why you are able to draw these raiders in and get rid of them. They expect what they are used to and your weapons shoot farther, more accurately, and faster than the old ones. If my people do not change with the times, the times may be hard for them."

The battalion had been away from home for almost a year, with orders to patrol the western borders with Poland, Austria/Hungary, and Moldova. It was usually boring duty, riding from post to post, making sure all was right in the little world they surveyed. Because there were no wars going on and little chance for plunder, Vacilly had opted to leave most of his normal troopers at home on garrison duty and take the newcomers out on the foreign duties this year. Most of the mounted troopers of the host this year had been the younger sons of German settlers. Andreas and his brother Johann had been two of them.

20

"What are you twenty-five?" he asked. "With the loot you have just received, you will have no problem buying that land next door to your father's. You won't have enough money to build a house yet, but you have, what, four cows and three horses?"

"Yes, sir," Andreas said. "I turn twenty-five here pretty quick. The wages you pay us would have been enough for me to buy the land. I think my share of the horses and loot should be enough to build a house with. A small one."

"If I know your mother, she's already lining up a wife for you," Vacilly said. "I may have someone that would suit. We will see."

"If you say so, sir," Andreas said.

"Our friends are early today," Vacilly said. "It sounds like there are many more of them than usual. Johann, quick ride over and tell the lads if the Austrians cross the river, to hold them as long as they can, then scatter and head back to base. Send three riders back to base now by different routes, and they are to report what is going on here. My, my, those are not Austrians at all, it looks like a squadron of Prussian Hussars all pretty and spotless. Come on, then, Sergeant, mount up, it's time to earn our pay."

"What's this then, Major?" the Prussian Colonel said. "Two boys and an old man? This is how the Russians choose to insult us?"

"These are Cossacks, sir," the Austrian Major said. "There are most likely a couple of hundred of them in the trees on both sides of the trail."

"Cossacks?" the Prussian said. "They look like farmers, Captain, deploy two lines of skirmishers along the river bank. We will talk with these Cossacks, if they are Cossacks."

"We'll stop just short of halfway, Sergeant," Vacilly said. "I'll do the talking. If they find out you're German, they are liable to shoot first and talk second."

"These troopers are well-trained," Andreas said. "Look how they deploy as infantry in a skirmish line, like we do. Fat lot of good it will do them with those short-barrelled carbines. I doubt if they can hit us, let alone the boys in the trees."

"That Hussar has the same uniform markings as your father and his troops had when they joined us twenty years ago," Vacilly said. "Somehow, I don't think he wants to join us though."

"The rest of the squadron looks like they are setting up camp over there," Andreas said, nodding across the river. "I have a feeling we are about to be joined by a bigger group soon."

"I begin to see why you have so much success," Vacilly said. "Look, another bunch of Prussians, lancers by the look of it, coming around the bend."

"Nice shiny helmets," Andreas said. "Wonder what the spike on the top is for? Knocking snow off of tree limbs?"

Vacilly couldn't help himself, he snorted through his nose loudly, almost choking in the hilarity of the comment. "Those are the famous Uhlans, Sergeant," he said. "I somehow don't think they would take your comment about their helmets kindly."

"Oh, I am supposed to be kind to them?" Andreas said. "Well, they have pretty horses."

22

"Good morning, General," the Hussar said, saluting the newly arrived officer.

"Is this the reception we can expect from those uneducated Russians?" the general asked. "Two dirty, unkempt farmers?"

"The major, here, assures me they are Cossacks," the Hussar said. "Not farmers, sir, and feels there are many more of them close about."

"Bah, I have seen Cossacks," the general said. "These are no Cossacks; come on, let's see what the farmers have to say, if they can talk intelligently."

"Captain Vacilly Ivanovitch of the Beresan Free Riders, attached to the Third Imperial Army, sir," Vacilly said. "How may I be of service to Your Honor today? Pretty troops you have there."

"Ask that fool captain where the rest of the delegation is," the general said to the Austrian. "God, he stinks, look the younger one has dirty hands and looks like he butchered a cow in that uniform."

"The colonel would like to know where the rest of the delegation is," the Austrian officer said in Russian.

"As far as I know," Vacilly said, "we are the only ones here. Of course, we have been on patrol for over a month; things change. Messengers are on their way back to brigade; we should hear back from them soon."

"Humph, a likely story," the Prussian General said, turning his horse around and heading to the other bank. "Tell that incompetent idiot to tell us when he hears from his superiors. These Russians could not organise a fart in a bean eating contest."

"The colonel respectfully requests that he be informed immediately you receive word, Captain," the Austrian said. "Thank you for your cooperation. I assure you, our intentions are of a peaceful nature and that you may stand down your troopers. At your service, Captain, good day to you." The Austrian then turned his horse and clattered after the Prussians.

With a puzzled look and a shrug at each other, the two Cossacks turned their horses around and leisurely walked them back to their own side of the river. After a shouted command from one of their officers, the Hussars deployed as skirmishers, broke ranks, and while some assumed sentry positions, the rest headed for the bivouac area. Reaching their side of the river bank, Vacilly gave the stand down signal to his troopers and dismounted by his fire. He and Andreas handed the reins of their ponies to a dismounted trooper to take back to the horse lines.

"Somehow I think that Austrian was sugar coating what that arrogant Prussian was saying," Vacilly said.

"You could say so, sir," Andreas replied. "Something about our lack of proper military bearing and how a Russian would have trouble organizing a fart after a bean eating contest."

"Right on both counts," Vacilly said and laughed. "We might as well set up camp here. I expect more visitors from our side will be here soon. Something big must be up."

Andreas, Johann, and ten other troopers made the half-mile trek upstream from the main camp to obtain drinking and cooking water for the battalion, watering the draft horses downstream before making their way to a suitable spot to fill the water barrels lashed to the inside of two wheeled carts, four to a cart. Starting their task in the grey, pre-dawn chill, now it was bright enough to see and the sun was beginning to poke its way above the treetops bordering the river. A light wind was blowing the smell of cook and campfires from both sides of the river away from them, and nothing but the sound of the wind in the treetops and the river gurgling down the banks disturbed their tranquility as they walked back and forth with their buckets of water, filling the barrels in the carts.

The rest of the regiment had appeared at the river crossing the day after Andreas's squadron had met the Prussians and set up a large camp. Larger than they needed for the three battalions of infantry and the rest of Vacilly's battalion. Finally, after a month of being constantly on the move, Andreas's troopers had been stood down and for a week now they had performed maintenance on themselves, their horses, and equipment. They had been given a bivouac far from the camp center and, to be honest, didn't mind it a bit.

At precisely the same time of the morning as every other morning, Prussian bugles sounded the wake-up and assembly calls breaking the silence of the morning as troopers assembled; sergeants and officers yelled orders, and the sound of axes splitting wood for breakfast cook fires dominated the landscape.

Not to be outdone, this was soon followed by the Russian bugles and swearing, turning the once quiet river crossing into a buzzing hub of conversation and noise.

Soon enough, a troop of cavalry appeared on the opposite side of the river intending on watering their horses.

"What the hell do you idiots think you are doing?" Andreas yelled at them in German. He and several other troopers throwing river rocks to splash just in front of horses' noses. "This is where we get our drinking water! Any fool knows to water horses downstream from the camp, not upstream."

"Yes, we understand," a trooper yelled back in English-accented German. "But their Lordships are insisting their horses have a better right to clean water than troopers do."

"Well then," Andreas replied in his German-accented English. "At least move downstream a bit from us, then. God forbid those pampered thoroughbreds drink human-tainted water. Was I you, I would fill their Lordships' water barrels after their horses' water and downstream from them."

"A man after my own heart then, you are," the trooper with sergeant stripes on his arm said with a weird lilting accent that Andreas learned after was Irish.

The English troopers were all dressed in a white canvas smock over their uniforms, the blue trousers just poking out from under the smocks.

"English are so weird," Andreas said, reverting to Russian.

"Looks like they're saying the same about us," Johann said, watching the English move their horses slightly downstream, pointing at the small Cossack group across the river from them.

"Right then." Andreas ordered as the last barrel was filled, "Back to camp, and cookie better have breakfast ready by the time we get there."

The ten troopers jumped into the three carts, jostling for the best spots, elbows flying and hands pushing, all in good fun, with jokes at each other's expense all the while. Soon striking up a lewd rendition of a Russian folk song. More laughter as they did so. The English cavalrymen just looked and shook their heads.

Even though they came from the same district, the young Cossacks received the same stares from their own infantry. All of them, militia companies made up from the peasant farmers and townsmen of the various boyars, or wealthy landowners, of their district. Unlike the Cossacks, they were only obliged to serve from the time the planting was done until the harvest was about to begin each year. Andreas and Johann knew many of the troopers and officers, but, of course, the officers being boyars' sons ignored them as being beneath their notice and became angry when the young Cossacks laughed at them.

"Alright, boys," Andreas said as they came to their squadron's bivouac. "After you drop off the water, get something to eat."

He and Johann did just that for their troop and were just sitting down and taking their first mouthfuls of beans and sausage.

"Great, here comes a ground pounder officer," Johann said, nodding his head in the direction of the approaching young infantry lieutenant as he marched up to Andreas in a purposeful way and stopped.

Andreas and his troop stood and saluted in the sloppy way they reserved for junior infantry officers.

"Senior Sergeant Bekenbaum, sir," Andreas said. "How can I be of service, sir?"

"Oh, a high-and-mighty senior sergeant now, Bekenbaum," the lieutenant said. "I can't imagine how a know-nothing, useless, square-head accountant like you managed that one. Or, rather, I can. Take me to Vacilly immediately!"

"Exactly who do you think you are, addressing one of my people like that!" Vacilly said, having walked up behind them unnoticed. "You can address your own men in that fashion if you wish, but if I ever hear you talking like that to one of my men again, I believe I will offer my services to another militia battalion and you can explain that to your father. And it is Captain Ivanovitch to you, Lieutenant."

"Yes, sir, sorry, Captain, I was only joking with the Sergeant, sir," the lieutenant said.

"Somehow, I don't think so," Vacilly said. "Now, what is it you want?"

"Sir, the major is requesting the captain's presence at the captain's earliest convenience, sir," the lieutenant stammered out.

"We had best not keep the major waiting then," Vacilly said. "Sergeant, you're in charge." Vacilly promptly turned on his heel and headed towards the infantry part of the camp, leaving the lieutenant to scramble after him to the quiet chuckles of Andreas's men.

Finishing their breakfast, Andreas gave his men their orders for the day and moved over to the tent that shared office and sleeping duties for him. He had a nice-sized stump for a chair and another for a coffee table, and he sat his hot tin cup of coffee on the table and perched on his stool digging in his pocket for his tobacco and pipe. All his paperwork was up to date and he had some rare free time on his hands.

Something big must be going on, Andreas thought. Two days before, another brigade had arrived; this one complete with aristocrats and their entourages, carriages, and baggage wagons holding large pavilions and copious amounts of furniture and servants. It could not be war, or both armies would not be so laid-back. There had been a constant flow of couriers running across the river in both directions, but there was no sense of urgency to any of it. It was all above Andreas's pay grade anyway, and he let his thoughts drift to other things.

They would be departing soon, and hopefully, he would make enough money selling his extra cattle and horses to purchase some seed and a plow for his new land. He would also have to figure out how much land to plow and how much to leave as pasture. His father and older brothers would help him with that. Now that he was a landowner, the pressure would really be on him to find a suitable girl and get married. His mother would leave no stone unturned to make a match suitable to the family. Andreas's older siblings had gone through the same ritual. So far, the matches had proven to be happy ones and he could only hope for the same.

I will cross that bridge when I come to it, he thought. The ladies seemed to find him agreeable, always fussing about when he came near, and he had enough sense to keep his flings discreet. The females seemed to have some ingrained possessive streak that was in some ways worse than men's, which Andreas thought amusing. He had really not had much to offer before, but things would be different now that he would be a landowner. He much preferred the local farmers' daughters over his friends' sisters anyway. They were more fun loving and took life a lot less serious. It seemed to him that the German girls spent a lot of time and effort in establishing pecking orders and class superiority. His musing was interrupted by Johann rushing up to him.

"Something is up across the river," Johann said. "It looks like more people arriving, lots of them."

Andreas hurried to a vantage point with Johann and observed the goings-on across the river. Officers were scurrying around meeting with non-coms and each other, and a large dust cloud could be seen rising above the trees. At that point, bugle calls had Prussians scrambling out of tents and assembling in formation just in time for the first of the advancing troops breaking out of the tree line.

The first outriders appeared out of the trees and at first glance, you could tell even through the dust of the trail, that these were first class troops. Now could be heard the tramping of many, many boots hitting the ground, in step and in unison. Next, coming through the trees in a column of four, marched a battalion of infantry, who at a command by an officer at their head mounted on a white horse, broke into the ground-pounding goose step Prussian troops used for formal parade marching.

Behind this group came a troop of Uhlans, complete with breastplates and shiny helmets, bright red pennants flapping beneath shining lance heads, followed by mounted officers in full regalia and a large expensive carriage.

At the appearance of the carriage, the formed up troops from the camp crashed to attention and the massed bugles played some sort of tune, while the four field guns boomed out a salute.

"So much for our nice quiet neighborhood," Johann said. "I guess the party can begin now, the big shots have arrived."

"Notice all the different uniforms?" Andreas said, pointing to the new groups of troops coming in after the first group. "Looks like a bunch of Frogs and Limeys there with them. Things are getting interesting."

"That's it, the neighborhood has gone all to hell," Johann joked. "I'm moving."

"Hey, you guys know where I can find Sergeant Bekenbaum?" a voice said from behind them.

Turning around, the two brothers saw a clerk with corporal's stripes.

"That would be me, Corporal, what can I do for you?" Andreas said.

"Major Halinov wants you in his exalted presence within the hour," the corporal said. "In your best uniform. I don't know what you did, but there seems to be an awful lot of fuss going on. Just a heads up."

"Oh, you're in the shit now, Brother," Johann said. "I wonder if it is too late to change my name."

Immediately upon arrival at the major's tent, Andreas had been marched with the major over to the command tent and left outside for an uneasy ten minutes. The major then came out and, after telling him to enter the tent and address the men sitting at the main table, had motioned him inside. Removing his head gear and drawing himself upright, Andreas marched into the large tent and coming to a foot-stomping, heel-clicking halt exactly three feet from the center of the table, and saluting in the approved manner said, "Senior Sergeant Andreas Bekenbaum reporting as ordered, SIR!"

Even though he was focusing his eyes three inches above the officer's head, he could see the man was older, his beard, mustache, and hair a beautifully well-kept grey. His Imperial Army uniform was immaculate with a large amount of gold braid and medals in view. The officer held him that way for what seemed like hours, but was only about thirty seconds, returned his salute, and growled, "At ease."

Andreas lowered his arm from the salute, moved his feet to shoulder-width apart, and placing his arms in the crook of his back, he assumed the position of parade rest his father had taught him to use when in the presence of senior officers.

There were seven men seated behind the ornate table in real chairs. They seemed to be sitting in order of descending rank from the center, with the officer on the far left in a plain uniform showing only his colonels rank, to the man on the far right who seemed to be a Catholic priest. They were all immaculately groomed and uniformed. The smell of expensive cigars, alcohol, and aftershave filled the room. A far cry from the home brew vodka, cheap tobacco, and horse sweat Andreas was used to smelling.

"Bloody Cossacks," murmured the officer second from the left, holding a perfumed handkerchief to his nose.

Another court dandy, thought Andreas, never spent a day in the field.

"You have been on active duty since mid-March, all of it in the field, Sergeant?" said the senior officer.

"Sir, yes, sir!" replied Andreas.

"That explains it then," the court dandy said.

"Tell me, Sergeant, what are the requirements for a man to be an officer in the militia?" he asked.

"Sir, in order to be considered to apply for an officer in the militia, the candidate must be a land holder, sir," replied Andreas.

"I understand you have an understanding to purchase some land after you have completed your years' service and paid the landowner the one thousand rubles still owing?" asked the officer.

"Yes, sir, but it is only three hundred rubles, sir," replied Andreas.

"We also understand you attended the seminary in Katherintal for three years and are fluent in a number of languages. German, French, and English, is it? In order of fluency, tell us how fluent you are in each language."

"Sir," Andreas said. "Russian, speak, read, and write fluently; German, speak, read, and write fluently; French, speak, read, write fluently; English, read and write fluently, speak competently."

Speaking in German, the dandy on the left said, "Probably with a horrible local dialect."

"No, sir," replied Andreas in the same language, "we speak High German at home, and I can understand most dialects."

"Your French?" asked an officer on the right in that language, "how are you able to keep up your fluency?"

"A number of my father's men married French women, sir, and I speak to them as often as I can," he said in French.

"The reason your English is not as proficient?" asked the officer in the center in English.

"Sir, I have only the English I learned in school. While I have a few English books I read to keep up my skills, I have no one to actually talk with," Andreas replied in English.

"He has a better accent than you do, Michilovitch," he said, addressing the dandy on the left who just smiled and bowed his head.

Gesturing to two piles of documents in front of him, the officer in the center said, "Examine the document on the left and compare it with the one on the right."

The document on the left seemed to be one document composed with French, English, and German text. Andreas shuffled the papers about until they came into some kind of order, read them, and then read the document on the right which was in Russian.

"Sir, they appear to be the same document, sir," Andreas reported.

"The translations?" asked the officer.

"One of the English pages seems to have been written in a style I am not familiar with, but basically they are all the same contextually," replied Andreas.

"Just so," the officer replied. "Now, Sergeant, what do you know of the requirement of candidacy for an officer in the Imperial Army?"

"Sir, only that I am probably not eligible, sir," Andreas answered.

"Well, I am glad to know that there is something that this young pup doesn't know," remarked the gruff oldster in front of him, with the hint of a glint in his eyes under the bushy grey eyebrows. "First, the candidate must be a Russian-born, baptized Catholic of freeborn parents, which His Eminence, there, assures me is true." At which, the priest at the end of the table nodded in agreement.

"Next, the candidate must exhibit a clear working knowledge of the Russian language both the written and the spoken word, which I believe has been proven here. It is preferable that the candidate have some form of formal education, His Eminence tells me that you were an honors student in grammar, mathematics, and Russian history in your tenure in the seminary. By your own words and again confirmed by His Eminence, you have virtually, from birth, been schooled in military matters, specifically, cavalry deployments and tactics. By, I believe, your father a twenty-year veteran master sergeant in a Prussian Hussar troop. In addition, you have served in the field as a proven and capable leader. To paraphrase Captain Ivanovitch, 'The damn pup is the best born leader I have ever met'." This remark drew a number of chuckles from the assembled officers.

"In fact, Sergeant, it appears to me that you have better qualifications than most of the officers I have serving with me right now. Will someone, please, get the sergeant a chair, my neck is getting sore looking up at him."

After a short interval, a chair was provided and Andreas sat on the edge of it in a stiff upright position.

"We are about to enter into some delicate negotiations with our friends across the river, Sergeant," said the high-ranking officer seated across from him. "His Imperial Majesty is most anxious that these negotiations conclude successfully and to the best advantage to Mother Russia that we can obtain. Now, collectively, we as a group have the necessary skills to accomplish this, but only you, and few others located in Moscow universities, have all the skills, and I am not sure that the people in Moscow are as skilled as you are.

"We would like you to provide oversight on translation of documents as well as analysis of what was intended by the original document. We would also like you to sit in on the negotiations themselves, to provide us with similar services. If you agree to this service, we would also require you to attend formal and informal gatherings, to mingle with your peers from the other side to gain as much informal knowledge as possible, while not divulging the fact that you can understand everything that is being said. What do you think of that?"

"Permission to speak freely, sir," Andreas said.

"Yes, yes," said the officer, "your enlistment is up at the end of the month; you have big plans to attend to back home; you really don't see how you could be of value given your present status. Horse shit! What you really mean is, what's in it for me?

35

Quite rightly, too, I might add. We are asking a lot of you, and you have a unique skill set that we desperately require."

"We have arranged with Captain Ivanovitch your early release from enlistment in his regiment. Your one thousand rubles in wages has been paid to the landowner you are purchasing the one hundred and sixty acres from. Sign this document in recognition of payment and acquisition of the property." A document was handed over to Andreas from a large pile of documents in front of the officer.

A quick scan of the document confirmed what the officer had said, and after signing them, Andreas handed them back to the officer who placed them in two separate piles.

"You are now a freeborn, common landholder with all the rights and responsibilities that go with it," the officer said.

"His Imperial Majesty's Government has empowered me to offer you the following, should you agree to provide us with your services to the end of negotiations, regardless of the outcome. One thousand acres of land deeded in your name, villages, buildings, animals, and peasants included. An additional one thousand acres of Crown-controlled land to be administered by you with fifty percent of any revenue generated by said property to be paid to the Crown. You will be required to provide and equip your own staff to administer your security and administration. You have been assigned a staff officer, and you will be required to obtain ten other ranks to provide your needs. The wages, uniforms, accommodations, equipment, and livestock will be provided by the Crown. An additional five thousand rubles will be paid in advance for any other expenses, no receipts required. After completion of negotiations and serving to the end of said negotiations, a further one thousand acres will be deeded to you and a further two thousand acres of Crown land will be assigned to you to administer. Is this acceptable to you?"

The officer handed Andreas another pile of documents, which he reviewed and after a few moments signed and handed back to the officer, who again divided them into two piles.

"Attention," bellowed the officer.

Andreas jumped out of the chair and assumed a rigid stance at attention dropping his head gear on the floor as he did so.

"Five rubles fine for that, Sergeant, paid in cash before you leave this room," the officer said, laughing.

"Sergeant Andreas Bekenbaum, you are hereby relieved of duty with the grateful thanks of His Imperial Majesty for your service."

At that, the priest, who actually was a bishop as well as the officer in the non-descript uniform from the left end of the table, approached him.

Producing a Bible, the bishop requested he place his right hand on the Bible and raise his left hand.

"Andreas Bekenbaum, do you freely and willfully pledge to serve, protect, and obey all lawfully given orders by your superiors and to obey, protect, and serve His Imperial Majesty Czar of all the Russians to the best of your ability?" said the officer.

"Yes, sir," Andreas said.

"Kneel; by the power vested in me, I, Crown Prince Nicolas, anoint you Andreas, Earl of Katherintal with all the rights, freedoms, and responsibilities that title entails. Stand."

Oh my God, what the hell have I gotten myself into, thought Andreas.

"Attention to orders," snapped the crown prince. The whole group of officers sprang to attention.

"Earl Andreas Bekenbaum, you are inducted into the ranks of the Imperial Army and promoted to the rank of major, temporarily attached to the Royal Horse Guards, effective immediately. Congratulations, Earl Bekenbaum, I look forward to serving with you."

"Now then, Major, we have more business to conduct today; so, by your leave, if you would, a gentleman is waiting for you outside who will assist you in getting settled in. Oh, Boris, here is your five ruble fine." He flipped a coin at the older officer. "Dismissed, Major, report back here in two days at 8 a.m. for further briefing."

Andreas saluted and as he walked out of the tent the crown prince said, "Well, Boris, I believe I will fine you one bottle of brandy for scaring that kid half to death; pay up and crack the bottle." Andreas stood bewildered outside the tent listening to the crown prince, Royal Imperial Army Chief of Staff, and the heads of the various army groups roaring in laughter.

"Congratulations, my lord," said Major Halinov, his group's commanding officer.

Andreas snapped to attention and saluted.

"No, no, my lord, we are of the same rank now; if any saluting is to be done, it should be me saluting you, as you are the lord and I am a mere commoner with a militia's majority," he said, snapping a smart salute.

"If I may say, my lord, there is nobody more deserving of the honor. You and your family have done much to help Mother Russia. Why, you alone single-handed have saved me from ruin. I only wish my son were half as good as you."

"Well, this is all still a shock," said Andreas, "I'm not sure if I am not dreaming."

"No, no, my lord, it all true," Halinov said. "I myself have been part of the discussions; some of the land I was overseeing for the Crown is part of your investiture."

"Oh, I am sorry, Mr. Halinov. I hope this won't cause any hardship for you or hard feelings," an aghast Andreas exclaimed.

"Oh, quite the contrary, my lord," he said with a laugh, "less headaches for me, and with all you have taught my bookkeeper and what your father has taught myself and my overseers, I stand to make more profit."

"Thank you, Major. As we are both in uniform and of the same rank, can we dispense with this 'my lord' stuff while we are in private? My name is Andreas."

"Very pleased to meet you, Andreas; I am Michilov," he said, sticking out his hand. "Now, Andreas, we need to get you properly kitted out, then I will introduce you to your new aide, and you can set about getting organized, alright?"

"Lead on, Michilov," said Andreas with a grin.

Their first stop was to the officers' baths, where, as he was being undressed by a platoon of attendants, he was measured from head to toe by tailors and shoe makers. "I'll be wanting those back," he told the attendant who was removing his old uniform.

"Yes, Your Lordship," said the attendant with a bow as he left.

"Full complement of uniforms, dress, mess, and fatigues. Aide du camp, Major, Royal Horse Guard," said Halinov.

With a bow in acknowledgment, the tailors and boot makers also left.

"By the time you finish your shave and baths, they should have the fatigue uniform ready. The others will be ready before your next meeting with the command group. So, I will leave you now to your bath. One of the attendants will fetch me when you're finished," and, with a bow, Michilov also left.

As he lay soaking in the body temperature bath, steam rising about him, he was approached by two barbers, one with scissors and the other with a razor.

"How would you like it done, Your Lordship?" asked the one with this scissors.

"Out of my eyes, over the ears, and off the collar. No beard, no moustache, no side beards," Andreas said.

Well, I have a lot to think about, thought Andreas. He would need to get his father to check out the land and condition of the properties, as well as to come up with some kind of administration plan and what type of crops to plant. Alright, I'll just take it one step at a time.

First he would have to go to Vacilly's camp and collect his ponies and see about obtaining ten troopers for his personal troops. He didn't think that would be too much of a problem. Johann would be the first to volunteer, and the other nine would jump at the chance to make some extra cash.

He would have to see about getting quarters for himself, the troops, and the horses. His aide could probably handle that. The rest will just have to be taken as it came.

True to the major's word, the tailors and boot makers were back just as the water in the bath was beginning to cool. Wow, if this is what the fatigues looked like, he hated to think what the full dress uniform was like. Snug fitting cavalry trousers with belt, form-fitted blouse with real buttons, not the pull-over he was used to. Cavalry boots of soft leather that reached to just below the knee. Double breasted jacket with gleaming brass buttons with majors insignia on the shoulder boards. Some kind of cape affair was suspended by a chain from one of the jacket's epilates and draped over his left shoulder. Not to forget, the brass rope over the shoulder and under the armpits of his right shoulder which designated him as aide du camp. This was topped off by the signature black lamb's wool cap that all Royal Horse Guards wore.

"Sword or sabre," offered another aide, holding out both for his inspection.

"Sabre," he replied. It was what he was used to, trained with as he was light cavalry. He would examine it later and compare it with his own before he would commit to this one, he thought as the aide buckled on the sword and belt on the outside of his jacket.

"Your other two fatigues, mess, and full dress uniforms will be ready in two days, my lord," said the head tailor, "as well as three more pairs of boots. I apologize for the quality, my lord, but if my lord will, we will take this uniform and alter it to suit once your other uniforms are ready."

"No apology necessary, good sir," Andreas said, "you have done quite well in the limited time that you had."

"Thank you, my lord. If you would kindly have your aide tell the armourer what type of spurs you require, I am sure he will be able to have you all set up in no time, sir."

"Thank you, I will," he replied.

"With your permission, sir?" the tailor asked.

"Yes, carry on." Andreas returned the man's salute and the whole gang trooped out the door of the bath house.

Now, what in world would I need spurs for? he thought. Never used them before.

Looking at himself in the full-length mirror on the bath house wall, he thought his mother would say he cut a dashing figure. He never before had owned such high quality clothing and these were everyday clothes? Why, it would take him most of the night just to polish the boots and all the brass.

"Ah, all squared away then, my lord?" said Major Halinov as he entered the bath house trailed by a lieutenant dressed in the same fatigue uniform as Andreas was wearing.

"My God, Major, where am I to find the time to polish all this brass and clean all of this?" blurted Andreas.

"Why, my lord, that is what one has body servants for," he said with a laugh. "I tell you what; you can hire two of mine until you return home. I won't need them, as I will be returning home with Vacilly in the morning."

"Thank you, Major, I would appreciate that."

"May I have the honor of presenting Lieutenant Ivan Michilovitch Halinov, your new aide, my lord?"

The lieutenant sprang to attention and presented a smart salute.

"My apologies for my lack of manners, Lieutenant," said Andreas, returning the salute and extending his right hand for a handshake. "Welcome to the happy group."

"No apologies required, sir, it is an honor to serve," he replied, accepting the handshake.

"Oh my," the elder Halinov said, "this will never do. No true cavalry officer of your station would be caught dead without his spurs. Lucky for you I have come prepared. I never use the damn things so you might as well. The lieutenant here will obtain some for you at his earliest opportunity, I am sure."

At that, the young lieutenant offered up a set of spurs for Andreas.

"Alright, that's handled then," said Andreas after he had buckled on the spurs. "Let's get out of here before I melt."

"The first order of business, Lieutenant, is to obtain two more horses for you. That old nag your father gave you might be good enough for the infantry, but you're in the cavalry now and it just won't do. I will handle that for you," Andreas said.

"I'll have you know that the man who sold me that horse assured me it was of the finest quality and was a well-trained cavalry mount," said the major in mock disgust.

"Well, he was when I sold him to you, but I think he may have forgotten how to be a cavalry mount following all you ground pounders around," said Andreas with a laugh.

"Well, of all the nerve, been an Earl for all of three hours and already mocking us, eh?" laughed Michilov.

"So, first order of business, Lieutenant, our happy little gang is about to grow to a sergeant, three corporals, and six troopers. We are going to need quarters for them and thirty-six horses. We are going to have to arrange for mess facilities and feed requirements. When you have that sorted out come and fetch me. I will be over at Vacilly's camp," Andreas ordered.

"Yes, sir," the lieutenant said, and after a salute he was off.

"Vacilly, there are two brass walking over this way," said Johann, "one of them looks like some kind of big shot."

"Indeed, you have the eyes of an eagle, Johann, make yourself scarce, Johann," Vacilly said.

"See if they know anything about Andreas, would you," Johann said over his shoulder as he headed to his tent.

"Well, well, look what the cat dragged in," Vacilly said by way of greeting, "you've got more doodads on that uniform than a dance hall girl in St. Petersburg on Friday night."

"Now, is that any way to address a superior officer, *Captain* Ivanovitch?" Andreas said.

"Sir, sorry, Your Majorship, sir." Vacilly sprang to an exaggerated attention complete with belly sticking out, right hand quivering in salute, and knees knocking.

As Andreas burst out laughing, Vacilly grabbed him in an enormous bear hug, lifting him off the ground. "Oh my God," he said, "Mother Russia must surely be desperate. Couldn't be more deserving, Andreas, your poppa will be proud."

"Ach, you'll be wanting to take me out on a date next, Vacilly, and get all mushy," Andreas said with a laugh. "So, you knew all about this then?"

"Oh, yes, we've been negotiating for days," Vacilly answered.

"Actually, it's more like weeks, Vacilly," said Michilov. "This bunch showed up in the main camp about a month ago," he said, "some sort of treaty negotiations. Everything was alright,

44

then they found out that the English and the French were coming too, and everyone got in a dither. They were searching all over for someone who had English and French skills and not having much luck. That's when His Eminence remembered you from your seminary days and asked me if I knew you and if you were still in Katherintal. So, I told him that, yes, I did know you and that, no, you were not in Katherintal, but on patrol with Vacilly. They were all set to send for you right then when they found out that you were not an officer. That's when things got real hot and bothered, with lawyers and protocol, people running all over the place. Finally, they came up with this solution and, well, here we are."

"I'm not sure anybody did you any favors, Andreas, you are the most junior of the lowest rung of field grade officers and an earldom is the lowest rung on the nobility ladder," Halinov said with a sad expression on his face. "The land you have been awarded is not of the highest quality, and the villages are the poorest in the province."

Vacilly nodded in agreement. "Yes, they handed you a pile of horse manure, for sure," he said.

"Well, look at it this way," Andreas said, "I'm better off than I was before, and the only way to go is up when you're at the bottom."

"Always the optimist, Andreas," laughed Halinov. "I must be off; like Vacilly, here, our brigade will be leaving for home in the morning. We should be home in time for harvest. I'll fill in your father about all this when I get home, Andreas." And with a final handshake, he was off.

"Oh, I almost forgot, Vacilly, I have an aide that is going to need a couple of horses. Do you have any remounts I could purchase?"

"Already taken care of, Michilov paid for them this morning," Vacilly said. "Good luck with that one, Andreas, I'm not sure about him. Too much of his mother's influence, I think."

"We'll make a cavalry man out of him," Andreas said. "He'll be out from under daddy's wing for a while, probably make a big difference."

"Might be you're right," said Vacilly. "Speak of the devil," he nodded back over his shoulder.

"With your permission, sir, the arrangements you asked to procure have been completed," reported the young lieutenant.

"Thank you, Lieutenant, at ease," Andreas ordered. "Now, Captain, we have been standing here for hours and you have not even offered us a chair or a drink. I'm thinking all of those things people say about you Cossacks being uncivilized are true."

"Well, we can't have that now can we, Your Majorship?" Vacilly said and he disappeared into his tent, returning with three tin cups and a bottle of vodka.

Pouring a finger's worth of vodka in each mug, he handed them out. "A toast to His Lordship, Earl Bekenbaum."

"Thank you, Captain, the honor of Cossacks everywhere has been upheld," Andreas said, "and now to business, I think, Captain. It is getting late. Have the lads fall in, if you will."

"Fall in, fall in!" bellowed Vacilly. "Come on, come on, you sleepy heads, you're keeping an aide to the chief of staff waiting!"

An eruption of controlled pandemonium occurred as men rushed out of their tents, grabbed their stacked arms, and assembled in two lines in front of the tents at rigid attention.

"All present and accounted for, sir. They are all yours, Major," said Vacilly with a salute.

Returning the salute, Andreas marched to the center of the assembled men trailed by the captain and lieutenant.

"My name is Major Andreas Bekenbaum of the Royal Horse Guards. I have been ordered to select ten of you to be my personal guards. I would prefer volunteers. All those who wish to volunteer for this duty, take one step forward."

After a moment's hesitation and virtually as one man, all ninety-nine men took one step forward.

"Alright, then. At ease," he ordered to the accompaniment of crashing boots and rifles. "Sergeant Johann Bekenbaum, front and center."

Johann marched to within three feet of him stomping to a halt, rendering the rifle salute, and yelling out "Sɪʀ!"

"Sergeant Bekenbaum, you will distribute the bag amongst the men."

"Sir," was the reply; he took the proffered bag and marched back to the two lines of men. Each man reached into the bag and took out one stone.

"Thank you, Sergeant, you will now accompany the lieutenant to your new assembly area, then return here to pack up and reassemble in your new area."

As the new sergeant and the lieutenant left the area, Andreas continued, "The rest of you, there are nine colored stones. Those of you with the colored stones will be my volunteers. You will not look at the stones until I have left the area. The volunteers will gather all of their gear and return to their new quarters with Sergeant Bekenbaum when he returns."

"Captain, you may fall out your troops."

"Company, attention! Fall out!" bellowed Vacilly.

"Thank you, Captain," said Andreas, "please, convey my best wishes to your family once you get back home."

"I will, Andreas, and to your mamma and poppa, too," Vacilly said. "God speed, Andreas, you're going to need it."

They both saluted, and Andreas headed back to the main camp with some sadness at not being a part of the gang anymore. He wandered the camp aimlessly, walking with his hands clenched behind his back until he came to the river crossing where all this had started weeks before. That is where they found him, looking out at the camp across the river. A rough hand grabbed him on the shoulder and spun him around.

"Bloody hell, Andreas, what the hell is going on?" asked Johann.

He was faced by his brother and Ivan the young lieutenant, both with looks of concern on their faces.

"There is some grand game being played, by those on that side of the river and those back in the command tent on our side," Andreas said. "The ones on our side have decided that I can be of use to them, and by dangling some, to them, minor baubles at me, I will be their loyal man, to make use of as they wish. We are in a dangerous place amongst powerful and dangerous men who will stop at nothing to get what they want." Thinking for a few moments, he continued, "If for one minute it would be to their advantage, our side would sell us out to that side in a heartbeat."

"What could possibly make you think like that?" exclaimed young Ivan. "You, and we, are well respected. The czar would never tolerate such behavior."

"Ivan, your mother has filled your head with romantic notions of chivalry and honor amongst the nobility," Andrea said. "While that may be true of the upper levels of society, for us at the bottom, not so much. The czar is probably not even aware that Katherintal exists, let alone the people in it. What do you know of your father's people, Ivan?"

"I understand that he had some kind of dispute with his family. He never talks about it, or them," Ivan said. "Why do you ask?"

"Your father and my father grew up together in a city called Cologne in Prussia. Your grandfather owns an iron foundry and factory there. Your grandfather planned for your father, as a younger son, to open a factory for the family in Westphalia, a state southwest of Prussia, and they had made some trips together there to begin negotiations. That was when Napoleon decided he required some troops and the kaiser agreed. Your father thought he would gain some good experience and some contacts for the family; your grandfather agreed and he purchased a commission in the Prussian Hussars for your father."

Andreas continued that his father, also as a younger son, felt he would like to join the same regiment, but his father refused him permission to do so. "So, Father ran away, changed his name, and joined up as an enlisted trooper. This caused Grandfather to disown him."

He went on that both their fathers had taken to life in the army and they steadily rose through the ranks, with Ivan's father—to the dismay of his family—deciding to make a career of it. They ended up in the same company together and when the kaiser decided to back the English against Napoleon, had participated in several major campaigns. Rising through the ranks, Ivan's father, with the financial backing of his father, had risen to be the colonel of a Hussar battalion, "and he took my father with

49

him. In fact, my father had risen to the rank of chief warrant officer or the top non-commissioned officer of the battalion."

Being stationed in a mostly agrarian environment during garrison duty, the two friends had noticed that the peasants working in the fields had much less freedom than what they had experienced growing up as Burghers, or citizens of a free city-state. The peasants were virtually slaves to the landowners who could and did do what they wanted to them. When a great famine hit most of Europe, things only became worse.

The Prussians began to exert their large military and manufacturing superiority over the other German states, trying by any means to unite all of the German-speaking states into one country. This led to a popular unrest among a number of smaller countries at the loss of freedoms experienced for their states joining the German confederation dominated by the Prussians. This culminated in a mass, armed uprising in Heidelberg, which forced the Prussians to intervene, sending the battalion to join the more famous Uhlan, or lancer, cavalry battalion and two infantry battalions from Prussia to quell the revolt.

When Ivan's father had been ordered not to enter the city to quell the armed uprising but, instead, to destroy neighboring villages, farms, and crops, killing anyone who got in their way, Michilov had protested to the commanding general, had his protest vehemently refused, and had immediately resigned his commission in protest. Hearing word from a sympathetic infantry officer on the staff, that higher command was contemplating arresting him for dereliction of duty, Michilov had left the area immediately.

"The rest of the married officers followed him," Andreas continued. "The younger and unmarried officers stayed and, after receiving assurances that their families would follow, the enlisted men made a run for it, eventually crossing the border at this very same spot. Your father and the other officers had already made contact with Vacilly, and a squadron of his troopers was waiting at this crossing to escort the rest of the battalion to their new land and families. Your father changed his name, bought his land with money from Germany, and here we are.

"The settlement has been using our contacts in Germany to obtain the firearms that we now have. This is how we kept the Cossacks on our side originally, and we traded weapons for livestock and seed. Now my father trades horses to the Germans, wheat to the Russians and other people through the market in Odessa, just as your father does."

"So, this is why you are Cossack and we are not?" Ivan said.

"Originally, yes, the rest of the regiment became Cossack, spread through the Beresan district in family groups of thirty or so. Then the Russians began to bring in other German families and where we, by necessity, have blended in with the culture, these others have not. They still think of themselves as German and look down on us, much the same way you boyars do.

"We use this to our advantage, Ivan. We have a certain reputation and mystique and we go out of our way to make it look that way. In reality, I think you will find that underneath our devil-may-care attitude you will find we are very professional and take things very serious. Oh, and one more thing, your father and my father are brothers. That makes you our cousin."

Chapter Two

Andreas was finally ushered into the command tent as the sun was reaching its zenith. These people have a funny notion of first thing in the morning, he thought. He was given a seat at once this time, and after the formalities of reporting were done, Marshal Molotov got right to business. Seated behind the table today were only the marshal and the dandy from the previous meeting. Lying on the tabletop were two piles of documents.

"Major," the marshal began, "His Highness sends his regrets that he cannot attend this meeting, but he has been regrettably called to a more pressing engagement. If you wish, you may read through the documents in the left pile at your leisure. There will be no changes to them made or considered. They were prepared by legal experts by all the governments concerned, and we don't know why His Highness thought any different."

After a moment of silence, the marshal continued, "Yesterday we received word from Moscow that we are to be joined by another delegation regarding a separate treaty. The documents for that are in the right pile. You are to review those documents and if any errors in grammar et cetera are found, you will make recommendations for changes and submit them to General Andropov here. You will accompany the general to his quarters, where he will brief you on your task. Dismissed."

With that, Andreas and the general, followed by their escorts, walked the short distance to where the general's tent was located.

"Major, hand those documents to the corporal there and he can take them to your quarters and then return here to wait for you," the general ordered. One of the guards stationed outside the general's tent opened the flap and with a 'follow me' gesture, the general entered the tent.

"Take a seat, Major," the general said as he removed his cap and sword belt, tossing them onto a nearby trunk. Unbuttoning his jacket, he walked over to a row of bottles lined up on a table not far from his field desk and chair. Selecting a bottle and two mugs, he returned to his desk, poured two generous measures, and handed one to Andreas. "Good health," he said, draining the glass.

"So, Major, when we are in private, I will address you as Bekenbaum and you may address me as 'General'," he said, grinning.

"His Highness has discovered there is a lake not far from here with spectacular views, that he really must view, that is his pressing engagement. The crown prince often has these flights of fancy, which we, his court, must comply with; you were one such of his brilliant ideas. Now we are stuck with finding something for you to do. Now, not to worry, you are an earl. Albeit, a minor earl from an unknown earldom far from the seat of power. We were going to have to find someone dumb enough to take it, and I doubt anyone from the Moscow inner circle will object to a nobody taking a nowhere earldom with no hope of profit or a life of leisure luxury. You will have your work cut out for you to make a profit and enough money to field the troops required of you by the imperial government. The czar is also about to announce that all serfs must be freed, so you will have to pay for your labor."

"Andreas, you will also be a social outcast with the landed elites. You are not of Russian heritage or of old money. Or, if you try to make inroads with the wrong people, this could lead to some big problems for you."

"General, I don't think this will be a problem. I have no intention of currying favor or to increase my prestige. I have more than enough already."

"The naivety of the young," Andropov said. "Oh, by the way, I am the official in charge of Beresan District, and you will be under my control at home as well as in the field. Now, to business."

Andropov explained to Andreas that the original premise of this mission was to seal a marriage contract for the crown prince that would ensure stability throughout Europe and Mother Russia. During the course of the negotiations, the English had laid a not so subtle hint that they would take it as a favor should Mother Russia find some other use for their North American territories. Going so far as to suggest some concessions in Asia and not objecting to the possibility of an expanded Russian Navy.

The czar had come to the conclusion that the best course was to sell the land to the Americans. They were offering more money than the English. Money the czar would require for building and maintaining his new navy. The English could not really complain; he was, after all, complying with the English stated request. What did Alaska have to offer anyway, some firs, trees, salmon, ice, and snow? After all, Mother Russia already had a lot of firs, trees, and an overabundance of ice and snow; so, why not?

"This is where you come in, Andreas," the general said. "The Americans are uncouth commoners who no self-respecting aristocrat would be caught dead with. You are a new-made aristocrat, which will impress the Americans and let them think that Russia is more like America and less like the other European nations. Your family's ties in trade and business, which no self-respecting aristocrat would go near, will also stand you in good stead with the Americans. So you are to function as liaison with the Americans and report anything you think or hear the

Americans discussing that will impact the treaty. All the while keeping the fact that you speak English secret.

"The Americans will be provided with accommodations close to yours and you are to make yourself ready to greet them at any time. Now, I have wasted enough time on you; take those papers with you and get to work."

I really like that young man, Andropov thought as he watched a confused Andreas gather his three troopers and head back to his camp. We need more leaders like him and less like the fools surrounding the heir aspirant.

It is a good thing that Mother Russia is so big and has so many people, Andreas thought as he walked. If the rest of the European nations knew how backward and ill lead She is, they would band together to destroy her.

When Andreas reached his tent, there was a captain and a private waiting for him under the scant shade provided by the small tent fly in front of the entrance. Both were wearing uniforms and insignia from the administration arm of an infantry battalion. On the ground, one to each side of the private, were two medium-sized bags with handles.

"Major Bekenbaum, sir?" asked the captain with a salute. "Please, sign here in acknowledgment of receipt, sir?" Thrusting a sheaf of papers at him.

Noticing the bags were sealed, Andreas looked at the papers and saw that he was signing for receipt of five thousand rubles, minus one thousand rubles for uniforms and equipment that had been issued to he and his men, mess fees for them both, and feed costs for his horses.

Typical, he thought, signing the papers and handing them back to the captain who saluted and abruptly left with the private in tow. Shaking his head at their retreating backs, he gestured to his two servants to gather up the bags and to toss them on the floor beside his small desk, which he noticed was now equipped with several small piles of paper. Two were the two treaties he was to review, but which were not now important, the other was for material lists of equipment.

He now had two hundred rifles, four hundred rounds of ammunition for the rifles, and two hundred bayonets and cleaning kits for the rifles. Two hundred lances, two hundred mess kits and nose bags for the horses, enough grain for two hundred horses, and three wagons in which to haul all of these supplies. In other words, enough to equip a complete company, which on the books he commanded. All of this equipment was at the quarter master's bivouac and would have to be retrieved. As this was either already paid for, or government issued, Andreas saw no problem with getting them, even though he only had twelve men at the moment. He signed all of the various forms placing them to one side.

Glancing at his two servants standing by the entrance to his tent, he sadly remembered why they were there and that he had neglected them for several days now, a fact he would rectify immediately. Moving over to his cot, he gestured to the folding camp stool he had just vacated by his desk and another by the tent entrance. "Take a seat," he told them, sitting on the edge of his cot.

They both sat, both visibly uncomfortable to be seated in the presence of an officer. Both were in infantry uniforms, as befitted their previous status, one a private, one a senior private.

"Tell me," Andreas said. "Are either of you married, have children? What are your ages?"

"I am twenty-five, sir," the senior private said. "My comrade is twenty-one. We are both married, and I have two children.

When we are not on campaign, we are servants in Master Halinov's service. We are Russians and our parents are field servants for the Master."

"So, you both have a minimum of twenty-five years of military service before you can hope for land then," Andreas said. "What of your training?"

"We can both read and write, sir," the senior private said. "We have adequate mathematics, and we have been given basic firearms and horse-riding training. We can drive a team of horses and wagons, sir."

Now that Andreas was a member of the aristocracy, he had powers to do with serfs what he wanted and after a few moments of thought he decided what he wanted.

"I would like both of you to enter my service permanently," he said. "Would you have a problem with that?"

Both men quickly glanced at each other before, once again, looking at the floor.

"As my lord wishes," the older of the two said with no expression on his face or in his voice.

Having observed how the landowners and aristocrats treated common serfs his whole life, Andreas knew they were not going to show any emotion for fear of any displeasure from him.

"As soon as we return home," Andreas said, "I will be recruiting a complete battalion of cavalry and I will require help with administration affairs. The battalion will be expanding rapidly, and I would prefer having men who know me and how I operate at the core of my staff in the new battalion. As the new earl, I have been granted certain lands to administer how I see fit and to make the czar a profit on those lands. As I require a staff, I will require leaders for that staff; so, I am going to promote both of you to sergeant if you agree to the following conditions. One, you will become, at a minimum, proficient in the basic cavalry skills required of a Cossack trooper. I will have no non-combatants in my battalion. Two, you will take possession of one hundred acres of land each and see to it that they become productive before we leave for next spring's deployment. Three, you will be loyal to the czar, Mother Russia, the Holy Church, your battalion, your comrades, and myself.

"Go, now, think about it, and let me know your decision. Make no doubt, this will be your decision, not mine. I will not force you to comply. If you do not wish to become members of my troop, when we return home, I will relinquish you back to Major Halinov's command and nothing further will be said on the subject. I only want people who want to be with me, not compelled to be with me. The duty will be long, hard, and at times boring. At other times, more frightening than you can ever imagine. I will be hard, but fair. Think long and hard before you give me an answer. Where we will be sent will be far from home and dangerous. That is what this new Cossack battalion will be facing until we prove ourselves. Go now, and send Sergeant Bekenbaum to me when he returns from training."

After they left, Andreas picked up the first pile of documents, which, basically, was a marriage contract between the crown prince and the daughter of an Austrian high-born house. It was of boring and basically uninteresting bureaucratic language that left both houses plenty of latitude for maneuver. The other document was equally boring in language, but had some interesting elements that made Andreas think he would enjoy meeting and interacting with these Americans. His thoughts were interrupted when his brother announced himself outside his tent.

"Sergeant Bekenbaum reporting as ordered, sir," he announced after given permission to enter.

After he answered Andreas's questions on the men's progress on training, Andreas outlined the plan for obtaining the supplies provided for them and told Johann to coordinate with the lieutenant the implementation of that plan.

"Speaking of the lieutenant," he said, "how is he holding up? He's not used to the type of openness we enjoy amongst ourselves."

"The lieutenant is progressing as well as can be expected of an infantry officer, sir," Johann said. "His sword skills are adequate, horse skills marginal, lance skills barely passable, rifle skills hopeless, whip skills non-existent. The lieutenant is applying himself vigorously to his training and shows a willingness and eagerness to learn. He takes instruction and suggestions well, sir."

"Thank you, Sergeant. Keep me updated on his progress. Take a seat, Johann, do you have any tobacco? I forgot to get mine before changing quarters," he asked.

"But, of course," replied Johann, "I'll trade you for a swig of that wonderful vodka you fine officers always have on hand."

With a pipe full of tobacco and a cup of vodka, Andreas outlined his intentions about his two prospective recruits and asked his brother what he thought. His brother thought it was a good idea and that the two men would probably jump at the chance. Andreas then outlined his immediate plans for their little group, which after a few moments of thought, Johann also agreed with.

"Alright, then," Andreas said. "Gather the lads together after mess, and we'll have a little chat then. I will be approaching the lieutenant and his attendant with the same offer. On a more personal note, I am formally asking you to join my little happy group. Will you come?"

Taking a couple of puffs on his pipe, Johann swirled his cup of vodka about for a moment, tilted it up, finished it off, and held it out for a refill.

"Well, brother," he said, "you know I am in the same boat as you. No land, no inheritance to speak of. I have to make it on my own. I want to marry Irene, and the three hundred acres you will grant me will go a long way in persuading her to agree. The lads have agreed to me being senior sergeant; so, yes, I'm in."

"Oh, you dastardly Bekenbaums," laughed Andreas. "You know very well you are only allowed two hundred acres as senior sergeant. You are extorting an extra one hundred acres from me because I need your vast experience. Alright then, two hundred acres of Crown land and one hundred acres of my land, not one acre more."

"I was taught bargaining by the best, my lord, my older brother Andreas."

"Wait until we get home, I will teach this Andreas fellow not to trifle with a major of the Life Guards." Holding out his hand, they shook on the deal, smashed their tin cups together, shot back the fiery home brew, and the deal was sealed.

"Alright then, back to business," Andreas said. "Send the lieutenant and his man to my imperial presence, then send someone to His Eminence and ask him if he would honor us with his performing the induction ceremony tonight."

"Oh, before I forget. How are your English skills?" he said in that language.

"Da speaking I am to be not so goods, can understood be, perhaps. The better the listening is. The why I am wondering," Johann replied.

"We are going to be joined by some Americans shortly," Andreas said, continuing in English. "I have a feeling they will be with us for some time. No doubt they will have some enlisted men with them. Be friendly, not overly informative, but answer their questions. I don't want you to speak to them in English, just listen when they are talking to each other. We can maybe get some valuable information from them when their guard is down if they don't think we can speak their language. I will be doing the same with the officers."

Johann agreed and, obtaining permission to leave, strode out of the tent. Andreas noticed his two attendants waiting outside and called them in. They came before him and stood at attention in front of him. Unlike how he and his brethren reported, they had their eyes downcast instead of being proudly at three inches above his head.

"Speak your mind," Andreas ordered. These two had much to learn, he thought.

"My lord," said the senior of the two men, "with your permission, we would like to accept the positions you have offered us."

"Very well, then, you are both promoted officially as of now. You are also granted one hundred acres of Crown land. You will prepare the paper work for your enlistment in the Life Guards as sergeants of my administration staff, and you are to draw and wear the appropriate uniform immediately. Until we return home, I cannot tell you where your land will be located as I do not know myself; however, you have my word that you will receive it. Is that acceptable?"

"Yes, sir!" they bellowed.

"Make it happen. You will report back to me in uniform one hour after sunset. I don't want to see you until then. Dismissed."

Andreas followed them as they exited his quarters, hoping to get some fresh air for a few moments, when he noticed his clearly extremely agitated lieutenant and his servant waiting impatiently outside. Sighing, he turned back to his tent, waving the two men to join him in his tent. I was wondering when this was going to happen, he thought. He walked back to his desk, casually picking up his whip from the top with his right hand halfway up its length.

"You have no right to take those men from my father's service!" Ivan roared out as he entered the tent.

"ATTENTION!" bellowed Andreas in his best parade ground command voice. Spinning around, he swung the whip snapping it expertly one inch from the lieutenant's right ear with a pistol-like *crack*.

The lieutenant snapped to a rigid attention, while the already at-attention enlisted man was visibly shaking in fear.

As he walked around to their backs, Andreas recoiled his whip tapping it on his thigh as he walked. Glancing out his tent flap, he waved off his guard detail who were rushing forward— the corporal with his sword drawn and the two troopers with rifles at the ready.

Walking up between them, Andreas said, "Private, I wonder if you could leave the lieutenant and I alone for a moment? Move over there in front of the tent across from here until I send for you, if you please," he said quietly.

"Lieutenant," he continued still standing behind his young cousin, "insubordination to a superior officer while serving in the field is a court-martial offense. Insubordination to your overlord, at any time, is a capital offense, punishable by immediate execution at the overlord's discretion. As you chose to have your servant overhear your indiscretion, he also is guilty of insubordination and eligible to be shot immediately."

Still standing behind the young lieutenant, his whip gently tapping his right thigh, Andreas thought about how to handle this situation. The usual practice among the Russian aristocracy was to severely reprimand the offending officer, make him pay a hefty fine, and to have him shoot the servant in front of the rest of the men. Any Cossack officer who did those kinds of things for minor offenses such as this would, at best, wake up in the morning minus most of his men and, at worst, not wake up at all.

Turning around, Andreas walked to the front of the tent and addressed his guard corporal, who had positioned himself in front of the opening, and asked him to bring the private to him. He then walked back to his desk and, tossing the whip onto it, turned around to face the, by now, both visibly shaken men.

"At ease, Private," said Andreas, "please, accept my apology for having to involve you in this affair. You are not at fault here and have done nothing wrong. Lieutenant, you are to have the corporal of the guard escort you to your quarters to await further orders; Private, you remain here."

After the lieutenant had acknowledged the order, had performed a rigid about face and marched out of the command tent, Andreas walked over to where his desk was and sat himself on his camp stool. "The original purpose of this meeting, Private, was to ask you if you would join our regiment. That offer is still open should you want it. You have my permission to speak freely."

"You want me to join your regiment, sir, to become a Cossack like the others?" the private blurted out in surprise.

"Yes, Private, that is the intention. Do you have a problem with that?" answered Andreas.

"No, my lord, I have dreamt all my life about being a Cossack. If it please you, yes, my lord, I would like to accept any position you have for me, sir."

"Alright, Sergeant, go with my two new sergeants and draw your new uniforms and present yourself to me one hour after sunset with them."

As the new sergeant left the tent at almost a run, any thought Andreas had of some time for quiet contemplation was shattered by the man walking out of the shadow in the corner of the tent by the entry way.

"You handled that well, Major," said General Andropov.

"Sorry, sir, I didn't see you there, sir," barked Andreas, springing to attention.

"As you were, Andreas," said the general, hooking a camp stool with a toe and pulling it over to him. Sitting down, the general pulled out a cigar from his inner coat pocket and lit it. "Any of that famous vodka you people have laying about?"

Hastily grabbing a bottle, he poured a shot for himself and the general. "Sorry, sir, I only have these tin cups, sir," Andreas said.

"Oh, the indignities I must suffer while amongst the uneducated," laughed the general. "I was on my way here to ask you for an indulgence when I noticed the upset lieutenant marching toward your tent," the general said. "It seemed obvious to me that some kind of confrontation was imminent. When the private exited the tent, I snuck in while your back was turned."

Andreas thought for a moment as he fished out his pipe, packed it with tobacco, and accepted the general's proffered cigar to light the pipe, handing it back to the general.

"General, I grew up in the same village as the lieutenant," Andreas said. "The lieutenant's father brought him along on this year's campaign to hopefully wean him away from his privileged ways. Unfortunately, this year's campaign was more political than martial and the lieutenant fell in with other over-indulged, privileged young officers and, if anything, had become more arrogant. His father asked me as a favor to take him on as an aide and, hopefully, teach him the ways of a true officer and gentleman. I had been expecting some sort of confrontation with him, but had hoped it would be in private, not the public display that has just occurred. If it had happened in private, I could have contained it, giving the lieutenant a small slap on the wrist and carried on. Now, however, I will have to come up with some kind of public reprimand, or I will risk an undermining of my authority over the other troopers."

"Yes, I see," said the general, "my father did much the same for me when I was his age. Did me a world of good. If I might suggest? A counseling session with myself and His Eminence might be just the thing? Of course, I would still expect you to hand him some form of minor punishment to show the troops. Now, the real reason I am here is to invite you to a state reception to celebrate the conclusion of the betrothal agreements for the heir. The party is scheduled for tonight, and I think it is in your best interests not to attend. The sooner you can slip from the heir's notice, the better it will be for you, Andreas. Once that happens, the heir's toadies will no longer think of you as a threat and they will stop finding ways to discredit you or out-and-out attack you. This little disciplinary matter will be a good excuse."

"I would have tried to find a way out of it, General," Andreas said. "I have no wish to become involved in the politics of the grand court. In any case, we will be inducting the new members into our new regiment tonight at a small ceremony. You are, of course, welcome to attend the ceremonies; you are our commander, after all."

"Thank you for the invitation, Andreas, but I fear I must decline. As I am not a 'blood Cossack', I am not allowed to attend the ceremony itself. I will, however, try and make it to the party afterward. If I can slide away from the heir´s party, that is. The other reason I am here is that the Americans have expressed an interest in how Cossacks function, and they are wondering if it will be all right for them to observe some of your training."

"We train every morning, sir," Andreas said. "We have made a training area in a clearing about five miles east of here. It's a couple of hundred yards off the main trail, and you should be able to see the new trail we have cut to reach it. The Americans are welcome to come and observe anytime they wish. As a matter of fact, we will be training the new people from scratch tomorrow. Oh, better make it a couple of days from now. Nobody is going to be in any condition to train for a day after the party."

"Good, good," said the general, "I will let them know. I will be requiring a thousand troopers from you for next spring. Is that going to be a problem?"

After a moment's thought, Andreas replied, "I can guaranty five hundred, sir. I think I would need permission from the Ataman for more than that."

"Somehow, I don't think that will be a problem, Andreas. In fact, the more troopers you can get the better. As part of the alliance just formed, the czar has committed to an allied expeditionary force to conduct operations next year. You will be part of that force. Andreas, you really don't know how much of an impact you have made, not only within your own brigade, but the other Cossack contingents here. Vacilly had nothing but praise for you, and your men took every opportunity to brag you up. You should have been made an officer long before this. Only your ancestry seems to have held you back. Now you must take this opportunity that you have been given to advance not only yourself, but of your whole community. Tonight's ceremony will be the beginning of that." With that, the general took his leave, saying he would collect his lieutenant for his counseling session and return him as soon as that was done.

"May I have a moment of the major's time, sir?" The request came from the entry to his tent shortly after the general had left.

"Come on in, Johann," replied Andreas.

"That dumb kid could not have picked a worse time for that," said Johann. "I tried to warn him the general was approaching, but he did not listen."

"It's all under control, Johann," Andreas said. "I explained the situation to the general, and after he returns from his counselling session with the general, I will administer a severe slap on the wrist and hopefully that will be the end of it."

He outlined to Johann that he wanted him to groom two horses from Andreas's string of three to prepare as gifts to his two new recruits. As their sponsor, it was required of him to provide their first mounts. He thought that taking one of Ivan's horses from him to provide the mount required for his new sergeant would be a fitting punishment, as well as save Andreas the cost of procuring a mount for him. Johann agreed and, after confirming that Andreas had no further immediate requirements, left Andreas to his thoughts.

After what seemed to Andreas to be a short period of time, his guard corporal informed him that the lieutenant was requesting an audience with him. After taking a moment to collect himself, button up his uniform jacket, and run his hands through his hair, Andreas gave permission for the lieutenant to enter.

"Lieutenant Halinov reporting for punishment as ordered, sir!" said a very formal Ivan.

"At ease, Lieutenant," Andreas said, "anything to say for yourself before I pronounce punishment?"

"No excuses, sir. I apologize to the major for my behavior and beg Your Lordship's forgiveness."

"In light of your inexperience and lack of proper military training, I am willing to overlook some of what occurred. To involve one of the men entrusted into your care in your indiscretion, I cannot overlook.

"Attention! For insubordination to a duly appointed superior officer, I hear by fine you one month's pay. For insubordination to your duly appointed overlord, you are hereby informed that you have forfeited our gift of a horse. For involving a subordinate in your indiscretion, you will provide a horse to that subordinate, which has already been selected by us and you will publicly apologize to said subordinate before the induction ceremonies this evening. Do you understand, and are you ready to comply with this punishment?"

"Sir, yes, sir!"

"At ease. Are you still willing to serve as our aide, or would you like to be reassigned?"

A wide-eyed look of surprise came across Ivan's face, "You would still have me?"

"Field grade officers are not in the habit of making ill-conceived decisions, Lieutenant, nor are they in the habit of repeating themselves."

"Yes, sir, I would like to continue as His Lordship's aide, sir!"

"Very well, then. Take a seat, Ivan," Andreas said, concluding the formal part of the interview.

After he had seated himself, Andreas continued, "Cousin, what plans does your father have for your future? Would he be upset if you pursued a military career, and, more importantly, would you like to?"

"Sir, my father and I have discussed the possibility of my staying with the army for a while," Ivan said. "We both feel that my spending at least five years, depending on dire circumstances at home, would be in my best interests, sir. So, no, my father will not be upset."

"I have just been informed that I will be required to greatly expand my command in the near future," Andreas said. "I will be needing good officers as well as men; so, yes, I can use you. There is, however, one catch. I can retain you as an administration officer, but I cannot give you command of a squadron of troops as the troopers will all be Cossacks, which you are not. Would you consider joining?"

"I had considered that," Ivan said. "But I do not know how, or if I would be allowed, to join a Cossack host."

"Well, first you have to ask," Andreas said, "then you have to find a sponsor. Then the host has to take a vote on whether or not to accept you, then you have to be initiated into the host. Even after all that, you may not become an officer. Cossack officers are elected by the host members, not appointed by an overlord."

"Sir, who do I ask and how do I find a sponsor?" Ivan asked.

"Do I take it you wish to join?" asked Andreas.

After his nodded response, Andreas continued, "Well, you have asked, you have found your sponsor, the lads voted yesterday to accept you, and you will present yourself in uniform minus rank badges and weapons to the initiation ceremony this evening. Of course, you will have to supply your own horse for the ceremony as my sponsor's gift to you has been forfeited as your punishment, but, not to worry, that has been arranged as well. Now, run along, young cousin; someone will be by to collect you."

Oh, my aching head, thought Andreas as he struggled off his cot. The only thing worse than a Cossack initiation was a Cossack wedding; those went for three days instead of the two days of wild celebration they had just gone through. Andreas had slipped away an hour after sunset of the second day; nobody was likely to have missed him, anyway. Everyone was beyond even knowing what their own names were anymore by that point.

Gingerly looking around, he saw that his uniform and shaving equipment were already laid out for him, a bowl of water and towel on the desk. He pushed off from the cot and shuffled over to the desk, taking a couple of handfuls of water and splashing them over his head and face. As he was completing his shaving, a bright-eyed and enthusiastic newly made sergeant bustled into the tent.

"A wonderful good morning to you, my lord," he cheerfully greeted. "Some hair of the dog, sir?" Proffering a cup and a bottle.

"God, no!" Andreas said. "Some hot tea would be about the thing."

The man laughed and assisted Andreas with putting on his uniform. "How the bloody hell can you be so bloody cheerful?"

"Why, my lord," the sergeant said. "Nobody was paying attention to us too much after the first two or three hours. We were able to sneak away just after midnight the first night. I was amazed my lord was able to get away at all."

"Ugh, no respect, no respect at all. A good servant would have taken all that punishment for his lord. Did my guards at least stay semi-sober?" he asked.

"Sir, yes, sir. The ones on duty now did not partake much in the festivities," he replied.

"Corporal, get your butt in here," bellowed Andreas.

"Sir, how may I be of assistance to His Hungoverness, sir?" asked the corporal.

"Ach, not you, too. What do I have to do to get some respect around here? My own bloody guards!" the beleaguered major said, slapping the corporal good-naturedly on the back. "Alright, party time is over. Roust the lazy bums out, corporal," ordered Andreas.

Striding outside, the corporal grabbed a handy pot and ladle and began banging on the pot hollering, "STAND TO, STAND TO!"

The seven men staggered out of their tents and came together in a sloppy line, in various stages of dress or undress. Buttons incorrectly buttoned, if shirts were even on. Pants legs with one leg in boots, the other outside. All were swaying slightly as they stood in front of their major, flanked by his two sergeants in full uniform. A tardy Lieutenant Ivan was being hurried along by his attendant, hopping on one foot pulling the boot on the other as he joined the group. One suspender hanging off his shoulder and no jacket or cap on.

"All present, sir!" reported the corporal.

Andreas walked down the line, a look of disgust on him as he inspected the ragged crew. Marching back to the center of the group, he stood looking at them for thirty seconds tapping his coiled whip on his right thigh. At least they had their weapons with them, he thought.

"If you're going to party like Cossacks, you're going to bloody work like Cossacks the next morning! Everyone, excluding my guard, two laps around the camp, at the double. That includes you, Lieutenant, and both of you sergeants," he said, glaring at his two attendants. "NOW!" he ordered, cracking his whip in the air.

As the group more or less shuffled off in what loosely resembled a run, Andreas addressed his three-trooper guard. "I believe there are some nice eggs and sausages here in front of my tent. Would you gentlemen care to join me?"

As they sat and enjoyed their breakfast, Andreas verified that the three men had made sure that all the mounts had been cared for and that there was an adequate supply of water for the hung-over men. They would be extremely dehydrated, not only from the run, but the large amounts of vodka they had consumed.

After they had finished eating, Andreas outlined the training for the morning to the corporal and walked over to the horse lines; saddling Bartholomew, his only remaining mount, he lead him back to his tent. Tying the horse up to the log set up for that purpose in front of his tent, Andreas entered; picking up his ammunition bandolier, he opened the cartridge box attached to it and selected six rounds which he placed in the ready loops on his jacket. He then picked up his government-issued Dreyse rifle, inspecting the firing mechanism and barrel, and slung it over his right shoulder to hang crossways on his back.

Remounting, he walked Bartholomew over to the rack that held the squadrons' lances, picked one, and placed it in the scabbard behind his right leg, making sure it was fully seated before he turned his horse in the direction of the practice grounds and walked him out of camp.

Bartholomew was showing him signs of his lack of exercise, and Andreas broke him into a canter as soon as they were clear of the camp, giving him his head, and the horse broke into a gallop. He let him gallop for a couple of minutes before curbing him back to a trot, then a walk. It was good to get free of the camp, at last. The sun was fully up now, and the chill of the clear morning mountain air was beginning to dissipate. Andreas could hear the wind rushing through the trees and the birds and the squirrels announcing his passage to each other. The smell of the trees mingled with the smell of his horse as they made their way down the trail.

Soon Andreas found himself at the training place they had set up. As a more or less autonomous squadron, they had to make their own arrangements for training facilities. He and his brother had found this spot when they were still attached to Vacilly's brigade. It was just under eight kilometres upstream from the main camp, a large, approximately five hundred-meter by three hundred-meter, clearing in the trees bordered by the river; it was perfect for their cavalry training needs.

Dismounting, Andreas tethered Bartholomew and found himself a spot under a tree to sit. Listening to the trees and the river gurgling along its banks, his mind wandered back to the events of the last few days. He had known that there were other Cossacks in the camp, serving as guards or escorts to the various dignitaries of the group. He had not expected that over five hundred of them would show up for the ceremonies. It was not often that they were allowed to gather together and socialize. Not only were there groups of Life Guards, but also members of the czar's personal guard, these men were all permanently attached to the regiments and seldom had the opportunity to go home or mingle outside of their own regiments.

The ceremony itself had been brief, conducted during a mass celebrated by the bishop and four attending priests from the four different Cossack groups there. It was after the mass that they sprung the surprise on Andreas. Calling all fifteen of them to the front of the assembled men, the bishop had asked if they had chosen a leader for their new host. On the verge of replying in the negative, it was the first Andreas had heard they were to be a Cossack host of their own. He was interrupted by all his men replying in the affirmative in unison. When the bishop had asked them who they had chosen to be their Ataman, they had shouted again, in unison, his name.

Andreas still could not believe that all this was happening to him. It was all some kind of a dream, or cruel joke. When he had finally been able to get a private word with the bishop, he had said that to him.

The bishop had smiled at him and, in almost the same words the general had said to him earlier in the day, said, "You really don't know the impact you have had on everyone around you, do you? Such is the way with the true leader. Such was the way of Our Lord Jesus. This is all real, my son; all these men, yours and the others, they are all here to honor you. All who you are, all who you will be, all you will take the Cossack nation to be."

"How can that be, Father?" Andreas replied. "I have won no great battles, taken no great battle standards or famous hostages. I have only this one small campaign season and only been in one or two small skirmishes."

74

"Three battles, outnumbered two or three to one against you; opponents who, for years, have frustrated seasoned veterans on both sides of the border, some of whom are in this place tonight. Not only did you beat them the very first time you encountered them, Andreas, the few that got away will be telling the tale to their comrades back home, and they will not be back to bother us for many years. Not only that, Andreas, you did it without losing a man or a horse, indeed, not even sustaining a major casualty.

"Vacilly served with many of these men against the English and French coalition in the Crimea. He and his battalion have earned great respect from these others. For Vacilly to praise a man is rare, and he has been bragging about you almost constantly to anyone who would listen. You have earned this, Andreas; now, go on and enjoy yourself."

Andreas's thoughts were brought back to the present by Bartholomew's warning nickering, and as Andreas stood up brushing off his uniform, the quiet of the clearing was disrupted by the hoofbeats and jingling of tack as his little troop entered it. He saw that they were accompanied by the general, two civilians dressed in English-looking clothes, and three military men in blue uniforms. All were mounted on Russian cavalry mounts and, other than the swords the officers wore, none were armed.

Two of the officers had yellow stripes running down their pants legs, on one collar of their jackets they had a US badge and on the other a crossed sword badge. They both had a pillbox style cap on their heads with the crossed sword badge in the center of it. The third officer's uniform was of a darker blue with red stripes running down the leg and red embroidering on the jacket and seams of the arms. He wore a white hat with black brim and, instead of the crossed swords badge, he wore a globe with fouled anchors badge.

Oh God, that's all I need, thought Andreas as he looked at his troops. Well, at least they cleaned up somewhat, he thought.

Drawing himself up to attention and saluting as they came to a halt in front of him, the general waved him a return salute and told him to relax. "As I mentioned earlier," he said, "these gentleman are representatives of the United States of America, and they have come to observe how you Cossacks train."

"I am pleased to introduce Mr. Johnson of the State Department, Colonel Olynick and Major Rostov of the First Cavalry, Major Asmanov of the United States Marine Corp, and Mr. Remington of the *New York Times* newspaper. Gentlemen, Major Andreas Bekenbaum, Earl of Katherintal, and Ataman of the Andreashost."

Andreas shook hands with the civilians and saluted and shook hands with the military men.

"Andreas, please, explain to these gentlemen the drills you are about to perform."

His guard troop was just then leaving up the trail leading to a large hill with eight lances divided between them. The other members of the troop were setting up bottles on three lines of six poles, a stuffed figure attached to a pole: one thirty meters in front of the other poles, and three rifle targets thirty meters further on and grouped thirty meters to the right of the track of the other targets.

"Normally, we run this drill in groups of three," started Andreas, "but in the interest of safety, because of recent events, we will be running it singly today."

"Yes, we all heard the recent events you mentioned; it is hard not to hear five hundred drunken Cossacks when they let their hair down," joked the general to the loud laughter of the assembled group. "Carry on, Major."

"One at a time the men will run their horses over that hill and back a total distance of around two kilometers. They will, then, in turn, lance the dummy, decapitate or break one of the six bottles with their sword, then hit the target with one rifle round. This is to simulate conditions they may face on a battlefield someday."

"Why are those three taking all the lances over the hill?" asked Major Olynick.

"Well, as I am sure you have been told, Major, we Cossacks like to enjoy every advantage we can obtain," Andreas said, smiling. "Usually, this is a competition amongst the men; we will be planting those lances in the ground five hundred meters on the other side of the hill. This will make sure they run the full five hundred meters, Major."

"Enlisted men are the same with us, Earl Bekenbaum." And they all had a laugh.

"The three troopers who are planting the lances will not be taking part in the drill today. As they were assigned guard duty last night and are not as hung over as the rest, it would be an unfair advantage." More laughs all around. "They will, instead, be instructing our new recruits on the use of the lance and cavalry sword. The new recruits will not participate in the mounted drills until they have at least obtained some basic skills."

At that, the drills began. Each trooper leaving one minute after the one before, with Lieutenant Halinov going last. The general gave Andreas a look when he saw that.

"Sir," said Andreas, "Lieutenant Halinov has only just began the mounted drills, he would only be getting in the way and holding up the others. That is why he is going last."

One by one, the troopers passed down the line, and soon, there was a pile of broken glass on the ground, the dummies were wearing a number of lances, and shots were ringing out on the rifle range.

"Very impressive, Earl Bekenbaum," said the State Department man. "You say you usually run this drill in groups of three?"

"Yes, sir," replied Andreas, "we make it a competition; the winners of each group going on until only one is left."

Just as the lieutenant was cresting the hill and the last of the troopers had finished firing at his rifle target, five riders came into the clearing. Two Prussian Uhlans, two English Horse Guards, and a single member of His Majesty's German Cavalry, also an English unit, albeit German.

They arrived just as the lieutenant started his run at the lance dummy. His wobbly thrust glanced off the dummy forcing him to drop it before he could draw his sword. He broke the third bottle he swung at and he almost fell out of the saddle dismounting before the rifle targets. Taking his time, he was able to hit the target on his first attempt; although, it was low and off-center.

"If that is any example of the vaunted Cossacks, no wonder you beat them at the Crimea," the older Uhlan said to the others in the group in German, "and he was an officer. Look at that other one over there. They dress him up in a Cossack uniform, but he is clearly an administration type. What dung cart did he steal that horse from? We Prussians would mop up the floor with them." All of them except the German, who only smiled politely, had a good laugh as they rode over to the general.

Saluting, the mouthy Prussian said in Russian, "Good morning, General, a nice day for a ride."

"Yes, it is, Major, did you see our little demonstration?"

"An interesting exercise," the Prussian said. "I believe the lieutenant did a credible job."

"Nice horses," said Andreas, "thoroughbreds?"

"But, of course, only of the finest breeding," the Prussian replied haughtily.

"Care to have a friendly little competition amongst allies?" Andreas asked. "Me and my horse against one each of our new allies doing the same exercise as that?"

Looking at each other and then at the general, the mouthy Prussian addressed the general, "Sir, no disrespect, but I feel that it is hardly a fair competition, perhaps with another officer from a different regiment?"

"Why," said Andreas, "how about if I were to offer two thousand rubles each to the men who beat me? Would that be enough incentive for members of such famous regiments to play?"

This seemed to pique the Englishmen's interest.

"That and the ability to brag how you beat a Cossack at his own game?" added the general. "Of course, we will understand, the Cossacks have a well-deserved reputation. Was it not Napoleon who said they were the best light cavalry in the world?"

That was enough for the Prussian. "I will give double should your man beat me," he said, puffing out his chest. One of the Englishmen followed suit.

Hook, line, and sinker, thought Andreas. "Corporal, three lances to position, please," he ordered, "you others reset the course."

"I see you have your carbines with you," he said, pointing at the rifle scabbards on their saddles. "Would you like to use those, or borrow one of our rifles?"

Both men indicated they would use their own weapons.

"General, if you would not mind explaining the rules?" asked Andreas, riding over to where he had left his rifle and dismounted.

Johann was waiting for him and took the reins. "Was that smart, baiting them like that?"

"I did not say that I am a jumped-up, popinjay administration officer who stole his horse from a dung cart, they did. I intend on rubbing that smart-ass Prussian's nose in it." Removing his jacket and buckling his sword belt so it positioned his sword handle high on his back, hilt over his left shoulder, then donning his cartridge belt and slinging his rifle over his right shoulder, he made sure his saddle cinch was tight and his stirrups the right length. Remounting, he made sure his sword was loose and he was seated firmly in his saddle.

"Just as I thought," came a comment from behind him.

Andreas turned his mount around and saw the green uniform of the King's German Legion.

"You are the one Vacilly told me about, yes?" he said in German.

"Yes, I am," Andreas replied in the same language, noticing the man was about his father's age.

"I thought so; he and I served together once long ago. I was with your father's regiment at the time. Be careful of that mouthy one. His father was the one that took over your father's regiment when your uncle resigned his commission."

"Even more reason for me to grind him into the dust," Andreas said, moving his horse to rejoin the group.

As Andreas took his place in the line, he overheard the German tell the Americans, "You are about to witness why Napoleon said what he said, gentlemen. That man is a bred warrior, trained from birth to be one thing. Cossack!"

"Ready, gentlemen?" asked the general.

Both the other officers' high-strung horses were dancing in anticipation, already sweating, in stark contrast to Andreas and his mount, who stood in calm readiness.

"Go," yelled the general.

"Tally ho!" yelled the Englishman, as both men spurred their mounts into a gallop.

Andreas saluted the general and started his mount off at a canter after the other two horses. Both the other men were cresting the hill as he hit the base of it. When he hit the top and started down, both men had reached the lances. The Prussian stopped his horse and with a little bit of work removed the lance, spun his horse around, and spurred back to the hill. As Andreas passed him, he noticed that the man's horse was beginning to foam and that he had awkwardly placed the lance under his right armpit.

The Englishman had dropped the first lance and was just leaving as Andreas arrived. Slipping his left leg out of the stirrup, Andreas leaned down, grabbed the lance from the ground, and swinging back up to the saddle, placed the lance in the scabbard behind his right leg without breaking stride.

He passed the astonished Englishman halfway up the hill, the man's horse slowing rapidly, while Andreas' mount had not broken a sweat yet. Reaching the bottom of the hill, Andreas spurred his mount to a gallop as the Prussian awkwardly speared his dummy; drawing his sword and breaking the second bottle, trotted up to the rifle range. Dismounting, he drew his carbine from the scabbard and headed to the targets.

Andreas reached behind him and withdrew the lance, lowering it in time to hit his dummy dead center, letting it drag the lance from his hand. He drew his sword fluently, breaking the first bottle in his line and letting the sword drop to hang from its sword knot on his saddle. He then dragged his rifle from his back, taking a cartridge from his bandolier, loaded his rifle, and, standing in his stirrups, placed the rifle to his left shoulder. Pivoting, he sighted on his target and fired. Not even waiting to see where he had hit the target, he re-slung the rifle on his back and, spinning his horse around, spurred back to the bottles. Removing his whip from his belt, he proceeded to break every single bottle on every post. All before the Prussian had taken his first shot. Slowing his mount down, he trotted back to the group of spectators.

"*Mein Gott*," exclaimed the German. Switching back to Russian, "Vacilly told me you were the best he had ever seen. I did not believe him. Is it also true about the Muslims?"

Andreas made no comment as he moved back to the tree where he had left his jacket. Dismounting, he again gave the reins to his brother while he removed the rifle and cartridge belt and put the uniform jacket back on.

"Getting a little sloppy, Brother. Two inches to the right on the target," his brother said.

"Hung over," replied Andreas with a grin.

"Just lazy," laughed his brother. "How much you take them for?" he asked.

"Four thousand rubles. Each."

"Eight thousand rubles! You're buying tonight, Brother."

"My grandfather and father told me about you Cossacks. I never believed them. Now that I have actually seen it, they were not even close to what I have just witnessed. That horse, what a magnificent animal. Wherever did you get him?" said the Horse Guard, dismounting from his exhausted animal.

"He is a five-year-old from my own string," Andreas said. "I brought him along to give him some experience. He is showing good progress. You know, you were at a significant disadvantage here. You gave me thirty kilos of weight advantage, with your chest plate, helmet, and horse rigging."

"Yes, yes, and the horse has not been used much these last weeks, nor is he used to the altitude," the Englishman said. "But, what a story I have to tell. Competing with the two best light cavalry regiments in the world! I was still the best dressed though, what?"

They slapped each other on the back, both men grinning from ear to ear.

"Mary, Jesus, and Joseph! Did you see that shot? Seventy-five meters on horseback at a full gallop, and he hit the target two inches off-center!" This from the Prussian as he led his horse on foot up to them. "That horse, my God, look at him, hardly sweating and breathing normally."

Switching to German, Andreas said, "Not bad for a stolen, dung-cart horse. Not so?"

Laughing, the Prussian soldier said, "You heard that, did you? I was hoping to see what I could do against you fellows and thought if I provoked you enough you might be distracted enough to give me at least a small chance. But, I really did think you were just an administration officer. You sandbagged me on that one. I knew I was in trouble when you came to the line. Will you accept my apology?"

Bowing slightly, Andreas stuck out his hand to the Prussian who gladly accepted it. "You know," he said, "I underestimated you there. I knew I would do better with my rifle over your carbine, but that horse of yours was better than I thought. I took a chance with that shot, hoping to distract you more than anything."

"Now, now, Major, no false modesty. Thank you for the compliment, but I understand you are usually better than that, must be the hangover, no" the Prussian said. "The horse? Well, that was my secret weapon. My family buys all its horses from the von Bekenbaum family in Cologne, who I believe obtains them from some Cossack family with a similar name."

Andreas gave a quick look over at his brother and shook his head. "There are many people among us with German last names," he said. "Senior Sergeant, please, see to our guests' horses. Give them a good rub down and cooling off."

As Johann delegated two troopers to look after the allies' horses, he personally took control of Andreas's mount as Andreas and the other two officers walked over to where the rest of the group were standing.

"Major von Hoaedle, here, was just telling us how your company destroyed one thousand Turkish invaders earlier this year," said Mr. Remington, the newspaper man. "Care to tell us about it?"

Looking at the German cavalry officer and shaking his head slightly, Andreas said, "It was hardly one thousand, Mr. Remington. You know how these things become exaggerated with the telling. I am sure by the time I get home it will be up to four or five thousand and eight or ten artillery pieces. It was actually four hundred Turks, and we caught them by surprise."

"Major Bekenbaum is being overly modest," said General Asmanov. "I have his full report, come by and see it. Fascinating reading."

Andreas spent a lot of time answering questions from the Americans who wanted to see the lances, the rifles, and the swords they used. All of the weapons except for the rifles, which were standard government issue, were uniquely Cossack in nature and manufacture. Mr. Johnson, the State man, asked Andreas if he could have his military men demonstrate some of the American weapons, which may be of interest to him. Always interested in weapons he was unfamiliar with, Andreas agreed and set up a meeting for the next morning. After a few more comments and making arrangements to have his winnings delivered, all of the visitors departed, leaving Andreas's small detachment to their own devices.

"Have everyone continue with the training, Johann," he told his sergeant. "Then you and Ivan come back here."

"So, whose horse was that?" Andreas asked.

"Looked like one of Papa's," Johann answered. "More questions when we get back home, I'm thinking."

"Mm, yes. Ivan, do you know anything about us selling horses to the Prussians?"

"I know my father buys some from your father, then trades them somewhere to get the iron and steel we need for the smiths," Ivan said.

"That would explain it, then. By the way, if not for you, I would not have made as much money on the bet as I did. Consider your punishment complete," said Andreas.

Ivan then asked about the skirmish with the tribesmen earlier in the year. Andreas begged off answering, saying he had to return to camp to do paperwork. Gathering up his three-trooper escort, he told Johann to continue the weapons training, mounted up, and headed back to camp at a much slower pace than he had come. Bartholomew had worked hard that day and deserved a leisurely pace home.

The next morning, the Americans arrived at the training ground to see men furiously attacking each other with thick, sword-like sticks. Horses rearing, pawing the air, and biting each other. The air was thick with dust and the sound of men and horses screaming in pain or pleasure, depending on the outcome of the one-on-one battles.

To one side were the four new men hacking at each other on the ground, learning the basics of sword work. It took hours of training each week to not only hone the skills of sword work, but to build up the stamina of arm and body that would allow them to master a foe. The sticks they were using were the same size as the real blades but heavier, and while an injury such as a broken limb or rib was possible, rarely were the injuries more severe than a bruised or sore body.

Andreas noticed that the American military men today had rifle stocks protruding from rifle scabbards mounted to their saddles, and they all appeared to have some kind of a pistol in enclosed holsters attached to belts wrapped about their waists. The belts were also holding two cartridge boxes. The newspaper man had the same belt, but with cartridges exposed in loops attached to the belt, shiny side up, much like the Cossacks themselves did with their ready rifle rounds.

They rode over to the tree Andreas had parked himself under to observe his men training, leaning his back against the tree trunk, leisurely puffing on his pipe. As the men dismounted, the officers removed the firearms from their scabbards and, handing the reins to the newspaper man to tether the animals, strode up to Andreas.

"Good morning, Earl Bekenbaum," said Major Olynick as all three saluted.

"Coming to kill some targets today?" enquired Andreas, returning the salutes with a lazy wave in the general direction of his forehead. "Don't mind me, I'm not much up to the formal nonsense today; besides, we are all the same rank. Are those American weapons? I have not seen the like before."

The marine major explained that all the weapons were of American manufacture. The one he had was a Sharps infantry rifle, .44 caliber; one cavalry officer had the carbine model of the same make, the other a Winchester Model 73 carbine, also of .44 caliber. He said that the Sharps were single-action, breach-loading rifles that fired self-contained cartridges. The rifle had a range of one thousand yards, accurate to three hundred, the carbine slightly less due to the shorter barrel. The Winchester utilized brass-encased cartridges, center fired, and was called a 'repeater'.

The Sharps were standard military issue, while the Winchester was not widely used. He then asked Andreas if they could give a demonstration. Andreas, always interested in weapons that might improve his situation, agreed and, pushing himself up off the ground, accompanied the foursome to the rifle range.

While the two cavalry officers went down range to set up the targets, one at three hundred yards, the other two at two hundred, the marine major withdrew five cartridges from his front cartridge box and lined them up on the tree stump the Cossacks had been using for that purpose. He handed one over to Andreas for his inspection. The round had a paper wad with the powder encased in a copper cylinder with a round silver-colored disk in the center of the bottom end of the case. That, explained the marine, was the primer. He then picked up the rifle and lifted a lid above the trigger, which exposed the firing chamber. He pointed out to Andreas that lifting the lid prepared the bolt to be fired, and showed Andreas the firing pin. Once a cartridge was placed in the breach, the breach was closed, the rifle was fired, and lifting the lid again ejected the spent cartridge case making the rifle ready to fire again. The breach was machined in such a way that it was self-sealing. There was no need for rubber seals like Andreas's men needed with their needle rifles. In addition, the firing pin was much more robust than the pins that the Russian firearms had.

When the other two officers returned, the major wrapped the rifle sling around his left forearm, went down to one knee, and, bracing his left elbow on his left knee, rapidly fired off his five rounds. Splinters coming off the piece of firewood being used for targets indicated he had hit it with all five rounds.

Next came the cavalry officer with the carbine model. He also fired from a kneeling position but, having no sling, fired just with his elbow on his knee. Despite being one hundred yards closer, he managed only to hit his target three times.

"Told ya ta practice," the marine said to him in English.

"Ah, pound salt, Asmanov, not all of us goes to sleep with our weapons," the cavalryman replied in the same language.

"Not all of us was born with a rifle in his hands or came up through the ranks like him, either," joined in the other cavalry major. "I myself much preferred chasing girls than playing with rifles at the Point."

"Yeah, ya college boys, eatcher hearts out," laughed the marine.

"Semper Fi, bud," the other two roared out, laughing.

"Would you care to try one?" the marine officer, switching back to Russian, asked Andreas.

"If you don't mind? I would like to try the carbine, its shorter barrel would be more suited for what I do," answered Andreas.

The cavalry officer handed the carbine to him and explained how the breach and the sights worked and handed Andreas five cartridges, which Andreas placed in his, for now, empty cartridge loops on his uniform jacket. Going down to the ground in the prone firing position, he fired his first round, the bullet hitting the two hundred-yard target slightly high and to the right. Adjusting his aim, he fired the next four in rapid succession more or less in the center of the target.

"This is sighted for two hundred?" he asked.

After receiving an affirmative response, he asked for another five rounds. Lifting the carbine so the sights were aiming three inches above the three hundred-yard target he fired, plowing dirt at the bottom of it. Aiming three inches higher, he fired the next four rounds which hit the firewood.

"Close enough to kill a man," he said. "What about that other carbine? The Winchester, I think you called it?"

The other cavalry major, then, came up and began pushing cartridges into a slot on the breach of the weapon point first. Visually, this rifle was more pleasing. It had a brass breach, trigger, and funny-looking, large trigger guard. There were also two brass bands holding the hexagonal barrel onto the stock.

After putting ten cartridges into the slot, the major also took one knee. This must be the approved way they are taught to shoot, Andreas thought. The major levered down on the large trigger guard, pulling it away from the stock, then back up, sighted, and fired. He did this ten times in a row hitting the target seven times in less than thirty seconds.

All sounds of sword practice were gone, and Andreas forced himself to close his gapping jaws.

"That is why it is called a repeater," the major said. "It holds ten rounds in its magazine. A spring forces the round into the chamber when you ratchet down; this also cocks the firing hammer. Lifting the handle back up, forces the round into the breach and seals it. Pulling the trigger releases the hammer, firing the round. Pulling the lever down again ejects the spent round, and the sequence starts again. The War Department does not much like these weapons, nor do many of us. The rapid fire does not equate the loss of accuracy, and we feel the troops would waste too many bullets," he said.

"Hmm, yes, I could see that being a problem," Andreas said. With poorly trained conscripts, he thought. "May I try?" he asked.

The major showed him how everything worked, and Andreas loaded the weapon. Once again laying prone, he fired the first round, adjusted his aim, fired again, then fired three more times as rapidly as he could realign the sights after reloading. He shifted his aim to the further target, this time sighting eight inches above the target to compensate for the shorter twenty-two inch barrel, and fired, striking the target low one inch and slightly to the right. He fired the last four rounds at rapid fire hitting the target all four times, but not in a consistent grouping.

I can see why they prefer being down on one knee, he thought, it's easier to reload. I think I will try that technique.

"Well, I can see what you mean about wasting bullets. One shot, one kill, what?" he said.

"Just so," the marine agreed, "that's our motto. Let's have a look?"

All three targets had large exit holes, which Andreas knew would make for life-ending injuries in a human. "Very impressive," he said. Better than our weapons, he thought.

The two cavalry officers found three more pieces of firewood and set them up. Walking back about twenty-five yards, they stopped.

"If you don't mind, we would like to demonstrate our pistols."

"Pistols? Those things are only good for decoration on some fancy, chair-warming bureaucrat. One shot and all they are good for is a club," replied Andreas haughtily.

Looking at each other and smiling, they all undid the flaps on their holsters, removed strange-looking pistols from them, and, turning sideways to the targets, pointed the pistols at arm's length and, as fast as the pistols returned to line of sight from the last shot, fired five shots each without reloading. The worst of them hitting the target three times. The silence in the clearing after the firing was not just from the lack of firing. None of the Cossacks had ever witnessed the rapidity of the firing they had just witnessed.

"Care to try this one?" the marine major asked.

The major cocked the weapon halfway, then using a push rod attached to the barrel, pushed each spent cartridge out of the cylinder, and then, one by one, reloaded the pistol.

"I don't have much experience with pistol shooting," replied Andreas. "Tell me more about this weapon."

He was shown how pulling the hammer back not only cocked the weapon, but moved the cylinder containing the cartridges around so that when the trigger was pulled it landed on a live round. Cocking again moved the expended round out of the way and again placed a live one ready to fire. Taking the proffered weapon, he found it was well-balanced and fit his hand well. Turning sideways to the target, he cocked the weapon back, fully extended his right arm, sighting at the target, and squeezed off a shot, the bullet going nowhere near the target.

"Told you," he said. "What size ammunition does it use?"

"The same as the Winchester," he was told.

"Interesting. I am getting the feeling that perhaps you may be wanting to sell these weapons to us?"

"Well, the United States government always tries to promote our products, and we feel that these are better than any you will find anywhere in the world," replied Olynick.

Andreas thought for a moment, then told the major that if he had one hundred rounds for each of his weapons, he would put the weapons through a field test right now. The marine major smiled, whistled to get a nearby enlisted man's attention, and waved him over. The man was wearing a similar uniform to the majors, with a number of brightly colored stripes on the uniform jacket. He was about one hundred and seventy pounds and just under six feet tall. The way he moved and looked around as he was walking, had the look of a veteran, a man that had been there and done that.

Returning the man's perfect salute, the major explained to him in Russian that he wanted the sergeant to help Andreas run a field test of the three weapons. While he was doing that, Andreas waved Johann over.

"Senior Sergeant Bekenbaum, you will select two troopers," Andreas said. "You will accompany this gentleman who will instruct you on the operation of these weapons. You will then fire one hundred rounds from each of these fine weapons and from one of our rifles. You will then report back to me on your impressions and findings. Delegate the rest of your duties to one of the corporals for the rest of the day. Understood?"

"Sir!" snapped back Johann with a smart salute.

"Gentlemen, I don't see why we need to stay here and subject our ears to more of this. Perhaps we can reconvene at my quarters tomorrow about this time and discuss this further?" said Andreas to the other officers, as Johann went off to carry out his orders.

As the four men rode back together to the camp, Andreas complimented them on their Russian language skills and perhaps that they may be Russians? At this, all three men laughed. No, they were all American-born, but their parents were Russians who had emigrated to America and they all spoke Russian at home. The only member of their group that was actually from Mother Russia was the gunnery sergeant who was doing the demonstration with his men. He had come to America with his family at a young age.

Andreas then learned from the three men that they were from different parts of the country and had not met before being selected for this diplomatic mission.

"That's not exactly true," said Major Asmanov, "the colonel and I met briefly at a place called Gettysburg, on different sides."

The colonel laughed. "Yes, I had forgotten that. Beat you good, too." Then seeing the baffled look on Andreas's face, explained, "The good major was fighting on the other side at the time. It was during the Civil War; I was with the government troops and the major was with the confederacy troops."

"Civil war, never a good duty. As yet, I have not been involved in any of that kind of affair; although, my government does from time to time deploy Cossacks to quell those kinds of things," replied Andreas.

The rest of the leisure trip back to camp was in silence. The three Americans reflecting on their Civil War experiences, Andreas trying to find a way to get a hold of those fabulous weapons the Americans had for sale. He thought he may have a glimmer of an idea when they reached their area of the camp and went their separate ways. Andreas to his quarters where he handed his horse off to the trooper stationed outside.

Heading to the main part of the camp, he asked the aide he found at the quarter master's quarters if he could see the quarter master and was soon ushered into the interior, where he found the quarter master seated behind a large pile of paperwork. The man was about forty and looked like he had not missed too many meals lately. His uniform jacket and shirt collar were unbuttoned, and he had a harried look about him.

"What can I do for you today, my lord?" he asked.

"Thank you seeing me on such short notice, I just have a fast question to ask," replied Andreas.

After receiving an impatient 'carry on' gesture, Andreas continued, "I am being asked to raise a regiment of fifteen hundred men for next year and will be requiring rifles and ammunition for them. I was wondering how I would go about doing that."

"The normal procedure would be to submit a request for the materials required to your overlord, who would then arrange payment and delivery arrangements. In your case, you fill out the forms, I tell you how much it will cost, you pay it and the shipping costs, and we deliver," came the response.

When asked the price, Andreas was told for one thousand five hundred rifles, bayonets, rifle slings, cleaning kits, and one hundred summer and winter rounds for each would be six thousand rubles. Plus another thousand for shipping. No, he did not care that bayonets were not required. The book said one rifle one bayonet. If Andreas chose, he could find another supplier, nobody cared either way.

Andreas collected the forms to fill out, thanked the man for his time, and headed back to his quarters deep in thought. When he reached his tent, he found the King's German Legion officer lounging in the shade provided by the tent fly in front of Andreas's tent. As he drew himself up to attention and saluted, Andreas noticed the man was about his father's age; although sporting a mustache and long side beards, both grey, he was otherwise clean shaven. His uniform, while clean and neat, was not flashy, showing only the badges and rank markings required. The sabre he wore on his left side was not ornate, and the pommel showed evidence of much use. Everything about the man said he was an experienced warrior.

"I don't believe we have been properly introduced," he said. "I am Rudy von Hoaedle, Major, King's German Legion, Cavalry Regiment."

"Andreas Bekenbaum, Major, one small Cossack troop commander of what I don't know yet," said Andreas, sticking out his hand with a grin. "What can I do for you today, Major?"

"Oh, I don't think you will be in the dark for long, my lord. They seem to have big plans for you." Gesturing to the two bags by his feet, which when he touched them with a toe, clanked slightly. "I have brought your winnings. I hope you don't mind; those two had trouble finding rubles, the money is in pounds sterling."

When Andreas showed surprise at this, von Hoaedle let Andreas know that the exchange was in order, the amounts correct, and that he would have an easier time exchanging the English money for foreign goods than the Russian money. Andreas informed him that he was amazed that so much money was so readily available.

Von Hoaedle shook his head sadly. "Life is different for members of that class," he said. "I have seen those two spend more than that on a night of carousing."

Both men were the eldest sons of very highly placed members of their countries' aristocracies. Military duty was a mere formality, and they had enough money and prestige to afford commissions in only the best regiments. In fact, the Englishman was about to purchase his colonelcy. The money he spent on that alone would pay half a battalion's salary for a year. Neither officer would ever spend any time in the field commanding troops. Even should war break out, they would be staff officers stationed far in the rear.

"It is for men like you and I to do the actual dirty work," von Hoaedle said. "Those two will order your troops like so many toy soldiers, not caring if they live or die. If their orders will lead to slaughter or not. If yes, it's your fault; if some how you succeed, they get the glory. Such is the grand game. They fear us, they admire us, and, thus, they despise us. For all their wealth and power, they know they can never do what we do. They gain loyalty by money and threat. We, by respect for who and what we are. The days of the glorious cavalry charge and mass frontal attacks are over. They and their like in high command refuse to see or believe it."

He went on to explain he had been sent to America to observe the civil war there. How modern long-range infantry and artillery weapons tore apart formations. At a place called Gettysburg, over one hundred fifty thousand casualties had been suffered in one day's fighting. The American cavalry had been used as scouts or mounted infantry men. Modern weapons tore apart cavalry at long range, taking away their advantage.

"I fear that once the old czar is gone we will all be in trouble," von Hoaedle said. "It is only him and the old English king that are keeping everyone in line. The next ones have no idea what real war is like, and the little foray the new kaiser had against the French only made him more arrogant. Your crown prince, I fear, is worse. He only cares for the good life and will delegate every decision to his toadies, who are only thinking of themselves. Mark my words, before your lifetime is up, there will be the biggest war Europe has ever seen." With that, he took his leave, and Andreas could not help but wonder at this strange and wonderful man.

Later that afternoon, the relative quiet of the camp was disrupted by the return of his small troop from training. Andreas walked out to stand and watch as his men settled in, cleaning themselves up, and making preparations for this evening's meal. They were in good spirits, laughing and joking. Good-natured ribbing was aimed at the young lieutenant and the two new members of their group, who had a number of bruises from their sword training. Catching his brother's eye, he inclined his head to the tent and walked in.

"How did it go?" Andreas asked.

"We fired fifty rounds, simulating a fire fight," Johann said. "Our weapon performed as expected. We lost the chamber seal after about thirty rounds. The Sharps started experiencing jamming problems after ten. The cartridge casing being of copper is too soft, so when the breach heated up, the extractor just tore off the copper. Had to use a knife to extract the round. Also, the top-loading breach could be a problem in rain or snow. The Winchester had no failures, barrel fouling was less than expected. Loss of accuracy, minimal."

"Did you ask about cold-weather performance?" Andreas said.

"The sergeant says they both operate well. Where he is from has similar weather conditions to what we have. Loading the Winchester takes but a few moments. I prefer it over the Sharps and prefer both of them over our rifles."

"Very well, then. Anything else?" Andreas asked.

"Overheard the man Remington and the sergeant talking. The Americans want to unload the Winchesters. The military does not want them, and they have a lot of them left over from the war. I think you could probably get a good deal on them," Johann said.

Andreas told him what von Hoaedle had said and that he agreed with him. It might be time to change how they did things. Perhaps the training of the new men should start with firearms, pistol and rifle, and stop the sword and lance training. Instead of sword training, substitute wrestling and knife use. Stealth and use of ground to cover movements. In short, abandoning their traditions and starting new ones.

"We have already started," said Johann. "Our victories over those tribesmen proved that."

98

Before Andreas could respond, his staff sergeant entered and handed him a dispatch from the general requesting his presence. Shaking his head, buckling on his sword, and placing his cap on his head, he headed to the general's quarters.

Entering the general's presence, he noticed the general was looking a little more harried than his usual harried self. Murmuring something about meddling fools ruining a promising good officer, he handed Andreas a set of papers.

"Your services as an interpreter are no longer required," the general said. "High command has determined that your services are more suited to the orders in the packet. You are to report with one thousand combat-ready cavalry troops, with support personnel, to the Imperial Navy Docks in Odessa, no later than February first for extended duty not to exceed one year. You will then be contacted by a member of His Majesty King George of Britain's Army who will guide you to your area of operations, where you will be in support of the infantry regiment in place. Your patience and indulgence during your current duties has been noted and appreciated. You are free to leave for home any time after tonight. Tonight, you will be attending a reception at my quarters. You may go now."

Saluting, Andreas headed back to his quarters, musing to himself on the abrupt nature of this meeting, which was so out of character for the general. Reaching his quarters, he sent for his lieutenant. Then he sat down at his desk with his head in his hands trying to comprehend all the events that had occurred to him in the last few weeks. Now he was being told to go somewhere, fight, and perhaps die. Not to protect his family or country, but to serve at the whim of an uncaring and whimsical heir to the throne. Traded to a foreign power for some minor favor or point of honor.

"Lieutenant, we are no longer required here," he told Ivan when he entered. "You will prepare the troop to return home in two days. You may tell the troops of the move. Dismissed."

Later, he was seated at a long bench between and across from young, English aristocrats, belonging to the fashionable regiments of the day. They were discussing not military matters, but their latest sexual conquests or investment opportunities. One young man describing how his father was evicting all the tenants of one of his villages in order to rent the buildings and land to a textile manufacturer. There was more money to be made that way than collecting rents from disrespectful and lazy villagers, after all.

After two glasses of a fiery beverage called brandy, the young officers began to brag of their military prowess and how their regiments would vanquish all before them in glorious cavalry charges.

Just as Andreas was searching for a way to extract himself from the increasingly uncomfortable position he felt he was in, they were approached by a portly, middle-aged Russian dressed in the uniform of an administration unit with colonels rank on his shoulder boards.

"Come, come, Major Bekenbaum," he said, "you must hold up the honour of Mother Russia. Tell these fine officers of your glorious defeat of the Muslim invaders. Of the might of a Russian cavalry charge!"

There was no way out now. All the young officers around him begging him for details.

"It was not much of an affair," he replied, "we caught them by surprise."

"Caught them by surprise, I should hope so," said the Russian colonel. "One hundred brave Russians killed four hundred for the glory of Mother Russia and the czar."

Andreas stood up, clearly making to leave, but the constant boasting of the colonel and the looks of awe on the young officers made him pause.

"Do you know how these brave invaders operate?" he asked in a quiet, measured tone. "Their favorite tactic is to sneak up on a village while all the villagers are in church for morning mass. They bar the church doors and set it on fire. Anyone escaping from the church they roundup, killing any males no matter the age. They rape all the women then kill them all except the prettiest. Then they kill anything alive and burn the village to the ground. Anytime they are near any kind of armed resistance, they flee.

"We tracked this group for a week, following their trail of burnt villages and farms. One night, our scouts returned telling us they were holed up in a ravine not far from us. The ravine had three steep sides and was fronted by a small stream. Their camp was set up at the base of the ravine about a hundred and fifty yards away from the stream. I positioned twenty-five men on the top of each of the three sides of the ravine. The other twenty-five of us dismounted in a skirmish line across the stream. I waited till they were all lined up nice and neat for their morning prayers and we shot them where they knelt. They had no chance. A few tried to get weapons or run. None did. We found their priest slightly wounded cowering under a tent. My intensions were to treat his wounds and send him home as a warning to any others who might think of raiding us in the future.

"When we entered the camp, we found forty women. Ten dressed from head to toe in black garments which only allowed their eyes to be seen. Five were scantily clad. Five were staked

101

spread eagle facedown on the ground. The first woman we released came up to me, grabbed the lance on my saddle, walked up to the priest, and stabbed him in the belly with it. All of the other women followed her example. Taking our lances or swords from us, first stabbing the priest in the belly, then, stabbing the fully clothed women in the belly. After that, they went amongst the fallen and made sure all of them were dead. There was no glorious charge, only butchery and death. The monsters deserved no better. When we left, we left them where they lay."

When he stopped talking, he was surprised at the silence in the room. All conversation had stopped while they listened to his tale. Before he could do any more, von Hoaedle, seated at the head table, stood and began to rhythmically thump his glass on the tabletop. He was soon joined by a grizzled old Cossack. Soon all the Cossacks and all the veteran combat officers were doing the same. They stopped almost in unison, raised their glasses in salute to Andreas, and shot back the alcohol, thumping the empty glasses back down on their tables before reseating themselves and restarting their conversations.

A clearly moved Andreas nodded at his awed dinner companions and made for the exit. As he stood outside the entrance, pulling on his cap and lighting up his pipe, he felt a gentle hand on his shoulder.

"Doing God's work is sometimes hard, my son," said the bishop who had followed him out.

"Father Rosenbaum, there was not much of God's work being done that day. One of the captured women told us that the priest was the worse one of the bunch. He dashed babies heads into walls himself making sure they were dead. A number of the villages they raided were Muslim villages. These were no holy men on a religious quest. These were greedy men out for blood and pillage. They were vermin of the worst kind and like vermin we killed them. I have no remorse for doing what I did, but to glorify it would be wrong."

"What of the captured women, my son. What happened with them?" the bishop asked.

"We gave them what clothing we had and brought them back to our camp. Vacilly sent them back to his home under escort. They will be adopted into his clan and husbands found for them. Any children that come out of their time of captivity will be fostered into another of our clans. This is our way. The Muslims had intended on selling them on the slave market once they returned to their homelands. The other women we had saved told us that blonde women brought high prices on the markets.

"Do not fear for my soul, Father. I did what had to be done. If I had not, they would have continued and next year would have been back with more men. Just like I kill the wolf or the bear that are killing our livestock in order to survive. I kill them, but I don't have to like it."

"No, my son, I do not fear for your soul," the bishop said. "Rather, I had fears for your mind. Sometimes a man can grow fond of the killing and become like those you destroyed. Sometimes the killing can cause such anguish that a man loses all will to live. You have proved to me that there is not much to fear of the first happening with you, and I pray that the second does not as well." With that, he gave Andreas his blessing and took his leave.

The next morning, as Andreas was sitting out front of his tent enjoying his after-breakfast tea and pipe, three Americans walked up to him. The First Cavalry colonel was joined today by the State Department man and Remington, the newspaper man.

"Good morning, Earl Bekenbaum," said the State Department man, who was carrying a battered, leather brief case with him.

"Would it be an inconvenience to talk business with you at this time?" he asked.

Motioning to his aides to provide seats and tea for the three Americans, Andreas said, "Well, no Mr. Johnson, I had, after all, invited you here this morning for that very reason."

Reaching into the breast pocket of his suit jacket, Johnson withdrew two cigars, offering one to Andreas. Lighting his cigar and taking a sip of his tea, Johnson continued, "How did you like the performance of the weapons? Is there anything that may be of interest to you?"

Taking a couple of puffs on the cigar, Andreas began, "I believe we would be interested in obtaining some of your Winchester repeating rifles and some of your Colt pistols. If the price is reasonable."

"Why I think that our prices would be very competitive to that of your other suppliers," he said. "How many would you be requiring?"

"One thousand Winchester rifles, not carbines; one thousand Colt pistols and holsters with belts, one thousand rounds of cartridges for the rifles, cleaning rods for the rifles and pistols, spare springs and firing pins."

Taking a piece of paper from his brief case, Johnson did some mathematics for a few moments. Thinking for a second, he said, "Six thousand five hundred rubles."

"Well, we can sit around here all day dickering on price and details," replied Andreas, "or we can come to a deal and spend the rest of our day relaxing, instead. I much prefer the latter. Four thousand rubles, in pounds sterling. Half now, the other half when you deliver the weapons and they pass inspection. Take it or leave it. If you need time to consider the offer, I will be here until we leave for home tomorrow morning."

Johnson got up from his stool and with a gesture, he and the colonel withdrew out of earshot beginning a discussion. Andreas, puffing on his cigar, held out his cup, which his waiting aide filled from the ready tea pot. Andreas nodded his thanks, then gave the aide a wink of his right eye, signifying all was in order. He noticed that Remington was still seated on his stool apparently sketching something on a notepad. After a few moments, he noticed he was alone with Andreas and jumped up off his stool, hurrying over to where the other two Americans were standing. Remington listened to the discussion and shortly said something which made the other two men pause. Then, with a shake of his head, Johnson ended the discussion by walking back and sat down again beside Andreas.

Waiting for the other two men to join him, Johnson said, "You have a deal, with one condition."

Narrowing his eyes slightly, Andreas motioned the man to continue.

"I to end of winter, your home come," said Remington in bad Russian. "You pay food, house, horse."

Andreas looked at the man, sizing him up. Then, just as he was about to speak, Andreas stood up, extending his hand and said, "Deal. Sergeant, vodka for all."

The three Americans sprang up and one by one vigorously shook his hand. His aide quickly returned with a tray holding three glasses of vodka with the open bottle on it. Saluting each other with the glasses, they tossed the alcohol back with one shot. Indicating the bottle, Andreas raised his eyebrows in a wordless question. All the Americans waved their hands in the negative, placing their empty glasses on the tray.

"Yes, it is a little early in the day for that," laughed Andreas.

"Where and when would you like the weapons shipped?" asked the colonel.

"Before freeze up would be best. My settlement is thirty of your miles on the west bank upstream from the port of Odessa, or sixty miles by road. Will that be possible?"

"Oh, no problem at all," he said, "they are being stored in a warehouse in Odessa right now. If you have the down payment with you, I can have the documents brought to you immediately."

Andreas nodded to his sergeant who held up a clanking heavy bag. "Why don't you do that, Colonel, while Mr. Johnson counts the money?"

A half hour later, the colonel returned with the marine sergeant driving a wagon with two crates in the back. Jumping down from the wagon, he handed Johnson two pieces of paper, which he signed and gave to Andreas.

Looking over the documents, one in English, the other in Russian, he saw that they both said the same thing and, with the same intent, told exactly the deal that had been worked out. Andreas signed both copies and dated them, handing the English one back to Johnson.

"In a gesture of thanks, we would like you to accept these twenty Winchester rifles and ten Colt pistols. Completely off the books, of course, they will not be a part of the tally for the order. But only if you help us unload them."

Laughing, Andreas let out a whistle and waved his troop over to help out with the unloading. Each crate held ten rifles, five pistols, and enough boxed ammunition, ten rounds to a box, for one hundred cartridges per rifle.

Indicating to his men that each man was to take one rifle, one pistol, and ten boxes of ammunition each, he left them to it. Once again, he asked the Americans if they would like some vodka or perhaps tea.

"I think I will take you up on the tea," said Johnson, "but only if you have another of my cigars."

After they were all comfortable, sipping on their tea and puffing happily on their cigars, Andreas looked over at Remington and in perfect English said, "You know, Mr. Remington, if your Russian does not get any better, you are going to have no luck at all with our girls."

"By God!" exclaimed Johnson. "And with a British accent, too! Beaten at our own game. Hoodwinked good, we were. They warned me you were a smart one."

"All fair in love, war, and business, Mr. Johnson," laughed Andreas. "As a small token of penance, I would like you to accept these modest gifts."

His aide approached with several objects as Andreas stood and, removing his lance from its place beside the entrance to his tent, he handed it to Johnson. Then removing his ceremonial sword from his waist, he presented it to the colonel. Waving his aide forward, he removed two Cossack swords and handed them also to the colonel, asking him to give them to the two majors in his group.

"I wonder, could you part with your sergeant for a few months?" Andreas asked. "I am sure Mr. Remington would feel more comfortable with someone from his own country along. He could serve as a bodyguard for him, as well."

"I don't see that as a problem," said the colonel, waving the sergeant over to them.

"Sergeant, you are hereby relieved of your duty and assigned as temporary duty to accompany Mr. Remington as his personal guard. You will place yourself under the command of Earl Bekenbaum for any duty that does not compromise the safety of Mr. Remington, or place you in a conflict of interest with the United States of America."

"Aye, aye, sir!" the sergeant said.

Holding up a whip and a sword, "Know what these are?" asked Andreas. The marine nodded. "Know how to use them?"

"Aye, aye, sir, my father trained me, sir," the sergeant said.

Switching to Russian, "Sergeant, please, give the senior sergeant my old duty uniforms, we are of the same size, I think," ordered Andreas, tossing the whip and the sword to him.

"We leave at first light, Sergeant," he said in English, "have yourself in the proper uniform and Mr. Remington ready to go by then. Mr. Remington, we will be traveling fast and light, pack accordingly."

Receiving permission to leave, both men rushed off to make their preparations.

"I wanted to ask you about that," said the colonel. "He never said anything, but I knew he would have liked to have seen where his father came from. Thank you."

"His clan was from farther north," Andreas said. "But we all live in a similar way. The pleasure is all mine, Colonel."

"Yes, it will mean so much to him," said Johnson, "he is a good man. Please, try to keep him out of trouble, my lord."

"The steppe is never completely safe, Mr. Johnson, but he should be fine with us."

"That's all I can ask. Thank you, again, Earl Bekenbaum. I still can't believe how you humbugged us." Laughing, they all shook hands again and the Americans left.

Johann came in right after Andreas walked into the tent. "How much did that set you back, Brother?"

"Four thousand rubles. Half what that crook quarter master wanted for our old rifles, without the pistols. I thought they might want to unload the rifle version. The extra two inches is still four inches shorter than our rifles, so it won't be a problem. Do they have sling swivels?"

"Yes," Johann said. "It won't be a problem modifying our slings to fit them. What are we going to do with our old rifles?"

"Oh, that will be no problem at all," Andreas said. "Those English and Prussian officers are crazy for anything Cossack. They were outbidding themselves, I got two thousand rubles in pound sterling for them."

"Brother, remind me never to get into a deal with you!"

"I want to be home by this time next week," Andreas said. "You ready for tomorrow morning?"

"Not a problem for us. The new guys and the Americans?" He shrugged his shoulders.

Simultaneously they said, "That what doesn't kill you, makes you strong."

Laughing, Andreas said, "They might wish they were dead after the first day or so. Keep your eye on the marine. He's been on ships too many years and being Blood Cossack, he may feel he needs to prove something."

"My lord, where are the wagons? I must load your things," said his senior aide.

"Johann," Andreas said, "have a couple of the lads show them how we pack and what we don't pack. In fact, have a couple others go show the lieutenant and tell him it's on my orders, so he won't give them any static. I'm going for a walk now. Have fun."

"Thank you for seeing me, General," Andreas said, sitting across from General Andropov in his private quarters. "I would like to thank you for all your help and advice these last weeks. I was able to secure some information from the Americans that may prove beneficial to you."

After receiving permission, Andreas continued, "It is my opinion the Americans are anxious to establish trade internationally and if the quality of their weapons is any indication, their engineering and manufacturing is very good. Perhaps better than the Germans. One of the men in their party is a newspaper man, and he is going to spend the winter with us. Another is a Blood Cossack, born in America. He also is going to be spending the winter with us. We will get more insight into what they are up to during that visit."

"Yes, you have done some good work for us, Andreas," the general said. "That little demonstration race and your comments at last night's reception made quite an impression on our new allies. We were hoping for someone to do that, and here you are. Not only making an impression, but making some money as well. I will have to keep my eye on you, or you will be after my job next."

"Not so, sir!" Andreas said. "I am way over my head as it is. Commanding ten men is one thing, a whole battalion is another, let alone a whole army group. I still have to consider how to manage the land and property I am now responsible for, in addition to training a new battalion."

"This is just what I was referring to," the general said. "Most officers of your age are only interested in spending money, chasing girls, and getting drunk. They consider this kind of duty as a hardship duty; they go through the motions of setting up patrols, go on a few when they must, and make sure all of their reports are full of nonsense about how brave and diligent they were in the performance of their duty. You, on the other hand, actually went out and did your job. We had been chasing that group of what you called bandits for three years. There was always some tale about a glorious charge that caused the enemy many casualties. They were always costly to us in loss of good men and young subalterns, never or rarely were any field grade officers casualties. Yet, every year, after sustaining great losses, the enemy was back, killing our farmers, burning our farms, and causing local food shortages. On your first year of campaign, you tracked down and you did not cause many casualties or lead a glorious cavalry charge that lost half your men. No, you killed six hundred highly trained enemy cavalry troopers, wiping them completely out, and did not lose a man or horse doing it. The proof was in the amount of horses you brought back with you and the amount of booty Vacilly showed me.

"This why we brought Cossacks in. You are better trained in cavalry tactics than our regular units. What you did, though, that was new and unexpected. Using infantry tactics, backed up by cavalry. Believe me, if you would have used normal cavalry tactics, the result would have been much different. Because you are better trained, you may have done alright with the first group, but you would not have survived the second. Those troops you were facing were well-trained in classical cavalry tactics, with sword and lance. They were also veterans. Yes, what they did to civilians was horrible and evil, that does not take away the fact that they are excellent troops and very brave when faced by combat.

"That you are thinking of how to best use your men, your tactics, your weapons. Trying to improve and modify your tactics to suit the citation. Looking out for your men as well as you can. Finding the best weapons you can. Thinking on how to manage your responsibilities as a landholder for the best return for the peasants, the government, and yourself. These are not the thoughts of the usual aristocrat. They leave that to others and take no responsibility or accountability for any of the decisions those others make.

"Should you survive the next few years, I believe you will go far, and Mother Russia will have gained not only a good commander, but a good aristocrat with productive lands and people." The general then stood and, indicating an impatiently waiting aide, shook Andreas's hand once more and the interview was over.

They had been ready to leave at daybreak; the camp was broken down, tents folded neatly and stacked for easy retrieval. They had only been borrowing them and someone else was responsible for storing and transporting them. His aides and the lieutenant's aide had pack horses for any gear that was too much for his and Ivan's mounts to carry. Ivan would be trailing a pack horse with the five spare weapons and all the spare ammunition for the group. Andreas himself would be trailing a pack horse carrying all the money and the small company's paperwork.

Each man's mount held, in addition to his saddle and weapons, a great coat tied to the pommel, a blanket, and two saddle bags tied to the cantle. Each man had two cartridge boxes attached to his rifle sling, holding ten rounds each. Another sixty rounds in oiled and protected packets in their saddle bags. Enough dried meat and bread for ten days and two canteens of water. Their blue uniforms were rolled up and in their saddle bags. They would be dressed in, to them, their normal apparel. Loose, long-wearing pants with leather inner legs and crotches. Mid-calf length leather boots with pant legs stuffed in, and loose-fitting, heavy canvas blouses over the pants, not tucked in. Pistol belts over the blouses above the hips. Experience had taught them to tie the holsters down to their legs to keep them from bouncing around as they rode. Some wore them on their right sides, being right handed, Andreas had his mounted on the left, so he could draw it cross body with his right hand. All the troops but one had reverted back to their traditional lamb's wool caps. Andreas left his officer's cap on, it would be the only thing marking him an officer.

They had been ready to leave for two hours, but the bishop had insisted on blessing them before they left. Unfortunately, they would have to wait until he finished morning mass, which today was being attended by the heir, which meant the whole court would be attending, which also meant the mass would take twice as long. The troops had loosened cinches and unslung rifles and were now in various attitudes of relaxation.

Andreas, with one foot on the corral fence, was gazing at the horses in quiet contemplation when the Americans made their appearance. Both men were mounted on thoroughbreds, one pack mule trailing behind each of them.

Greeting the two men, Andreas gestured at their animals. "I'm not sure they will be able to keep up," he said in English. "We will be moving fast with few breaks."

"The mules are stronger than they look," said Remington.

"He not talking was of mules. Horses here to stay should," said Johann, walking up behind them. "Pretty horses, short time fast go. Better those, all day go," nodding at the corral.

"Do you all speak English?" the sergeant asked. "What else about you people don't we know?"

Andreas shrugged his shoulders. "Not all speak English. It would be better for you if we and you speak as much Russian as possible. You will pick it up faster. He is right, those thoroughbreds will tire quickly. We will be covering sixty miles today and eighty every day after. Pick any two of those Arabians in the corral, we will be switching horses every day and there are plenty."

They had received four each from the encounter with the raiders; with the three mounts they all had brought with them, there were sixty free horses in the corral. After receiving a negative response from the man, Andreas smiled to himself. Another one in love with beauty not substance, he thought.

Not willing to be drawn into a discussion on blood lines and horse breeding, Andreas continued, "We have tried to keep them as exercised as possible, but many of these horses have been in this corral for many weeks now. There are sixteen of us. I will want three riders as advance scouts. That leaves thirteen of us to control sixty horses who, as you can see, are anxious to leave. When they are let out of there, they are going to want to run, so we will encourage them to do so. They are well-trained and should stick together. To ensure they do so, we will station outriders on each flank and the rear, and have two troopers on our best runners leading out front. You two will be positioned on the right flank. Keep up the best you can but don't kill your horses. You can catch us up after. In fact, if you could keep an eye out for the lieutenant and the three aides, I would appreciate it. The way the day is shaping, we won't be going far today, but we will see."

114

"Ah, from the sound, it would appear we are to be graced by His Grace shortly." Switching to Russian, "Johann, here they come; cinch them up and get ready for inspection!" he ordered. They could hear chanting coming from the main camp, slowly growing louder as the procession got closer.

The troopers quickly and skillfully pulled cinches tight and made sure that packs and equipment were as secure as possible, pulling tunics down and straightening hats. Andreas and Ivan handed the reins to their pack horses to waiting troopers who lined up in two equal ranks two yards apart. Andreas and Ivan walked their mounts to the center of the front line, two yards in front, with Ivan on Andreas's right. The ten remaining Cossack remounts, having performed this ritual before, lined up also in two loose ranks, even the Arabians had stopped milling about. The chanting was becoming louder, and the priests turned the corner into the lane leading to the corral. The center of the first three priests held a Russian cross aloft, flanked on the left by one holding a smoking incense urn, the other a bottle of holy water. Following them was the bishop in all his fully gowned glory holding, front cover out, a large Bible, flanked on each side by priests in their formal garments. The priests were singing in that soul-wrenching sound that only massed male Russian voices could duplicate. Bishop Rosenbaum sang a solo passage that required a response. Instead of the expected five voices, came. . .

Oh shit, thought Andreas, followed immediately by, muttered from the ranks, "*Gott in Himmel*" and "*Mein Gott*" and a very loud "*Shiza*" from Johann.

"Quiet in the ranks!" barked Andreas; drawing his sword, he presented the sword salute and shouted, "TROOPS, ATTENTION, ROYAL SALUTE, PRESENT ARMS!"

Fifteen pairs of boots crashed to the ground in unison as the heir in his formal uniform, flanked by the chief of staff, rounded the corner followed by the rest of the military staff, members of the court in the camp, their aides and staff, and all of the foreign ambassadors and their staff. All dressed in their best and shiniest uniforms.

The priests walked across their formation stopping on the formation's left side. The crown prince stopped opposite Andreas, flanked on one side by the chief of staff and on the other by General Andropov. The rest of the group lined up behind and opposite the small Cossack formation. At a final massed response to the bishop's last recital, all present were standing silently, Andreas's men at rigid attention.

"Company ready for inspection, Your Highness!" barked Andreas.

The heir returned Andreas's salute, and together they walked down both lines; the grand duke stopping every so often exchanging a few words with a trooper. Reaching the end of the second line, he started to the front again but stopped beside Johann.

"Nice to see at least one man upholding Cossack tradition," he said.

Instead of his cap being squared away, Johann had his at the rakish angle normally afflicted by Cossacks. Clicking his heals together, Johann gave a quick bow of his head and resumed his stance of rigid attention, albeit with a smile on his face.

The next part of the performance was the bishop blessing each man and his mount with the sign of the cross, then moving across, he blessed the animals in the corral. The final act of the performance was about to begin.

Taking two steps forward and taking each man in a glance, the grand duke began, "Troopers, this in your first campaign season, you have proven to the world the might of Mother Russia. That if you invade us and do us harm, we will hunt you down and we will annihilate you. We are generous with our friends and deadly to our foes. You have upheld and surpassed the traditions of your predecessors. We are proud of you; the Holy Church is proud of you; your families are proud of you. Keep yourselves ready; we will have need of you to uphold our honor in the future.

"Go now. Go home to the bosoms of your families and friends. You go with our thanks and our prayers. God save Mother Russia; God save the czar!"

"WHOA!" roared the assembled company.

Saluting the grand duke, Andreas motioned to Ivan and they both mounted their horses.

"Company prepare to mount!" Waiting till all the men were ready, then, "Mount!"

When all the men and mounts were settled, Andreas turned back to the grand duke and gave the sword salute. "Permission to leave the field!"

The grand duke returned the salute and nodded his head.

Saluting again and returning his sword to his scabbard, Andreas swung his horse back to face his men.

Now the show could begin and they could get on their way. The horses in the corral could sense the mood, the Cossacks' remounts moving to the entrance, the Arabians began milling about but keeping their distance from the others.

"Scouts! Prepare to deploy. Deploy!"

The three troopers assigned to scout duty for the day rode their horses forward a few paces, pivoted to the west, and, in line abreast and a kick of the heels, in three strides were off at a full gallop. Andreas then nodded to Ivan to take over and turned Bartholomew to head to the rear of the corral, paralleled by Johann on the opposite side. The lieutenant gave the order to deploy to the rest of the group and they split up into the formation they would be using for the rest of the day. Three experienced troopers went to the middle of the trail; the others spread out in equal numbers spaced out down the length of the trail on both sides.

Andreas removed his cap, pulled the chin strap off the brim, and, replacing his cap, cinched the strap so his cap would not come off. It was still too new to have fitted itself to his head. Pulling his whip out of his belt and uncoiling it, he looked over at Johann who was waiting on the other side of the corral with his whip laying lazily in the dust and a huge grin on his face. The Cossack horses lined up at the gate began tossing their heads and stomping their feet, while the Arabians started edging closer to them.

Making sure the troopers were spaced out evenly down the trail, Andreas nodded to Johann and they began to slowly twirl their whips about their heads. Faster and faster the whips twirled. Nodding to the two cavalry troopers they had borrowed from another regiment, the two men began heaving on the rope tied to the gate of the corral to open it, ensuring they had a place to run. Now the horses were in a state of anticipation, neighing and tossing heads all around; the Cossack mounts still blocking the entrance and enforcing discipline on the Arabians with kicks. The whips kept whirling, whooshing as they swung through their arcs. Then. . .

Crack! Crack! Crack! As loud as a pistol shot, both whips cracked the air above the horses.

"Yeaiii! Yeaiii!" both men yelled out, and the ground shook as sixty horses thundered out of the corral at a full gallop down the trail. All of the other outriders put heels to sides and, with whips cracking and voices yelling, the whole company was galloping down the trail.

As they passed the assembled entourage, Andreas saw the whole group leaping, whooping, and hollering, waving caps in the air, none more enthusiastic than the grand duke himself, who tossed his cap in the air and was jumping up and down waving his arms in glee.

The only thing better than watching a herd of horses at full gallop, manes and tails blowing in the wind and hooves thundering on the ground, was to be part of it. The wind in your face, the feel of the powerful muscles between your legs, and, as you lay your head alongside his head, the warmth and the sound of his excited breath. As man and horse become one.

Expertly gathering his whip, Andreas bunched it up and looking over at his brother, he thrust it up high over his head. "YEEHAWWW!" he screamed out in glee.

Free, for the time being, free. Free of responsibility, free of making decisions, free of overlords. Free to run. "YEEHAWWW!"

After two miles, the horses were showing signs of slowing down, so they were allowed to slow to a trot. They would keep this up for an hour then slow to a walk for half an hour, and then back to a trot. This was the pace they would be keeping for eight hours a day until they reached home. The outriders had only been there to keep the herd together in the first while. Once they were used to working together, the horses would keep in touch and stay together on their own.

It was about two hours from sundown when they reached the area the scouts had chosen for them to stop for the night. There was a small stream to provide fresh water and a large area for the horses to graze. No one could relax until the free horses had been watered, just to make sure that they would settle down and not want to keep moving. Leaving a three-man team to watch over them, after that the troopers dismounted, removed the saddles and packs from their mounts, and rubbed them down to graze with the other horses.

Andreas had noticed that the three scouts had automatically moved to help the three new men who, not used to being in the saddle for that long, had actually collapsed when they had dismounted. Even though the three men were the butt of more than a few derogatory remarks, Andreas knew this meant the rest of the men had accepted them as one of their own. Otherwise, they would have been left to handle things on their own, which was what was happening with the Americans.

The two Americans had taken his advice and switched horses to the Arabians. From the way they moved and handled their horses and equipment, it was clear both men were accustomed to horseback travel and Andreas felt it would not take to long for them to get used to how the troop operated.

Seeing that his men had things well in hand, Andreas was free to attend to his own equipment and quickly set up his bedroll and laid out his riding equipment so it could air out. Ivan had moved his gear next to Andreas's, and they both were going through saddle bags looking for their contributions for that night's meal.

Johann walked over from where he had set his gear up and plunked himself down cross-legged beside them. "Well, Cousin, the local farmers will not have to worry about their daughters with you tonight, I think," he said with a laugh.

"Oh, I don't even want to think about all the new places I'm going to get calluses," Ivan replied with a groan. "At least I'm used to riding, not like those three poor recruits."

"The lads will look out for them," said Johann. "It will be tough on them for a few days, but their bodies will adjust. It was the same for all of us the first few times. Why, I remember our glorious leader, here, was wont to fall off his horse when he came back from learning all that high and mighty stuff at that fancy school."

"This is what I was warning you about, Lieutenant," said Andreas, "get too close to your men and they lose all respect for you."

All three men snickered. "Well, you high-and-mighty officers, the food is ready; come now or go hungry."

It was well after dark before Andreas rolled up in his blankets. He was asleep almost before his head hit the saddle he was using as a pillow.

Two nights later, after everyone had finished their meal, Andreas took his cup of tea and walked over to where the Americans had set up camp for the night. The two men had kept to themselves during the day and camped separate from the rest of the group.

"Do you mind if I join you?" he asked in English.

The two men gestured him to a spot by their fire and he sat down.

"Have we done something to offend you?" Andreas asked.

"Why, no, my lord, whatever would make you think that?" Remington asked.

Andreas just pointed at the main group of men and then gestured with an open hand at the small camp the two men occupied and shrugged his shoulders.

"No, no," said the sergeant in Russian, "we would like to apologize to you, sir, for whatever we have done to upset you. We did not mean any disrespect, sir."

"Ah," said Andreas after a moment in English, "this is one of those, what is it called now? Yes, one of those 'cultural differences' I was warned about."

"Johann, you ungrateful wretch!" hollered Andreas in Russian. "Our guests are thirsty, and you are hording all the vodka. We are coming over there, and you better have some left or I'll kick your butt."

"Stand in line, Brother, better men than you are waiting to kick it," he yelled back.

"Again, I apologize, gentlemen, when you are invited to join us when we are traveling, you are also invited to share our camp. I did not think to tell you that. Gunnery Sergeant, I am sure you have a name, no? All this 'my lord'-ing and 'major sir'-ing are quite tedious. We all know who is who here, no reason for all the formality. I am Andreas."

"Peter Chimalovich, sir," the gunnery sergeant said. "Thank you for inviting me along, sir; my father has many stories of his life here, and I welcome the opportunity to witness firsthand how my forefathers lived."

"Fredrik Remington, my lord, I mean, Andreas. I noticed you speak German amongst yourselves. I thought Cossacks were all Russian?"

"Technically, you are correct, Fredrik," Andreas said. "Cossacks are Cossack, a nation within a nation if you will. All our families are from Cologne and while the Cossacks welcomed us into their community, we are not Cossack. While we were all born in Russia and have all been raised to be and act as Cossack and our battalion was led by a Cossack, we were only auxiliaries. This little group of fifteen is the first to be made Cossack."

After that, the two Americans were seen mingling freely with the troop talking with the troopers, and as they moved out of the forests and onto the steppe, the travelling became easier and the men more relaxed. In the evenings, Remington was always busy, sketching on pads he had packed away or writing on other pads. Fresh game was usually available, and so far, they had not had to dip into the dried meat packed away in saddle bags. Soon, the vast empty steppe was dotted by isolated farmsteads and small villages. At first, herds of cattle, then larger and larger fields of grain. It was clear they were moving into a populated area.

While the long days and speed of the trip were beginning to take a toll, the men's spirits were rising as they knew they would soon be home. Andreas also wanted to get home, but now, did he have a home? When he had left, he and Johann had been sharing a small outbuilding on his father's farm to live in. Now, he would have to find somewhere to live, not only for himself, but his two aides. Hopefully, there was a suitable site to build a home on the land he was now responsible for and that it could be built and provisioned before winter would set in.

Tonight would be the last but one, camping out on the steppe. The next night they would only be a short distance from home. The troopers wanted to make a grand entrance to their village, so they would time it so that they arrived just as Sunday mass was over. This night, the men were excitedly speaking of home and what their plans would be and wondered at what had happened since they had left. Andreas spent most of his time apart from the group, he had much on his mind.

Andreas was up and saddling Bartholomew before daybreak. The horse had responded to his whistle in the dark, tracking him down amongst the shadowy shapes of the horse herd in the pre-dawn light had been unnecessary. As he was slinging his rifle over his left shoulder, he was approached by the horse guard.

"Need any help, sir," the guard asked.

"I have everything under control, Private," Andreas said. "Please, inform the lieutenant he is in charge today and have the senior sergeant take my packs for the day. I will meet you at the next camp spot."

Riding slowly out of camp, Andreas waited for some distance before breaking into a trot. As he rode, he had the makings of a plan for his future. It was clear to him that those in power would use him until he became a threat or was no longer useful to them. This pattern had been followed with his people for generations. When the groups became too powerful, the Russians split them up, by force if necessary. If they rebelled, they were crushed mercilessly. From what he had heard, the rest of Europe was much the same. A person had not much choice in his future, you did what your government told you to do. Unless you were an aristocrat or incredibly lucky.

America was different. Yes, the wealthy had much power, but anyone who worked hard and was smart could live well, if not become wealthy. A man could pursue any endeavor, not just what the government wanted him to do. The western part of the country had just been opened for settlement and land was plentiful and cheap.

Riding on in silence, the sun had come up and was warming his back. Dismounting, he removed his great coat, rolled it up, and tied it snug to his cantle. He had been riding at a faster pace than the rest of the group would be going and would soon be in the little valley by the brook where they would spend their last night, about ten miles from home. As he remounted and started climbing the small hill that concealed the little valley, a smile crossed his face as he thought of the joyful reunions, the parties, and the real bed they would have the following day.

He was reaching the middle of the hill when the day's calm was shattered by the noise of what sounded like a violent confrontation happening on the other side of the hill. More out of caution than anything else, Andreas unslung his rifle and trotted to almost the top of the hill when a women's angry shriek followed by a man's cry of agony pierced the air.

The scene he saw when he crested the hill was one of violence and despair. Two men, a woman, and a boy were lying in pools of blood on the valley floor. One of the men was writhing in agony holding his intestines in his hands. To the right of this, a man held a teenage girl off the ground from behind with a large knife to her throat. Just in front of him was a horse-drawn, two-wheeled cart with a family's goods in it and four saddle horses, ground tethered.

A scream of rage forced Andreas to look to the left, where he saw a woman in her early twenties being dragged on her back by her hair by two men to a log that was laying not far from them. These were followed by a portly, middle-aged man. The two men forced the woman facedown over the log and as Andreas realized what was to come next, he fired a round from the Winchester at the feet of the middle-aged man.

He calmly rode down to the now quiet scene, dismounting near the wounded man. The other man, woman, and boy were clearly dead, throats cut. There would be no saving the wounded man; Andreas shot him in the head, ending his suffering.

"Be gone, Cossack, this is none of your affair," ordered the portly man, clearly the leader of the group. "What I do with my property is my business not yours."

"Property?" asked Andreas. "Ah, you mean the women? They are your daughters or your wives?"

"No, they are serfs who have run away," the man said. "I intend on teaching them a lesson and taking them back to show my other serfs what happens when they think they are free."

"You do not agree with what the czar has said about freeing serfs?" Andreas asked.

"The czar never comes out here. I can do what I want," he said.

At a gesture from the man, the two men holding the woman on the ground let her go and stood up, pulling large knives from their belts. The portly man had a small sword in his hand, which he gestured with to Andreas.

"What are you going to do about it anyway, Cossack? You are alone; your rifle is empty. If you come for us, my man there will cut that girl's throat and come for you. If you go for him, we will come for you. You can't win. Get up on your horse and ride away. They are only serfs, not worth dying over."

Looking over at the man holding the girl with the knife at her throat, Andreas saw the grin on his face, aimed the Winchester at him and shot him in the left eye, the .40 caliber bullet knocking him backwards two paces before he fell to the ground. Putting another round into the chamber he spun around and shot the man on the right in the chest, and as the man on the left charged him, shot him in the chest as well. Levering another round in the chamber, he pointed the rifle at the portly landowner.

"Who can't win now?" asked Andreas. The man was clearly shaken as urine was staining the front of his pants and running onto his boots.

"Get on your horse and get out of here before I change my mind," Andreas ordered.

The man dropped his sword and grabbed the nearest horse. Galloping off, he yelled back, "This is not over, you dirty Cossack, the new earl is coming tomorrow."

"I'm counting on it," Andreas murmured to himself.

Hearing hoofbeats coming from behind him, Andreas spun around, going to one knee and sighting his rifle on the two riders pelting down the hill. Recognizing two of his troopers assigned as scouts for the day, he placed the rifle on safe and, rising to his feet, looked up at the top of the hill. The remaining scout and Chimalovich were on one knee sighting their rifles down the hill while Remington, still mounted, was working furiously with pad and pencil.

Waving the all clear, he motioned the men on the hill to join him and turned to check on the two survivors of the attack. The older of the two women had the younger clasped tightly to her breast and was gently stroking her hair with one blood-stained hand. The front of her blouse and skirt were covered in blood, as was her face. Alarmed, Andreas asked her if she was injured. She took her head from her sobbing sister's head and looked at him with determined and defiant eyes.

"You let that fat bastard get away," she said. Spitting in the direction of the man with the spilled entrails, she continued, "this blood is his, and I would have done the same with the one you let go for killing my parents and my brother."

"I have plans for that one," said Andreas, "his fate is sealed."

"You fool," she sneered. "He is a powerful landowner with much influence. Do you think the new earl is going to listen to you or me? We are nothing compared to him. Better to have let them kill us."

"The law is the law, dear lady," Andreas said. "Now, why don't you take your sister down to the stream and clean that blood off you while we take care of your kin?"

Snorting and giving him a look that would have killed him on the spot had she been anything other than a human, she gently led her sister down to the stream.

As all the other men grouped around him, Andreas assessed the situation and began issuing orders.

"One of you head back to the rest of the troop, tell them what has happened and that they are to push straight on through to home for tonight. I want another scout to go home; tell them we are coming in and stop at my mother's house and let her know the two females will be needing assistance."

The scouts sorted out who was doing what and headed off at full speed to carry out his orders.

"See if there are any blankets in the cart," Andreas said. "We will cover the bodies of the parents and the boy with them. We'll tie the bundles in the cart to those four horses there and put the bodies on the cart to take home with us for burial. Those other four bastards can stay where they are laying. Let the crows have them."

"Come, miss, we are ready to leave," Andreas quietly said to the two women sitting on the stream bank.

When they reached the cart, Andreas gently picked up the younger sister and placed her on the cart seat. The defiant one slapped his hand away and climbed up to the seat herself. Before he could order one of the men to drive the cart, she grabbed the reins herself and slapping the reins on the horses' rump, started down the path that lead to Andreas's home.

Four hours later, their solemn little procession wound its way down the main street of Katherintal towards the church located in the center of the street. The normally vibrant town on market day, silent, with the residents lined up on both sides of the street leading up to the church, making the sign of the cross as they passed. Father Litzanburger, dressed in his vestments, was waiting for them in front of the church doors and began to pray as they stopped in front of him. A group of young men took charge of the three bodies and accompanied by the priest and his attendants, gently conveyed them into the church. A group of women took charge of the two sisters, the cart, and the four horses carrying their possessions and headed in the direction of the Bekenbaum's town residence.

Andreas spotted the offending landowner speaking with great passion to a group of the town's elder statesmen gesturing wildly. The group came to some kind of agreement, nodding their heads, and as they headed Andreas's way, the landowner gave Andreas an evil grin and stalked away.

The group of elders, headed by Ivan's father, stopped in front of Andreas's horse. "I wish your homecoming would have had a more pleasant outcome," he said. "The man is accusing you of some very serious things, Andreas. He is insisting on a full trial with the earl as soon as he arrives."

"Very well," Andreas said. "Assemble the council. The rest of the troop is right behind us; we will assemble two hours after they arrive. Send someone to inform my mother of this and to have the two sisters at the meeting to give their testimony. I also want that jackass landowner kept under protective custody, so he can't find any witnesses to swear to the truthfulness of his lies."

The group broke apart to carry out Andreas's wishes and only his uncle was left.

"You remember Mr. Remington, Uncle?" Andreas said. "He is going to be our guest until spring; I wonder if you could arrange some accommodations for he and the good sergeant here? I fear I am going to be otherwise occupied today."

Riding the mile outside of town to his father's farmstead, Andreas tied his horse up to the hitching rail in front of his and his brother's modest shack and, removing his saddle bags, entered. Throwing the saddle bags on his bed, he grabbed two buckets sitting by the stove and walked over to the water pump filling both. He put one on the ground for the horse and placed the other on the rough bench between the two beds in the shack. Removing his personal care kit from the bags, he pulled off his shirt and shaved off his week-old beard. Then he gave himself a quick sponge bath before heading back outside and pouring what was left of the bucket of water over his head.

The full dress uniform he had sent ahead when the battalion had left for home was hanging cleaned and pressed in the makeshift closet he and Johann had made. His boots, complete with silver spurs, were polished and sitting underneath. Taking his time, he dressed carefully making sure all of his badges were in order and buttons done up. Taking six cartridges from the ammo pouch attached to his rifle sling, he quickly polished the brass casings and shoved each one with care into the bright red decorative loops attached to the uniform jacket, three to a side.

Buckling his sword and pistol belt over his jacket, Andreas remounted his horse and rode back to town. Stopping in front of the town hall, he handed the reins to an attendant, climbed the few steps to the building, and entered. He was ushered into a waiting room off to one side of the main room and stood waiting with an attendant to be called.

Across the room from him, with their own attendant, sat the two sisters nervously. Both in clean fresh dresses, their long blonde hair tied back and coiled around their heads with fresh flowers tied into it. The older sister scrutinized him for a moment, then her eyes went wide and she was about to say something, when Andreas raised a finger to his lips and winked.

"Have you heard the one about the man who was scared to say the truth at a trial because he feared he would be punished?" said Andreas to his attendant loudly. "He asked Our Lord Jesus for guidance, and this is what he was told, 'Speak the truth always, and the truth will set you free'."

Just then, the door to the council chambers opened, and the attendant at the door motioned for the sisters to follow him. They rose from their seats smoothing their dresses. The older sister glanced over at Andreas with a questioning look and gave a little curtsy. Andreas smiled a toothy grin, placed his left hand on his midriff, and, sweeping his cap off his head with his right hand in a grand gesture, bowed from the waist in return. The older sister straightened right up, lifted her head, and, younger sister in tow, proudly marched into the main chamber.

After the door had swung shut again, the attendant Andreas had told the story to asked, "What happened? Did the man tell the truth?"

"What happened? Well, they hung him, of course. He was a murderer, after all."

Before anything else could be said, a booming voice could be clearly heard through the door.

"They are clearly lying. You can't possibly believe this filth these serfs are spouting. Besides, all this means nothing; the earl is not here and none of this is legal."

A general uproar erupted in the chamber, and after several seconds of gavel banging, the noise quieted down, and after a few moments, the door once again opened with the attendant standing to the side.

"If it please my lord?" the man quietly asked, gesturing into the room.

Andreas stepped up to the open door, took his cap off and tucked it under his left arm. Tugging his tunic down, he then marched briskly to the front of the packed council chamber spurs jangling at each step. Reaching the spot where Father Litzanburger was standing, he smartly about faced so that he was facing not only the panel of elders seated behind a long table, but the standing room only council chamber.

Holding a crucifix towards Andreas, the priest asked, "Do you swear before God and this assembly that all you are about to say is the truth?"

Making the sign of the cross and kissing the proffered crucifix, Andreas responded that he would.

"State your full name and position," ordered the most senior of the elders.

Looking the offending landowner in the eye, he said, "Andreas Hanrayovitch Bekenbaum, Ataman Andreashost, Earl of Katherintal District."

"If it please my lord, could you explain to this enquiry your observations and actions in this unfortunate incident this morning?"

As Andreas related the sequence of events and the actions taken, the offending landowners' domineer went from blustering confidence to mild panic as the realization of what and who Andreas was sunk in.

"Why then, my lord, was the gentleman in question not summarily executed as the other perpetrators were?" Andreas was asked.

"We felt that as the gentleman had not personally, physically attacked us, a trial by his peers would be more appropriate for a person of his status."

"Why then is my lord not chairing this enquiry?"

"We felt that our presence on the board would unduly influence the impartiality of the proceedings."

"Are there any more questions for Earl Bekenbaum? Thank you, my lord, for your indulgence in this matter and if it please you, you are free to stand down."

Andreas gave the board a stiff nod for a bow and silently marched right out of the building and rode back home to find Lieutenant Ivan lounging on his porch.

"Nasty business," he said, dismounting and tying up his horse. "Maybe I should have just shot the man."

Entering his spartan dwelling, Andreas removed his formal uniform, carefully hanging it back in his wardrobe and donned the comfortable work clothes that he had not used since leaving in the spring. Pulling on his scuffed, comfortable old work boots, he rummaged through his saddle bags, found his horse grooming tools, and went back outside. By the weak light from the porch lamp that Ivan had lit, Andreas removed the horse tack and started brushing down Bartholomew.

"An ugly business, buddy," Andreas told the horse. "You are lucky you only have to make me happy and you get all the feed you want."

"His name is Olag Zaboe, he is a Hungarian," said Ivan. "He has managed through bribery and other means to amass a lot of wealth and power. He treats his serfs poorly and has ignored the czar's order to free the serfs."

"From what I could see, those people he was abusing were freemen, not serfs," Andreas said. "Even had they been serfs, they were not his serfs and they were not on his land. He had no right to do what he did. Attacking a member of the czar's army, no matter the rank, is a serious offense. The man was overconfident in his supposed power."

"Not the homecoming we were expecting," Ivan agreed. "Seeing it on the frontier is one thing, at home by one of our own is something else. While my father was at home, he was able to keep this Zaboe under control, but when he is leading the regiment on campaign, the rest of the council were afraid to stand up to him. Zaboe probably thought you were the typical young Russian aristocrat here for a couple of days, then back to Moscow. All this would have been swept under the table."

Finished with his grooming and leading Bartholomew over to the corral, Andreas let him loose. In typical horse fashion, he promptly rolled on his back in the dust undoing all Andreas had just done.

"I wonder why we bother," said Andreas, shaking his head. "Are the troopers all back at their homes?"

"Yes, all except Johann," Ivan said. "He is staying with Olynick tonight, so you have the place to yourself. Your aides are in my parent's servant's quarters for now. Let me know when to send them over."

"Everyone needs some time off, Ivan; you too," Andreas said. "Have everyone assemble here in three days, say after lunch. I think you should come for breakfast; we have to organize a few things first. Are you staying at your father's house? Good, get some sleep; have some fun. I'll be here. I foresee many meetings in my future, so no rest for me. I have had a long and trying day, so if you don't mind?"

Coming awake with a start, Andreas grabbed for his pistol until he realized where he was, home, safe, and in a real bed. Albeit, fully clothed and on top of the blankets. Standing up and stretching the kinks out of his back, he walked out to the porch step and watched as all the farmhands and their families, dressed in their Sunday best, descended from carts or stepped off horses after Sunday mass.

"You see, Heinrich, an officer and a gentleman for a month and already he doesn't feel he has to talk to the peasants or go to church."

"Papa!" exclaimed Andreas, spinning around and hugging his father. The gentle expression of affection lasted only a moment before each man was trying vainly to lift the other off the ground.

Breaking off, they both laughed, the elder man slapping Andreas on both shoulders.

"You've gained weight, you old coot; I'm going to tell Mamma not to feed you so much."

Getting a rough shove in the back, Andreas turned around and hugged his elder brother.

"So many questions, where do we start?" his brother asked.

"Vacilly and Michilov have told us most of what happened, but there are many gaps. We will have all winter for that," his father said.

"Everyone in the family is good? I have had no word all summer," Andreas asked.

"Mamma is fine," his father said. "She will really be looking now to make an honest man out of you. You are an uncle again; Ingrid had a boy in July. Heidi married that Hassman boy. He has moved to Odessa and set up his wheel shop there. Last word, she is due her first child January. Heinrich here can't leave his wife alone, number six is due October. A bunch of boys are nipping at little Marie's heels, so soon it will be only you and Johann left."

"Oh, Johann is all hot and bothered by Irene Klieshoff. I don't think he will make it past harvest," said Andreas.

"I hope he has enough money to buy a farm," his father replied.

"Oh, that won't be a problem. He has one hundred acres and enough money to build a house and start a herd," Andreas said. "Speaking of which?"

"You have four promising foals and six calves this year," the elder Bekenbaum said. "A couple of neighbors want to talk to you about studding out your stallion, and one has talked about trading stud services of his prize bull for a couple of your cows."

"I think I will have to find or build a house, sooner than later," Andreas said. "I now have two aides to fend for and a lot of meetings and planning sessions to hold."

"Time enough for all that, I think," his father said. "Michilov will be coming over soon to let you know what decision was made last night about that Zaboe fellow. Let's go fill our bellies before he comes over and ruins our appetites."

Andreas had barely walked in the door before he was mobbed, "Uncle Andy, Uncle Andy."

"Help, help, send for the guard I'm surrounded," Andreas said, lifting his hands in the air. Laughing, he gathered his niece and two nephews up in his arms, hugging and kissing them all. Setting the two eldest down and hoisting the youngest on his hip, before he could take another step, he was engulfed by his youngest sister Marie.

"Oh, my brave Andy, I'm so glad your home and safe," she exclaimed between kisses on his cheeks.

Walking into the kitchen, he handed his young nephew to his sister and greeted his sister-in-law rubbing her bulging belly.

"Rosvite, I'm going to get you a big stick to keep that brother of mine in line," he said, laughing.

"More like I need the stick to keep her off me," roared his brother, who received a wallop on the arm from his face-reddening wife.

"Let my son greet his mother as a good son should," demanded his mother.

"Ah, Mamma, just as beautiful as the day I left," he said when he could finally break away from her fierce hug.

"Oh, Andreas, why are you wearing those old clothes? You have such a beautiful uniform." Tears of joy and pride running down her cheeks.

"Oh, Mamma, don't ever change," he said, holding her close.

All of the conversation had been as usual when amongst themselves, in German. As he was about to say something else witty, his glance fell at the end of the table and he fell silent. Standing there in their pristine white dresses were the two sisters he had saved. The dresses were embroidered in red, with red aprons that had swirls of green and yellow flowers stitched on them. Their long blonde hair had been braided and coiled about their heads, red and yellow waist-long ribbons were woven into the braids, one on each side.

"Excuse my manners, ladies," he said in Russian, releasing his mother; he stood taking in their beauty.

"Oh, you have not been properly introduced," continued his mother in German, "Andreas, this is Elizabeth and Katia Halenczuk, our guests; Elizabeth and Katia, my son Andreas."

"Pleased to meet you, my lord," said Elizabeth in perfect German.

"The pleasure is all mine, Miss Halenczuk, and I am sure my mother will tell you, the only 'lord' at her kitchen table is Our Lord Jesus," Andreas said, bowing his head.

"Quite right; now, everyone to the table, the food is getting cold," ordered his mother.

Andreas sat quietly eating the ham, eggs, and potatoes piled onto his plate. As he ate, he glanced around the table and realized how much he had missed all this. The local gossip of the community, who was sick, who was doing well, how the harvest

138

was coming, and plans for the day and the future. He found his eyes being drawn to the end of the table where Elizabeth sat, eating delicately and quietly talking with Marie and Katia. Once, when he glanced over, Marie saw him and leaned over whispering in Elizabeth's ear. Her eyes shot up looking at him before quickly going down to her plate, while she turned a light shade of red. Marie and Katia giggled as teenage girls are wont to do when sharing secrets, which only made Elizabeth turn a deeper shade of red before giving both girls an evil look.

Andreas spent the rest of the meal avoiding looking at that end of the table, but once, unable to resist, he quickly glanced over and caught Elizabeth shyly observing him. He wondered at the changes in the young woman. The fire brand of the day earlier, ready to lash out with great violence, had been replaced with a quiet, lovely, and polite young lady with perfect manners. Women, he thought, like his father was always saying, can't live with them, can't live without them; don't try to figure them out, you never will.

After the meal and a cup of rare coffee, Andreas's cup was refilled and he was banished from the house. His mother absolutely refusing him to help in the cleanup, saying it was undignified for a man of his position to be doing menial work. He took his cup and, walking over to the corral, he placed it on a fence post and filled his pipe. Standing with one foot on the lower fence board, he looked at the horses in the corral while smoking his pipe and sipping his coffee. His thoughts were disturbed by Bartholomew bumping his head on his shoulder, rubbing up and down. Placing his mother's precious china coffee cup on the ground safely out of the way, Andreas grabbed the animal's head in both his hands, rubbing his ears, and laid his head on the horse's neck.

"It's a sad thing," he said, "when a man only has a horse for a friend. Someone to confide in, to share his thoughts and dreams with."

Not for the first time, Andreas felt something was missing in his life.

"How do you it?" said a soft feminine voice beside him.

Andreas turned to see Elizabeth standing beside him looking in the corral. She had changed out of her Sunday clothes into the more normal clothing they all wore; the ribbons gone from her hair, but the hair still wound around the crown of her head, which came to just above Andreas's shoulder. Unlike most of the big-boned girls Andreas was familiar with, she had an athletic build, slight without being skinny, and what he could see of her arms showed she was no pampered lady.

"How do I do what?" he asked.

She turned and looked at him with piercing green eyes, which were brimming with the tears she was valiantly holding back.

"How can you kill a man one day and the next, carry on as if nothing has happened?" she asked. "I took that knife and stuck it in that man, killing him. A woman is supposed to give and nurture life, not take it."

As the tears started running down her cheeks, Andreas took her in his arms hugging her, gently stroking her hair as she buried her head in his chest and broke into body-shaking sobs. As he laid his cheek alongside hers, he looked back across to the house. His sister-in-law was herding her protesting children back into the house, while Marie had her right arm around a concerned Katia's waist, comforting her.

My God, he thought, have I become so callous. Am I becoming one of those veterans who had no value for human life or suffering. No, even thinking these thoughts proved that wrong.

As her body slowly stopped shaking and she began to calm down, with a soft rumbling, the stallion gently forced his head between them rubbing his head on Elizabeth's shoulder.

"Oh, come now, Bartholomew, you think you need to have all the attention," said Andreas, rubbing between the horse's eyes. "Look what you have done, you've gotten your smelly hair all over the lady's pretty dress." Knowing in his heart that gestures of emotion like that from his horse were rare to anyone but Andreas himself.

Breaking away from him, Elizabeth grinned shyly and absently brushed the front of her dress, before grabbing the stallion's ears and shaking them.

"Typical male," she said, "you need all the attention for yourself. Oh my God," she said, "I am so sorry, my lord, I did not mean to burden you, and, oh, look what I have done to your shirt."

"First off, when we are alone like this, my name is Andreas, what we have shared together gives you that right. As for the other?" He shrugged his shoulders. "Many is the time I wish I could do the same as you have just done. Bartholomew here gets tired of hearing it all the time. Life must and has to go on, miss. There are mouths to feed, animals and people who are counting on me to make them feel safe. We have a saying around here that helps keep us focused, miss."

"Elizabeth, not 'miss', Andreas. Yes, I know, 'That which doesn't kill you makes you strong'."

"Ah, you have been eavesdropping, Elizabeth, bad girl," Andreas said, smiling. "My father has just the cure for that. Papa, you quit hiding around that corner and bring that brandy over here." Elizabeth and Andreas laughed as the tension left them and his father walked sheepishly over to them eyes downcast, but with a glint in them.

"Bloody officers is all the same," he said, mischief in his voice. "Keep all the pretty girls and the good booze for themselves."

"And rightly so, Senior Sergeant," Andreas said in mock severity. "You enlisted men do not appreciate pretty girls or good booze."

"Why I outta," said his father, raising his right fist and shaking it at the couple in mock anger as the two young people broke out in laughter.

Before another word could be spoken, thumping hooves, rattling horse tack, and wagon wheels signaled the approach of visitors. A smart buggy, drawn by two horses and escorted by Ivan on horseback, made its way down the laneway to the farmstead. Driving the buggy was his Uncle Michilov, beside him Father Litzanburger, and in the back, Andreas's Aunt Wilhelmina.

"Forgive me for disturbing you at home on Sunday, my lord," Michilov said. "The council has reached a decision on the enquiry and if it please you, I have been bid by the council to give you that decision and await your guidance on our findings."

As Elizabeth made to leave, Andreas gently placed his left hand on her left shoulder preventing her from leaving. "Speak freely, Mr. Chairman," Andreas said. "Miss Halenczuk has a right to hear."

Andreas felt a shock run up his arm and stop at his heart as his hand made contact with her shoulder. He felt her breath stutter and her shoulder tremble briefly as his uncle began the report.

"As my lord wishes," his uncle began. "The council has found the man Olag Zaboe guilty of ordering and participating in the death of three citizens. We have found him guilty of illegal confining and causing physical harm to two citizens, and we have found him guilty of ordering the death of his overlord."

As Andreas felt Elizabeth begin to weaken, he slipped his arm around her waist hoping to hold her if she fainted.

"We have also found no evidence of wrongdoing by citizen Elizabeth Halenczuk or her sister, Katia. In addition, the council has found that my lord's actions of that day were completely justified."

"What recommendations does our council have for us in way of punishment?"

"In view of the serious nature of the crimes, the council recommends stripping the man Olag Zaboe and his family of all rights, privileges, and citizenship. That all their possessions, wealth, lands, and property be surrendered to the Crown for dispersal, and immediate exile from Russia. Finally and with the permission of the church, we recommend the man Olag Zaboe be executed for his crimes at my lord's discretion."

"We agree with our council's findings and recommendations," Andreas said, effecting the imperial We. "We order our council to dispatch our constables to immediately arrest and escort the family Zaboe to the Hungarian border with nothing but the clothes on their backs. In addition, we order the man Olag Zaboe be held in custody with no access to visitors until such time as he is executed. We also order the man Olag Zaboe be hung by the neck until he is dead as soon as it can be arranged. His remains are not to be buried in holy ground, nor is the grave to be marked."

He held the priest's eyes the whole time he spoke the last comment, seeing no disagreement in them.

"The funerals for the Family Halenczuk, my lord?" asked the priest.

Andreas looked down at Elizabeth who, placing her hand over Andreas's on her waist, straightened up and in a clear voice said, "My parents and my brother will not be buried until that monster is no longer of this world."

"The lady has spoken," Andreas said. "So shall it be. The execution shall take place at noon tomorrow; the funerals, after morning mass Tuesday. Lieutenant Halinov, you will return to town and inform the council of our decisions and see to it that they are carried out immediately. Then you are to return here and report."

"My lord," said Ivan, turning his horse, kicking his heels back, and galloped to town.

"Senior Sergeant," Andreas asked. "We feel that we must once again impose on your hospitality. Could you please inform your good wife that we wish to entertain our guests with some tea?"

"Of course, my lord, no problem, my lord," the elder Bekenbaum said. "Father, Mr. Chairman, and lady wife, if you please."

As his aunt and uncle followed his father to the house, Father Litzanburger approached Andreas.

"My lord, if you wish, I can hear your confession."

As Andreas's arm around Elizabeth involuntarily tightened on her waist, he felt her thumb gently stroking his hand.

"Father, I shot those men down like the animals they were." He felt his anger rising along with his voice and forced himself to calm down.

"While I agree, my Lord and Savior would not approve."

He continued, "In my heart, I am at peace with God, have no regrets, and would do it again. Now, please, let us talk no more of this and enjoy the feast I am sure Mother is laying out for us."

"My lord," said the priest, nodding his head and walking into the house.

It was then that he realized he still had his arm around Elizabeth's waist and he awkwardly removed it, muttering an apology. Placing both his arms on the top rail, he laid his forehead on them and, forgetting his surroundings, placed all his efforts at controlling his raging emotions and the tears that threatened to overwhelm him.

It was then that he felt an arm around his waist and a gentle kiss on his neck beneath his left ear. "Andreas, thank you," she whispered into his ear and eight months of horror and sorrow, depravations and degradations could no longer be held back.

As he stood there, his head on his arms, the tears staining the ground as he silently purged himself, he felt the warm comfort of her arm as she slowly moved it up and down his side and the softness of her hair as she laid her head on his shoulder. Taking a deep breath, holding it for a second, and slowly letting it out he stood up, put his left arm about her again, and, leaning his head against hers, said, "Where have you been all my life?"

"Nowhere special," she said softly.

The spell was broken by his young niece crying out in protest, "But, Oma, Uncle Andy and Lizbet need their tea."

He looked around and saw his mother hustling the protesting girl back in the house.

They both self-consciously removed their arms and stood up straight.

Turning to her, he brushed her hair back from her eyes as she straightened out his shirt.

"What a sorry sight you are, your shirt is all wet and wrinkled," she said with a smile. "What kind of earl are you, setting that kind of example."

"Sorry, me lady, it'll not happen again, me lady," he said with a mocking bow.

"See that it does not; now go, and next I see you, be more presentable," she said in mock severity. With skirts swirling, she marched towards the house and, looking back at him, gave a flick of her hips and a toss of her head before being engulfed by his and her sisters in a three-way hug.

Oh God, Andreas thought, if she didn't have me before, she's ensnared me now.

After changing into a clean shirt, Andreas was ushered into the front room, where men were always banished when women had important matters to discuss. Pouring a beer from the pitcher on the table by the wall, Andreas took a deep pull before refilling it and taking his place amongst the group of men gathered there.

"You could do worse, you know," said his uncle.

"Yes, she has good hips and looks to have her wits about her," said his father.

"It's not her hips he's thinking of—va va voom," joked his brother, waving his arms in a gesture every man knows.

"Ha, look at him; she's got him good." All the men laughed as his brother waved his right arm around and making sounds like a whip. "Heel, boy, heel."

"You should know. Rosvite has you jumping every time she bats her eyes at you," Andreas shot back at him as they all broke out in laughter.

"We've all been there, eh, Heinnie," said his uncle.

"Women," said Andreas's father.

"Can't live with 'em, can't live without 'em!" they all roared out, raising their beer mugs up.

"Oh, sure, while the loyal lieutenant is out diligently carrying out his orders, the rest of the officers are lazing about, getting sloshed, and talking about women," said Ivan, who had walked into the room just as they had made the toast.

"Who you calling an officer, you young pup," said both Heinrichs. "The only thing better than a rookie lieutenant. . ."

". . . is no lieutenant at all!" they all roared out, raising their mugs again.

"Somebody is in for it," said Ivan when they had stopped laughing long enough to speak again. "All the women, even the two new ones, are clustered together making some kind of plans."

"Oh shit," said Andreas.

All three of the older men and the priest looked at each other, then swinging their arms around and making sounds like whips in the direction of Andreas.

"Hiya, boy, hiya," they rang out. Then taking turns, each man with much embellishment and grand gestures mimicked all they had seen Andreas and Elizabeth do, filling Ivan in on what he had missed.

"You poor man. You're done for now, cousin," Ivan said, raising his cup of beer in mock salute.

"No respect," said Andreas.

"No respect at all," the other men finished for him as, once again, laughter engulfed the room.

Finally, as the men settled down, his uncle addressed him. "I think we have found a solution to your residence and headquarters problem," he said. "That fool Zaboe has a very fine villa right in the middle of your mandated lands that is now free of tenants. As the lord of this province, it is within your rights to take it over."

"After the funerals, we will ride out there and have a look," Andreas replied. "If it suits, that would solve a lot of my immediate concerns. Ivan, I am afraid I am going to have to ask you to return to town and muster up the troop. I want no problems tomorrow; have them muster here at first light in full uniform and weapons."

"Already done," Ivan replied. "Johann should be here soon. He's bringing the packs and the spare weapons with him."

"Well done, Ivan, if I don't pay attention, you'll turn into a useful officer after all."

"Mamma said to check if you need more beer, you're too quiet in here," said Marie from the kitchen door.

"Perhaps later, Marie, thank you," replied Andreas.

Nodding, she shut the door behind her and a few minutes later an explosion of feminine laughter erupted in the kitchen.

"Glad to hear they're having fun in there," Michilov chuckled.

"I am going to need your advice and counsel, Uncle, Father," Andreas said. "I have been ordered to field a battalion for a full year's service, starting in April. At the moment, my battalion consists of ten troopers, three administration troopers, one rookie officer, and me, a jumped-up sergeant with no experience."

"That's not true, Andreas," said his uncle. "In one year, you fought two significant engagements, outnumbered, with inexperienced troops and not only survived, but had no casualties. You used superior tactics and terrain to your advantage, and to compensate for inferior weapons. In one year, you have done more than most officers do in their lifetime. Your father and I participated in a number of big and famous battles, but we never faced more than a hundred or so experienced troops and we always lost men, sometimes a lot of men.

"You command respect, Andreas, men want to do things for you; those are things that can't be taught. We can help you with large unit tactics and logistics, but if anything, you can teach us. Even in our day, firearms were becoming so powerful it was almost suicide for us to line up and charge them en mass. You have changed your tactics to suit the new reality, and with your new weapons, it will be some time before anyone can catch up to us. We will guide you where we can; the rest, well, it's up to you."

The running of little feet and general uproar in the kitchen heralded the arrival of Johann, and a few minutes later, followed by Peter Chimalovich, he entered the front room, both men carrying pitchers of beer, kicking the door shut behind him with his heel.

"Greetings all," he shouted out, "did you check out the dish in the next room? If I wasn't hooked up with Irene."

The four men in the room started the whip motion again, pointing at Andreas.

"Oh, Brother, I leave you alone for two days and look what happens," Johann said, shaking his head. "Look at all the trouble you get yourself into."

As laughter again erupted in the room, Andreas saw Peter standing with a puzzled smile on his lips.

Switching to Russian, Andreas began, "Peter, welcome, the older man in the corner there is my father, Heinrich, and the one next to him is my brother, Heinrich the younger; Father, Brother, this is Gunnery Sergeant Peter Chimalovich of the United States of America Marine Corps. His father is a Cossack living in America now, and I invited him to stay with us so he can see where his forefathers lived."

The elder Bekenbaums rose and shook hands with Peter. "Welcome to my home," said his father in accented English. "Thank God another enlisted man, we were outnumbered by all these officers here."

"So, who's the girl? What a looker, the younger one, too," continued Johann.

"Those are the two that Andreas rescued from that vermin Zaboe," said his father.

"Wow," said Peter, "I thought I recognized them. It was hard to tell under all that blood and dirt."

"Sure, sure, the gallant US Marines and valiant Russian hero to the rescue; now we know why," joked the younger Heinrich.

Discovering that Peter spoke Russian, every one switched and the conversation shifted to everyday concerns until they were called in for supper. After the men had completed their after-supper chores and the women had finished the kitchen clean up, the family conducted their customary Sunday evening stroll around the farm. The nieces and nephews excitedly telling Andreas and Johann about this cow or that and whose chickens were laying better than the other.

Andreas soon found himself walking beside Elizabeth in an island by themselves. He walked along with his hands clasped behind his back, she with her right hand holding her left arm. Andreas would occasionally point out a farm feature, and she would ask a question about how they did something or why. As they walked, Andreas felt things he had never felt before. He had trouble thinking of things to say, or stumbled over his words. He had a weird feeling in the pit of his stomach, and at times he had trouble breathing. He hoped he was not coming down with something, he had too much to do.

Soon they were back in front of the main farmhouse and bidding farewell to the Halinov family, including Father Litzanburger and Ivan. The family started to drift off to bed, and Andreas was left standing on the porch with only his mother and father. As his father lit the porch lamp, Marie came out with three steins of beer and kissed them all good night.

"Sit, Andreas," ordered his mother. "Elizabeth seems to be quite taken with you. How do you feel about her?"

"Mamma, please," Andreas said. "She has just had a traumatic experience, and I just happened to be there. I would not dare to presume and take advantage of her. Besides, I have no

151

house or place of my own, and next year—don't dare to deny, Papa—I am being sent on a dangerous mission somewhere for a year and may never come back. She seems a nice girl, but I know nothing about her or her family, and she is a little old to be unmarried."

"Her grandfather was one of your father's sergeants and her mother went to school with Heinnie," his mother said. "She married one of Vacilly's officers young, and Elizabeth is their first born. She is now mistress of their lands and so is hardly penniless; she has good pedigree, and you need an heir."

"Mother," said his father gently, "I agree with Andreas on this one. Yes, she is all of the things you have said, and it would be a good match for both families. Andreas, like it or not, you are now an earl and that comes with responsibilities, some of which need a wife. You also need an heir, or some villain like Zaboe could take it all away from you. But, Mother, he is right. It is too soon; she has suffered much, and her people are not even in the ground yet. Give her time to get her feet on the ground, and we will talk about it then."

"Humph," his mother said and abruptly stood up and stomped into the house, softly closing the door behind her.

"You're off the hook, Papa; if she was mad, she would have slammed the door," Andreas said.

"Yes, she knows," his father agreed. "She had been promised to another man before I came along, and she didn't even know about it. If it had not been for my pedigree and your uncle's influence and money, you would have a butcher for a father. Honestly, man to man, how do you feel about Elizabeth?"

"I don't know. I feel like a fool around her," Andreas said after a moment of reflection. "I can't breathe; I have a hard time not stumbling on my words. The hair stands up on my arms, and

152

if we touch, it's like a million needles punching my skin all at once. My God, you should have seen her. They were dragging her on her back by her hair when I showed up, and she was still trying to get at them. She had already gutted one of them, and she was so angry when I let that fool go I was afraid she was going to kill me. You're right, she is a good match and I mean to make her mine. But only if she wants it too, and only after she has time to grieve."

The next two weeks were a flurry of activity for Andreas. The hanging and funerals had gone according to plan; he had approved of taking over the now vacant villa as his home and headquarters. His meager possessions, animals, the spare rifles and ammunition, and his money had been taken to the villa along with his two aides. His aides had met with all the villa's servants and farmhands and run off any that were unsuitable. He had held a meeting with all the district's elected and hierarchical leaders and outlined his intentions and a requirement for eight hundred troopers and three hundred supply and service troops.

Johann and Peter had become close friends, and Peter was picking up speaking German rapidly. Andreas was learning as much about America as Peter was of Russia and the more he learned, the more he wanted to go there.

Finally, he had time to get back home for a family Sunday dinner and was happy to see that Elizabeth and Katia were still living there. Johann sprung the fact that he and the love of his life, Irene, were going to get married in the spring and that he was going to build a house on the land he had received from Andreas from their original enlistment agreement.

During their after-dinner walk, Andreas found that he and Elizabeth were completely alone. He stopped walking and Elizabeth turned towards him.

God, but she was beautiful, he thought.

"When are you planning on going home?" he blurted out.

"Oh, there is no rush," she answered. "We really should be home before winter, but your family is so kind and I would like to stay for your brother's wedding."

"But, what of your father's lands?" Andreas asked. "Who will make sure the harvest is in and the animals cared for? I can send one of my people, or go myself, to see that all is in order."

"Sweet Andreas, always thinking of others," Elizabeth said, smiling. "No, there will be no problem. My father-in-law is looking after all of that for me."

"Ah, father-in-law." His hopes dashed in those three words, and his world came crashing down around his ears.

"Yes, he is one of Vacilly's closest friends," she said. "I have no doubt everything is already done."

"Very well, then, I will concern myself no more about it. We should really be getting back to the house," he said, starting in that direction.

"Wait!" she said, grabbing his arm and spinning him around, a look of fire in her eyes. "Just because I was married and am no longer a virgin, I am no longer good enough for the great Andreas, hero of Mother Russia?"

Then she saw he was not resisting her, his shoulders slumped and had an air of dejection she had never before seen in him. Her grip on his arm lessened from the bone-crunching hold and with her right hand she lifted his chin so his tear-rimmed eyes were looking in hers and not at the ground.

"You didn't know, did you?" she said softly. "He was eighteen, I sixteen," she continued. "My father had arranged the marriage two years earlier, and I met him a week before we were wed. Three days after the wedding, he went off for his summer service. He never came back. Killed in one of those glorious cavalry charges that your father says you avoid. His father has allowed me to keep his estates, and he and my father were going to ask to arrange for another marriage for me. That is why we were on our way here."

Taking his left hand and covering her right, he lowered his head until his forehead was touching hers.

"I thought my world had just come to an end," he said softly. "Here lies Andreas, Hero of Russia, the stone would have said. Undefeated in war, killed by a broken heart."

"Really?" she asked, her heart pounding so hard she thought it would burst her chest.

"Really," he said.

That's how a concerned mother, father, and two sisters found them. Forehead to forehead, one hand clutched on their cheeks, the other on each other's waist.

"Andreas Heinrich, I brought you up better than that! Unhand that poor girl right this second!" demanded his indignant mother.

Turning around so that he was facing the crowd, he slipped his arm around Elizabeth's back and she around his.

"Drat, caught in the act," Andreas said. "Well, there is nothing for it, in order to protect the poor girl's honor, I will have to marry her now."

Elizabeth's legs collapsed and his arm around her kept her upright.

"She is an orphan and a widow, after all, and I, the great earl, must ensure she is well looked after, and her estates too, of course. She is rather good looking, Father, don't you agree?"

Spinning her around and holding her with both his arms on her shoulders, he looked her in the eye, "Before God and these witnesses, I, Andreas, ask you, Elizabeth, to be my wife."

Putting her arms on his shoulders over his arms, she said, "Before God and these witnesses, I Elizabeth, say yes, and if my father-in-law agrees, I will be your wife."

"And I, Vacilly, will only approve if I don't have to pay one penny more for her dowry than you crooks are already getting."

Andreas looked at Vacilly's beaming face, then back to Elizabeth. Releasing his right arm, he extended it to Vacilly who shook it vigorously. Encircling her with his arms around the tops of her legs, he pulled her tight to him lifting her off the ground until they were eye to eye.

"What a fool, I would have given him everything," Andreas whispered to her.

"He knows," she replied. "I told him. I also told him that if he did not approve, you would rip his heart out, and if you did not, I would."

"Beautiful and deadly," Andreas said.

"Just like my husband," she replied, and wrapping her arms about him tightly, she kissed him.

"How long had you bandits had all this planned?" Andreas asked the two old friends when the three of them had finally been able to escape to the porch for a smoke.

"When I broke the news of your promotion," Vacilly said. "Your mother got all in a panic about finding you the right girl. I did not think much about it until I checked in on Elizabeth to see how she had fared over the summer. I thought to myself how lonely she must be. My son and she had not really even got to know each other before the fool went out and got himself killed. And I thought to myself, 'Self, Elizabeth would be perfect for Andreas.' I approached your parents and, as a formality, I told her father, who insisted on being the one to bring her here to meet you. Then that nonsense in the clearing happened and the rest, well, you two worked it out.

"Andreas, I have come to cherish her as the daughter I never had. Ever since my Olga died, Elizabeth has always made sure I was looking out for myself and not getting into too much trouble. You have become as a son to me and selfish old man that I am, I wanted so much for you two to find each other. It could not have worked out better."

"At first, she was very cold to the idea of meeting you," his father said. "Letting that bandit get away had not endeared her to the man who had done it. Then at the trial, she said you gave her courage to testify. Momma said Elizabeth told her, when you walked in for breakfast that first day and the children and Marie mobbed you; well, you had her heart right then. These weeks she has spent with us has endeared her to us all. Rosvite says the children adore her, and Mother and she are like old school chums. Mother acts half her age. Andreas, if in your heart you do not think this match is right, if all you are doing is feeling sorry for her, stop and think. Do not do anything that will hurt her and you."

"Do you know that feeling you get when you have been on the trail for some time?" Andreas asked. "The one you develop between horse and rider? That is the way I feel when I am with

157

Elizabeth but ten times stronger. When we stood at the corral that first day, I had only wished to give her a shoulder to cry on, she had been through so much. Then, with two words, she drew out all the pain and anxiety I had been going through all those many weeks. Somehow, some way, I had to make her mine; she completed my life, and I knew that without her I would be nothing, the rest of my life."

Looking up, Andreas saw both these strong, tough warriors looking off in the distance, tears running down their cheeks.

Two days later, Andreas was summoned to his father's home. Any excuse to spend time with Elizabeth was reason enough to get away from all the organizing of the estates and upcoming campaign. When he entered the yard, he noticed more horses in the corral than usual and a lot of activity. Farmhands gathering horse tack and a row of packs lined up along the corral rails.

After the greetings and a cup of tea, Andreas was left facing what he called the council of war. His mother, Rosvite, Marie, Katia, and, shyly, on the far end of the table, Elizabeth.

"It has been decided," his mother announced regally. "The bands have been posted in the church and your wedding is to be in three weeks. Like a typical male, you have left us little time to plan, but we have just enough time to accomplish it. Rosvite and Katia will organize things at Vacilly's end. I and Marie will turn your undoubtedly pigsty villa into as respectable a condition as we can. The wedding itself will be held at Vacilly's house, as is traditional, on Friday, and the main reception is to be in your villa, Saturday. The guest list has been set and invitations sent out. Any questions? Good, now you and Elizabeth go and do something, we have work to do."

Clicking his heels and saluting at attention, Andreas barked out, "Yes, my commander, right away, my commander, this trooper requests permission to withdraw, my commander."

Grabbing Elizabeth by the arm and running, they almost made it to the door before Andreas received a wet dish rag in the back of the head. Reaching the porch, he pulled her close, lifting her in the air and swinging her about before she grabbed his head in both hands and kissed him passionately.

"Now, put me down before you break something," she squealed. "Come sit, we don't have much time; we are leaving soon, and I must get ready for the trip. No, you can't come. Your mother is insisting on keeping tradition."

"Lizbet," he said, holding both her hands in his, "are you sure about all this? We can still call it off."

"Are you having second thoughts?" she asked. "I know I am not young and I come with a past."

"No, no. It's, well, it's like this," Andreas began. "They are sending me out in the spring and you know they always send us where it is most dangerous. There is a good chance I will be killed, and I am not sure I want to put you through that again."

"Andy, surely what has happened these last weeks has shown that life is never safe," she said. "You could fall off your horse and break your neck. I could catch fever and die. We could both be caught in a blizzard and die. God will take us when he will. We will have all winter together and take the days as they come. I will hear no more about it."

He pulled her close and kissed her. When Katia came on the porch in what seemed to them to be but minutes later, she found them on the bench, her feet tucked under her skirt with her head on his shoulder, and he holding her hand with one arm around her shoulder.

"Liz, it's time to go," Katia said softly. "You must get ready if we are to be home before dark."

Elizabeth took a deep breath and let it out slowly; she kissed Andreas lightly on the lips before reluctantly breaking from his grasp and entering into the house.

"Lord Andreas?" Katia asked, no amount of coaxing could break her of calling him that. "I have never seen my sister so happy, never. You won't beat her like Papa did to Mamma and her, will you?"

She had her hands clasped before her so tight they were turning white, and her face was so distraught Andreas could not help himself. He gathered her into his arms and gently stroked her hair.

"God, no," he whispered. "On my mother's soul, never."

He was still holding her, rocking her gently, when Elizabeth returned to the porch. Katia broke free from him then, running up to her sister and giving her a big hug before running off the porch and vaulting onto her horse.

Elizabeth, like her sister, was wearing loose-fitting, long pants tucked into calf-length riding boots, her tunic, over the pants to her thighs, held by a belt about her waist and sleeves rolled up just under the elbow. Her long blonde hair was pulled back into a ponytail that hung halfway down her back. Raising one exquisite eyebrow, she advanced on him placing one hand on a hip, with the other she brushed at the tear stains on his shirt.

"I'm going to have to make you more shirts if you do this with every woman you meet," she said.

"Sorry," Andreas said, "you don't get off so lucky; she's not my type, but I hear she has a good-looking older sister that likes to show off her figure with tight belts."

"All in good time, Trooper, all in good time," she said, slapping him gently.

Arm-in-arm they walked to her horse, where they stood awkwardly, not wanting the time together to end.

"Do you think you have a big enough escort?" Andreas asked. "I could call up my father's troop if these ten fierce warriors are not enough, my lady."

"Be nice, my lord," Elizabeth replied. "These are my own men. They feel horrible about what happened even though it was not their fault. My father had sent them home, forbidding them to escort us. Come, you are their commander; you should greet them."

Leaving her by her horse, Andreas walked over to the lounging troopers who immediately grabbed their rifles lying against the corral boards and lined up at attention. Their leader, on the left of the formation, snapped a crisp salute, which Andreas just as crisply returned.

"My lord, escort assembled and all accounted for. Ready for inspection, sir."

Andreas trooped the line looking each man up and down and in the eyes. All the men were in their late thirties, their equipment well-worn but still very serviceable. These men were all tried veterans, tough as nails and soft as shoe leather.

"Very well, Sergeant, have the troop prepare for departure, at my lady's leisure."

"A word, my lord?" the sergeant asked.

"Go ahead, Sergeant."

"My lord, as God as my witness, her father ordered us home, Major. We never . . ."

"Enough, Sergeant," Andreas said. "My lady has vouched for you. How long have you served her?"

"Nine years, sir, we are all that is left whole from her husband's troop, sir. She is like a niece to us, sir, we will all die before letting her come to harm, sir."

"Very well, Sergeant, I commend her to your care. I only hope I can one day earn your trust like my lady has. Thank you, Sergeant."

"First, I have an overlord for a new father-in-law," Andreas said. "Now, I have ten combat veteran troopers for godfathers. I fear I will never be able to sample my lady's favors at this rate."

"No fear there, my lord," Elizabeth said. "Now, help me mount before I do something very unladylike, for instance, ripping your clothes off and having my way with you right here."

"Oh God forbid," Andreas said with mock horror. "Not even those ten fierce warriors would keep my mother from ripping you to shreds." Only his lips over hers stopped her laughing.

He trotted into the villa's courtyard two hours later. As he dismounted and handed the reins to a groomsman, he saw two wagons with five long boxes each stacked in them, parked against the carriage house.

Stomping the dust off his boots, he yelled out in Russian, "Sergeant Malenkov, you slacker, your lord and master has returned from the wars and is thirsty."

The sergeant came onto the porch with a beer stein foaming over the side in his hand.

Taking two quick swigs of the pale beverage, Andreas continued, "Very good, Sergeant, you will not be drawn and quartered, yet."

"How went the battle, Major?" the sergeant asked.

"Not well, I fear," Andreas said, shaking his head. "We are about to be invaded and there will be no stopping them. The only possible outcome is unconditional surrender. The senior sergeant's wife and her minions will be here in two days and will take over the main house. It would be well if all traces of us were gone by then."

"Of course, sir, already in progress," the sergeant replied. "The previous tenant had converted a warehouse that will suit us nicely."

"I may have to promote you sooner than I thought, the way you are going," Andreas said. "What's in the boxes on the wagons in the yard?"

"I believe I will defer to the visitors, sir," the sergeant said.

"Visitors, you left visitors in the house unattended?" Andreas said in mock dismay. "What if they steal the eating utensils? The senior sergeant's wife would be most cross. Most cross, indeed. I may not be able to save you from being drawn and quartered."

"Gentlemen." Andreas walked over to the American majors, his hand outstretched. "How good to see you again. I see the good sergeant has provided you with refreshment; it is only beer, I fear."

"Thank you for seeing us, my lord," said the marine major.

Looking around in panic from side to side, Andreas said, "Sergeant, did you let a lord in here, too? The bugger is probably stealing all the china."

"I am sorry, Andreas," said the major, "old habits, and the beer is very good."

"What's in the boxes?" Andreas asked.

"Those are the first hundred of your consignment. The rest will be arriving two wagons a day."

"Ah, yes, I had forgotten about that," Andreas said. "A lot on my mind these days. I will have my brother and your sergeant inventory them. Come, let's sit on the porch; it's not so oppressive out there. I repossessed this place from a very bad man who will not be needing it any more. The décor is not to my tastes, but I am sure the senior sergeant's wife will fix that in no time. Have a seat, gentlemen."

"That was the nasty business Remington has been telling everyone in Odessa about?" Major Olynick asked. "That was a very brave thing you did, Andreas."

"Nonsense," Andreas replied, "either one of you would have done the same. I had them outnumbered, three tough guys with knives and an overweight fool, against me, a Winchester, and my horse. No contest."

"That's not the way Remington is telling it and he says he saw it all," Olynick insisted.

"He was up on a hill three hundred yards away," Andreas said.

Spotting two men riding into the court yard, Andreas got the sergeant's attention and nodded at the men who were dismounting. Switching to English he yelled out, "Hey, you two enlisted men, get your lazy butts over here!"

"Ya, who's calling who lazy? Looks like my brother has been swilling beer and chasing his girlfriend all day, while the rest of us . . ." Johann said.

Both men came to rigid attention with Peter saluting.

"At ease, Gunnery Sergeant, you're not in uniform and you're on leave," Andreas ordered. "While you, Senior Sergeant, are going on report for insubordination to an elder sibling. No pudding for supper for you. The majors here have brought us a hundred of our new toys; so after your beer, I would like you to get them squared away. Grab some of the farmhands to help you."

"Now, the majors here have had the bad manners of showing up in uniform," Andreas continued. "See if you can outfit them up in some normal clothes so we can be done with all this 'sir' and 'major' and saluting stuff. In the meantime, I will sit here and swill my beer drowning my sorrows on my loss and, even more distressing, the soon arrival of the senior sergeant's wife."

The two Americans had brought their own civilian clothing and before Andreas had finished his second beer were back, along with the two sergeants.

"So, what's all this about; what did you lose and who is this senior sergeant's wife? Anything we can help you with?" asked the marine major.

Wiping off his chin from the beer he had spilled on it laughing at the major's question, Johann answered, "Why, the fool has lost his heart, and the senior sergeant's wife is our mother, of course. The wedding is in three weeks, here, of course."

"Congratulations, do we know the lucky lady?"

"Why, not only does the dashing earl rescue the damsel in distress, and she is a beauty, she is," Johann said. "But, he gets her to fall in love with him, so he can get all her land and money."

"But, of course, she is but a poor orphan and widow, and he was just doing his duty as earl of the district, looking out for the poor girl's best welfare," said Peter.

"That's my story and I'm sticking to it," Andreas said. "What do you mean the wedding is to be here? Only the reception was supposed to be here."

"Oh no, my brother," Johann said. "Word got back to Odessa, the duke and the bishop are insisting on attending the Hero of Mother Russia's wedding, so the venue is changing. So all the Bekenbaum women will be here in two days to make our lives hell for the next two weeks."

"Oh, that's it then," Andreas said. "Sergeant, bring the whole bloody keg; if I have to unconditionally surrender, I'm doing it with a hangover."

Contrary to what Andreas had said, he sat sipping his beer asking the Americans questions about their homeland. The sun had gone down but the night was still warm, and they sat talking and joking in the dim light of a lantern hung in the rafters of the porch.

"Gunnery Sergeant, your enlistment is up at the end of the month," the marine major said. "If you come back to the consulate, you can re-sign there."

"Actually, sir, I believe I well let my enlistment run out," Sergeant Chimalovich said.

"In that case then, go to the consulate; they'll give you a steamer ticket and you process out when you get to port," the major replied.

"I believe I would like to stay here for a while, sir, if that would be possible."

"In that case, you would go to the consulate, they would process your papers, give you your back pay and steamer fare back home, and you would be on your way. Who you have to contact to stay here I can't say. Andreas?" the major said, looking at Andreas.

"Normally, you would have to contact an immigration officer and file all the reasons why and where and for how long you were staying," Andreas replied. "I believe I can do that for you. Do you plan on looking for a job or career; I can help you with that as well. I happen to know of an auxiliary military unit that is looking for qualified, experienced officers. If you're interested, I think I can arrange a captaincy."

"What's the pay like?" the American sergeant asked.

"Thirty US dollars a month is the going rate," Andreas answered. He was about to change the subject, as there had been no response when the cavalry major spoke.

"Is that for real?" he asked. "Or is that only because you like the gunnery sergeant?"

"No, that is the standard rate," Andreas answered. "I know it is not much money, but for most of us it is only a part-time job and most officers have land that gives them income. The money for the position, for them, is just extra cash."

"Would this unit perhaps need a couple more experienced officers?" the other cavalry major asked.

"Yes, I believe so; they are a new unit, with new recruits, and very few officers at all," Andreas replied. "Are you interested, as well? I thought you were both committed."

"Officers can resign their commissions at any time after five years' service. We don't have five-year renewable contracts like enlisted men. Who do we contact to join up and how do we go about it?"

"It is normally a complicated affair," Andreas said solemnly. "Character checks with your government and things like that. For the senior sergeant there, as he was born here, I can just tell him he is to report tomorrow as a captain. For you three foreigners, I would suggest first, you tell your government that at the end of the month you are leaving their employ and you show up and report to your new commander the next day. Better make it the day after. You will all be attending the new commander's wedding and will most likely be in no condition to report the next day. Come to think of it, the new commander may not be visible for a couple of days. Welcome aboard, gentlemen."

After a few more beers, Peter had taken the two officers to their quarters and the two brothers were sitting alone.

"Were you just joking about me being a captain, Andreas?" Johann asked.

"No, as of now, you are a captain," Andreas replied. "We need officers; I intend on making that offer to Ivan, as well. Let the other nine troopers know I would like them to be lieutenants, if they want it. You will learn a lot from those two Americans; they have already been using the tactics we started to use here."

"Thank you, Brother, I can really use the money. I will be able to build a house for Irene and I before we leave," Johann said.

168

"One condition, don't tell anyone until after my wedding," Andreas said.

"God, no, Momma is going to be full of herself as it is," Johann said. "Let alone having two officers now in the family, there will be no living with her."

Chapter Three

The next day, Andreas moved his uniforms, clothes, and equipment into the vacant foreman's house, and as the rest of the troop showed up after their vacations, they took over one of the bunk houses for an officers quarters. Work was started on converting one of the warehouses into an administration building, and another was selected for an enlisted-mans barracks and mess. Another two wagons had arrived with the new weapons and they were inventoried and repacked in their crates.

Andreas's mother had appeared with Marie and Rosvite and as expected, took complete charge. Furniture was being moved, walls and widows cleaned, trips to town to buy paint. The farmhands and house servants were kept busy cleaning and doing repairs. Guest houses were aired out and cleaned, and the barn, selected for the party, had the stalls removed to create an open space to dance, and temporary tables and benches created for the guests ranged along the outside walls.

Livestock was driven in from the outlying fields and penned up, while wagonloads of vegetables were stored next to the kitchen complex. A small army of butchers, cooks, and bakers arrived from the outlying areas, and the air about the villa was filled with the aroma of fresh baked bread, boiling cabbage, and roasting meat. Wooden kegs of beer and cases of vodka were stacked behind the makeshift bar in the barn, while the wine was commandeered by his mother and placed under her protection in the main house.

The first guest to arrive was General Andropov, Thursday before lunch, with his escort and aides. After greeting the general and showing the general's aides where the general and they would be quartered, Andreas took him to the main house to meet his mother and sisters. Choosing discretion over valour, both men retreated to Andreas's headquarters.

"A sad state of affairs when a man can't sleep in his own house," Andreas said. "I have been banned from my own bedroom, or maybe that room has been changed to another for all I know."

"Women and weddings," the general said. "At least you only have one mother driving you insane, at my wedding the mothers were bickering about the affair constantly."

"The Duchess is well, my lord?" Andreas asked.

"Oh, yes, and all the little Andropovs as well. She is looking forward to meeting the Hero of Russia and his lady. Unfortunately, the speed at which you customarily do things made it impossible for her to be here from Moscow in time. You have been commanded to appear at my residence for a complete weekend once she arrives.

"Now to business," the duke continued, "while we have some time for ourselves. That big box over there against the wall contains the uniforms you ordered out there in the wild. Have your people remove the aide de camp insignia and put on your new unit badges and the badges that are in a box in the crate. Make sure you have the proper badges in place for your wedding.

"The large box on your desk has the orders for your district in next year's deployment. The important orders are on the top and are for you alone. The others can be distributed to the unit commanders to deal with.

"To summarize your particular orders: On or about March first, you are to assemble one thousand cavalry troops, mounts, remounts, and support troops for extended foreign duty. You are to proceed to the port of Odessa for embarkation on transport ships. This will be classified as hazardous duty and pay scales will be adjusted accordingly. You will be under British command but retain autonomy within your own ranks. Rations, transportation of rations, and liaison personnel are to be provided by the British. By order of the czar and in writing, you are authorized and encouraged to disregard any orders that would clearly result in sustaining catastrophic losses. That means, if those fool English cavalry men want you to charge massed infantry or guns like they did at Balaclava, you can tell them where to get off. It does not mean to avoid contact altogether, that would be classed as cowardice and would be punished accordingly. Questions?"

"Is there any information on where we are going to be sent?" Andreas asked.

"Not for sure," the duke replied. "The British are having problems with some fanatical religious groups in Northern India and Afghanistan. I think they will put you in port in Iran and overland you to the border region between India and Afghanistan. Trade routes from all three countries converge in that area. I think they mean to bring their main forces up from India and use you as a blocking force. It's rough country," he said, "but not much worse than you are used to. Will you be ready?"

"Word has been sent out to the district leaders asking for candidates to arrive a week after the wedding," Andreas said. "We will pick the most qualified and send the rest home. After the selection process, we will begin tactical and intensive weapons training. We will be a long way from support, so the troops had better be the best."

"Very well, then," the duke said. "Now, where are you bandits hiding the booze? I have heard someone around here has

172

premium German beer they are hiding from their duke and general."

"Sergeant, if you ever hope to be promoted to an officer and not drawn and quartered," Andreas yelled at the office door, "you better have the general's personal beer keg in here before we all die of thirst."

The rest of the afternoon, Andreas and the duke were kept busy greeting arriving guests and renewing old acquaintances. It was after midnight before an exhausted Andreas collapsed on the cot set up in his office and passed out.

Everyone had been under strict orders to leave him alone that morning, and he lay on his bunk with his arms beneath his head staring at the ceiling. Today, finally after three weeks, she would be here. When he thought about it, his heart would start pounding and the anticipation of seeing her again would almost drive him mad. The smell of something delicious wafting beneath his door stirred him to action. On the verge of berating his long-suffering aide once again, instead, Andreas heaved out of bed and walked into the outer office.

"Where did we find the coffee?" he asked.

"Oh, I believe the sergeant is really in trouble," his aide said. "His Lordship is being nice this morning. That American officer in the fancy uniform dropped it off this morning. He says that he has a couple of pounds a month shipped over from America."

"Well, Lieutenant, I thought that from one officer and gentleman to the other, a little politeness would be nice," Andreas said. "But if the new lieutenant doesn't want to be busted back to private in a front-line infantry unit, he better pour me a cup of that coffee right now."

Instead of waiting, Andreas placed a hand on the shocked man's shoulder preventing him from getting up and walked over to the stove and poured two cups of the steaming coffee. Placing one cup on the desk, Andreas sat in a chair across from the desk, inhaling the aroma before taking a sip.

"You should know by now, Stan, I always try to do what I say," Andreas said. "You have worked hard for me. Johann says you are becoming a good horseman and your marksmanship is up to par. All the things I told you to do. Ivan will be busy training himself and his new officers, and I need someone here to do the same. You will be having a full staff shortly and, in addition to administration training, you will be responsible for their weapons training. Everyone in this battalion, clerks, cooks, blacksmiths, wagon drivers, will be certified proficient in firearms training or they won't be in my battalion."

Johann walked into the office to see a beaming Stanislaw reaching over his desk and vigorously shaking Andreas's hand.

"Major, pour your own cup of coffee," Andreas said. "The earl has a rule that he only pours coffee for junior officers once in a blue moon, and he poured one for the new lieutenant here, so you're out of luck."

"Ya, ya," said Johann, walking over to the stove before he stopped dead in his tracks. "What did you just say?"

"I said pour your own coffee," Andreas said deadpan. "Was the last major that deaf, Stanislaw? Perhaps we should call him back and bust this fool down to chicken herder."

"What are you making me a major for?" Johann said. "I don't even know how to be a captain."

"I have a sudden need for four majors," Andreas answered. "Ivan will be one, the two Americans, and now you. So, now, we

174

have two foreigners, one boyar, and a Cossack. The Americans will help you with the officer bit. You have been through everything I have, so you deserve it. We will be working with the English and there are four of us who speak it, so there you are. Oh, Peter? I need Peter where he is for now." Andreas began to pace around the room, stopping to look out the window, then pacing again.

"Been doing that a lot lately?" Johann asked.

"Just most of the morning," Stan said. "Maybe I should have put a lot of vodka in the pot. He'd be passed out by now."

"That would have worked," Johann agreed. "Elizabeth would have your manhood for it, though."

"Yes, I had thought about that," Stan said. "We could dump a pail of water on him?"

A lathered horse skidded to a halt in front of the office, the rider vaulting off the horse before it stopped.

"They have stopped two miles out, my lord," the rider blurted out. "One hour, hour and a half at the most."

"Thank you, Private," Andreas said. "Please, convey the news to my mother. Have someone look out for your horse first." He poured another coffee and sat down legs stretched out in front of him, eyes closed.

"We should have said that two hours ago," Stan said.

"Wouldn't have worked two hours ago," Johann said. "He always does that before something big is going to happen, clears his mind."

"Andreas Heinrich, what are you doing?" his mother demanded, storming into the room. "Why are you just sitting

175

there; you are not even dressed yet. Get moving. Am I going to have to pull your ear? You think now you are a big shot I won't do it?" With a flurry of skirts, as fast as his mother had stormed into the office, she was gone.

Standing up and stretching, Andreas said to his brother, "Alright then, get the lads ready, no pistols, only swords, full uniforms. Oh, and before I forget, here are your new shoulder boards." He tossed the majors insignia at him.

Andreas walked into his temporary bedroom and stripped off his normal clothing. Blue pants with red stripe first, then spurred, knee-length cavalry boots, polished so that he could almost see himself in them. Next, a white shirt buttoned to the neck. At that point, Stanislaw entered the room and helped him on with his tunic. Dark blue with blood red embroidering, brass buttons gleaming. There were ten Winchester cartridges placed in two five-cartridge, blood-red loops on his chest, one loop to each side, gleaming brass casings facing up. Stanislaw wrapped the red officer's sash around his waist and hung the sword belt above his hips. Sword on the left, hilt to his midriff. The final touch was the white, lamb's wool cap.

Stanislaw took a step back, looked Andreas up and down, and with a final brush of Andreas's new colonels shoulder boards, nodded and, following a spur-jangling Andreas, walked out of the office, headed for the main house.

Nodding to the people he met, Andreas stopped at the porch and stood leaning against one of the posts holding up the roof. Slowly, people began filtering into the yard quietly talking, standing along the front of the house and front yard. Ivan and Johann joined him on the porch both sporting officers sashes and their new majors shoulder boards. The remaining twelve of his men were gathered in a loose group in the center of the laneway about five yards in front of the house, their low voices occasionally breaking out in laughter as someone would crack a joke. Tugging at tunic bottoms or the adjusting of swords and plucking at sleeves betrayed their nervousness.

The beat of a drum started in the distance, its beat mimicking a horse at a fast walk. The strains of a balalaika could also be faintly heard in the distance. Then, as the children of the villa pelted into the yard from the road leading to the villa, a single male voice could be heard beginning to sing. At the end of the first chorus, he was joined by a mass of male and female voices singing in unison one of the Cossack ballads, in the soul-reaching way they were famous for.

Andreas's family came out of the house dressed in the ceremonial clothes that betrayed their German heritage. Women and girls in white dresses; seams, hems, and dirndls embroidered in bright flower patterns; blonde hair tied in two tight braids lying across both shoulders, bright yellow clogs on their feet. Men and boys in cross-belted lederhosen; white, knee-high socks, short tunics, and feathered caps. They arranged themselves in front of the steps leading to the door, Mamma wrinkling her nose as she looked Andreas up and down. As she passed him, Marie gave him a smile, a wink, and a kiss on the cheek before joining the family at the right end of the line. She was giving a small bouquet of flowers to each of the three eldest of Rosvite's children, whispering last minute instructions to them.

With impeccable timing, the singing stopped at the end of a rousing chorus, just as the lead scouts turned the corner of the lane leading up to the house.

Four abreast they rode, in perfect formation. Right hands gripping pennant-tipped lances upright, shafts held tightly to their dark blue breaches and highly polished boots. They split, two to a side, and rode midway to the house, where they stopped and turned their horses inward, facing each other across the lane.

Next, in columns of four, came the advance guard. Twenty veterans with long beards and mustaches, impeccably groomed horses gleaming, and tack shining in the sun. Five paces behind came Vacilly and Bishop Rosenbaum flanked by the drum and balalaika players. The four troopers behind them were the color party, Imperial Russian flag on the right and Cossack flag on the left, two guards flanking them.

Andreas gave a nod to his troopers, who spread out casually across the lane in line abreast, turning sideways to the oncoming group, arms crossed on their chests, hands on sword hilts, blocking their progress.

The advance guard stopped ten paces in front of the dismounted troopers in a simulated standoff. It was then that Andreas, flanked by his two officers, casually walked to the front of his troopers and stood square to the mounted troopers, arms crossed on his chest, weight on his left leg, right leg slightly forward, toe tapping impatiently on the ground. The advance guard expertly split ranks going to the sides, Vacilly and the color guard advancing and doing the same.

Then came row after row of men and women, young and old, all mounted on their best mounts, gold and silver jewelry glinting in the sunlight. These too split and moved to the sides lining the entire laneway. The silence was total, not a person or child making a noise. Horses completely still.

Then around the corner she came. At least he thought it was her. Four veteran troopers in front, four in the rear, and one to each side of two women rode slowly down the laneway. Katia, her hair braided in flower covered braids coiled around the crown of her head, red and yellow ribbons streaming down her back, rode on the left. As her eyes fell on Ivan to Andreas's left, she looked quickly down, color coming to her cheeks, and Andreas heard Ivan gasp as he saw her.

The other woman's horse had flowers woven into its bridle and a blanket of flowers in front and to the rear of the saddle. She was completely covered in a gold-embroidered, sheer, white lace veil, only her lace-gloved hands and red-booted feet were visible as the veil draped over the rear and sides of the saddle.

The four troopers in front split ranks leaving just enough room for the two women to slowly ride up to where a still stern-looking Andreas stood, sweat running down his back bone. Three troopers from the rear rank dismounted and quickly moved to the women's sides, one to Katia and two to the veil-covered woman and assisted them to dismount.

The veil-covered woman, assisted by Katia, arranged the veil around her before walking to Andreas and performed a deep curtsy, heads bowed.

Andreas bowed from the waist, equally deeply, sweeping his right hand outward.

"Welcome to my humble home, my lady," Andreas said.

"Well met, my lord," said the woman, who by her voice was definitely Elizabeth, holding her left hand out, palm down.

Reaching out his right hand and grasping hers, he gently kissed her knuckles. "Three bloody weeks I've been waiting, and I can't even see you, let alone greet you like we both want to," he whispered.

"All in good time, my love," she said mischievously, gently slapping him twice on the cheek. Then rising and holding her hand at shoulder height, he escorted her towards the steps to the house.

He stopped in front of his bowing and curtsying family. "My lady, may I present my family?"

Prodded by Marie, the three children approached and, shyly bowing and curtsying, held out the bouquets to Elizabeth.

"For you, Lizbet, me and Marie picked them special for you ourselves," said Andreas's niece proudly.

Elizabeth bent her knees until she was at the children's eye level. As she accepted the flowers, she gently stroked each child's cheek, holding the girl by the chin, she said, "Thank you, Heidi, they are beautiful."

Andreas could tell from the quiver in her voice that she was close to tears.

Running back to Marie, Heidi tugged on the hem of Marie's skirt and in an audible whisper said, "Auntie Marie, did you hear; she said they were beautiful."

Carefully rising and gingerly climbing the steps, Andreas and Elizabeth, followed by Ivan escorting Katia, entered the house.

"Get this damn thing off of me, I'm dying in here!" Elizabeth said, arms flailing beneath the veil, trying vainly to pull it off until Katia came to her rescue.

Finally clear of the offending garment, she rushed into Andreas's arms, kissing his neck, cheeks, forehead, and finally his mouth. Receiving no response from Andreas, she looked anxiously into his eyes.

"Andy, love, what's wrong?" she asked.

He held her shoulders and, saying nothing, turned her around until she could see the beaming middle-aged couple standing behind them.

"Oma, Opa!" she cried, breaking free of Andreas.

Andreas grabbed Ivan by the arm and left the house, quietly closing the door behind them, shutting off the sight of the four family members, grandparents, and granddaughters clutching each other, crying.

The scene in the yard was completely changed. People from both groups freely mingling. Old friends renewing acquaintances, new friends being made. Groups were breaking off, collecting pack horses or joining friends, and heading for their homes.

The sole exception was Elizabeth's honor guard, who although dismounted, were still in ranks holding their horses' bridles.

Andreas motioned to Johann to follow and headed across the yard directly towards the formation of veterans who popped to attention, the senior sergeant saluting. Both officers returned the salute, and Andreas approached the sergeant hand outstretched, gripping the man's hand in a strong grip.

"Senior Sergeant, I can't express my gratitude enough for safely bringing your lady first to her home and then to mine."

He then went down the line shaking each man's hand and looking each in the eye.

"Gentlemen, please accompany Major Bekenbaum," Andreas said. "He will show you your barracks and where you can stable your horses. Please, be gentle with your barracks mates, they are young and have tender ears, but they are mine and I would like them in one piece, if you please."

Andreas walked back to the house where he joined his older brother, father, uncle, Vacilly, the bishop, and the general. All the women relatives had gone into the house, and the abandoned and banished men were talking generalities and reminiscing about old days. Andreas, other than being the butt of the odd joke, took no part in the conversations. Looking around, he saw an even more forlorn looking Ivan and walked up to him, booted him on the ankle to get his attention, and motioned for him to follow.

Walking back into his deserted office, he found a case of vodka with five bottles still in it, picked it up, and headed for his troopers barracks. Ivan opened the door for him, and they walked in on a group of men, tunics off, shirts unbuttoned from collars, all laughing at some joke Andreas had not heard. He placed the case on a nearby table and leaning against the table, watched the two groups of men interacting.

"Attention! Officers on deck!" Peter had spotted them, and everyone in the room immediately stopped what they were doing and popped to attention facing Andreas and Ivan.

"Gentlemen, I would like to thank all of you on the job you did today," Andreas said. "You made your country, your district, your families, and, most importantly, your commander proud." Turning around, he pulled two bottles out of the case and held them up. "Now, if somebody doesn't pour me a drink, you'll all be demoted to chicken herders!" he yelled.

A great cheer went up and a mad rush for the bottles, and glasses for Ivan and Andreas were found. After everyone had a drink in his hand, Andreas signaled for silence by raising his glass in the air. "Mother Russia, the czar, and the best damn men in the army. Hurrah!" he yelled.

"Hurrah!" the room bellowed and shot back the drinks, and empty glasses were immediately refilled.

Elizabeth's senior sergeant next raised his glass. "My lady Elizabeth. Hurrah!"

Next was Johann. "The condemned man, the Hero of Russia, our comrade in arms, my brother, Andreas. Hurrah!" Shooting his drink back, he fired the glass into the corner where it and twenty-five other glasses shattered against the wall.

Ivan handed out the other three bottles, and the room settled back into an air of celebration. Motioning Johann and Peter to join him, Andreas found a seat on the end of a bench on an empty table.

"So, no matter what Momma says, this is what we are going to do tomorrow," Andreas began. "Ivan, you will be standing next to me. Your job is to catch me if I fall down, and you are to escort the bride's sister, all night if need be. Peter, you are to wear that wonderful marine uniform of yours; you will stand next to Ivan and shoot him if he lets me fall. You are to escort my sister Marie, all night if necessary. Johann, you are to stand next to Peter. In addition to shooting both of them should they let me fall, you are to provide a screen from Elizabeth of Peter's uniform. I don't want her changing her mind and taking him over me. You will escort Rosvite until after the first dance, when, if Irene has not run off with Heiner, you may exchange partners for the rest of the evening. Any questions? Good, because I'm not changing my mind. Now, go, mingle, be merry. Oh, and Peter? There are no ships here, attention on deck is not the correct way to make that order. Attention under the floor perhaps, but not attention on deck, if you please."

"Ah, so the colonel is not completely blind, after all," said Johann after Peter and Ivan had left to join their comrades.

"I hope you are not upset, Johann," Andreas said. "You know and I know that you are really my best man."

"Not to worry, Brother," Johann said. "You just took me off the hook. That was a good thing you just did; you seem to have a natural instinct in these matters. Ivan and Katia don't know they have a thing for each other, yet. So we give them a little nudge, eh? Uncle will be happy you have placed Ivan in such high regard, more bonus points.

"Peter and Marie know they have a thing for each other, but Mamma would not approve. Putting him there will make her see things in a different light, especially after he joins the regiment as a captain. It also shows everyone else he has your trust and confidence, making it easier for everyone to accept him. Very smart. Me, well, everyone already knows where I stand. No problem, Brother, I am just happy to be a part of it."

"Actually, Johann," Andreas said. "I had only thought about getting the two couples together. I didn't think about those other things. Makes sense, though. I thought you told me you didn't know anything about being an officer."

"I don't, I just know how you think."

"Could you bring Elizabeth's sergeant over here for me?" Andreas said. "I want you to hear what I have to say to him."

"You wanted to see me, sir?" the senior sergeant said.

"Have a seat, Senior Sergeant," Andreas ordered. "You told me you have served my lady for nine years now? How much active duty did you have before that?"

"Five years, sir," the sergeant answered. "We were a front line unit before the incident. We are happy serving your lady, sir, but it is not exactly real soldier work."

"If you were given the opportunity, would you and your men go back to active duty?" Andreas asked.

"Yes, sir, if your lady did not need us anymore, sir. We are sworn to her service."

"I am putting together a new unit, Senior Sergeant," Andreas said. "It will be a front line unit, and I would like you and your men to be candidates. The requirements will be extremely tough, and anyone not meeting those requirements will not be accepted, no matter who or what they are.

"Talk it over with your men, think about it for a few days, and then let me know. Anyone that wants to try, I will talk to Elizabeth for. Those that do not can stay in her service. I want to make it clear, Sergeant, anyone who does not meet the requirements will not be in the main regiment. Understood?"

"Yes, sir, thank you, Lord Bekenbaum," the sergeant replied.

Dismissing the man with a nod, Andreas rose from the table. "I need some air, Johann," he said. "See to it that the two love lost and yourself are ready for tomorrow. No excuses, I really will have your balls if you are not."

"Nothing to fear, Brother," Johann said, laughing. "I'm more scared of Momma and Elizabeth than you."

Nodding and patting his brother on the arm, Andreas walked out into the crisp October night. He found himself once again standing by the corral holding his horse, one foot on the bottom rail, both elbows hooked over the top. Bartholomew caught his scent and with a snort trotted over to get his ears rubbed.

"Tomorrow is the big day, buddy," Andreas told him. "I have oiled and polished all your tack, and your blanket has been cleaned and aired. I see someone has given you a bath, and your mane and tail are all combed out. All the stallions and geldings are going to be jealous, the mares and fillies are going to be fighting over you."

"Just like his master," Elizabeth whispered into his ear, gently stroking the hair at the back of his neck.

185

Instantly, he was in her arms.

When they came up for air, he looked over at Bartholomew and saw that he had been joined by Elizabeth's mare.

"You traitor," Andreas said, wagging his finger at Bartholomew. "You were in on this, weren't you?"

"I knew I would find you here," Elizabeth said. "Most men would be drinking themselves into oblivion, but not my man. Always brooding, always alone."

"Not anymore, not since I met you," Andreas countered. "Right from the start, I knew I would never be alone again. At first I thought, well, maybe she is just infatuated with the Hero of Russia nonsense. But you have seen me at my worst and at my coldest and at my weakest and my best. You have accepted all that I am; how can I do anything else but to love you?"

"Yes, I have seen your fierceness, but only when you had to be fierce," Elizabeth said. "You do not brag about it; you do not go out of your way to find it. Not knowing who I was or what I am, you loved me and were willing to risk your family's displeasure to be with me. You have shared my pain and I yours. I have always been told that God works in mysterious ways and this proves it."

They kissed again and she pushed his chest with both her arms creating space between them. "I must get back now before your mother discovers the sleeping bride is not sleeping after all," she said.

"Too late," replied Andreas, nodding over her shoulder to where his mother, Marie, and Katia were standing.

After seeing Andreas had noticed her, his mother started advancing in their direction. Elizabeth gave him a quick kiss and

186

trotted head down until she passed her. Reaching the two girls, she swayed her hips provocatively looking over her shoulder at him, before the three girls hurried away, giggling like mad.

Andreas, ready for the tongue lashing, turned back to the corral to see the two horses moving to the other side of it.

"Traitors," he called after them, "first sign of trouble and you run away."

His mother slipped her arm around his back, gave him a quick squeeze, and laid her head on his shoulder.

"The night before our wedding was spent running as fast as we could to the next town," she said. "Your father had bribed the priest there to marry us, or was it your uncle? No matter, it was done and we were married. We were and still are madly in love. This is all beyond our wildest dreams for you, Andy. She has a beautiful soul and you will make beautiful babies. God has smiled on you, my son, my beautiful Andy." She kissed him on the neck behind his ear and then grabbed him by the arm, "Now, I have something in my eye and can't see for the tears, so help your old mother home."

They walked back to the house arm-in-arm, her head on his shoulder until they reached the porch steps. She reached up on tiptoes, ran her hand through his hair, and kissed him on the cheek.

"Now, make sure you are on time, sober, and dressed properly tomorrow, or I will box your ears, see if I don't," she said as she reached for the door knob.

"Well, well. I turn my back for two minutes and my wife runs off with a younger man. After all I have done for you," his father, sitting on a chair in the dark, said.

Opening the door so that the light from the interior of the house shown on her fully, she took two steps into the house with the same provocative hip swing Elizabeth had used earlier, looked over her shoulder, stuck her tongue out at his father, and hip checked the door shut. Massed female laughter erupted on the other side of the door.

"Do they teach each other that, or do they do it naturally?" asked Andreas.

"I believe God showed Eve how to do that to keep Adam in line," his father said. "It works, too. Lord, how I love that woman."

"Do you ever regret it?" Andreas asked.

"No, never," his father said. "I sometimes miss my parents and my other brothers and sisters, but no, I would do it all over again."

"I met a Prussian; what was his name now?" Andreas said. "Yes, von Kleeman, he said all was forgiven for you and Uncle Mikhail; you could go back home now."

"Von Kleeman—your age, was he?" His father spit off the edge of the porch at the mention of the name. "His grandfather was the bastard that ordered us to burn those people out, and his son was the bastard who was hunting us down afterward," the elder Bekenbaum said. "They are in tight with Bismarck and the kaiser; I wouldn't trust him as far as I could spit him. My father says the same thing; in fact, they made peace by marrying one of my sisters to that young pup's father. No, I will stay here, and so should you.

"Andreas, you have every right, especially now, to use the 'von'," his father continued. "My father never disowned me like we tell everyone. It is an old and honorable name."

"No, the name my father gave me may not be old," Andreas said, "but it is just as honorable, as is the man who gave it to me."

"One more thing, Andy," his father said gravely. "That young pup's grandfather is also your grandfather; he is your mother's father, and he will never forgive her or me and mine for what we did, never."

"Oh shit, does Mom know?" Andreas asked.

"Yes, Andy," his father said, "she knows. There are very few things I keep from your mother, especially anything to do with her family. That bastard would put us in the worst positions against the strongest opponents, hoping I would be killed, or he could charge me with cowardice and have me shot. Your mother despises him, and I believe she would kill him herself if he showed up here."

"That shit was sucking up to the general and the damn British Horse Guards commander the whole time we were in camp," Andreas said. "Damn it, von Hoaedle warned me about him."

"King's German Legion? That von Hoaedle?" the elder Bekenbaum asked. "Fought with him at Waterloo, good man to have on your side. Mikhail didn't tell me he had seen him. Yes, the general told me the British had asked for you by name."

"Shit, shit, shit, it's all making sense now," Andreas said. "That bastard. He's still trying to get back at us."

His father took him by the shoulders and looked deep in his eyes. "I should never have let this conversation get this far," his father said. "Never, ever get angry, Andreas, get even. When we get angry, we don't use our heads, we make mistakes, and our people die. Be patient; your time will come, be ready for it.

"Now, a beautiful, wonderful girl is up there in her room, full of love for you, dreaming of tomorrow and the rest of her life with you. Let this thing go for now. Take her love for you and your love for her, listen to your heart. Believe in her, believe in yourself, and love her always." He pulled Andreas to his chest more to keep Andreas from seeing the tears in his own eyes, but also to console him.

Neither man seeing the two women, the old bride and the new, standing arm-in-arm looking out the open window having heard everything. Sharing the grief and the burdens each woman had just heard their men disclose.

Johann, Ivan, Peter, and Stanislaw walked into the office expecting to rush Andreas in a last-minute frenzy to be ready for the ceremony. They should have known better. Andreas was sitting in a chair looking at the flames visible through the open door of the stove. His hands held a cold cup of coffee, in his mouth a long gone out pipe, his stocking feet straight out, reaching for the stove. He was shaved and his hair combed, the tall riding boots shined, sitting next to the chair. He had donned his uniform breaches, suspenders over his white blouse, the top three buttons of which were undone. The formal tunic was draped across the back of the chair, his officer's sash on the small table beside him, sword and belt leaning against it.

"I told you, Stan, he does this all the time. I bet you a week's pay he's been sitting there since daybreak," Johann said.

"Sucker bet, Stan, you'd lose," Andreas said. "Somebody put the pot on the stove, there is enough left for one cup each. Anyone have a light? I don't want to get ashes on this damn dark blue uniform."

Peter picked up a slender piece of kindling and held it in the flames until it caught fire, then handed it to Andreas, who lit his pipe with it.

"How the hell do you do that?" Andreas asked.

"Simple, pick a piece of thin wood and stick it in the fire," Peter said.

"Not that, you dummy," Andreas said. "How do you get, let alone keep, that gleaming uniform that way. Somebody pull down the shades, he's hurting my eyes. Johann, when we leave here, find the biggest dung heap you can find and shove him in it. I'll not have him stealing away my Elizabeth with that uniform."

"No fear of that, my brother," Johann said. "You will be sleeping with a baroness tonight, I fear."

"Ah, no, my brother," Andreas said in disagreement. "I was kissing a baroness last night. Tonight, I sleep with a Gräfin."

"All these bloody titles, confusing," Johann said. "Right, 'Earl' in English means 'Graf' in German and Russian."

"Or 'Count' in English and French," Andreas said. "I don't much like Count though. Enough of this already, it's giving me a headache. Tomorrow, no more fancy marine uniform, my friend; tomorrow, your ass is mine."

"Marie may not like that, Brother," Johann said. "I think she already owns it. She might rent it to you, though. What are you laughing at, Ivan? Brother, our cousin is laughing at our sister."

"He better not be," Andreas said. "I'm going to be Katia's guardian in an hour, and I may not want her to have his ass. Speaking of that, have you had a look at that Irene, Peter? Va va voom."

191

"Where did you say that dung heap was, Brother?" Johann said.

"Enough, it's time to prepare the condemned man for his execution," Stan said.

"Of course, Commandant Stanislaw, right away, commandant," the other three men said.

Mounting their horses, the groom and his three groomsman rode to the open air church prepared for the ceremony. The four men dismounted in unison and handed the reins to stable boys waiting for them. Unhooking swords from belts, they handed the scabbarded weapons to the guardsmen stationed at the entrance, and, four abreast, walked instep to the front of the assembled guests and in unison knelt before the altar performing the sign of the cross, heads bowed in a brief moment of prayer. Standing, they turned to their right and moved to the right side of the altar and turned, facing away from the assembly in a position of parade rest. Feet shoulder-width apart, white-gloved hands clasped together in the pits of their backs.

One of the group of men could be overheard by the front row making a comment that there was still time to run, they could be across the border by night fall. Andreas's mother made a return comment about the positioned guardsman who had orders to shoot on sight anyone leaving the church without her permission. Both comments eliciting quiet chuckles from the front row, a smile from the bishop and his attendants, and shoulder shaking from suppressed laughter from the four men standing waiting for the bridal party.

Someone at the back signaled the bishop, who motioned the assembly to rise from their seats on the long benches that had been built for the ceremony. The crowd and the groom's party turned to face the entryway. Rosvite led the parade, today dressed as all the bridesmaids would be in white, red embroidery, red flower-patterned aprons, and red boots. As they were in church, the ribbons in their hair could not be seen because of the white linen scarves covering their heads and reaching back to the tops of their legs. Even after three children, she was still lovely and today she was concentrating hard on keeping a slow, even pace. Next was Marie, followed by Katia.

After a slight pause, the bride and her escort began the long trek up the aisle. Vacilly in his best immaculate blue uniform, not a hair on his head, beard, or mustache out of place, beaming face held high, marched proudly beside her. Her right, lace-covered hand delicately placed in the crook of his left arm.

Today, she was in dark blue to match Andreas's uniform. Through the sheer, blue, lace veil that went down to her ankles in front and trailed three feet behind, the gold-seamed dress, embroidered apron, and gold-colored boots could be made out. When they reached the front, the bishop asked Vacilly to present the bride to the groom. In a practiced motion, Vacilly and Katia expertly folded the front of the veil back to fall along Elizabeth's back revealing her face and the front of her gown. Bowing to the bishop, then to Andreas, with two hands he presented Elizabeth's left hand for Andreas to accept.

Everything after that was a blur. Words were spoken, they knelt and rose on cue. All he could think of and was aware of was the beautiful woman standing next to him. The soft touch of her hand or her arm when they brushed each other, the smell of the flowers in her hair, and finally, it was time for the vows.

"Do you, Baroness Elizabeth Halenczuk, take Ataman Andreas Bekenbaum in holy matrimony for as long as you both shall live?"

"Yes," said Elizabeth in a barely audible whisper.

"Do you Ataman Andreas Bekenbaum take Baroness Elizabeth Halenczuk in holy matrimony for as long as you both shall live?"

Andreas looked deeply into Elizabeth's searching, tear-rimmed eyes and, holding her trembling hands, clearly and firmly said, "I, Andreas, son of Heinrich, son of Michael, clan of Bekenbaum, take Elizabeth as my wife so long as I shall live. What is mine is hers. She and hers are as me and mine, what is done to one is done to all. So say I, so say us all."

"So say I, so say us all." Came the massed response from Andreas's gathered family, friends, and retainers, stunning the bride's side of the aisle with the strength and the solidarity of the response.

"In the name of the Father, the Son, and the Holy Ghost, in the eyes of God and man, I now pronounce you man and wife."

Instead of turning to face the assembly and be introduced as they had rehearsed, the bishop motioned for the couple to kneel. The general rose from his seat next to Andreas's father, carrying a sword, walked to stand next to the bishop, who began to pray.

"Bless this man and this woman, may their decisions be just, and their justice fair; may they treat their people humanely and may their rule be long and prosperous." He then anointed their foreheads with holy oil in the sign of the cross and stepped back.

The general stepped forward and broke the seal and unrolled the document he held.

"I, Viscount Andropov of Ukraine, by order of Alexander, Czar of all the Russias, hereby bestow the lands, properties, and welfare of the people of Katherintal District to the custody of Andreas Heinrich Bekenbaum, to rule in my name. I give you this sword as a token that your words are as mine. Rise, Graf Andreas of Katherintal."

"I, Viscount Andropov of Ukraine, by order of Alexander, Czar of all the Russias, crown you, Gräfin Elizabeth Bekenbaum of Katherintal." And with some minor fumbling, the bishop placed a small crown on Elizabeth's head. "Rise, Gräfin."

Now the couple was bid to turn around and face the assembly, all of whom were now standing.

"People of Katherintal, I present to you, Graf and Gräfin Bekenbaum of Katherintal."

The entire assembly knelt bending their heads. The viscount moved in front of them, and first Andreas, then Elizabeth slipped silver signet rings on the pinky fingers of their right hands. He then clicked his heels together, nodded his head, and left.

One by one, the head of each family from Elizabeth's side of the aisle, starting with Vacilly, came to them, knelt, spoke their names, kissed their rings, and followed the viscount. Next came the non-German members from Andreas's side. Finally, the bishop gave them the sign of the cross and he too left, leaving only the officers of his uncle's battalion and their families who arranged themselves in four ranks before him, the wedding party joining them.

"*Auchtung!*" barked Andreas's father, and the entire group stomped to attention. It was then that Andreas noticed that all the men were dressed in their Hussar uniforms and that there was something wrong with his father's.

"Present!" his father barked, and one hundred sabres rasped clear of their scabbards and lay on their shoulders. His father and mother marched forward and both went to one knee in front of them, his father laying his ornate sword at Andreas's feet.

Looking at both of them in the eyes, his father raised his right hand.

"I, Heinrich, son of Heinrich, son of Heinrich, son of Fredrik von Bekenbaum, Graf of Cologne, do pledge my fealty to Graf Bekenbaum of Katherintal. What is mine is yours; what is done to you and yours is done to me and mine. So say I, so say all of us."

With a crash of boots and a rattle of sabers as they were presented in salute, "So say I, so say all of us," they shouted.

Andreas picked up his father's sword by the blade and presented the hilt to his father. "Rise Graf and Gräfin von Bekenbaum."

"To hell with this!" he yelled; tossing his sword to the ground, he pulled his father up and hugged him fiercely. "What the hell, Papa, Senior Sergeant, my ass."

"Tomorrow, Son, tomorrow. Now, let me go," his father said.

Releasing his father, his mother was in his arms next openly weeping. "Gräfin, this is no way to behave, my lady. Everyone would think you were a sergeant's wife."

"Not today, Andy, no jokes today," his mother said. "Go to Lizbet, Andy. It's her day, not ours."

Elizabeth was surrounded by all his father's officers and wives, and while she was smiling and accepting their congratulations, her eyes were always on him. As he made his way through the crowd, his brother came to him.

"What the hell was that about?" Johann asked. "I knew about your ascension, but this?"

"You're one up on me," Andreas said. "I just came here to get married. Now, let me get my woman."

He finally reached her, standing behind her, listening to her talk in her Russian-accented German, while she listened and returned the compliments she was receiving. When she turned to see where he was, he moved, staying out of her sight. She kept smiling and talking, but her eyes kept darting about searching for him. With his left hand, he brushed her veil aside, revealing her neck, which he gingerly kissed while placing his right arm around her, pulling her close to him.

"I'm the luckiest man alive," he whispered into her ear.

She spun around and placed her hands on his shoulders. "Where have you been?"

"Just admiring my lady, Gräfin," Andreas responded.

"Admire me later, kiss me now," she whispered back and to the cheers of the onlookers, he did.

After four hours of mingling with guests and relatives, Andreas began to work Elizabeth to the door of the barn. When he lingered too long, she worked him towards the door. Soon they were forgotten in the shadows and with a quick glance, they darted out the door.

Hitching up her skirts, Andreas was treated to a glance of her bare thighs as she sprinted towards his office before he turned and ran for the corral. Grabbing Elizabeth's bridle and the whip he had stashed before dawn, he quickly tracked the mare down, expertly swinging the whip, wrapping it around her neck before she could break away. Used to being caught this way, she stopped and Andreas quickly bridled her, taking her back to a rail and tying her there.

Running to where he had hidden the saddles and blankets, he grabbed both, dropping his down, he rapidly and expertly saddled the mare. Turning around, he saw Bartholomew standing patiently

197

waiting. In a short time, he was walking both horses to his office. Loose tying the mare, he took the riding jacket he had tied to the back of his saddle and put it over his uniform jacket buckling the leg straps around his thighs. Putting a foot on the porch step, he unbuckled the hated silver spurs from his boots and tossed them in the open door.

Shortly, Elizabeth hurried out onto the porch, dress replaced by riding breaches, the top buttons of her tunic open. She was unpinning her braided hair from around the crown of her head as she walked. Andreas helped her into her riding jacket and they both mounted, riding slowly down the lane to the main road. Any revelers that saw them thought they were other partiers and paid them no notice. As soon as they had reached a safe distance from the villa, they broke into a gallop heading away from the villa and into the fields beyond.

Reaching the tree line, they slowed to a walk. Elizabeth undid the braids confining her hair and deftly tied it in a quick knot and passed it over her shoulder.

"Oh my, that was a very nice view. Can you do that again?" asked Andreas.

She slapped him with her reins and laughed, pulling her coat closed. "It's too cold to go topless," she said, leaning towards him and they kissed long and slow.

They soon reached the trail that Andreas had been searching for and turned up it. The trail went to a hunting cabin Andreas had found. Over the preceding three weeks, he had secretly cleaned it up and made it habitable, mostly at night. Katia had given him a bundle of Elizabeth's things the day they had arrived and he had brought them and warm blankets on a pack horse while everyone else had been partying the night before.

"There is kindling in the fireplace by the back wall, Liz," he said as they dismounted.

As he unsaddled and turned the horses into the small corral, she was able to find her way in the moonlight to the fireplace and quickly had a fire going providing a dim light in the small cabin. She stood and as she removed her jacket surveyed the one room. A small table was by the door, with two homemade chairs tucked underneath. Against the wall, close enough to the fire to stay warm, yet far enough away from it to be safe, was a small bed with warm blankets and a fresh straw mattress. Andreas walked into the room and quietly shut the door.

"I'm sorry it's not nicer," he said.

Walking up to him as he was taking off his jacket and tunic and was hanging them on a peg in the wall, she hugged him from behind and kissed his neck. "It's perfect," she said. "It's ours, and we are alone. I will have a lifetime of fancy houses and servants. This night is ours and ours alone."

He sat on the edge of the bed and tugged off the cavalry boots he had worn since morning. Picking up the boots, he carried them over near the fireplace in his bare feet and dropped them on the floor.

"Oh, that feels like heaven," he said, wriggling his toes as a pair of smaller riding boots came sailing across the room to thump against the wall next to his.

"It does, does it? What do you think this will feel like then?" she said huskily.

Andreas turned around to see a vision of beauty. She was standing, bathed in firelight, her hair cascading around her shoulders, riding breaches off showing off legs that went forever. Her tunic went to mid-thigh and only two buttons at the bottom held it closed, leaving all but the tips of her breasts showing. She advanced on him slowly, one foot in front of the other swaying her hips as she came.

She stood, close but not touching, in front of him, looking down at her feet. Andreas stood speechless, for the first time in a long time. Then she looked up at him, and he felt the strength leave his legs.

"What's the matter, my lord? Cat got your tongue? Maybe I can find it for you." She grabbed the back of his head with one hand and pulled it down to her kissing him hard, while her other hand pulled his up and placed it inside her tunic on a firm breast.

As their passion blossomed into a raging fire, she tore off his tunic, buttons hitting the floor, and fumbled with his belt buckle helping him step out of his breeches. Jumping up to straddle his hips as he carried her to the bed where they fell, he pinned her on her back and while kissing her breasts, she took hold of him guiding him into her and they became one.

The next morning, she awoke to see him looking at her, brushing her hair away from her face in soft movements. She lay gazing into the blue, almost grey eyes and not for the first time wondered what had drawn this magnificent man to her.

"You were right," he said, twirling a lock of her hair.

"Right about what?" she asked.

"That definitely felt better than when I took my boots off."

"Silly boy, of course it did. It's cold in here." She rolled out of the bed and fed some more wood to the fire.

That's when he saw them. A mass of long, thin scars ran across her back just above her buttocks. They were newly healed, still red against her white skin. He reached out and ran his hand gently across them and as he did, she stopped still, not moving or making a sound.

"Your father?" Andreas asked.

"The day you found us, my father was drunk," she began. "My brother convinced him to send my escort away, and he was lying in the back of the cart passed out when those men stopped us. They dragged my sister and I out of the cart, and my brother laughed as he cut my mother's throat. Then he killed that poor young boy, one of my father's grooms I think, while another one threw my father out of the cart and killed him. While two men held me against the cart, he took a cane and beat me until my legs collapsed and he let them let me fall. He and that man had come up with some kind of scheme where they would marry me to one of his sons to get hold of my property." She stopped and slowly raised her head.

"Which one was your brother?" Andreas asked.

"The one with his belly slit," she snarled, "I grabbed the knife he had let fall on the ground while he was beating me and shoved it into him."

She took a deep breath and let it out with a sigh. "I will understand if you send me away and never want to see me again."

He touched her shoulder and said, "Liz, come back to bed, it's cold in here without you."

Keeping her back to him, she slid back under the covers. Andreas carefully covered her and, leaning on one elbow, brushed the hair from her face and wiped his thumb on her cheek before leaning over and kissing the tears from her eyes.

She rolled over and took his head in her hands, looking deep into his eyes.

"I love you, Liz, with all my heart and all my soul, I love you," Andreas said softly.

"And I love you, Andy, with all my heart and all my soul." Her gentle kiss rapidly turned into passion as once again he followed her lead. It was only afterwards when he realised that was the first time she had ever said she loved him.

When he woke up, he found her looking at him this time. Her bright green eyes reflecting the sun off gold flecks radiating from the irises. She pecked him on the forehead then on the mouth; this time, it was he that took the lead and it was slow and measured while they each learned the other's body and what each other felt. He laid atop her afterwards, weight suspended on elbows, feeling her soft warmness, and her hands moments ago grasping and pulling his back, now gently rubbing. Bartholomew softly nickering broke his mesmerized spell and with a groan, he rolled off the bed, feet hitting the cold floor. The fire crackling and snow melting around her boots by the door showed him Elizabeth had been up earlier. Searching the small room, he found his breaches in a heap by the fireplace and tugged them on, stepping on a button on the floor while he did so.

"My lady, it seems as though someone has pulled off all the buttons on my pants," he said as he walked to the side of the door where he had placed his comfortable old boots a few days before and slid them on.

"Come back over here and I'll show you how I did it," she said, giggling.

"All in good time," he said, mimicking her voice and with a toss of his head and an exaggerated swing of his hips, imitating her actions, he walked out the door grabbing two buckets standing just outside it.

Bridling both horses, he led them to the nearby brook and, while they drank, filled both buckets. A light skiff of snow was on the ground, and he could see his breath slightly in the crisp November morning. Carrying both buckets, he plunked them down just inside the cabin door before leading the horses back to the corral. Putting a handful of grain in each horse's nose bag, he picked up the saddles that he had left lying in a heap on the ground in his hurry the night before and draped them and the blankets over the porch railing.

Elizabeth, his shirt on hanging down to beneath her exquisite knees, had just filled the cast iron pot and tea pot, hanging them on hooks for that purpose and swinging the hooks into the fireplace, was standing watching them.

He walked up behind her and slid his hands over both her breasts.

"Aiee," she yelped and spun away from him. "Your hands are cold!"

Laughing, he kicked off the fancy breaches and walked over to his saddle bags and pulled out a pair of normal trousers.

"Oh my God." She gasped out with such surprise, Andreas was instantly alert. Eyes darting about looking for a weapon, ears straining for any abnormal sound, mind racing for a plan, he spun around hoping for a clue from Elizabeth. She stood hand over mouth, looking at his right side, and he relaxed. She came to him tracing her hand gingerly on the new scar tissue that ran down his right side, from beneath his shoulder blade to just above his hip.

"Everyone says there were no casualties," she said softly.

"There were none. I am embarrassed by this little thing," Andreas said. "After the second battle, I was walking through the bodies looking for any of my men that may have fallen in the last charge. One of the enemy had been feigning death and he sprang up before me and swung his sword at me. I twisted aside and he landed this lucky blow, then I tripped over a body and lay there at his mercy; I could do nothing." He stopped talking, his mind's eye retreating back to that day. "The man made a mistake. He forgot the first lesson when fighting a Cossack," Andreas said, the scene vivid in his mind's eye. "Never get between a Cossack and his horse. Bartholomew killed him."

By now, she had wrapped her arms around him looking up at him.

"The only ones that knows about this are Johann, Irene, Bartholomew, and now you," Andreas said. "We felt it was more important for the men to believe no one had gotten hurt."

"Come back to bed, my love," she said. He kissed the top of her head.

"Even the hero of Russia has his limits, Liz," Andreas said, laughing. "I fear you may have worn it out. Come, we really should be getting back; the lads will be trying to kill each other if I'm not there putting the fear of God into them." He bent down and kissed her as she reached down and stroked his inner thigh.

"Oh, look," she said, staring at his crotch and pulling him down to her, "I haven't broken it, yet."

As they rode leisurely down the road hand-in-hand, the sun was beginning to sink, but it was still warm.

"Andreas, can you tell me about the words you said in your vows?" she asked.

"Up until my father said them to me," Andreas said, "I had thought they were just something we said at weddings. I pledging

204

to protect you and go to your family's aide and acknowledging your claim to me and all my possessions. Now, I know it is based on something more and older. Did you know anything about what was going to happen?"

"No. I mean, not really," Elizabeth said. "I knew they were planning something special, but with your family, I never know when they are planning something special or something mischievous. I still don't understand much."

"My father always told me he was a younger son," Andreas said, "and that he had run away from home to join the army, had met my mother, and they had run away together. There seems to be something wrong with that story, and I mean to get to the bottom of it when we return."

"Be gentle with them, my love. There must have been a good reason," she said. "Where did you learn all those things you do with me? You must have had lots of girls."

Andreas smiled, "Not really, love. A few, not many and not for a long time."

"I was a virgin on my first wedding night," Elizabeth said. "He was very drunk and passed out. In the morning, well, it was over almost before it began. I could never see why all the girls made such a big deal about it and was never interested again. Until last night," she added.

Andreas laughed, "And this morning and this afternoon."

They were still laughing when they rode into the villa's yard. Returning lewd comments by friends and family with ones of their own. A pair of grooms ran up to them, and the happy couple turned the horses over to them after retrieving the saddle bags from the rear of their saddle cantles and the riding jackets from the front; these they handed to two smiling maids, who, giggling, ran them up the stairs to the bedroom area. The smell of dinner drew them to the family dining room, where they were reunited with their family members.

A manservant ushered Andreas to the head of the table while another took Elizabeth to the foot, positions normally reserved for his mother and father. Today there was little of the friendly kidding and ribbing, everyone waiting for Andreas, who seemed to be serious today.

After dinner was complete, the dishes cleared, cups of coffee and tea poured, and servants banished from the room, shutting the heavy oak doors behind them, Andreas stood up and walked to the other side of the table.

Placing his hands on Elizabeth's shoulders and looking at his mother and father, aunt and uncle, he said, "All right, then, the full story, if you please."

His father began the story, with his uncle or mother and aunt contributing when they felt it was time to do so. The story in the main was the same, but with reversed roles and minor differences. Sisters had married brothers for one thing. Michael had not been disowned, just changed his name to make it harder to trace him. Both had been officers with Heinrich being the commander.

His father and mother had been arranged to be married; they had met several times over the years and had fallen in love. Both were the eldest children, with his mother's family having a barony. His grandfather had not agreed with some of Bismarck's and the kaiser's policies, and his mother's father, thinking to curry favor, had annulled the marriage agreement. His parents had indeed eloped, as had Ivan's parents, who having served as chaperons for his mother and father, had also fallen in love.

The baron could do nothing about it, his rank being below Andreas's grandfather's, and the kaiser had sided with his grandfather in the matter. In the army, it was different. His mother's father not only was on the war staff, but he had wormed his way into the good books of the field marshal. He exploited every opportunity to put Heinrich and Michael in harm's way.

When they had escaped to Russia, they changed their ranking so that Michael would get the better land and be able to set up an inheritance for his family. When their father had died, Heinrich had inherited the titles and lands, and being sent as 'liaison man' to Cologne each summer for his yearly Russian military service, he had been able to keep up his residency requirements as well as to maintain the family estates and businesses.

Knowing that Heiner would inherit everything, Heinrich had done everything he could to ensure both Andreas and Johann had every advantage to make it in their own. They had never dreamed it would have become this successful.

Heiner and his family would be leaving in spring, going back to Cologne. Heinrich had already cleared his abdication in favor of his son with the kaiser. His life was here now, and he had no wish to return to the new Germany. The fealty ceremony had more to do with binding the two families together in such a way that the Prussians could not find a way to wedge themselves into Russia.

Leaning his forehead onto the crown of Elizabeth's head for some seconds, Andreas moved to her side, caught her eye, and raised an eyebrow. She smiled and nodded her head. He kissed her and walked back to the head of the table, sitting down.

Sighing heavily, he said, "Most of the confusion has been resolved, thank you. Thank all of you for all you have done for me my whole life. Especially, I would thank you all for letting my lovely Elizabeth into our family and loving her as you love me." Looking around the table and seeing everyone still had at least a little brandy left in their glasses, he raised his glass and looked everyone at the table in the eye as they rose and lifted their glasses. "To us, the family Bekenbaum."

As the glasses thumped back onto the table and everyone sat back down, he said in a loud voice, "All this talking has made me dry. What does a Graf have to do to get a beer around here, die of thirst? I thought being a Graf meant having some respect."

"Which Graf are you talking about?" asked Johann. "I'm all confused, there are three of the cursed idiots here."

"No respect," said Andreas.

"No respect at all," said the whole table, laughing hard.

The next morning, the whole family, except for Johann, Ivan, and Katia, departed with many a tear and hugs, the most heart rendering to see was Marie and Peter. Finally unable to bear anymore, Andreas was about to say she could stay, when Elizabeth left his side and gently but firmly pried Marie away from Peter and guided her to the family's carriage, sobbing. Peter on the verge of joining her, was stopped by Johann's hand on his shoulder, whispering in his ear.

All the drama over for the day, Elizabeth and Andreas announced to the servants they did not wish to be disturbed for the rest of the day, and they climbed the stairs to their bedroom, where Andreas lost count of the number of garments a high-born lady felt she must have on at any one time.

After dinner that evening, an intimate affair on a much smaller table, with only Elizabeth and Andreas present, Elizabeth, yawning, excused herself from the table and headed upstairs.

"Manfred," said Andreas to the head of the household staff, "could you, please, send someone to invite my officers for an informal breakfast tomorrow?"

After receiving assurances that it would be done, Andreas also headed to the bedroom, where he was ambushed by a nude Elizabeth, who found out how few garments, and how easy they were to get out of, a male wore.

"Do you understand English, Liz?" Andreas asked in that language the next morning as they lay arm-in-arm in bed.

"Understand? Da. Speak?" She shrugged her shoulders.

Continuing in English, "American English is a little different but understandable; if you don't understand everything, ask me later, ok?"

"Oh-kay?"

"It means 'alright'. I will be discussing some things pertaining to you and I want you there."

"Oh-kay, dress now?"

Andreas and Elizabeth were seated at the lengthened table; Elizabeth at the head, Andreas on her right. Both dressed in everyday riding outfits and both, to the shock of the servants, with the top two buttons of their shirts undone. Johann, Ivan, Peter, Patrick, William, and Stanislaw, similarly dressed, entered the dining room and arranged themselves around the table in no particular order. As soon as they were seated, the servants began bringing breakfast, putting the plates down in front of each person.

"Good morning, gentlemen," Andreas said, "hopefully, your English is good enough to follow us today, Stan? All conversation and correspondence on what we are about to discuss will be in English. The walls have ears, but none of them are English, yet.

"Volunteers for our new battalion will be arriving shortly; indeed, some have already arrived. All conversation and orders to any in the battalion, except us, will be in Russian at all times. Two groups are guaranteed positions in the battalion. My original nine and Elizabeth's ten. Mine, because they have already proven themselves to me and have been trained with the new weapons, and Elizabeth's, because they are all veterans and have firsthand experience on how not to do things.

"Patrick, your task, in addition to the main training task, is to turn my twelve, that includes Ivan and Johann, into competent officers. You have been an instructor of officers before, so that is that. Peter, you are our firearms man; I want only certified marksman in my battalion front line troops. William, mounted infantry drills along with Johann. Johann, and perhaps Elizabeth if she has time, I want evaluating the troopers' horses. Stan, you and Elizabeth will pick the most qualified administration staff, and Stan will evaluate the support staff. Ivan will be assisting you with the physical training as well as fire arms training. Support and admin types do not have to be marksman, but they need to be better than front line infantry troops.

"No one, and I mean no one, including everyone in this room, will be front line troopers in my battalion unless they meet the physical, marksmanship, and horse suitability minimum requirements. I don't care who they are, who they are related to, what status or rank they have, everyone is a recruit and will be treated as such. There will be a number of people here for the money or status, or plunder and adventure. I want them gone. Peter and William tell me that the US Marine Corps has the toughest physical training in the world. We will copy that training.

"Stan, your people will also have to complete that training, or they won't be here either. Elizabeth's men are older so may have problems with the physical part. Any that don't, send them to me. I still need baggage train guard troops, they can run those. Any questions?

"Ok, every Saturday morning, here for breakfast, like this, we go over the week's progress."

"Pardon?" said Elizabeth, raising her hand like a school girl. "How you say this, Medico? Doctor?"

"Shoot, I forgot that," Andreas said. "Thank you, Elizabeth. Stan?"

"Yes, they come," Stan said, "I ask for already."

"Very good, anything else I forgot? Elizabeth, you don't have to raise your hand."

"Sorry. Woman's, um, medico, like Crimea," she was vainly trying to find the right words.

"Nurses?" said William.

"Da, da, nurses," Elizabeth said, nodding her head. "Man's wives, maybe?"

Andreas looked around at the other officers who all nodded in agreement. "Agreed. Once again, thank you, Elizabeth. Alright, if any men who make the final cut have wives and the wives agree to train as nurses, they can come. But, again, only if they are tough enough and can handle firearms."

Elizabeth sat straight up in her chair. "Woman tough like man."

Then she abruptly stood. "Some time, woman more tough like man." And she abruptly marched out of the room, leaving the men in stunned silence. A short time later a horse could be heard galloping out of the yard.

"Well, I guess we know where she stands on that subject," said Andreas. "Anything else?"

"Ok, then," Andreas continued. "Everyone who is going to be here will be here by Wednesday, that's the cut off day. Anyone after, is out of luck. Do what you have to do to get ready. Thursday morning, my office, full uniform. Good morning, gentlemen, thank you for coming. Ivan? Please, tell the groom I won't be joining my lady for our Monday morning ride, after all. He can put Bartholomew back in the stable."

It was dark when she came back, sneaking up the stairs in her bare feet. Andreas stayed sitting in front of the stove, feet up on a plush ottoman sitting in a well-stuffed, high-backed chair. He had decided the best thing to do would be to let her alone. He had a blanket, the chair was comfortable and the fire warm. Now that she was home, he started dozing off.

"Andreas?" She was standing in front of him dressed in a dressing gown.

"Hello," he said sleepily, as he reached out and took her hand.

"I'm sorry, Andreas, I, I don't know how to say this."

He pulled her gently to him and she sat with her bare legs across his thighs, one arm around his shoulders, looking in his eyes for some kind of reaction.

"I thought you were mocking me," she said. "Your voice was so firm, so flat. So, so not like the Andreas I know."

"That was the business, Liz," Andreas said, "and the business we were talking about is not pleasant. There can only be one

212

leader and his wishes must be carried out or there is confusion. When there is confusion, a lot of people, including the leader, will die. I asked for and received feedback. Your idea was sound; the rest of the officers had no objection; I put in mandatory requirements; and the decision was made to implement your idea. If the idea was not sound or I required more information, I would have said it the same way.

"The general does the same; he gives the orders, I do the best I can to implement those orders. If he asks my opinion I give it, but at the end of the day, he makes the right decision as he sees it. There is no time for emotion, people die. Can you understand that?"

"You make it sound so cold, so calculated, Andreas," she said. "Is, is that how you live? Am I just a business decision?"

He sighed deeply, brushed her hair from her eyes and said, "My Liz, when I did not know who you were, or what you were, no matter your social status or the consequences I would face, you were going to be my wife. Somehow, some way I was going to make that happen. No, love, that was, and is, all pure emotion."

"Will you allow me to come to more meetings?" she asked.

"Yes, you ran your own estate for nine years. That is not unlike being in command of a company. You have a different perspective and are willing to share it. The decisions we make affect the welfare of everyone. If I ask for debate or information, I expect it to be relevant and pertinent to the subject at hand. State your case the best you can. If it will help the situation, we go with it. If not, the subject is dropped; we move on."

"Do I have this right, Andreas? Business yes, personal no?" When he nodded, she continued, "When is personal?"

"This is personal, is it not? Now we complicate things, yes?"

213

She had that look in her eyes and that sly grin on her face. "Yes, this conversation is one kind of personal." She kissed him, her hand going between his legs. "This, another kind of personal. And this is the kind of personal, if I catch you with another woman." She grabbed his testicles and squeezed firmly before bouncing up and trotting to the door, looking back at him.

"Why, you . . ." He was out of the chair in a flash chasing her up the stairs.

Officers' meeting was held Monday evening in Andreas's headquarters office two weeks later. Winter had set in, snow and cold were the norm. Daily tasks for the recruits included clearing the yard, parade ground, and ranges of accumulated snow. There was no letup in the training, no matter the weather conditions. They pushed the recruits to their limits every day. Of the almost three thousand that had showed up on the first day, only fifteen hundred were left. Five hundred had left the first day and a steady trickle had left every night. A few had been discretely told to go home and others had been singled out in front of the group and roughly dismissed.

Andreas and all the officers joined in on the daily five-mile run, which had gone from just the man running, to adding rifles, then ten pound packs. Now the physical training would include an obstacle course designed to mimic field conditions.

"This is it, gentlemen," Andreas said, "the final week. Push them hard. At noon on Friday, the final cuts will be sent home. Saturday, graduation, Sunday, send them home until New Years. Stan, your report please."

"The tradesmen were no problem," Stan began. "Physically, they are used to most of it. Rifle training was a mere formality for them. The clerks, different story; I only have half what I need. Is

214

there any chance I could utilize any of your cuts? Also, I have been thinking, perhaps we could also use some of your cuts for baggage train guards."

Andreas looked over at William, gesturing palm up to him.

"All our five hundred weakest will suit as guards," he said. "Clerks, I will have to find out who can read and write. How many men will you require, Stan?"

Stan shrugged his shoulders. "All of them?"

"Bureaucrats, you're all the same," Andreas said, smiling. "Thoughts about that? Peter?" They always started with the least senior member.

"All the troops left will suit; obstacle training will weed out a few more, though, and I'm not sure about the writing part," said Peter.

Patrick concurred with Peter.

"I agree with Stan," said Ivan.

Johann rubbed a finger over his right eyebrow, thinking for a second. "All the men left meet most of what we are looking for. There are about fifty men who would be troopers, but because of their youth or poverty, have a problem with horses. If we could find a way for them to obtain proper horses, I'd take them as front line troopers. Yes, I concur."

Andreas contemplated what they had all said. "Ok, everyone that is left passes. Take your fifty aside, Johann, explain the situation to them: they find better horses, we supply them with better horses and take it out of their pay, or they go as guards or clerks. At general assembly today, tell everyone they have passed, but the bottom five hundred of them will be guards or clerks.

215

"That will make them compete harder this last week," Andreas continued. "We all know we will be sustaining casualties; this will give us some reserve capability. William, can we obtain five hundred more Winchesters and Colts?"

"Shouldn't be a problem, sir," William said. "I'm going down to Odessa for my leave, so I'll arrange it then."

"Good," said Andreas. "Now, about Elizabeth's ten, will they make the cut?"

"Unless they all have heart attacks," said Patrick. "They leave a lot of the younger guys behind. They are in the top fifty, sir."

"I was hoping I could get them as my personal guards," Andreas joked. "Good, keep them in the same unit, non-coms for sure, any of them officer material?"

"All of them, sir," replied William.

"Make it so," he ordered. "Is there any other business?"

"If the colonel could spare a moment on a personal matter after dinner this evening, sir?" asked Ivan.

This puzzled Andreas, his cousin knew he was always welcome at his home. "Certainly, Major, it will be my pleasure."

As they trooped out of his office, Andreas caught Johann's eye and nodded towards Ivan and raised his eyebrow. Johann shrugged his shoulders and walked out the door.

Dinner had been a pleasant, if a somewhat more formal affair. Elizabeth was wearing a full-length, blue, satin dress with a buttoned high collar. Katia was wearing a similar style dress, but in a cream color, with a blue ribbon holding her hair back in a ponytail. Andreas, as usual, was wearing his riding outfit as they

216

called it. Riding pants and an embroidered-seam shirt not tucked in.

Katia had come out of her shell in recent weeks, and dinner was always normally a fun time of day. Katia had a keen sense of humor, never at a loss for words. Today, it looked like she was just going through the motions. She was attentive and joined in at the appropriate times, but more subdued.

After dinner was complete and they retired to the salon for their customary after-dinner chat, she was even more withdrawn, barely responding to Andreas's attempts to poke fun at her.

"My lord?" the head manservant asked from the door of the salon. "Major Halinov to see you, my lord." Turning and bowing slightly, he motioned Ivan into the room.

Ivan in full uniform, complete with sword, cap under his left arm, and silver spurs attached to the heels of his shining boots, marched to within five paces of Andreas and came to a boot-clicking and head-nodding halt at attention. He thrust three sheets of paper in Andreas's direction and said, "Colonel Bekenbaum, three officers' requests for permission to be married, sir."

Any officer under the age of twenty-five required the permission of the regiment's commanding officer to be allowed to be married. Andreas stood and accepted the papers, throwing them on the small table beside his chair without looking at them.

"We could have handled that in the office tomorrow morning, Ivan, there is no need for all this formality." Andreas noticed sweat beading on Ivan's forehead and that Katia and Elizabeth too had stood. Katia very nervous, Elizabeth with a tiny smile on her face.

"No, sir. I mean, yes, sir."

Andreas noticed his cousin was very nervous and had something else on his mind. "Spit it out, Cousin, before you explode," he said.

"Graf Bekenbaum, I, Major Ivan Michilovitch Halinov, ask the Graf's permission to marry Gräfin Bekenbaum's sister, Katia Halenczuk," Ivan blurted out.

Looking quickly over at the two sisters, he saw Elizabeth with her arm around Katia, a smile on her face, and Katia, biting her lip and bouncing up and down slightly in anxiety. They're all in on this, he thought, I'm going to make them sweat a bit.

Standing up straight, assuming a haughty and arrogant lord's perturbed expression, he said, "This is highly irregular, Major. She is young and I am not sure ready for marriage at this time. The Gräfin and I have not discussed the possibility of her marriage at this time. We will take your request under advisement and compare your request with any other possible matches that can be made for the welfare of the district.

"Now, if you would have come to me as a normal person and said, 'Cousin I'm madly in love with your sister-in-law and want to marry her', I probably would have said yes." He spread his hands out to both sides. "But . . ."

Andreas felt the sharp toe of his wife's dainty slipper hit him in the calf.

"Cousin, I'm madly in love with your sister-in-law and think she loves me, too. Can I ask her to marry me?" Ivan stammered.

"What's taking you so long? Ask her already; the poor girl's about to faint," Andreas said barely able to keep from laughing.

Katia flew into Ivan's arms.

Elizabeth put her arm behind Andreas's back and kissed him lightly.

"That was not very nice, my lord," she said.

"That will teach my lady to keep secrets from us and ambush us and make the poor lad suffer like that," Andreas replied. Then, he did laugh.

Friday the recruits had been told the results of the competition would be posted outside their barracks after the evening's mess. The results would be posted alphabetically, not in order of finish. Ten sheets of one hundred names for the men that would be front line cavalry troops on one board, five sheets of one hundred names on another.

They had been given Saturday morning to prepare for the graduation ceremonies. Each man had been given two brass badges to be worn on shirt collars. Both had rifles to be worn on the right collar. Bears had been given to the support troops to put on their left collars and eagles to the combat troops. Those that had been chosen as officers had been given red sashes.

Part of the combat recruit's tasks for the week had been to clear and keep clear a large pasture. The support troops had assembled a reviewing stand and bleachers. Families that had been able to make the trip on winter roads were seated in the bleachers, anxious for a glimpse of the loved one that had left weeks before. Among them were Andreas's mother and father, his uncle and aunt, his brother and sister-in-law, and Marie. Katia was seated beside Marie and, curiously, Irene and her parents seated alongside.

Seated on the reviewing stand were Andreas in his full winter dress uniform, with Father Litzanburger on his right and Elizabeth on his left. Elizabeth had on a sable coat and sable hat, her badge of office on the center of a red sash angling from left shoulder to right hip.

A shouted command warned the waiting people and Andreas's party stood and walked to the front of the stand. Elizabeth and the priest stopped one pace behind Andreas, who stood at parade rest, arms tucked into his back, feet shoulder-width apart.

Another command was shouted and Andreas snapped to attention as the sound of many feet hitting the ground in unison could be heard. The support troops marched onto the pasture from the left, Stanislaw in their lead marching proudly, his head held high, the sun glinting off the sword he held unsheathed on his right shoulder. Behind him in ten columns, one behind the other, ten wide and ten deep, marched one thousand men, gleaming rifles on right shoulders, arms and legs swinging in perfect unison.

As Stanislaw reached Andreas, he swept his sword off his shoulder snapped his head to the right and presented the sword, point angled downwards, to Andreas, who snapped a perfect hand salute in return and held it.

"Eyes right!" Stanislaw bellowed and as each line reached Andreas, nine heads snapped to him, heads held high. The columns smartly pivoted and arranged themselves in two rows of columns, five wide on Andreas's left side.

The second-to-last column had come to a crashing halt, the combat troops entered the square.

These columns marched with bayonets fixed, rifles in both hands, slated to point over the right shoulder of the trooper in front. Sword bearing officers marched at the right side of each leading line, as the officer reached Andreas, he snapped his sword in salute and the whole column jerked their heads to the right.

Once the last column had come to a halt in the same formation as the first, except on the right of Andreas, William shouted out, "At ease!" and both formations crashed rifles to the ground held at an angle from their bodies in their right hands, left arms behind their backs.

"Officers, front and center!" barked William, and the officers marched to the space between the two formations and slightly in front.

"At ease," he told the officers, then marched up to Andreas, saluted with the sword, and barked, "Battalion all present and accounted for, sir! The battalion is yours, sir!" He saluted again, about faced, marched to the center front of the officers, about faced again, and assumed the position of parade rest.

Andreas took a deep breath. "Battalion! Attention!" He waited until each man had rifles grounded and tucked into right arms. "Battalion will prepare for prayer . . . Now!" Two thousand heads bent down. "Father, if you would be so kind," Andreas said in his normal voice.

"Heavenly Father," Father Litzanburger began speaking as loudly as he could, "we ask you to bless these men and guide them to serve honorably and with integrity in all that they do. We also ask you to look out for them and keep them from harm. We ask this in your Son's name. Amen. I bless this battalion, in the name of the Father, the Son and the Holy Ghost, amen."

"Thank you, Father," said Andreas as the priest stepped back.

"Battalion! Attention!" Crash, went two thousand boots.

"Battalion! At Ease!"

"Comrades," began Andreas, "six weeks ago, five thousand men came here in hopes of standing where you stand right now.

Only two thousand survived this six weeks of training. Training, I have been told, was tougher than that men of the United States of America Marine Corps have to endure. You have performed better than they do at their training; I have been told by Captain Peter who should know because he served in and trained them. I expected no less; you are Russians, not Americans.

"Honor and integrity, the good Father said. I say, the men who wear the bear and the eagle will serve with honor, integrity, and tenacity. I say well done, you have done your country and your families proud. Congratulations."

"Battalion! Attention!"

"Major, you may dismiss your men."

"Battalion!" barked William. "Three cheers for the Graf and Gräfin!"

"Hurrah! Hurrah! Hurrah!" two thousand voices yelled out.

"Battalion! Prepare to dismiss! Dismiss!"

"Hurrah!" For the last time, then bedlam, as men congratulated each other and began searching for friends and loved ones.

Andreas and Elizabeth took the opportunity of all the milling about to steal away from the crowd. They had not had much opportunity to be alone in the last few weeks, and it would be nice not to be the center of attention for once. They had the house to themselves, as all the servants had been given the day off to attend the ceremony and the, no doubt, parties to be held afterward.

The day had turned sunny and warm for the time of year, and the couple slowly walked down the lane to the house together. Elizabeth walked with her hands in her fur hand warmer, and

Andreas with his arm around her. When they reached the house, Elizabeth pulled off the hat and the sash, Andreas helping her off with the heavy coat. They walked through the kitchen and into the parlor, Andreas unbuckling and tossing his sword on his chair. Elizabeth carefully draping the coat over the chair's back, folding the sash neatly, and placing it and the hat carefully on one side of it. She shook out her hair, allowing it to spill across her back and shoulders, while Andreas put more wood in the stove, then removed his great coat, lamb's wool hat, and tunic, casually tossing them onto the same chair while he undid the tight shirt collar.

He walked over to the sideboard, lifted the bottle of sherry there, looked at Elizabeth, and raised an eyebrow. She nodded as she sat down on the loveseat tucking her feet under her skirt. Today, she was wearing a black, ankle-length skirt and a white blouse with a high collar tucked into the skirt. A black ribbon with a brass bear badge tied on her neck under her Adam's apple. She too undid the tight collar around her neck. Having poured the fiery liquid in two glasses, Andreas walked back to the loveseat, handing Elizabeth her glass before sitting down beside her.

They sat like that for some time, Elizabeth with her head on Andreas's shoulder and he with his arm around her, sipping out of the glasses and enjoying the stillness of the house. Elizabeth put her empty glass on the end table and took Andreas's from his slackening hand as he began to doze off. She deftly undid two more of his buttons and slid her right hand into his shirt while kissing his neck softly. Andreas had just found her mouth and, having undone some more of Elizabeth's buttons, placed his left hand into her blouse, when a commotion broke out in the kitchen.

Ivan and Katia staggered into the parlor doorway. They had already thrown off their overcoats and were kissing passionately while moving clumsily. Ivan had opened Katia's blouse and had

223

one hand inside it, she pushed him roughly into the door frame and was fumbling with his tunic buttons.

"Was I that brazen?" asked Elizabeth in a loud voice, which stopped the passionate couple in the doorway dead in their tracks.

"Why, no, my lady," replied Andreas, "by now, you would have had your blouse all the way off and would have ripped the buttons off my tunic. I think the major will find that a bed is more comfortable than a doorway."

The embarrassed couple looked over to see Elizabeth, hair astray, with her hand stopped in the process of removing Andreas's belt and Andreas's inside her blouse over one of her breasts.

After a second, Katia stuck her tongue out at them and grabbing each side of Ivan's tunic, ripped it open, buttons tumbling on the floor. Then she giggled and grabbing his hand, they ran up the stairs.

"Where were we?" Elizabeth asked.

"I believe my lady was about to ravish her unsuspecting husband," replied Andreas, and she did.

The time of departure was rapidly approaching, training with the new weapons and tactics was complete. Any of the men that wanted to were allowed to go home for two weeks, but most had opted to stay.

Elizabeth had taken control of the nurses, there were fifty of them. Every morning they were out jogging five miles, sometimes with heavy packs. Every day, Elizabeth, Marie, Katia, and Irene were with them. The Sunday after graduation, a triple wedding had been performed for Ivan and Katia, Johann and Irene, and

Peter and Marie. The three couples were now residing in guest houses at the villa, but meals were generally held at the main house.

The elder members of the Bekenbaum family's return home was even more tearful than usual. Over the winter, it had been decided that Heiner would return to Cologne, where he would take control of the family interests. While everyone went through the motions of making promises of return visits, in their hearts, they knew it was unlikely to occur. So, with heavy hearts, the families bid each other goodbye.

Andreas and the male members of his newly expanded family all knew that a confrontation was imminent between them and the female members of the family. All of them wanted to bring their wives along, but all of them also knew the rigors and dangers of campaign and wanted to spare the women they loved from those hardships. So far, they had been able to deflect the subtle hints they had been getting from the wives to be included in the expedition. The day was rapidly approaching when they would have to be told that they were not coming. That day came sooner than they were expecting.

As part of the women's graduation ceremonies, Elizabeth had insisted on the women doing an exhibition of their martial capabilities in order to quell any rumors the men may have on how easy it had been for them to join the regiment.

At the appointed time, Andreas and his staff were assembled on a stand overlooking the field they used for mock battle training. Sitting in the bleachers behind were about a hundred men. There mostly out of curiosity.

A small cloud of dust and the thunder of hooves informed the onlookers the demonstration was about to start. In twelve columns of four, the female troopers trotted onto the field. The male instructor riding alongside the first row, and two women selected to be officers for the day alongside other rows. Dummies had been set up in various positions to simulate an ambush.

Reaching the middle of the ambush site, the male instructor hollered out, "Contact left!" The women immediately dismounted, three women handing the reins of their horses to the fourth still-mounted trooper, who spurred the animals out of danger. The dismounted women unslung their rifles, and while assembling into fire teams, loaded their weapons. Half the teams went to one knee firing at visible targets, while the other half sprinted up a few yards, then flopping on the ground and firing while the first group reloaded and leap-frogged them to start the sequence again. They rapidly completed the task of clearing the ambush and curiously stayed lying in the prone position.

"Very well done," said Andreas to the group around him, "almost as good as our combat boys." He had just started to scan the women to see if Elizabeth had found a way to be included in the drill when the sound of horses galloping could be heard coming from the left.

Four riders, long hair flying behind them, came flying into the practice ground. "Oh shit," said Johann.

Each rider was five yards behind the other, standing in their stirrups and bringing Winchesters to shoulders. The first was Irene, followed by Katia, Marie, and finally Elizabeth. Unseen by the onlookers and supposedly by the attack drill, ten yards to the right, was another ambush. As each of the galloping women's weapon came to bear, she started firing, hitting more times than missing the targets set up. Pivoting as they passed, they kept firing until out of range or out of ammunition. The four women slowed to a trot and impressively formed a column and retraced their steps to pivot and stop five yards in front of the command group.

Elizabeth, in the center of the group, said in her heavily Russian-accented English, "Woman just like man. Some time, woman better like man." She smiled, saluted, and joined the line of women troopers who paraded past the command group, accepting the salute of the command group and the cheers of the onlookers.

After they had left the field, Andreas looked at his commanders and especially his fellow husbands and said, "Well, I guess that puts an end to them staying home."

The four husbands, Andreas, Johann, Ivan, and Peter, sat lounged around the stove in Andreas's office until well after dinner. They had long ago discussed what they were going to do once they went home and had been talking about anything but that ever since. A runner they had sent to discreetly inquire had just returned, saying that all four women were still in the house together and Andreas stood, buttoning up his tunic.

"Alright then," he said, "once more into the breach, comrades, once more into the breach."

The four men walked into the parlor, Peter, still the junior officer, belted out, "Attention! Officers on deck!"

The four women sprang from the chairs they had been lounging on and assumed the position of attention before the grim-faced officers in front of them. The only woman without a look of desperation was Elizabeth, who stood with jaws clamped shut, defiantly looking Andreas in the eyes. All the women had changed out of their uniforms and into their best party dresses, with open backs, bare arms, and plenty of cleavage in evidence.

Andreas, his arms behind his back, slowly surveyed each woman from top to bottom, a stern look on his face.

"Ladies," he growled, "you have allowed yourselves to be manipulated into a grave situation. One that, on a battlefield, could well result in a large loss of life. Disregard of the chain of command is frowned upon for good reason. It erodes the commander's authority and the morale of the troops. Done skillfully and in times of emergency, it can be a great asset. This is one of those times." He nodded to his officers, who, like he, removed their hands from behind their backs and pinned two simple brass ornaments on their wives' dresses. A bear on the left and a rifle on the right. "Welcome to the regiment, ladies," Andreas said.

The four men saluted the women, about faced, and walked out to the porch, where they heard unsoldierlike and unladylike screams of joy and thumping of feet as their wives jumped up and down in the parlor with glee. One by one, the ladies came to collect their husbands and take them home, leaving Andreas standing alone, one foot up on the bottom rail and leaning both arms on the top, gazing into the moonlit yard.

"Excuse me, sir," said Elizabeth, "this trooper would like to express her appreciation to the colonel, sir."

Andreas turned around to see Elizabeth leaning on the porch door, her dress unbuttoned to her navel, and crooking her finger at him.

The battalion arrived in Odessa on a Thursday afternoon, riding through the city to their designated bivouac areas near the docks. They had made an impressive sight, combat troops split in two groups of five hundred. Each split in the middle by the supply, services, and medical troops with their two-wheeled wagons piled with supplies. Any trooper not riding on wagons was mounted; all the troopers were armed, rifles slung across new blue-uniformed backs.

By order of the general, the command group had been sent to one of the posh resort hotels for accommodations. The staff of the hotel were shocked when, instead of arriving in the luxury coaches they had been expecting, the group arrived on horseback, trailing pack horses. All twelve officers, including four women, were dressed in grey uniforms, rifles slung across their backs, and pistols hanging from left hips, butt forward. The male officers had saddle bags slung over their shoulders, which thumped against their backs as they climbed the stairs to their rooms.

Andreas and Elizabeth were ushered into a suite that rivaled one of their guest houses in size and even included a large bathtub in a separate room, which had hot and cold running water. They had barely surveyed the suite, when answering a knock on the door, the couple were greeted by three men and a woman. Two men were carrying one of the packs from the pack horses, which the woman directed them to place in the bedroom, after which they bowed quickly and left. The two people remaining explained that they had been assigned as the Graf's body servants for the duration of their visit.

It wasn't until Elizabeth removed her tunic and let down the hair she had pinned up under her cap that the servants realized she was a woman. "I could really use a bath," she said.

Another knock on the door revealed a lieutenant in an aide's uniform. His eyes went wide when he saw Elizabeth in troopers trousers with a pistol strapped around her waist.

"Graf," the man said, "the viscount and viscountess, are requesting the Graf and Gräfin's presence for a dinner and reception this evening."

"At what time?" asked Andreas.

229

"S-s-sorry, my lord, six, my lord."

"Very well," Andreas said. "Please, arrange for suitable transportation, Lieutenant, the Gräfin can hardly be expected to arrive wearing her party clothes riding a horse now, eh?"

"Yes, my lord, thank you, my lord," the aide said and he rapidly exited the room.

"Was I ever that dumb as a lieutenant?" he asked.

"No, dear," replied Elizabeth, "you were never a lieutenant."

Then she dashed into the bedroom, the female servant trailing her, and began tossing clothing out of the pack. Selecting the ones she wanted to wear tonight, she asked, "Is there any way I can have these pressed before six, perhaps you could send up an iron?"

"Not to worry, my lady, we have a full staff here. If you would allow me?" She held out her hands, and Elizabeth handed the clothing to her. "It is only a simple pressing they require; they will be back within the hour."

"Andreas, don't just stand there!" Elizabeth demanded. "Give the man your uniform; I won't have you looking like a common trooper tonight."

Knowing better than to argue, Andreas opened one side of his saddle bag and after rummaging around a bit, removed a tightly rolled package of clothing, which he handed to the manservant.

"Thank you, my lord," the man said, "and, my lord? We will have your current clothing laundered, pressed, and put away for you by the time you return this evening."

"Why, thank you, very considerate of you," said Andreas.

Three carriages had been sent for them and they arrived shortly before six to the viscount's official residence. Andreas and Elizabeth were in the first carriage along with Johann and Irene. The men were wearing their full dress uniforms, officers sashes, and spurs, except Andreas who absolutely refused to wear spurs.

The women were wearing the same party dresses that they had tried to beguile their men with the night of the demonstration, with their bear and rifle badges pinned shining to the straps of the gowns. Andreas and Elizabeth had their sashes of rank attached to their clothing from left shoulder to right hip. Elizabeth had pinned her badges to the sash high up by her collar bone.

The groom escorting them stopped before the open double doors and rapped his cane loudly on the door frame.

"Graf Bekenbaum and party," he announced as he escorted them to the head table up the center aisle. The whole room was standing, and as the party passed them, everyone bowed or curtsied. Reaching the head table, Andreas stopped before the viscount and bowed his head briefly.

"My lord Viscount, I have the pleasure to introduce my wife, Elizabeth," Andreas said.

Elizabeth performed a deep curtsy and when she rose the viscount brushed his lips across her right hand. "A pleasure once again, my lady. Graf and Gräfin Bekenbaum, my wife, Ilana."

Andreas bowed and took her proffered hand to his lips, while Elizabeth once again curtsied deeply.

"My lord Viscount," said Ilana, "why have you been hiding these exquisite creatures from me out in the wild country?"

Ilana took Andreas by the hand and placed him in the seat next to her, on the other side of him was an older woman who was the mayor of Odessa's wife. Most of the dinner was spent with Andreas listening to Ilana prattle on about the parties of the season he had missed, how exquisite so and so baroness's flower arrangements were or Duchess Whosit's party had been a flop because they had an inferior band playing.

The mayor's wife was finally able to ask Andreas a question when Ilana was distracted by a servant asking her a question. "Will my lord Graf have much time in the city?" she asked.

"I am afraid not, my lady," Andreas answered. "I believe the viscount has scheduled us to leave Saturday on the tide. I have much to arrange in that time and fear this will be the only time available for me to relax."

"Oh, that is a shame. Odessa is quite beautiful and has many wonderful sights," she said. "I wonder if my lord could tell me about the badges you wear on your collar?"

"Oh, they are nothing special. Everyone in the battalion has one similar," Andreas said. "No one in the battalion is allowed to be in the battalion unless they earn the marksman's badge. That is what the rifle stands for. The other collar will have a bear on it to signify support troops, or an eagle to signify combat troops."

"How very quaint," said Ilana who had overheard the last comment, "and look, their wives have replica badges the same as their husbands."

"I fear my lady viscountess has misunderstood," Andreas said. "Our lady wives, as members of the medical company, are entitled to wear the bear, not the eagle like their husbands. The only way and I do mean, the only way, they were allowed to wear those bears was if they first earned those rifles."

Andreas must have spoken more loudly than he had intended, because the entire head table and first two rows of diners before them had stopped talking and were looking at them. The four wives were sitting straight in their chairs, shoulders squared back, proudly showing off their badges.

The viscount rose from his chair and the room fell silent. "Our guests have traveled a long way to be here with us tonight; indeed, as I am sure you are all aware, they arrived mere hours ago. I would like to thank the Graf and his lovely wife for letting us all welcome them here tonight on such short notice. I am sure they are all quiet fatigued after the long journey. They have much to do and little time to do it in, so I pray you excuse us and them, while we escort them home, and hope you join us in wishing them a safe return from the duty Mother Russia has called them to."

The viscount led the Bekenbaum party, not through the main public doors, but through the doors that led to his private quarters.

"A moment of your time, Andreas?" he said once they had reached the hallway beyond. "I won't keep him long, Elizabeth. Ilana, please escort our guests to the parlor and offer them some of that fine French brandy."

Oh, I'm in for it now, thought Andreas.

The door to the study shut behind them and the viscount walked over to a sideboard and poured two glasses of brandy, handing one to Andreas.

"You are one of the most patient men I have ever met, Andreas," the viscount said. "Ilana was running out of things to say, trying to drive you nuts. Who would have thought little tiny broaches would do the trick? She really is not that shallow, but appearances sometimes must be kept. How long did it take you to get here, four hours? For those fools out there, a trip of thirty miles would take three days. Do you think you could spare Elizabeth for a day? Ilana would like to spend some time with her."

"It should not be a problem, my lord," Andreas said. "There are only fifty troopers she is responsible for, as long as she is ready for Saturday."

A knock on the door revealed a British naval officer.

"Ah, Commodore Peacock, this is Colonel Bekenbaum; he is the commander of the forces you will be transporting," the viscount said in English.

After the men exchanged pleasantries, the British officer said, "We could make it in one trip if we packed everyone and everything, very tight. The trip is only four hours."

"It will take longer to load and unload though?" Andreas said. "I don't see much of an advantage then, maybe three, four hours and more chance for injury to animals and people. Two trips would be better, I think."

"How are you planning your loads?" Peacock asked.

"Fifty, fifty, I think. We'll get the first group unloaded, I want them on the road first thing the next morning. If we can load the second group right away, they will only be eight hours behind."

"Very well, Colonel, first light Saturday then."

They exchanged pleasantries for a few minutes and then the commodore made his exit.

"I wish we had more time, Andreas," the viscount said. "But the British are quiet anxious. They have been in port two weeks already waiting for you. The battalion will be landing on the west coast of Georgia and heading inland from there. Georgia has been under Russian control for some time now; you won't have any trouble transiting there, I think. After that, Iran, who knows with Iran? One minute they are with us and against the British, the next with the British and against us, then against both of us. This time, I think, they are having problems with that same group of fanatics the British are, so you should get cooperation there. After that, Afghanistan, I can't help you there."

The viscount picked up a thick packet of papers and handed them to Andreas. "These are the maps we have of the area, and I have taken the liberty to mark the shortest route for you. Of course, local conditions may not be ideal and you might have to deviate. The overland portion of the route is around three thousand miles. How long do you think it will take you?"

"About sixty days, I think," said Andreas after a pause to do the calculations. "I'm building in a ten day cushion, just in case."

"Very well. I think it is time we reunite you with your lovely wife. Married life seems to agree with her; she has a special glow about her that was not there before."

The transit from the viscount's office to the parlor was short, and they found Ilana gaily chatting up the party. The viscount and Andreas reached their wives, and Andreas gave Elizabeth a peck on the cheek to signify everything was alright.

"Well, my dear," the viscount told his wife, "I believe we have neglected our other guests for too long, and Andreas really has a lot to accomplish tomorrow. Ilana, Andreas has graciously consented for Elizabeth to visit with you tomorrow."

"Oh, that will be so nice," replied Ilana. "The other three ladies, as well? I think, yes, I will not hear otherwise. I will have a carriage at your hotel for, say, nine? Good. You have some clothing other than uniforms and these fancy party gowns? Breakfast first, then a tour of the best sights, I think." Ilana had taken Elizabeth by the arm while she was speaking and artfully ushered Andreas's party to the front door. Andreas and Elizabeth were the last to leave, Ilana reluctant to let them go. The couple stood in the doorway watching them leave.

"I am growing rather fond of that young man," the viscount said. "I hope he makes it back all right."

"I think I could love Elizabeth as a sister," Ilana whispered. "She's pregnant, you know."

"What? And that young pup is taking her with him? I knew he was young and somewhat arrogant, but that is too much. I will forbid it."

"You will do no such thing, my dear," she said, patting his arm to calm him down. "She hasn't told him yet. She hasn't told anyone yet. I wouldn't either if I was her."

"I seem to recall that you did do that," he replied with a smile, and they walked back into the party arm-in-arm.

After the wives had left the next morning, Andreas held a breakfast meeting with his command group in his suite. The meeting was conducted in English, which Andreas hoped would make it more difficult for any eavesdroppers to overhear. He handed a package of maps to each man.

"We begin loading at first light tomorrow," he said. "William, you will take your group along with Ivan's and Johann's and half the support troop. William will be in overall command until I link up with you with the second group. The naval commander tells me it's a four-hour trip one way. As soon as you are unloaded, I want you on the move. The second group will be Patrick, Peter, myself, and the rest of the support group. We should be eight, no more than ten hours behind you. Daily objectives are marked out on the maps. At the border between Georgia and Iran, if we haven't linked up yet, wait there for us. If we need to change routes or anything else that should occur, send a scout back to us. The British should be waiting for us with local guides at that point. Questions? Alright, enjoy the rest of the day as best you can. I think it will be last day off for some time. Oh, Peter?" He tossed a box at the man. "Maybe you can afford to buy my sister a new house now and stop sponging off me. Congratulations, Major."

Andreas spent the rest of the day doing last-minute calculations and studying the maps he had to familiarize himself more on the routes, looking for anything that may cause him problems. The supplies they had with them should last until they reached Iran, and he was hoping the British would be ready for resupply. If they were not, did he have sufficient funds to purchase them? Shortly after two that afternoon, he felt himself getting drowsy and was soon asleep, papers and maps scattered all around him.

A light touch on his shoulder and kiss on the lips woke him up. The sun had set and the room was only lit by one lantern by his chair, which was enough to show him that Elizabeth was only wearing a blouse and it was only closed by the bottom two buttons. The rest of the night was a blur.

Dawn was not even a thought as they lay entwined together, gently exploring each other's bodies.

"How long until you think you will catch up with us?" Elizabeth asked.

Andreas shrugged, "A week, ten days at most. The roads are supposed to be good. I will miss you a lot, Liz, and I know you will miss me too. I think you will find, though, that the days will fly by. We will both be too busy; before you know it, I'll be there."

"The days may fly by, but the nights will be long," she said with a sigh. "Once more, my love, then I must go."

Afterwards, she kissed him and hugged him so hard he thought he felt ribs cracking before she left the disheveled bed and entered the bathroom. She's gained a little weight, he thought. Winter inactivity does that; a couple of days in the saddle should cure it, for her and for him.

She came out of the bathroom, fresh smelling from her bath, hair pinned up under her cap, buttoning up the uniform tunic over her blouse. She buckled up her pistol belt and slung her Winchester over her left shoulder and her saddle bags on her right. The box that contained her clothing had already been taken away. Andreas hugged her, and they kissed one last time.

"Please, don't come to the boats, Andy," she pleaded. "I don't want the girls to see me crying, and if I see you, I may not leave."

Kissing the tears from her eyes, he said softly, "It would never do to have two colonels crying, my Liz." Then, she left.

Of course, he lied. He watched her with her nurses load the ship, then watched the ship till he could see it no more, Peter beside him.

"You know, I used to laugh at the married men always talking about how much they missed their wives and their homes," Peter said. "I'm not laughing now. Thank you for the promotion, sir."

Switching to English, Andreas said, "Ok, enough Peter; we are both field grade officers. We are alone; I am your brother-in-law and, hopefully, your friend. I have a name, use it."

"Sorry, Andreas, this is all so new. The titles, being an officer, I still catch myself saluting lieutenants."

"Ya, it takes a little getting used to," Andreas said. "That happens to me sometimes, too. Christ, it's not even been a year. Last year this time, I was not even a sergeant, looking forward to the glory of my first campaign. Hoping the money I made would allow me to buy my first plot of land, and I could start thinking about looking for a wife. If you think you're dazed and confused, spend an hour in my boots."

"I only took the job to come over here because of the bonus money they promised me," said Peter. "After the cruise, I was going back home to Minnesota to buy a farm by my folks and, like you, find a nice girl and start a family, probably a good Cossack girl if my mother had anything to say about it. Mothers." Both men laughed at that.

"I wanted to promote you when I promoted Ivan and Johann, but William felt it would be more beneficial during the training phase for you to stay, Captain. He was right. William is teaching me a lot about being an officer," continued Andreas.

"He was a general in a militia cavalry unit before they asked him to transfer into the marines. If his wife wouldn't have died during the war, I don't think he would have stayed. His family was well off and connected before the war," Peter said.

"What happened?" Andreas asked.

"His family lived in a border region, there were raids on both sides; one night raiders attacked his father's home. They killed everyone. Burned the farmhouse around them and killed them as they came out," he said quietly.

"And yet he and Patrick are friends. Weren't they on different sides?" Andreas asked.

"Different story. They were both in regular units, not night bandits killing civilians. And one more thing," Peter said. "They are brothers-in-law. They married each other's sisters and both sisters were in the house that night."

"Oh my God!" said Andreas. "Brother against brother, what a terrible thing."

"Ok, enough of this, Brother," said Peter, "my stingy colonel has not paid me yet. Maybe if we poor sergeants can pool our money together, we can find enough money to drown our sorrows in some cheap but decent booze."

Six days later, they were setting up camp when the scouts came back in.

"Colonel, they are camped maybe two hours up the road," the lead scout reported.

"Very good, thank you," Andreas said. "We should link up at tomorrow night's camp then. Have tomorrow's scouts let them know we are coming and to not let up their pace."

"Sir," the scout said, saluting and moving away.

It was hard, but he could not push the men any harder; they had a long way to go—another day away from Liz would not kill him.

The horses alerted them they were getting close. It was harder to keep them on pace, they wanted to surge ahead and were snorting and tossing their heads. Some of the stallions started whinnying, and in the distance, return whinnies could be heard.

As much as he wanted to go, Andreas kept Bartholomew in check, halfway back alongside the first wedge of his cavalry troopers. This was as close as he would permit himself to come until just before the end, when he would drop back to the center troop. They were at the end of the one-hour walking period and care would have to be taken, when they broke into a trot once again, that the horses would not run away on them. Most of the men had whips ready just in case.

Peter was at the head of the troop alongside the troop's captain and he looked back at Andreas and grinned, then stoically looked back ahead, after yelling at one of the troopers to keep his animal in line.

The lead bugler signaled the pace change, and as the half battalion came up to a trot, Andreas pulled Bartholomew aside and kept him at a walk. The columns of eight took up the full width of the road, and as each troop of a hundred passed him, someone in the troop, usually in the middle, would yell some joke or another at him as they passed. Andreas would good naturedly yell back a response, which normally left the whole troop laughing.

When the sixteen men assigned as the front guard troop of the support troops reached him, Andreas allowed Bartholomew to advance to a trot, positioned alongside the front rank. The two-wheeled carts that carried their baggage, supplies, and spares were four abreast, the two horses pulling them at a trot with ease. The wagons were arranged four columns to a troop with sixteen guards separating them, then would come the final two troops of combat troopers. It would take five minutes for the half battalion to completely pass a single point in the road when they were at the trot.

Once Andreas was satisfied with his position, he yelled at the men beside him, "I think a song would be nice."

The men beside him started to sing a highly altered and lewd version of the Don Cossack ballad and soon the whole half battalion, women included, was joining in.

When they reached the other half battalion, they had already made camp, tents pitched on each side of the road in neat lines, wagons drawn up in squares in the center of the tents. A group of troopers was arranged loosely at the edge of the camp watching them arrive. Among them was Marie, flanked by Irene and Katia. Katia was clearly holding herself in, bouncing up and down in nervousness. Elizabeth was nowhere to be seen, and Andreas began to worry a bit.

The troopers expertly wheeled off alternate troops to opposite sides of the road, senior officers handing off to subordinates, and the field grade officers gathered in the center of the road, observing the troopers' movements. Once all the troopers and wagons were lined up and Andreas received the report that everything was in order, he gave the order to dismiss and set up camp. Then he and the senior officers rode up to the same group from the first half battalion, received their salute, dismounted, and handed horses to aides. At that point, there was no holding Marie back as she charged Peter, jumping into his arms with her legs around his hips.

"Alright you two; get a room, will you," laughed Andreas.

"Oh, we will, we will," said Marie when she came up for air, then dragged Peter off in the direction of the tents.

"Jumped-up sergeants, no sense of right and wrong," Andreas laughed. "Anything I need to know, Major?"

"No, sir. No catastrophes, no break downs, nobody has died or deserted. All rather boring, sir," reported William.

Andreas put both hands on his hips and arched his back. "I can use the extra two hours of sleep, I can tell you, Major. One of the ships had some kind of problem on the way over, put us behind schedule a bit. We have been eating your dust for seven days now; tomorrow, we take the lead. We'll switch off every day after that. Anything else, Major? Then I believe I will take my leave and find out where my aides are pitching my tent." He noticed the major was smiling and was about to ask him about it, when a lieutenant cleared his throat behind him.

"Begging your pardon, Colonel," the aide said. "But the colonel is requesting you to come to her quarters so she can report in private, sir."

Andreas looked at the reddening young man, "Where would the colonel's quarters be located, Lieutenant?"

"That one, sir, the one by the tree line by itself," he said, pointing at it.

"Very well, thank you, Lieutenant, no need for an escort, I can find my way. Dismissed, you can go back to your comrades. I don't believe the colonel will require your services tonight." After dismissing the rest of the grinning officers, Andreas casually walked to where the lone tent stood and rapped on the tent side.

"Colonel, you requested my presence?" he asked.

"Get your ass in here! What took you so long?" Elizabeth said.

Once again, another night was lost in a fog.

They had been sitting on the border for two days now. It was ludicrous, two thousand heavily armed people, being kept from crossing one piece of ground for another, by five underfed, underpaid, and under-armed border guards. The fact that the reason the two thousand were coming to their country was to help them, did not seem to matter. The guards said they could not cross, so they did not cross.

Just before noon, a plumb of dust betrayed the arrival of visitors from Iran and ten riders appeared. Andreas and Elizabeth saw the arrival, but thought nothing of it until one of their lieutenants came to their quarters.

"Colonel," the man said, "a British officer and Iranian officer are requesting your presence."

"Which colonel," said Andreas, knowing full well it was him.

"They didn't say, sir. The Iranian just demanded that I fetch the colonel."

"Which is it? Demanded or requested?" asked Andreas.

"The Iranian demanded, the British requested," the now-confused lieutenant said.

Both colonels looked at each other, shrugged their shoulders and grinned. The couple rose, donned their uniform tunics and hats, buckled on their pistol belts, and walked to the border crossing.

At the crossing were eight King's German Legion troopers lined up in a row behind Major von Hoaedle and an officer in flowing silk robes, with gold bracelets on his wrists and gold rings hanging from his ears.

Making sure they were on the Georgian side of the border, the couple stopped, saying nothing, Elizabeth following Andreas's lead.

In English, Major von Hoaedle said saluting, "Major von Hoaedle of the King's German Legion, sir, this is Major Aslimbad of the Iranian Guard."

Andreas did not move or say anything. The German major was about to say something else when he noticed the Iranian was not saluting and said something under his breath at him. Then the Iranian presented a reluctant salute, which Andreas returned.

"Colonel Andreas Bekenbaum and Colonel Elizabeth Bekenbaum of the Andreashost Russian light cavalry, how can we be of service?" he said.

"A woman? A woman not only unveiled and not in a burka, but in a man's clothing and armed? I will not treat with such. It is an insult, the Holy Koran forbids it," the Iranian said, but he did not leave. Then he noticed a group of women similarly dressed and armed, watching. "Infidels, you will not cross with these women like this; they will change their garments or they will not cross the border."

"I'm sorry, Major," Andreas said. "These women are necessary for the efficiency of my battalion; it is essential that they come with us."

"I did not say they could not cross," the Iranian said. "I said they could not cross dressed like that. The Holy Koran forbids it."

"Really? I do not wish to disrespect your religion. Perhaps the copy of the Holy Koran I have has been mistranslated. Here, I have marked the passage for you." Andreas passed his well-used copy to the major.

The Major scanned the book and handed it back.

"No, it is translated properly," the man said. "These women must be clothed properly or they will not cross."

"Are they dressed provocatively, Major?" Andreas asked. "Are they showing any skin or other parts of their bodies other than their faces or hands? Then they meet the requirements the Prophet Mohammed set out in the Holy Koran."

"No, they shall not pass dressed like that," the man insisted.

"I have already told you, Major, it is necessary for them to come with us, and it is necessary that they be dressed like they are," Andreas said.

"Then none of you shall pass," the Iranian said.

"As you wish," Andreas said. "Please, convey my regrets to your commander Major von Hoaedle. I fear the czar will not be able to complete his bargain with your government due to this man's unacceptable demands."

Then looking at the Iranian, said slowly and with menace, "You, sir, may tell your government that the Czar of Russia will not be pleased that he was unable to complete his bargain. There will be consequences and they will not be pleasant. In addition, I have been chosen by the czar personally to conduct operations in his name. I choose to spend the rest of my term patrolling this border. Any person trying to cross this border, anywhere, without proper authorization, will be shot and their property seized. Any person crossing this border with proper authorization will have all goods searched. Any goods found not properly accounted for will result in the confiscation of all property. All persons and goods crossing this border will pay a toll.

"Good day, gentlemen." And without waiting for or rendering a salute, turned back to his camp issuing orders to mount an immediate patrol.

"Sir, the British Major and an Iranian Colonel and that major are requesting permission to come over the border and meet with you," said the same lieutenant that had reported earlier in the day.

"Fine, bring them up, first have the cook bring up a pot of coffee, five cups, and some bread," replied Andreas. "Send somebody to fetch the colonel, if you please."

246

There was about three hours of daylight left in the day. They must be desperate or someone is making a lot of money smuggling around here, thought Andreas, as he walked out of the tent and sat outside under the tent fly. Elizabeth came hurrying back to their quarters, and Andreas had her sit in the chair beside him, had a small table and three chairs placed opposite them, and waited.

When the three men approached, Andreas and Elizabeth rose and returned their salutes.

"Thank you for receiving us, Earl and Countess Bekenbaum," said the Iranian Colonel.

"Welcome to our simple accommodations, Colonel," Andreas said. "Please have a seat. Coffee? I am afraid I can only offer some simple muffins; we are in transit and a front line unit, so our food is limited and simple," replied Andreas.

An aide poured the coffee and handed out the muffins, which each person took a sip of and a bite. The two Colonels talked of generalities for a few minutes, then Andreas decided that it was time for business.

"What can I do for you, Colonel?" he said.

"I am afraid relations between us have gotten off to a bad start, and would like to see if there is anything we can do to remedy the situation," the Iranian Colonel said.

"As I explained to your major earlier, Colonel," Andreas said. "We are a combat regiment. Every person in this regiment is vital for its operation. Everyone, including the women, in this regiment, is a combat-trained cavalry trooper. We are not here to invade your country, or settle in your country. We are here to kill bad people for your country. If you don't want us, we will go back home when the year is done."

"I am afraid my major overreacted and was not clear on what was expected of him, Earl Bekenbaum. We have a very different culture and the appearance of armed women unsettled him." The colonel nodded at the major.

"I would like to apologize to the earl and, especially, the countess for my behavior this morning," the major said.

"No apology necessary, Major, we understand the cultural differences," said Elizabeth in her now better, but still heavily accented English.

"Our needs are simple," continued Andreas. "We simply wish to transit your country, arrive at our destination, kill the enemies of our countries, and then go home. Nothing more. Anything more, I will leave to the politicians. I am a soldier, not a politician."

The next morning, Andreas led his troops into Iran for the next stage of their journey. Reaching the supply point the British had set up for them in the early evening, Andreas asked von Hoaedle to join he and Elizabeth for dinner.

"Graf, Gräfin," said von Hoaedle, clicking his heels together and nodding his head as he approached their table under the tent fly.

"Come sit, Major," Andreas said. "Elizabeth, this is my father's old friend Rudy von Hoaedle; Rudy, my wife, Elizabeth."

"A pleasure, Gräfin Bekenbaum," said Rudy, bowing as he sat.

"My pleasure as well, Baron von Hoaedle, and it is Elizabeth, Rudy," she replied in the German the two men had been talking.

"I must say, Andreas, you Bekenbaums certainly know how to pick your women," Rudy said. "Even dressed in that unflattering uniform, you are exquisite, my lady."

"Flattery will get you everything, my lord." Elizabeth laughed back at him.

They continued the light-hearted banter throughout the meal, catching up on events since they had last met. They had finished eating and were sipping their tea. Rudy was regaling them with stories of Andreas's father's exploits as a younger man, some of them extremely funny.

"You know, Elizabeth, my Greta was much like you," Rudy said. "She had to come with me on campaign, not as you are mind, but she was with me for most of the Napoleon Wars. In fact, my eldest son was born just after Waterloo, in camp."

Elizabeth started a smile, then her look went to a startled one and she clutched her stomach with her right hand.

"Oh," she said, "I believe this rich food may not be agreeing with me. We have been on dried foods for so long; I may have overindulged on all this fresh meat and produce. If my lords will excuse me?"

Both men rose as she left, then settled back down to finish their tea.

"You know, Andreas," Rudy said. "The British were unprepared for the speed at which you have been progressing. I warned them about how you people operated, but they are stuck in their own reality. Thirty miles is a long day for them, sixty almost unheard of, let alone for days on end like you are doing."

"I would go longer if I could. Iran bothers me," said Andreas. "We will rest here for a day, resupply, and do any repairs, then head out again. How are your men holding out?"

"I, unlike the British, know how you people operate," Rudy said. "We have remounts with us, and we share rations with your people, so I don't have to worry about that. I only have a company with me, and we are combat loaded, so no baggage train to worry about. Yes, we can keep up, no problem."

Andreas nodded. "Good, thank you for joining us, Rudy; if you will excuse me, I really should check on Elizabeth."

Rudy took his leave, and Andreas entered the tent he shared with Elizabeth to find her sitting on the edge of their cot, her tunic off and belt buckle undone, hands rubbing her belly gently. She had been crying and as she saw Andreas, tears began to well in her eyes again.

"Liz, I will send for a doctor at once." She grabbed his arm as he was turning to leave.

"No, my love, this is nothing to concern him with. Come to me," she said, pulling him gently to her. He knelt in front of her, and she took his head in both her hands and looked at him. "I'm pregnant," she said quietly, tears beginning to run down her cheeks.

He looked at her with astonishment.

"Please, don't send me home, Andy, please!" she pleaded.

"Send you home, why would I want to send you home?" he said. "I'm going to be a father? Oh, Liz, thank you! I am so happy for you. How, when?"

She laughed in relief and joy. "Dummy. Did your father not tell you what happens when a stallion mounts a mare? We have

250

been very busy. Your son or daughter should be arriving in August."

True to what Rudy had told them, the British had not been ready for them when they reached Kandahar in Afghanistan. They had been met by an infantry captain who was in charge of the hundred man garrison stationed in Kandahar, and was clearly overwhelmed by the site of two thousand-plus riders and wagons descending on his town. The troopers had set up their temporary camp outside the city proper and while the May nights were still cool, no one was unduly concerned.

Andreas had found that Elizabeth had been shopping with the viscount's wife in Odessa, as she had material which she had used to alter her uniforms and tunics to fit her ever-growing belly. Once the doctor had been assured that they would be in a permanent camp soon, he was no longer concerned about Elizabeth and the baby's health as the long days on the trail were no longer troubling him.

Rudy had sent a detachment to Kabul, the capital, to inform his commanders of their arrival. Four days after, the detachment had returned with word that the rest of Rudy's battalion and a British Light Horse Brigade would be joining them shortly. Three hours before nightfall, the remaining four companies of Rudy's battalion, complete with a pack train and remounts, arrived and set up camp adjacent to the Cossack battalion.

"Well, it looks like the Germans have come to play. I hope the British look as good," said Andreas to his command group as they stood watching the German battalion arrive.

"The British will look very good," said Patrick. "Past history would tell us performance is rather less than good however."

"Yes, they have a system where the officers are promoted by family connections and wealth, rather than by merit. At the lower end of the command chain, they have some good officers, professional soldiers, but they are generally ignored by the ones in higher positions," agreed William.

"That is why we are attached to, instead of being 'under control' of them," said Andreas. "We can take their orders under advisement and can modify them to suit ourselves, or indeed, disregard them altogether if we feel it necessary."

The next morning at reveille, the British hoisted a brand new Union flag to the top of their citadel in the city. A constant series of signals all morning at regular intervals were being sent from the semaphore station located next to the flag. If that had not been enough to signify that something big was going to happen, the Germans were busily grooming horses to a shine and polishing tack and uniforms. Andreas and his command group, not having been informed of what was going on, sat under the large fly set up in front of the command tent, leisurely talking and joking.

"You Bekenbaums seem to be starting your own army," said William with a glint in his eye. "The way you are going, by the time you retire, you'll have your own platoon."

All four of the Bekenbaum male relatives had received news that their wives were pregnant.

"Must be the long winter nights," said Patrick. "Or, maybe the water."

"Not at all," said Johann, "it is clearly a case of superior male manhood."

"I think it's the inability of them to keep it in their pants," said Elizabeth who had come to sit beside Andreas.

Once all of them had stopped laughing, Peter choked out, "Or, maybe it's our wives waving their fannies in front of us all the time." Which started them all going again, after Elizabeth had thrown a bun at him in mock indignation.

Soon Rudy's five hundred were moving out, lining both sides of the road leading to the town gates, standing beside their horses in loose formation. Twenty red-coated infantry men marched out of the gates, led by their now-mounted captain; they also lined both sides of the road in front of the gates. A column of dust betrayed the arrival of something down the road. A smudge of red at the head of the dust soon revealed itself to be mounted cavalry in columns of four.

"No problem with them surprising us," said Ivan. "They're what two miles away?"

"Yes, that red really sets them up," said William.

"Much like the blue you Yankees wore. We could see you coming a long time before you knew we were there," said Patrick.

"Yes, the color of your uniforms made it hard to spot you at a distance, much like the light grey we are wearing here," agreed William. "Should we assemble an honor guard, Colonel?"

"I think not, Major, no one has bothered to inform us of what is going on," answered Andreas. "Besides, William, we have a better view here and really my lady's delicate condition is not suited to all the dust and smelly horses."

They all started laughing again, after Elizabeth had punched Andreas on the shoulder, just as the first of four open-top carriages, carrying high-ranking officers and their ladies, was passing in front of them.

Shortly after that, a British lieutenant was ushered into their presence. He came to a foot-stomping halt, five paces in front of them, an open-handed British salute held to the side of his gleaming white pith helmet. The chin strap of the helmet was positioned between his chin and his lips. Everything about his uniform from the red tunic with white, pipe clay belts and shiny brass buckles, to his blue trousers with yellow stripe and clattering sword hanging on his hip, to silver spurs buckled onto knee-length cavalry boots, was gleaming.

Andreas acknowledged the salute with a wave in the general direction of his forehead.

"What can I do for you, Lieutenant?" asked Andreas in English, choosing the American pronunciation of the rank.

Handing Andreas a sealed envelope, he said, "The colonel and his senior officers and ladies are commanded to attend Officers Mess this evening at seven, sir. Transportation for the ladies will be provided."

"Thank you, Lieutenant. Please advise your commander that transportation will not be required," replied Andreas, dismissing the man with another salute in the general direction of his forehead. Opening the envelope and withdrawing the card inside, Andreas quickly read it before tossing it on the table.

"That's what it says all right, 'commanded', not 'requested'."

He heard Elizabeth's sharp intake of breath.

"Not to worry, Liz," he said, tapping the invitation below the signed name. "We are Russian soldiers serving in our sovereign's name, assisting a friend of the czar. We have been in the field in combat readiness for over two months now and have just been insulted by that friend. We go as we are. Combat ready Cossacks in a war zone. Colonel, if you would inform your sisters? I believe we should go for a stroll about six thirty. Maybe we will stop in and pay our respects to the British at that time."

Rudy and his four captains in their dress uniforms clattered by the laughing group of Russians, casually walking in the direction of the British officers mess and shook his head. Someone was about to be taught a lesson, and it won't be Andreas, he thought smiling.

"The Russians," announced the mess sergeant who ushered them into the dining area. A sharp gasp emanated from every one assembled in the hall.

In sharp contrast to the immaculate dress uniforms and fancy party dresses the men and women already assembled were wearing, Andreas's party walked in, ladies on gentlemen's arms, in field uniforms, complete with pistols in the pistol belts strapped to their waists.

Instead of going to the table reserved for them to the side of the hall, to the mess sergeant's dismay, Andreas and his party casually walked up the center of the aisle and came to a stop fanning out to each side of him in front of the head table. They stood there, not moving or saying a word. Andreas waited until the man in front of him was about to burst in indignation.

"Leftenat Colonel," he said quietly but firmly, pronouncing the rank with the English pronunciation, "I don't know how it is in your army, but in mine it is customary to salute a superior officer. It is also considered bad form for an inferior officer to issue orders to a superior officer. My report to your headquarters shall reflect that I do not hold this disrespectful behavior against them. Now, if you will excuse us, the countess and I will resume our after-dinner walk. It is really a nice night for a walk, don't you agree, my lady."

"Oh, yes, my lord Earl. The evening breeze is so very refreshing after the heat of the day," replied Elizabeth, also in English, as the party turned and casually strolled out of the building.

Every morning for a week after the dinner, Andreas was in the saddle and accompanied by ten troopers, and a different officer each day left Kandahar as the sun was breaking the horizon. Every man including officers and Andreas went fully armed, Winchesters slung over their backs, and pistols at their hips. They visited each village they could find, meeting with village leaders and explaining the reason for their presence. That they were not there as invaders, but to help them, if they could, from the raiders that were attacking their villages and herds.

At first the people were skeptical, but soon word got around that this foreigner was different. This foreigner was educated and quoted from the Holy Koran. Even when tested by imams, he gave the proper responses. Even though he was a great lord and warrior in his own land, he treated everyone, no matter their status, with respect and dignity.

Word soon began to spread, first from Kandahar, then from the rural areas, that the foreigners had doctors that would try to help anyone. That they even had female medical people, so their wives and daughters could be treated for medical conditions. Indeed, the great lord's lady was often on hand to provide assistance herself.

Each day, Andreas would return after dark. Each night, he read the ever more desperate messages from the British commander requesting an audience. Each day, he added them to the pile of previously unanswered messages.

"Good morning, sir," Andreas said. "May the blessings of God be upon you."

The local imam had received an education in Russia and was fluent in the language.

"And may they also be upon you," he replied. "Come sit, the local leaders are all present and wish to speak to you and hear your wisdom."

"I am but a young man," Andreas said, "with much to learn, but if I can be of help, I will do my best."

"This is all that God asks of us," the imam said, "to do our best. Some coffee for you and your aide?"

Andreas had brought along Ivan today, to show not only where the villages in this sector were, but for Ivan to meet the locals so that both he and they could begin to get to know each other. Both men took their places on the rug placed on the floor of the meeting place; sitting cross-legged, they accepted the strong coffee and talked of the weather and their families for a time.

"This is what we wish your advice with," the imam said after Andreas had asked how the crops and herds were progressing.

"We have been approached from rich and powerful foreigners that wish us to grow the poppy on our fields," the imam said. "They promise us great riches, much more than we have now. Riches to buy more wives, horses, and guns. Riches to become free from the white man."

"All men strive to make life easier for themselves and their families," Andreas said after a moment of thought. "I myself have had to make such a decision, not with poppies, they do not grow on our land, but with another crop that would provide great riches.

"If you grow the crop to provide great riches, you will become dependent on others for your food. They will charge you more money than what it would cost to provide it yourselves. Once other villages see you are making good money growing poppies, they too will grow poppies and the money you receive will become less. Soon, no one is making great riches and no one has any money to buy food."

Andreas took a sip of coffee allowing the imam to translate his words. There was much nodding of heads from the older men, but some of the younger ones became vocal with much gesturing of hands. One of the young men standing and pointing at Andreas angrily.

"This one says, you just want to keep us poor like all white men," the imam said. "So you tell lies to make us do your bidding."

"I am here to kill raiders, not steal your lands," Andreas said. "I have enough wealth and land; I need no more.

"I would ask the young man this," Andreas continued, pointing at the angry man still standing glaring at him with his arms crossed on his chest. "If a man takes ten cows to market in the fall on Saturday when all other men are taking their cows to market, does he get full price?"

The young man made a gesture that Andreas understood to be negative.

"But that same man takes the same ten cows to market on Wednesday when no other men are selling cows, and what happens then?" Andreas asked. "So, it will be with the poppies," he continued. "You will have so much land growing poppies, the price will be low and you will have to plant more to be able to buy food and so it will go."

"Why not make sure all your people can eat well?" Andreas asked. "The goats and cows have good pasture and hay. You have grain for the winter for yourselves and the animals and a little more to store for bad times and maybe to sell. Then, take some small pieces of land and grow a little poppy to make extra money if you wish. Does this make sense?

"While other tribes grow much poppy, you make more money selling grain and herd animals, plus a little bit from poppy," Andreas said. "You make the best of both worlds."

Now the glare had come away from the young man's eyes to be replaced with a look of thoughtfulness, and he sat down stroking his well-manicured beard with one hand as others debated Andreas's words.

"What is in this for you?" the young man said finally in English. "Your British overlords are pushing us to grow the poppy as well as the invaders, but you do not."

"I have no British overlords," Andreas said in English. "I come here to kill raiders, just as I have said. What is in it for me? The more raiders I kill here, the less I have to kill at home. The less my people have their crops burnt, their grandfathers killed and women stolen. That is what is in it for me. If you can feed yourselves and make enough money to buy weapons to protect yourselves, then my sons and grandsons will not have to come back here over and over again to help you. That is what is in this for me."

The young man looked at him for a moment and then rose, motioning the others to join him.

"Stay here," the young man said. "Have more coffee. We wish to discuss this matter more fully and will return shortly."

Instead of having another cup of coffee, Andreas rose and, beckoning Ivan to follow, went to check on his troopers and his horses.

"Have the horses been watered?" Andreas asked his sergeant.

"Yes, sir," the sergeant replied. "They let us use their well and we have all eaten, sir."

"I am not expecting any trouble," Andreas said. "Be prepared just in case."

"We always are, sir, you taught us well," the sergeant replied.

"It's getting boring out here," a young trooper in the back said. "I had more chance of dying from a cow kicking me back home."

"Yes, you are correct, Private," Andreas said. "Dying of boredom is a boring way to die."

"Oh, Jesus," said a corporal. "Do they take you guys' sense of humor away when they make you big shots?"

That and a few more comments got the requisite laughs Andreas was looking for, and the comments kept coming, mostly about themselves. The returning village leaders were greeted by troopers pounding Andreas on the back and all of them laughing hard.

The delegation came up to Andreas and the young English speaker began to talk.

"Your words are wise for one so young," he said. "We have decided to heed them. We also have experienced much raiding and killing. The animals that do this are the ones pushing for us to grow the poppy. They say they will leave us alone if we do. A large group of them are coming this afternoon for an answer. We would like your help to give them one."

"What kind of an answer?" Andreas asked.

The young man pulled the sword from his belt and showed it to Andreas. "This kind!" he yelled and the other leaders followed his example.

"They will use the same tactics, they know no other," Andreas said to his sergeant as they watched the raiders pull their lances out of scabbards and make sure swords were free.

There was about six hours of daylight left. Enough time to die in, Andreas thought.

"We will charge them, fire three rounds, then run like hell," Andreas ordered. "Got it?"

Including Andreas, there were five of them lined up across the trail. They were facing about a hundred mounted riders, each with a lance and a sword and shield. Seeing that Andreas intended on blocking their path, the riders deployed into line, six abreast, knee to knee, and several rows thick. At a word, half of them began to walk toward Andreas's small group and he waited until they were three hundred yards away before motioning his men forward and quickly into the gallop.

The raiders had seen these tactics before and kept their pace to a walk, they would charge after Andreas's troopers fired the first shot, thinking that's all there would be. At a hundred and fifty yards, the troopers pulled out and aimed their Winchesters over their ponies' heads; at a hundred yards, Andreas waited for the split second all Bartholomew's hooves were off the ground and pulled the trigger, each of his four men doing the same, and in four strides, they spun the ponies around and headed the other way. Fifteen of the enemy were lying on the ground, shot themselves or lying under shot horses; the rest of the enemy spurred into a trot, intent on revenge, followed by the other fifty raiders. They rapidly approached a spot on the road where it had been dug into a small hill, and as the enemy riders entered the cut in the ground, Andreas's other troopers rose and poured .44 caliber bullets, one every two seconds, into the mass of horse and man flesh beneath them. Any riders that escaped were met by Andreas and his four troopers, now dismounted and with ten rounds each in their reloaded rifles.

The enemy that turned to escape were met by the angered locals charging from the rear, swords slashing down on them. It was a slaughter. No amount of coaxing or gesturing by Andreas after could stop the locals from putting down any wounded or captured invaders and he soon gave up, pulling his troopers back and out of any danger of a local deciding to take them on.

"Any casualties, Ivan?" Andreas said.

"No, not even a scratch this time," Ivan said.

"Right, lads," Andreas said, going down on his knees and removing his cap; the rest of the troop doing the same.

"In the name of the Father, the Son, and the Holy Ghost," Andreas said, making the sign of the cross. "Father, thank you for your guidance and your protection for your sons to do your will and allowing us and your Muslim children to defeat those who had only evil in their hearts and who distort your words to Our Lord Jesus Christ and the Prophet Mohammed to do evil in this world instead of good. We ask your forgiveness, Lord, in the taking of these misguided lives and ask you to absolve us. We thank you, Lord, for your protection and allowing us to come unscathed from this skirmish. In the name of the Father, the Son, and the Holy Ghost, amen."

The troopers echoed the 'amen' and they all stood to see the local tribesman also on their knees, their imam saying words to them in their own language. He and they then rose and began to make preparations to leave. The imam walked up to Andreas extending his right hand.

"You must be a great leader of your faith as well as a warrior," the imam said, shaking Andreas's hand and hugging him. "I translated your words to my people and they had a big impact on them."

"No, I am not," Andreas said. "I am but a man who happens to be good with words and a knack of being in the right place at the right or wrong time, depending on your point of view. My people, like yours have great faith, and it is only right to thank God for His guidance. Beyond that, I am not much of a religious man."

"Yet, you have studied scripture, the priest in Kandahar tells me you almost became a priest and I know you have studied the Holy Koran. I have heard you quote it."

"I did not say I was not a believer," Andreas said. "I am not a religious man. In the seminary, I was taught there is only one true way to God. Yet, here you are, saying the same thing, as does a Jewish Rabbi, a Buddhist Monk, and half a dozen other religions. There is only one God and He has only one mission. All religions teach the same thing. Yet, they all say each other are wrong and many wars are started because of it."

The imam translated what Andreas had just said to the growing number of local elders that were gathering around him and Andreas. There was much nodding of heads in agreement.

"Yes, I see this even among our own people," the young leader said in English. "The Sunni attack and kill the Shia, yet we all follow the Prophet Mohammad. I see this with you as well. The English fight the Catholics, the Catholics fight the Greeks, yet you all follow your prophet Christ. This is all wrong and, as you say, God has many voices but only one message. Come, enough of this. We must celebrate this great victory over a common enemy."

"Thank you, my men and I appreciate the offer," Andreas said. "But, sadly I must say no. My wife is pregnant and soon I will have a son or daughter, and my men are like children. If their father is gone too long, they get into mischief. The English cause me many headaches."

The young man laughed and translated that for the others, they also nodded their heads and laughed; one of the older men made another comment that the others agreed with.

"They tell me they are not surprised that you have trouble with the English," the English speaker said. "The English trouble us all. Only that you have much patience and self-restraint. My people admire this trait as well. Go with God, Lord Andreas. We understand and know that you are always welcome among us."

A tired, dust-, sweat-, and gunpowder-streaked Andreas reached camp to find an open carriage parked in front of his command tent. Two civilians and a clearly agitated lieutenant colonel were seated across from Elizabeth under the fly that covered their dining area. A half-full glass of brandy was before each man sitting on the table, a tea cup and pot before Elizabeth. Two of the locals that had begun showing up to provide their services were standing attentively to the side, a female for Elizabeth and a male for the men. Elizabeth was wearing the apron covered dress and headscarf she wore when working at the medical clinic and was laughing at something she was looking at in a book on her lap.

Dismounting before the fly, he handed the reins to Bartholomew to a trooper and in Russian said, "Look after him for me, please. Alright, Ivan, come with me. Let's find out what our friends, the British, have in store for us today."

As the party at the table heard them approach, the men rose and turned toward them.

Andreas broke out into an immediate ear-to-ear grin and thrust his hand out to one of the men. "My good friend, Remington, how good to see you again," he said in English, his right hand pumping the other man's, while his left was thumping him on the back. "Look, Ivan, it's our good friend Remington."

Ivan also broke out in a grin and stuck out his right hand and vigorously pumped Remington's. "It's so very good to see you again, my friend," said Ivan, also in English.

Andreas walked over to Elizabeth and kissed her on her proffered cheek.

"What does my lady find so amusing?" he asked her.

On her lap was a hand-drawn picture of Andreas swinging Elizabeth behind him on the saddle of his charging horse with one hand, while shooting a sword-slashing villain in the head with the pistol in his other. The caption below read, 'The Hero of Russia rescuing his Lady.'

Andres just smiled and wagged his finger at Remington.

"Oh my dear, how rude of me," said Elizabeth. "My lord Earl, may I present Mr. Wiggam, Her Britannic Majesty's Counsel General for Afghanistan; Mr. Wiggam, my lord Earl Bekenbaum of Katherintal."

The two men respectfully shook hands.

"My lord Earl Bekenbaum, I have the pleasure to present, Lieutenant Colonel Featherstone, Her Britannic Majesty's Commander of Her armed forces in the region," said Wiggam.

This time Featherstone presented a parade ground salute, which Andreas returned in the same fashion before sticking out his hand for a quick handshake.

"Gentlemen, Major Halinov, one of my company commanders," Andreas said and Ivan shook hands with the two men.

"Come sit," he said, "Ivan, a glass of brandy?" he asked as the servant filled his glass.

"I must apologize for my appearance, gentlemen, I have been in the saddle all day conducting a tour of the area," he said.

"A tour of the area, my lord?" burst out Featherstone, "but it's not safe with only ten troopers."

"Yes, we'll come to that later, Colonel. Now, what can I do for you, Mr. Wiggam? I'm sure you did not come all this way just to be entertained by tales told by my dear lady and Mr. Remington."

"Harrumph, yes, well, er. I have come to mediate some concerns between your forces and ours, my lord," he said.

"Concerns? I have no reports of any concerns. My lady, have you any reports of concerns from your command?" asked Andreas.

"No, my lord, I have no concerns to report," she answered.

"You have my assurance, Mr. Wiggam, that any concerns we hear regarding the conduct of any one under my command will be dealt with immediately, and with great severity," Andreas said.

"No, no, my lord, let me rephrase it. We seem to be having a problem with co-operation between our two forces," said Wiggam.

"Ah, cooperation," said Andreas, raising his left arm and waving two fingers toward him.

The male servant placed the stack of correspondence in front of Wiggam, who began reading them. The cards were stacked in reverse order, newest first, earliest last. Each one was dated and signed in Featherstone's own handwriting.

As Wiggam made his way through the pile, he became more and more concerned, with a final involuntary "Oh my God!" leaving his lips as he read the last one, gently placing it on the table, clearly trying to compose himself. Andreas had no intention of letting him off the hook.

"I don't know how you run things in your army, Mr. Wiggam, if one of my officers acted in that manner towards me," he slammed his Colt pistol on the table, "I would have shot him with that pistol in the forehead where he stood."

"As far as it not being safe out there, Colonel," he said, sneering on the word 'colonel', "how would you know? If your behavior in Kandahar is any indication, you spent the last two months in Kabul, partying every night and berating and beating your soldiers for some minor infraction every day. Who do you think you are, some kind of Earl? I tell you, Mr. Wiggam, if I treated my people like that, they would hang me on that tree over there. In the past eight days, while this fool has been composing letters, I have been out there. I have met with village leaders in forty villages. Those visits have resulted in solid leads of our enemies' movements. So solid, that in the last two days, we have foiled two raids resulting in over one hundred enemy dead. My two doctors and small medical staff have treated over one hundred local people, while your four doctors swill gin and treat the officer's venereal diseases.

"Cooperation, Mr. Wiggam, I'll tell you how Her Britannic Majesty can cooperate with me. Why don't you and your amateur army get the hell out of here and let professional soldiers do their jobs!"

The last comment was punctuated by Andreas slamming a gunpowder and blood-stained, clenched fist on the table beside the obviously newly fired Colt. That was when everyone noticed that the sleeve that held the arm was stained deep red to the elbow, as was Ivan's right arm; the same stains in an arc pattern over chests and down backs from the blood flung off of sword blades.

Elizabeth's hand on his arm let Andreas know he was losing control of himself. He took a deep breath to steady himself.

"I apologize, gentlemen, it has been a long day and I forget my manners. Ivan, please, see to it that our guests are properly entertained. Gentlemen, my lady, I bid you good evening." Nodding to the assembled people, he picked his pistol up off the table, holstered it, and left, walking the ten yards to his quarters. He didn't hear Elizabeth when she came in and covered his fully clothed body, he was fast asleep.

Chapter Four

When he reached the horse lines in the pre-dawn light, he found Bartholomew ready for him and five of his troopers had been replaced with five green-jacketed King's Loyal Germans. His officer for the day was Rudy.

"Lose the lances, they are useless," were the only words Andreas spoke until the sun had risen over the horizon and they were several miles outside Kandahar.

"How many of your people speak Russian?" Andreas asked Rudy in German.

"Besides myself? Two, maybe three," replied Rudy.

"I will supply you with interpreters, many of the locals speak Russian. Others speak English, so we can work together after a while. These people have met and trust most of my people already, and I am hoping that we can get them to trust you as well and extend our ability to patrol the area," Andreas said.

The day went like the others, meeting with elders, drinking coffee, and sharing a bit of cake or dried fruit. One man in one village tried to give Andreas a goat. Andreas had earlier helped the man to resolve a dispute with his neighbor that had been going on for years. The two argumentative men had left arms around each other like long lost brothers. They left the final village of the day headed back to Kandahar. The village children chasing after them, men and women waving as they rode by.

"You have such an easy way with people," Rudy said. "They want to trust you."

"We are here to help them. I don't want anything from them; we don't steal from them, we don't harass or violate their women.

I respect their religion and value their opinions," said Andreas. "Rudy, most of us come from villages just like these. Barely scratching a living out of the ground, trying to feed our families, and make it a little better for our children. We are deeply religious because that is all we have. So when a leader comes along that cares, that tries to help, we give them our loyalty. It's the same with these people."

Andreas could see the German troopers nodding their heads in agreement. "Do you see, Rudy? Your troopers know, or have you been in the army so long you have forgotten what it's like?"

"No, Andreas," Rudy said. "I remember. Our land was better than this, but our peasants were the same. Living harvest to harvest. My father was a good lord, but some of our neighbors, well, they were like that colonel you just had a run-in with. Careful of him, Andreas, he has powerful friends."

"Rudy, in October I go home," Andreas said. "I will most likely never see him or his lot again. By this time next year, I will be powerful enough and have enough money to buy him and his father out twice over. Fool that he is, he has probably spent most of his inheritance already."

"My troopers are happy you people are here," Rudy said. "The English troopers are leaving them alone for once. They are going after your lads instead."

"That could end badly for them," Andreas said. "We shall have to see."

The weeks went by and the Cossack camp began to have a more permanent look. The locals had built a brick structure to house the medical facility, which every morning had a line of ten or twenty people in front waiting for treatment. The German

270

doctor and even one of the British doctors had come to help. Elizabeth was becoming larger and larger as her time grew nearer, and Andreas fell more deeply in love every day.

The daily patrols were increasing, and as the local people began to trust them, Andreas was able to stay in camp more. Letting his subordinates take over the patrols. Village leaders came to call them 'green jackets' and 'grey jackets' and looked forward to their visits. There had been more skirmishes with raiders and the raiders, not as well armed or trained, suffered greatly. The frequency of enemy movement reports from the locals increased, which resulted in more skirmishes and more enemy losses. Remington had taken to traveling with a patrol two or three times a week, and his sketches and stories were filling up many pages in his notebooks.

The only troublesome area was with the British. Tensions were building more each day, no matter how much Wiggam tried to intervene. At one point, he admitted to Andreas he was trying to get Featherstone relieved, but was having trouble with it because the man had done nothing really wrong and had friends in high places.

The British officers had started to wander around the compound, and Andreas began to hear reports from his men of disrespectful officers berating his men in English then laughing at them. Andreas could tell something was going to happen and it was not going to be good.

"Rudy, we have been receiving reports of enemy movement in this new area," Andreas said, pointing at the map on the wall. "I want you to plan a major patrol tomorrow, my people and your people. All of your guys and half of my Eagles. I want to integrate a few of my pack train guards into some of the patrols, mostly with your people. I will be using them for replacements for casualties, so they need some experience."

271

"Alright, have them at my horse lines by daybreak," Rudy said. "What the hell?"

Andreas was up and out of his chair grabbing his whip as he ran out of the tent and toward the noise of a confrontation.

It was over by the time he reached it. Four British troopers were laying on the ground and three more had three of his troopers standing behind them with arms around their necks and daggers jammed under English chins. Andreas swung his whip cracking it over his men's heads causing them to drop the English troopers and jump to attention in a line. Andreas swung the whip again; this time, snapping beside an English ear as the man spun to engage the trooper that had just let him go. The three English men spun around to see Andreas still swinging the whip and Rudy pointing a pistol at them and joined Andreas's men in line at stiff attention.

"What the hell is going on here!" Andreas said in German, jamming his nose into the face of the nearest of his men. "We do not fight each other! We fight the goddamn raiders! What is behind this?"

"My fault, Graf," the corporal of the group said. "I lost my temper, sir. No excuse, sir."

"Take off those eagles! I expect more from my troops! One of you is worth more than ten of these!" Andreas pointed at the English. "You saddle and groom the horses for the horse guards for the rest of the week and all pay for the week is forfeit. You will run five miles each morning with full packs and weapons loads before breakfast. Maybe then I will reconsider!"

"Gentlemen, I apologize for my men's behavior," Andreas said to the English troopers. "Please, take your comrades to our infirmary and our doctors will look after them."

The three English troopers looked at each other in astonishment.

"Ah, thank you, M'lord," the English corporal said. "It wasn't all their fault, sir. We had somewhat to do with it, sir."

"Nonsense, Corporal," Andreas said. "You are in my camp, and my men have dishonored me and their regiment with their behavior. Now, please, let me make up for it by treating your injuries." Andreas made good by escorting the English troopers to the medical tent himself.

"Please, extend my apologies to your commander for this incident, and I guarantee this will not happen again," Andreas said to the corporal as a doctor started looking at the English troopers.

"It looks to me that your boys were just protecting themselves, Colonel," Rudy said.

"Yes, I know this, Rudy," Andreas said. "I demand more from my people than you do from yours. We are a long way from home and support. We need all the friends and help we can get. But they should have killed at least one of those Englishmen and severely wounded the rest. I was not kidding, Rudy, my people are better than these half-trained English."

The next day four British officers came strolling through their camp, drunk in the afternoon, and going by the medical building, started harassing one of the nurses. Elizabeth and the British doctor came out of the building and Elizabeth started to try and protect her nurse, yelling at the officers in English. One of the men knocked her to the ground and the nurse she had been trying to protect shot the man. Andreas was in camp that day and went running over as soon as he heard the shot.

Elizabeth was lying on the ground holding her stomach supported by the doctor, and the nurse was holding her pistol on the four men when Andreas arrived on the scene.

"I demand you arrest that bitch immediately for shooting me," said the man, a captain, to Andreas when he saw him. "The other whore, too, who the hell do you think you people are to question your betters?" The man's companions were trying in vain to get him away or calm down.

"Do you know who I am? My brother is the commander of you Russian piss heads." The man had a minor scrape on his face from the stone ricochet of the shot.

"The 'bitch' you harassed is a major in the Russian army," Andreas said quietly. "The 'whore' you just knocked down is a colonel and a countess and my wife." Andreas pulled out his Colt and, putting the barrel to the man's forehead, pulled the trigger.

Reaction to the shooting was swift. The other three British officers had dragged away the body and Andreas, having been reassured by the doctor that Elizabeth was alright, had returned to the command tent, sitting under the awning going over some reports. His pistol was lying on the table beside a cup of tea. He was just about to send for Johann to ask about a report, when Featherstone, accompanied by a harried Wiggam and ten of his troopers all with carbines in hand, marched up to the tent. Smiling a wicked smile, Featherstone dragged out his sword, pointed it at Andreas, and said loudly, "Arrest that man!"

The troopers with him looked around them at the growing crowd and did nothing.

"Arrest that man, I tell you, or I will have you all flogged!" he said, advancing towards Andreas.

Andreas, putting his hand on his pistol, stopped the man in his tracks. Keeping his hand on his pistol, Andreas raised his left hand and made a circular motion with it. The sound of one hundred rifles chambering a round made Featherstone pause and look around.

"I knew you were a fool," said Andreas in the quiet tone he used just before trouble was about to occur, "but I didn't realize you were stupid, too. I do not recognize your authority to arrest me. Now, go away and put that sword away before you hurt yourself with it, foolish boy." He took his hand off the pistol and waved it dismissively at Featherstone, and picking up his report, began to read it again.

Three days later, a British general with a large escort of lancers wearing turbans and accompanied by two civilians rode into Kandahar in a flurry of dust. Soon after, an English lieutenant, with aide de camp decorations, handed Andreas a sealed envelope and left. Inside the envelope were two messages, one in English the other in Russian, both signed by the general, the English ambassador to Afghanistan, and the Russian ambassador to Afghanistan. Both said the same thing: That he was to hold himself ready to testify at a board of inquiry being held today.

Andreas marched to within five paces of the table, came to attention, and saluted, looking three inches above the general's head. He was in his full dress uniform, complete with sash and ceremonial sword, Hero of Russia medal pinned to his chest, but minus the hated spurs.

"Colonel Andreas Bekenbaum, Imperial Guard Cavalry, reporting as ordered, General!" he barked, holding the salute at rigid attention.

The general returned his salute formally. "At ease," he growled.

Andreas snapped his feet to shoulder-width apart and rammed both his arms behind his back, hands clenched in the small of his back.

The general was seated in the center of the table flanked by the two ambassadors. He was about sixty years old. The sides of his grey mustache went to his jaw line and were joined by his side beards as they curled at the jaw line from the other direction. His uniform was the blue with red and yellow facings of the Royal Horse Guards, and the decorations he wore betrayed that he was a veteran of more than one war. His highly polished brass helmet lay on the desk in front of him, glinting in the sunlight coming in from the widows. He held a sheet of paper in his hands and was studying it.

"The purpose of this inquiry, Colonel, is to establish the facts surrounding the tragic events of three days ago and to recommend or implement any course of action we find necessary."

"Did you see Captain Featherstone strike a superior officer?"

"No, sir!" answered Andreas.

The general made a check mark on his piece of paper.

"Did you see or hear any of the confrontation that preceded that event?"

"Sir, other than the sound of the first shot, no, sir!" Andreas said.

The general made another check mark on his sheet of paper.

"Did you immediately go to and assume control of the situation, asking for a report?"

"Sir, yes, sir!" Andreas answered.

Another check mark.

"Did the captain then order you to, and I quote, 'Arrest that bitch she shot me and the whore on the ground too.'"

"Sir, yes, sir!" Andreas answered.

"At that time, what was the severity of the captain's injury?"

"Sir, he had a scrape on his cheek from a rock ricochet. I can only assume the major shot at the ground intentionally or by accident, sir. The major has been reprimanded for her poor marksmanship, sir." Andreas said.

"Humph, yes." The general cleared his throat and continued, "Did you, then, remove your sidearm from its holster, place it on the captain's forehead between his eyes, and shoot him?"

"Sir, yes, sir."

"Cold bastard, aren't you?" the general said. "Don't answer that, and strike that comment from the record," he told the clerk scribbling away at the corner of the table.

"The officer that the captain struck, do you confirm that she is a duly commissioned Lieutenant Colonel of the Imperial Russian Army, that the baby she is carrying is yours, that you are legally married, and that before you were married she was an honored and respected baroness in her own right, responsible for two baronies?"

"Sir, yes, sir!" Andreas said.

The general made another check mark on his piece of paper, then drew another sheet before him, wrote on it for a minute, signed it, handed it to first the British, then the Russian

277

ambassadors who read and signed it. An aide took the paper from the general, gave it to the clerk who copied it, and handed it back.

"Attention to orders!" the general barked and Andreas sprang to attention, his eyes once more above the general's head.

"This inquiry finds that the actions of Colonel Bekenbaum in the matter at hand are completely justified. Furthermore, we find Captain Featherstone guilty of conduct unbecoming an officer, gross insubordination, and of striking superior officers during the performance of their duties while on active service in a time of war. By the powers granted to me under the military code of justice, I posthumously strip Captain Featherstone of all rank and privileges, he is dishonorably discharged from Her Majesty's Service, and is sentenced to death."

"At ease, please, state for the record your full name and titles."

"Andreas Heinrich Bekenbaum, Earl of Katherintal, Ataman Andreashost."

"How many troops are under your command?"

"Two thousand cavalry troops, sir."

"Let me rephrase that," the general said. "How many troops in total are you responsible for?"

"Ten thousand cavalry, twenty thousand infantry, and five gun batteries, with the same amount of my father-in-law's troops, sir."

"You are in charge of sixty-five thousand combat troops, and you are not a general?" the general asked.

"No, sir, I refused the commission, sir," Andreas said. "I do not have the experience to lead that amount of troops in a combat situation, sir."

"My God, you would never see that in our army," the general said. "Don't write that down, you fool," he said to the clerk. "The major that shot at Featherstone. What is her relationship to you and what is her background?"

"Sir, she is my brother's wife, and her uncle is my lord Viscount of Odessa, sir."

"How many troops are under his command?"

"I am not sure, sir, perhaps one hundred thousand."

"I am reliably told by your ambassador, here, that it is closer to five hundred thousand," corrected the general.

"Is it not also true that the viscount is the cousin of the grand duke and heir to the throne?" the general asked.

"I believe so, sir."

"Then that would mean he is related to her Britannic Majesty Queen Victoria. Lastly, is your older brother Heinrich, Graf *und zu* Bekenbaum of Cologne? The commander of one hundred thousand German troops and head of Bekenbaum Steel and Transport?"

"Yes, sir," Andres said.

"My goodness, the lieutenant colonel certainly knows how to pick his enemies," said the general, looking at the clerk who held his pen in the air, signifying he had not written that down.

"Attention, Colonel," the general said in his normal voice.

"Lieutenant Colonel Featherstone, front and center," the general ordered. When Featherstone presented himself and saluted, the general did not acknowledge the salute for several seconds.

"Attention to orders!" barked out the general. "This court charges Lieutenant Colonel Featherstone with conduct unbecoming an officer, exceeding the mandate of his orders, gross negligence of duty, improper conduct to superior officers, and excessive punishment of his subordinate officers and enlisted men. The lieutenant colonel is found guilty of those charges and by the articles of war, the officer being under my command on active duty during a time of war, Lieutenant Colonel Featherstone is stripped of his command, rank, and all privileges, dishonorably discharged from Her Britannic Majesty's service, and held under close arrest until he shall face a criminal court in Britain. This court is closed!" With a final bang of his gavel, the general and ambassadors rose and left the room while two guards led Featherstone away.

After dinner, Andreas and Elizabeth were enjoying a quiet evening together, both sitting legs outstretched. Elizabeth was attended to by three local women who would not allow her to lift a finger. She was dressed in a loose-fitting, colorful gown that the local women had produced, with four more similar to it. Andreas was dressed in his familiar riding uniform, tunic off, top two buttons undone. Elizabeth had been released from doctor's care earlier, with strict orders to stay away from the clinic. Crunching of gravel heralded the arrival of visitors. Andreas jumped to his feet as he saw the general, the British ambassador, Wiggam, and Rudy approaching. The three serving women would not allow Elizabeth to rise.

"No, no," said the general with a smile. "This is just an informal visit merely to convey our personal regrets for the recent events.

"Oh my God!" he exclaimed, seeing the bruise on Elizabeth's face. "We had been told he only shoved you to the ground. Not, not this. I am truly sorry, Countess."

"Oh, sit down," said Elizabeth, becoming perturbed by all the unwanted attention. "Offer the men a brandy, Andreas, don't just stand there. As for this," she touched her bruise, "my sister gave me worse and hit me harder when we were growing up. If I could have gotten my pistol belt wrapped around my belly, I would have shot the bastard myself and saved Andreas the trouble."

"On behalf of Her Majesty, please, accept our apology, Countess," said the ambassador.

"Yes, yes, ok, I'm really tired of all this nice, nice B.S. I'm not a china doll, you know." She struggled up out of the chair. "I'm off to bed." She kissed Andreas and, with her three servants, waddled into the tent.

"I need to keep her away from Americans for a while," said Andreas, "her English is picking up a lot of their bad habits."

"We are going to make you overall commander of this group," said the general. "You have a good grasp on the situation and, with the exception of the Third Hussars, you have a good working relationship with our troops."

"I would rather not, sir, I really don't have enough experience," replied Andreas. "Why not make Major von Hoaedle the overall commander? He is a veteran with a lot more experience and is a part of your command chain already."

"Thank you, Andreas, but no," said Rudy. "A major cannot give orders to a colonel and members of my regiment are not allowed to command British troops."

"That rule is all poppycock, too," said the general. "I served with the major; he gave the commands, I followed, we won; I got all the credit. How about this then, Rudy, you are promoted to the vacant Lieutenant Colonel's position, you command under direction of Andreas and he takes your advice?"

"Oh, what a tangled web we weave," laughed Rudy. "That should work. You know, I learned all I know from Andreas's father, and I only spent two years with him, not a lifetime like Andreas. Andreas has already shown me some things I did not know before, but sure, I will work with him."

"That's settled then," said the general. "Combined with your reports, Andreas, our intelligence is telling us the enemy is massing its forces just across the border. We think they want to make a statement, so will be attacking here in force. You have been experiencing larger raids lately. I think they are probes. The way you keep defeating them, they cannot let you continue without losing credibility with their men. I will also be leaving behind one of my captains. He is from one of our colonies; his government has high hopes for him and sent him here to gain some experience. Perhaps assign him to one of the Americans? They speak a similar language, I believe.

"Very well, then, I have had a long day and I must be off to Kabul in the morning, Mr. Wiggam will be staying behind to keep an eye on things. Thank you for the brandy, good evening."

"Alright, gentlemen, we can't start the meeting at the regular time," Andreas said. "It seems we need a replacement from the medical department; the ladies that have decided they are looking out for Elizabeth will not allow her to participate, so here we wait.

I have also decided to include the new British commander in our Sunday ritual, and he's not here yet either."

"Oh great, another pretty boy Brit," said Patrick. "I hope this one has half a brain. Here comes the walking target now, he's got Rudy with him," he continued.

A red-coated and pith-helmeted officer was accompanying Rudy to the tarp-covered table.

"Morning, Rudy," said Johann, "*Ut* oh, excuse me, Colonel, sir."

"Now, the neighborhood has gone to hell," said William, "too many colonels around here, I'm moving."

"*Ja, ja,*" said Rudy, throwing a sloppy wave in Andreas's general direction as way of a salute.

Before anything else could be done, Irene came skidding to a halt beside the other two new arrivals.

Andreas held up his hand as Irene was about to speak. "English only at this meeting," he said.

Irene nodded, gave a salute and held it. "Acting Colonel Bekenbaum reporting, sir."

"Oh, I'm getting a headache," said Johann, earning him a punch on the arm from Irene. "I'd like to report abuse of a junior officer, Colonel."

"Suck it up, Johann," said Andreas, looking at the new officer still standing at attention. "You are?"

The red-coated officer raised his right foot and stomped it on the ground and snapped a smart salute. "Captain Ian McDonald, First Canadian Cavalry Regiment reporting for duty, sir!" yelled out the captain.

283

"Good, I'm not the junior officer anymore," said Peter.

"Aye, bloomin' colonial," said William.

"Do they even have an army in Canada?" said Patrick.

"What's a 'Canada'?" asked Ivan.

Andreas stood, returned the captain's salute crisply, then stuck his hand out for a handshake. "Welcome to our little command, Captain, take a seat."

"Not you, Irene, stick out your right hand." He then tapped her on the wrist with two fingers.

"I told the general I would reprimand you for your lack of marksmanship the other day, and now I have; you may find a seat."

"Ok, starting today," Andreas said, "we integrate those Hussars into our patrols, get them out there to learn how to be soldiers. Johann, Ivan, I want ten-man deep reconnaissance patrols. We need to know when and where the enemy are staging and going to. If we can hit them hard first, that would be good. Try and find a spot for that. Stan, if you could schedule some time with William? His Civil War experience may assist you with defenses around here; they may flank us or we may have to fall back to here for last ditch. The general feels we will be hit any time after the first of August, we need to be ready. We need to hold them long enough for the British infantry to catch them in the rear.

"We have been extremely lucky. Including red jackets, we are going to start having casualties; those coats are bullet magnets. Irene, will your people be ready? Once it starts for real, it's going to get real bad real quick."

"Da, as good as we can be," Irene said.

"Rudy, how good are the Hussars' carbines?"

"Not much good over a hundred yards, Andreas, maybe a hundred fifty, effective range about three hundred."

"I think what we will do is have four groups of five hundred and do leap-frog maneuvers," Andreas said. "We need to draw them into a frontal charge. We'll start off using standard tactics; once they commit, we change to our new tactics. It will probably end up in a running battle. If they flank us, we withdraw and try again. Everyone but the Hussars I want practicing it. Rudy, you and I will discuss my idea on how to utilize them later. Anyone have anything else? Ok, everyone but Peter and Ian, go do what you have to do."

"Well, my young Canadian friend," Andreas said. "We are about to find out where you are going to fit in around here. Peter, one of my horses for Ian, here, and firearms for yourself. Come on, Ian."

Andreas grabbed his Winchester and followed by Ian, walked towards where the horses were held. They mounted and rode outside town to where the target range was located, tied up the horses to the rail there, and walked over to where a series of man-sized targets were located.

"Know what this is?" asked Andreas, showing Ian the Winchester.

"Sir, Winchester repeating rifle, .44 caliber center fire cartridge, muzzle velocity. . ."

"Yes, yes. Here," said Andreas, handing him his rifle and a box of bullets, pointing at a target fifty yards away. "Five rounds, please."

Ian took the rifle, put ten cartridges in the magazine, and carefully sighted on the target from the standing position. The first shot was high to the right, but on target. The next four were in the center.

"Ok, good. Peter, hand him yours."

Ian laid Andreas's rifle on a makeshift table and picked up Peter's. Andreas pointed to another target one hundred yards away. Ian sighted on it, first shot to the left, the other four in the center. Andreas had him switch rifles again, this time pointing to the two hundred yard target. This time, Ian went to one knee, all five shots hitting the center of the target. The last was at the three hundred-yard target with Peter's rifle. For this one, Ian wrapped the rifle sling around his left arm, laid on the ground, and carefully shot his five rounds. The bullets struck the kill zone in the center of the target, but were slightly scattered.

"Now this." Andreas handed Ian his pistol butt first and pointed at a target twenty-five yards away.

Carefully sighting, Ian placed all five rounds in the center of the target and expertly reloaded it.

Taking Peter's Colt, he was instructed to shoot the fifty-yard target and four of the five shots were in the kill zone, the fifth was still on the target.

Andreas raised an eyebrow and pointed at the weapons.

"I was on the evaluation team for these weapons at the Department of Defense, sir," Ian said. "I've fired hundreds of rounds through them. The rifle version of the Winchester was a good choice; the extra two inches of barrel makes it more accurate for not much more weight or loss of mobility."

The two Cossack officers next had Ian perform a series of mounted cavalry drills, which proved he was a more than competent horseman.

"We will assume you know how to use a lance and sword, what with the British love of the things," said Andreas.

"Yes, sir, first in my class, sir," Ian replied.

"Alright, welcome to the battalion, Ian," Andreas said. "We have a rule here; no one can join the battalion who does not pass those tests. Peter, show Ian where he can quarter, and then bring your gear over, Ian, and report back to me. How many horses do you have?"

"Only the one I rode in on, sir," Ian said.

"Peter, have someone find him a couple of remounts." Andreas dismissed both men and walked back to his headquarters, he was becoming concerned about Elizabeth.

When he arrived, she was sitting under the tarp sipping a cup of tea. When he bent down to kiss her cheek, she pulled his head to her and kissed him long on the lips.

"Ah, my lady is in a much better mood this morning," Andreas said.

"Yes, my jailers made me sleep until just now. I'm sorry I missed the meeting, my love," she said, not letting go of his hand while he sat next to her.

"The bruising has gone down a lot, love, it's almost back to normal. Is the little monster behaving today?" Andreas asked. They had taken to calling the soon-to-come baby 'the little monster'.

"Oh, yes. He is not so angry anymore; now I think he is just impatient, like his mother. We have a new officer?"

"Yes, a captain, from someplace called Canada," Andreas said. "It's a British colony somewhere. His accent is not quiet English, more like American. The Americans seem to know about them; it must be close to America. He did very well at the range, qualified expert, in fact."

"Is he like those other British officers?" Elizabeth asked.

"Not that I can see, Liz. He seems very polite and respectful, but he is still young. He must be very well connected to be a captain at that age. Ah, speak of the devil."

As was their habit when alone, they had been speaking in German; Andreas switched to English.

"Captain Ian McDonald of Canada, my wife Elizabeth. Elizabeth, Captain Ian McDonald of Canada," introduced Andreas.

Ian snapped to attention and bowed his head. "A pleasure, Gräfin Bekenbaum. On behalf of myself and my country, I would like to apologize for the behavior of my predecessor," he said in perfect High German.

"The pleasure is all mine, Captain," replied Elizabeth also in German. "You do not have a last name that would suggest Germanic heritage."

"We live in a German community; my mother and her family emigrated from Brunswick. My father grew up in the next town and purchased the farm next to my mother's father's farm," Ian explained.

"So, you are landowners, then, that would explain your captaincy at such a young age," Elizabeth remarked.

A sad smile crossed the young man's face, "Yes, we are landowners, if you can call two hundred acres a lot of land. We make enough to feed and clothe ourselves, pay our taxes, and send our children to school. There is usually a little left over for other things, but we are not rich. Our parish priest noticed that I did well in school and sent my name in to the government as a possible candidate for the new officers training. I was selected, and the whole community pitched in to help pay my room and board."

Elizabeth looked at Andreas and said fondly, "Sounds like someone I know. It must be difficult being so far from home?"

"I miss my brothers and sisters," Ian said. "There are ten of us. The girl I was seeing is probably married by now, but we were not very serious, and I have been away from home for four years now."

"It must be a challenge serving with those class-conscious snobs though," said Andreas.

"Some days are worse than others, sir. They can be brutal to those they feel are inferior to them. But like my mother says, 'That which doesn't kill you. . .'"

"Makes you strong," Elizabeth and Andreas finished for him, laughing.

Seeing Stan walking by, Andreas called him over. "Stan, could you run the captain, here, over and kit him out in some tunics and proper head gear?" he asked in English. "I don't mind if he gets shot, but he will be standing next to me and our enemies are not good shots and might hit me by mistake. You can have the rest of the day, Captain, be here for dinner and lose the red jacket."

"I think you like him," said Elizabeth after the two men had left.

"Not as much as I like you," Andreas said. They spent the rest of the day together under the watchful eyes of Elizabeth's now four female servants.

As expected, the raids stopped. Reports from travelers told of increasing numbers of armed men congregating on the other side of the border. The long-range patrols now included four or five armed local tribesmen that showed the troopers areas of likely ambush, places they could regroup to if they had to, and escape routes. Andreas kept visiting local villages, Ian beside him, although only one or two per day. Elizabeth entertained Ian at night, swapping stories of home life. Ian was slowly becoming a part of the inner circle, as first Elizabeth then Andreas warmed to him.

The Sunday morning meeting saw Andreas passing around a sketch of how he wanted the troops deployed when the inevitable clash occurred. Ideas from the group were debated, and changes to the plan agreed upon and made.

"Ok, Ian, you've been here long enough," said Andreas as he tossed a small box at him. "The eagle goes on the left, the rifles on the right. Welcome to the battalion, Ian."

Johann and Ivan, sitting on either side of Ian, pummeled him on the back, then pinned the insignia in the proper places on his tunic collar. Everyone banged on the table and hollered their congratulations, while calling out for a toast.

Suddenly, Elizabeth gasped, grabbed her belly, and looked down. The four serving women broke into immediate action, one sprinting into the tent, one yelling at the male servers, and two gingerly picking Elizabeth out of her chair and heading off in the direction of the medical compound.

Just after midnight, a worried Andreas was summoned to the medical tent. A group of local women some twenty strong had surrounded the tent, letting no males, not even the doctors, come near. Now as he walked toward the tent, women were calling out, all smiles, some dancing. Local males were coming out on the street, surrounding him, laughing and pummeling him on the back, some were firing rifles in the air. The night sky was filled with people milling about excitedly.

The head imam of Kandahar was waiting for him outside the tent and, together, Andreas and the imam entered and walked to Elizabeth's side. She was clearly tired; someone had washed her hair and her face, and a blanket-smothered package with only a tiny face poking out of it was in her arms, snuggled on her breasts. One of the female servants, the eldest, whispered into the imam's ear, then smiled at Andreas and backed away.

"My lord, Andreas," the imam said in flawless Russian, "your son is healthy, has taken his first breath, and his first milk. His mother did not suffer and should recover quickly. They are both sleeping now, and the ladies would like us to leave, so mother and child may rest."

Andreas softly walked to the cot that held mother and child and knelt by their side, making the sign of the cross, the imam came and knelt beside him.

"Thank you, Lord, for allowing this boy to enter our world and for allowing his mother the joy of watching him grow to be your loving servant, Your Will be done," prayed Andreas softly, head bowed.

The imam also began to pray; the women in the room falling to their knees when he had finished, they all bent to the ground and kissed it three times. The imam rose and beckoned Andreas to follow and they left the tent as quietly as they had entered. The

291

imam explained that he had given the same prayer of thanks that Andreas had and asked why Andreas was so glum. Andreas was walking head down with his hands behind his back, when what had happened sunk in. He had a son; his wife was fine; he was a father. He stopped in his tracks and looked about at all the smiling faces about him, at his friends standing close, at the smiling imam.

He pulled his pistol from his belt and jumping up and down, both arms raised in the air, emptied the chamber into the sky, yelling, "I have a son; I have a son!" And the party was on.

Just after midday, six women from the medical company supervised by the four sisters-in-law, pulled Andreas out of the chair he had passed out on at dawn, carried him over to a nearby water trough, and dumped him in it.

"How dare you!" Andreas's sister Marie yelled at a sputtering Andreas. "You lying here drunk, while Lizbet is crying, thinking her husband doesn't love her any more. You haven't been to see her yet. How about your beautiful son? Don't you even care?"

"Whoa, whoa. I was there last night; the imam and I prayed by their side, then we were thrown out by you women," he said, trying to defend himself.

"That is no excuse; you should have been there when she woke up," scolded Irene, punching him in the arm.

Katia came and put her arms around him. "She knows Andreas; she woke up while you were praying," she whispered in his ear. "Come now, get cleaned up, she is calling for you."

Half an hour later, a cleaned up Andreas was ushered into Elizabeth's presence. She was sitting in a chair holding their son close to her breast. Her blonde hair spilling golden across her shoulders. She was smiling, stroking the baby's cheek. Andreas stood watching mother and son from the doorway for some minutes, before something drew Elizabeth's eyes to him. Sudden tears began to well in her eyes.

"You have a son, my lord," she said, her voice quivering.

"Yes and he is already claiming what is mine. What will he be like when he gets older?" Andreas said with a laugh.

"Get your butt over here," Elizabeth laughed, holding her free arm out to him. When the serving women came in, they found the couple—Andreas sitting on the floor his head on his wife's shoulder, both looking in wonder at their child.

"I want to see Captain McDonald and the three troopers on punishment duties at their earliest convenience," Andreas ordered his officer of the day.

"Sir, you wanted to see me, sir?" Ian said, saluting.

"Grab a coffee and a chair," Andreas said in English. "I am about to give you your first three Cossack troopers."

"Corporal Schmid and party of two as ordered, sir!" the corporal said in German, standing at stiff attention in the center of the group. All three men with caps under left arms, heads staring above Andreas's head.

Andreas tossed a small box at the corporal.

"You are out of uniform, gentlemen," Andreas said. "I have decided to give you back your eagles, but on condition. You will be the good captain here's bodyguards. If you perform adequately, I will allow you to rejoin your squadron."

"Captain, you will take charge of these three probationary combat troopers and will report back to me on their progress on becoming once again combat-ready troopers. Dismissed."

Chuckling to himself as the four men, left he wondered who would learn the most, the uptight young officer or the laid back troopers.

"Why, Lizbet? It only requires a priest and some of our friends." Andreas was always uncomfortable being on public display and this time was no different.

"No, you are their lord, they deserve to see and acknowledge his heir," she had said. "I will hear no more on the subject."

So here they sat, waiting for the last troops to form up, dressed in their best dress uniforms complete with sashes and swords. A large number of locals were grouped along the fringes of the assembled troops, dressed in their best clothing, quietly observing. The British, including Rudy's battalion, were in their dress uniforms assembled to the left of Andreas's troops in their red glory.

Only one splash of color marred the blue uniforms of the Cossack battalion arrayed before them. Ian had donned his best mess red uniform and was assembled beside Peter.

Finally a nod from William and a call to attention from him signaled Andreas the time had come. Standing up and assisting Elizabeth out of her chair, then, hand-in-hand they walked to the front of the podium. Elizabeth handed their son to him and Andreas carefully placed him in the crook of his left arm, his white blanket standing out on Andreas's dark blue sleeve. In slow, even, carefully worded Russian, Andreas began rotating around in place so everyone assembled could view the baby.

"I am Andreas, son of Heinrich, Earl of Katherintal, clan of Bekenbaum. This is Stephan, son of Andreas, heir of Katherintal, clan of Bekenbaum. What is done to he and his, is done to me and mine. So say I."

"So say us all," came the massed response. "Hoorah! Hoorah! Hoorah!"

Then Johann began to sing in his deep baritone voice a slow Russian lullaby about the people and their love for their prince. After one line, the entire two thousand took up the song, leaving Andreas and Elizabeth struggling to keep their composure.

Stephan, true to his father's views on all things of this nature, slept through it all, even the priest pouring holy oil on his forehead and blessing him did not disturb him.

They had three days of peace. The fourth day, a reconnaissance troop sent out before dawn rode in, horses flecked with foam, riders worn. The reason they had come to Afghanistan was here.

Chapter Five

Andreas sent William, Patrick, and ten troopers, each trailing two remounts, out to verify the numbers and direction the enemy was coming from. He had the semaphore station send the preliminary report on its way to Kabul and began his final preparations for the action to come.

As night fell, the patrol was back and sweat-stained William and Patrick came directly to the command tent, passing their horses to the other troopers.

"I haven't seen that many cavalry since Gettysburg," William said. "There is fifteen thousand easy, all cavalry. They are coming slow, down the main route."

"Alright, better than hoped for. More of them than we were planning on, but such is life. We need to change the plan somewhat. Somebody get Stan, it's time for everyone to earn those rifles."

The brigade left at midnight and were in position before dawn. Now, they waited.

Today will be a good day, thought the emir as he finished his coffee. We will surround Kandahar, then the following morning, finish it off. Allah willing, the fool British would come out and fight like men. More likely, they would sit behind the walls like the cowards they were. No matter, it would be over and he would go back home a hero and raise one hundred thousand men because of this victory and finally drive the hated British from his land. The order was given and fifteen thousand men moved out in the direction of Kandahar.

Two hours later the scouts reported the British had come out, they were just over the hill waiting and as they crested the hill, Allah be praised, there they were. Lined up in two formations, one five hundred yards in front of the other. The first row had five hundred green-jacketed soldiers on the right and five hundred grey-jacketed on the left. These were cavalry, dismounted in a long skirmish line, every fourth man fifty yards behind holding three horses. These would not hold long.

Behind them were the hated red coats, one thousand men drawn up in two lines as expected. The fools did not even line up in squares or have bayonets attached to their rifles. This will be over quick, thought the emir as he watched the British commander, curiously in a grey uniform and a rifle held upright, braced on his thigh, riding slowly up and down behind his men. Now was the time, and he gave the order to form up.

Andreas watched the enemy horde ride over the hill and begin to form up, not in spread out formations as he had feared, but into a solid block of riders walking their horses knee to knee. He watched how they deployed, flags and pennants flying, lances being readied and swords being drawn, and he smiled. The Germans in the green uniforms began to sing, followed by the British in their grey stable jackets. When the head of the horde had reached three hundred yards from them, they fired two volleys from their carbines then mounted and raced back to the wings of Andreas's formation. The Afghan tribesman, who had joined the allies, began harassing the massed cavalry from both flanks as had been planned. The enemy began to bunch closer in to each other and soon they were packed tight together.

Andreas rode up and down the two lines of his now red-jacketed men. Up close you could tell the jackets didn't fit very well, some of them couldn't even be closed and the sleeves were

297

not down to the wrists, but from a distance, they would look like regular British soldiers. Stanislaw had taken the jackets from every British soldier in Kandahar for this ruse and it was working. It was vital that the enemy host be drawn on them. The odd man was fidgeting; who could blame them? He himself could feel his stomach churning at the sight of the large block of enemy approaching. As he rode, he started humming the Cossack song, and it wasn't long before all his men were singing it. Not the lewd version they used when on a long march, but the full version.

At four hundred yards, the enemy began to trot their horses and Andreas gave the order to load; each man chambered a round and replaced it, loading one into the magazine. The sound of horses' hooves like thunder and the ground began to tremble. The singing men picked up the pace of the song to match the pace of the oncoming horsemen, and they sang louder. Andreas cringed as the sound of singing voices appeared to be echoing all around the little valley. He ordered the men to present and the lines shimmered as they turned sideways and leveled the rifles at the enemy. At three hundred yards, he ordered the front rank to fire and five hundred Winchesters crashed out knocking a large number of the approaching horsemen from their saddles, the second rank fired with the same results. As expected, after the second rank fired, the enemy spurred into a charge. What they had not expected was the repeating rifles.

Row after row of horsemen went down screaming as .44 caliber bullets struck men from saddles and horses from feet. The rows behind would trip over the row in front and the bullets kept coming. After the front rank had fired five rounds, they reloaded while the rear rank kept firing and a constant five hundred bullets hit the approaching cavalry every three seconds. Horses could no longer climb the piled bodies and as they began to fan out, the second surprise was on the horse men, as five hundred rifles opened up on each unprotected flank. Bakers, butchers, blacksmiths, and all the tradesmen from the bear battalion ripped into them as fast as they could reload their rifles. They had lain hidden from view, their grey tunics blending in with the tall grass on each hill side. Then the carbines of the now dismounted cavalry troops began to hit them.

The front ranks of the enemy could not advance; they could not go out to the sides, and the rear ranks kept pushing from behind. The bullets kept hitting, knocking men and horses to the ground screaming. The advance had stalled and soon the rear ranks tried to pull away. Those that were not gunned down by the massed three thousand rifles were slaughtered by Afghan lancers as they tried to run away. Of the fifteen thousand horsemen, fourteen thousand lay dead or dying, the emir among them. None had reached closer than two hundred yards from the two red lines.

Rudy had lost two of his men, their horses had fallen during the mad dash back to the lines and been over-ridden by the horde. His men were searching for their bodies, any hope of them being alive slim. Four men from the Horse Guards were also missing. Twelve of his men from the support troops had been wounded from panicked horsemen trying desperately to escape the carnage had broken the support troops lines. Four of the wounded had broken limbs from being run over or kicked by horses. Eight had slash wounds of varying degrees, the worst being one severed arm and a leg. The wounded were being loaded on carts brought forward to transport them back to Kandahar under heavy guard.

Even had Andreas had the capacity to treat the massive casualties of the enemy, there was no way they would be able to do so. Thousands of local villagers descended on the fallen men, intent on looting and exacting revenge on the fallen for all the suffering they had endured during the raids. No amount of pleading for mercy by his troopers was listened to and on several occasions, Andreas's men had been threatened. Being unable to do anything and realizing it was rapidly becoming dangerous, Andreas pulled the troops out and headed back to Kandahar.

For the first hour on the trail, the silence was only broken by the sound of horses' hooves hitting the ground and rattling tack, or the occasional snort of a horse. The men and women who had taken part in the battle, lost in thought over what they had just witnessed. Four hundred and fifty lines of armed troopers, eight abreast stretched along the trail in silence. Andreas drifted up and down, first ensuring his inner circle, friends, and family were safe. Each man acknowledged each other with a nod and a look. Everyone Andreas encountered had a vague faraway gaze, deep in their thoughts.

Reaching the front of the line, crossing over, and allowing Bartholomew to be overtaken again by the columns, Andreas saw that as each column passed the troopers looked over at him, searching his expression, looking for something in him. When he reached the middle of the column, he verbalized his thoughts, at first softly, then louder, in a chant they had all learned and used their whole lives, every Sunday morning, but with his own words.

"We thank you, Lord, for protecting us this day, for allowing us to go home safe. We ask you, Lord, to look out for our injured, to ease their suffering, and help make them whole. We ask you, Lord, to accept into your bosom, our fallen comrades, who died to keep others safe. We ask you, Lord, to forgive our enemies, who were led astray of your great purpose. And we ask you, Lord, for forgiveness of the destruction we wrought this day."

He then started to chant the Lord's Prayer, which was picked up by all the three thousand in Russian, German, and English. After five minutes of silence, a trooper in the middle ranks began to slowly, in Russian, sing the Don Cossacks song, which was picked up by the two thousand Cossacks and slowly rose in cadence as the horses, picking up on their rider's mood, began to increase their pace. Soon at a trot, the mood shifted to one of joy and celebration.

They had survived.

Andreas spent the hour before sunset speaking with his inner circle, getting their verbal report on what they had seen. The North Americans had already written down notes on what they had experienced, and after receiving assurances the others would submit their written reports the next morning, Andreas had dismissed them. He spent most of the night writing his report. He singled out one of Rudy's troopers who had stood by one of his mates, firing continually while the man remounted his horse. Another was a British Lieutenant, who, at great personal risk, had spurred his horse back, grabbed a comrade who's horse had broken it's leg, and in the face of the approaching enemy, swung the man behind his back and galloped back to the safety of the lines.

The last mention was of McDonald. Three times he had stridden in front of the lines and shot enemies who had somehow evaded all the carnage of the main charge and had threatened to break the lines.

Andreas worked late into the night, his eyes burning from strain and lack of sleep when he felt he was finished, closed the large notebook, and went into the tent he and Elizabeth shared. He had not heard her come in, and she was sprawled on her belly across the cot they shared, tunic thrown across a chair, but otherwise fully clothed. Her face and hands stained black from the gun powder, disheveled blonde hair scattered around her. He brushed her hair behind her ear and gently kissed her cheek, tasting the gunpowder on it. Picking her tunic off the chair, he sat down folding it neatly, smelling the gunpowder, dust, and sweat on it. He sat watching her, lovingly stroking her tunic, smoothing out the wrinkles. How blessed he was, he thought, that this woman had chosen him among any numbers of men. This beautiful, intelligent, and courageous woman who, only weeks before, had borne him a son and then fought fiercely in a huge battle. He reached up to his collar, removed the eagle pinned there, and pinned it on the collar of her tunic above the bear and walked out to sleep in his chair under the stars.

He woke with a start, reaching for a nonexistent pistol, in his mind hearing hooves thundering and rifles blazing. Then realizing it was a dream looked about him. Elizabeth was seated across from him, Stephan at her breast having his breakfast. Today her open shirt and tunic were over a long skirt. Her face and hair shone in the sunlight and her green and gold-flecked eyes were lovingly focused directly in his blues. He saw the eagle he had pinned on her collar the night before sitting on the table in front of him.

"You and your bears earned those yesterday," he said.

"No, Andreas, no," she said. "We all wear our rifles and especially our bears with pride; we did well, no one can dispute that.

"It was not we who stood in the path and stood our ground in front of that wall of galloping horses, lances and swords pointed directly at us. It was not we who would have been wiped out had you failed. It was not me who rode his horse calmly up and down the line behind his men, giving them courage just by his calm presence behind them. It was not me who gave his rifle to the man in front of him when his rifle failed. It was not me who shot dead the enemy that was about to lance poor Ian when his rifle was empty, with his pistol on horseback.

"It was you who gave us all the courage to do what we did. If you could do it so calm, so reassured, who were we, on the outskirts, to do no less? No, my love, you showed what it means to wear the eagle. All of us thank God for providing you to us, and we know God was on our side. Did you know you had six holes in your tunic and your cap was shot off your head?"

"No, love, I don't remember any of that," Andreas said. "I did not even know I had fired my weapon. I have never been so scared in my life. The reason I was riding was because if I went down on the ground my legs would have collapsed, they were shaking so bad. I didn't want anyone to see how afraid I was."

"The first time I was in the line I shit myself," said a gruff voice behind him. The British commander had walked up on them unannounced.

"I was eighteen, a brash, pampered, and spoiled aristocrat, whose father had indulged by buying him a commission in a top battalion. We were in a double line, not unlike yours, five thousand of us facing down Napoleon's best infantry battalions. Son, anyone that tells you they were not scared was not there."

"My God, man, fifteen thousand horse and only your one thousand blocking them? I've been to the battlefield already. I could tell from the spent casings where your lines were and from the piled up, tangled bodies of horses and men, where you stopped them. Those were not raiding tribesmen, Andreas. They were highly trained cavalry troops that had already met and defeated some of our best Indian troops. We came here expecting, at best, to raise a siege. Instead, we find a defeated and smashed enemy and, I fear, the end of the great cavalry charge.

"If your government does not value you enough to reward you for this, I assure you, mine will. Earl and Countess

303

Bekenbaum, my country and myself thank you for what you have done here in our service."

Then he stepped back, called his aides to attention, and gave the Bekenbaums a parade ground salute before turning and marching away.

It was a time of joy and anticipation. Katia and Marie had given birth to healthy boys, and several of the other married women in the nursing core had given birth as well. The doctors had cleared all the wounded for travel, and preparations were well on the way for the battalion's return home.

British and Russian troops were now interacting as brothers, and while there were, at times, the occasional tussle among the men, it was more about young men having fun. Often a Russian and a Brit could be found in a scrap together as opposed to a scrap against each other.

"Countess, how ravishing you look. I can hardly believe you have just given birth to a beautiful baby boy," a British officer's wife said. "This beautiful red gown suits you; where ever did you find it?"

"Some of the local ladies sewed it for me. It is rather nice, they did a wonderful job on it," Elizabeth said.

"Who would have ever thought it?" the English woman said. "They are always dressed so drably."

"Not so, they wear very colorful and flattering clothing at home and under the hijab," Elizabeth said. "Their culture does not permit them to show it in public, is all. It is much like your taboo against a woman wearing pants or riding a horse without a side saddle. It really is ridiculous and pointless, if you think about it."

"Oh my, yes," said an older English woman. "How I envy you not wearing a corset and hoops. The bloody things are such a pain. What a wonderful party. Your ladies are so talented and the decorations are marvellous. Much better than in that smoky old fortress. So airy and bright."

"We have not had much chance to celebrate," Elizabeth said. "We have been so busy since we arrived. The girls insisted on it and I could do not but agree. The enlisted wives are doing the same on the other side of the camp."

"It is a shame that we all got off on the wrong side of things at the beginning," the younger woman said. "I am having so much fun. Your people's sense of a good party is much better than ours. Not so formal and stuffy."

"Life on the steppe is hard, for noble as well as farmer," Elizabeth said. "We have to rely on each other to survive, and when we have a chance to celebrate, we take it. Come, the meals are done and the dancing will start. We have been invited to the enlisted party, and much that I wish I could partake of the dancing, I am really not dressed for it."

The group of officers and diplomats, British and Russian with their wives on their arms, moved out of the pavilion where they had consumed their dinner and slowly walked the short distance to the other side of the camp, where several large tarps had been strung together to form a large canvas roof over several fires. Groups of men and women were gathered around the fires, and musicians were playing their homemade instruments, some people singing along, others sharing gossip or good stories with each other. Some of the women were dancing around the fires where singing was happening, and the men were clapping hands in time to the music.

"I have seen this dance before," Wiggam's wife said. "It is a folk dance, I assume? They do it so gracefully, almost as if their feet are not even moving."

"Yes, it is a folk dance, almost a courtship dance, actually," Katia said. "The girls are showing they are available, but you can see by how they hold their heads they are not interested in being bothered by the lads just yet."

"The steps are easy; come, I will show you," Elizabeth said. "Irene, Katia, Marie! Come, let us show our guests how we dance."

Taking Mrs. Wiggam by the hand, Elizabeth strode to one of the fire-lit circles and started to move, one hand on her hip and her eyes cast to the stars.

"See, we swirl a little this way, then a little that," she said, guiding Mrs. Wiggam. "We flick our hips to the right, then to the left, then we spin to swirl our skirts, just high enough to show an ankle."

The group were starting to get the hang of it, and the watching crowd were slapping their hands loudly to the beat, shouting out encouragement to the ladies, and when the song finished, the ladies were treated to loud applause and shouts of approval.

"I feel like a young girl again," Mrs. Wiggam said flushed, her ample breasts heaving. "Our farmers have similar dances back home, but they would never permit us to join in."

"Not for the first time do I feel sorry for you, Mrs. Wiggam," Elizabeth said. "Your society is so structured, so strict. Russian nobility is much the same. Not so with us."

"No," Irene said. "Live for today, have fun and joy, because tomorrow we may die." She was draped all over Johann, her large belly portraying to the world she was close to her delivery date.

The music started up again, and Elizabeth, caught up in the moment, started swaying and soon found her feet moving once again—Katia on one side and Marie on the other. This time there was something more in their movements, they were gesturing outwards, then inwards. First the right hand then the left. The beat was slow and measured, then stopped for half a beat and picked up speed.

Three men entered the circle, the observers whooping in appreciation. Andreas, Peter, and Ivan began the male counter movements to the dance. The women looked anywhere but at them. One by one each man made a dance step and challenged the others to match it. One by one they did.

The music picked up speed, and the three men picked up their pace with it, now spinning, now jumping, all around the three women, who now danced back to the edge of the circle leaving the center to the men.

The three brothers-in-law were in a world of their own, hearts and minds deep in the music and the clapping hands, as one at a time they sank to their knees and swirled their legs around, then jumped to a squat, arms crossed on chests and started kicking their legs out, springing up off the ground and squatting again over and over. The first one out was Patrick, he had not done this dance for many years; the next was Andreas, he had been behind a desk too long the last few weeks.

All that was left in the center was Ivan, and he took full advantage of it, moving around the perimeter, then back to the center, faster and faster he went. Then the song slowed down again and Katia joined him, linking arms, her right with his left out at shoulder height until the music slowed almost to a stop and they came together face to face as the last beat thrummed.

"Kiss her you fool, or I will!" Andreas yelled.

The crowd roared as Ivan kissed Katia in the center of the ring, picking her up of the ground. And roared even loader when she punched him on the shoulder right after, but kissed him right back.

"Our culture does not allow for the same mixed dancing and celebration that your people had last night, great lord," the young tribal leader said in his accented English. "But we hope you enjoy our effort to thank you and your people with this modest feast."

"Not at all," Andreas said. "Good food, good conversation, good friends, this is all a man can ask for."

"My people have taken your advice about the poppy and other things, great lord. We will strive to be self-sufficient and, being far from the center of power, we may even succeed. But you have given us the chance and the training to do better for ourselves and our children. Our imam has seen how you do things and he agrees. Our women have seen, as we have, how your women can be strong, yet still women. This, we see is what makes you strong, and we shall do much of the same.

"We are afraid of new things or change. This is hard for my people, but our old ones understand that it must be so and we have vowed to become different. This is thanks to you, great lord. Many times my people have tried to become part of the modern world, but many times those that resist change attack us for this. You have given us the time and the skills to build resistance to those who would take us back in time. We thank you for this."

"Thank you for listening," Andreas said. "There are those in my own country that do not listen and, thus, are doomed to fail. I am not a great leader, my friend. I am but just a man who has had the luck to be in the right place at the right time."

"May this continue to be so, Andreas, we need more men like you."

"From your lips to God's ear," the imam said in way of a toast.

Correspondents from all the major European countries had descended like locusts, pestering everyone who had been at the battle, and Remington's sketches of events were in great demand.

Everyone in the inner circle, including Remington, were having a good laugh at one artist's rendition. It showed Andreas, surrounded by his men, some dying at his feet, straddling Elizabeth who was clutching his legs with one hand the other holding a staff, Russian flag billowing in the wind, while Andreas was shooting down a glaring enemy on a terrified horse with upraised sword.

Below the sketch was the caption, 'The gallant Hero of Russia rallies his troops.'

As Andreas posed in mock gallantry one hand on hip, head upraised, Elizabeth went to her knees before him, clutching a leg with one arm, the other reaching the heavens.

"My lord, my brave Hero of Russia, save me from these savage beasts," she cried in mock terror. Then, sniffing his rear she said, "Oh my, what's that terrible smell?"

"I'll have you know, dear lady, that the Hero of Russia's shit never stinks," Andreas said.

It was five minutes before all present could control themselves, then Johann made sniffing noises and they were all laughing again.

As a condition for an interview with an English newspaper, Elizabeth had a number of photographs taken. One with Andreas sitting in his full dress uniform, hand on sword. One with he and Elizabeth in full dress uniform. One was taken with Andreas and Elizabeth holding Stephan. Another photograph was taken with the family members all in uniform. One with the command group and, finally, one of the Eagles and one of the Bears as groups.

Finally, at the insistence of the photographer, a picture was taken of Andreas and Elizabeth mounted on their horses, in field uniforms, rifles slung on their backs and hands on holstered pistols.

Then, suddenly, they who had done and endured so much without so much as a scratch suffered their first loss.

Irene had had a rough pregnancy and was overdue when she went into labor. It lasted all through the day and most of the night before the almost exhausted Irene gave birth to a healthy baby girl. Johann's initial joy turned to concern, as the doctors, no matter what they did, could not stop the internal bleeding. Two days later, surrounded by the family, she died.

No amount of coaxing could pry Johann's arms from around her until Andreas knelt beside him, put his arm around him, and laid his head on Johann's shoulder. Then, Johann took a deep breath, gave one last kiss to her pale lips, brushed a stray strand of hair from her forehead, made the sign of the cross, and stood. Both brothers, arm-in-arm, tears silently streaming down their cheeks, walked into the night.

Two days later, Johann, holding his newborn daughter, watched as they lowered Irene's lovingly made coffin into the ground beside the two bear troopers who had died from their wounds. The grave was filled, the last hymn sung, and the volley fired. The battalion and all the well-wishers had all left. Johann stood gently caressing his daughter, looking into the distance.

"God's will be done," he said, then Andreas and Elizabeth on each side of him, walked away.

The next day, the battalion left for home.

Chapter Six

By the end of October, they were camped outside the port in Georgia waiting for their transport back to Odessa. Unlike the trip into Afghanistan, the trip home was not slowed by continual delays waiting for supplies or held at borders. There had been no choice but to delay for two days in Tehran, the capitol of Iran. The Shah had insisted on meeting Andreas and, this time, Elizabeth, hosting them to a grand reception, where he expressed his thanks and showered them with gifts of gold and rich silks. The raiders had been hurting his country as well, disrupting trade routes and burning villages.

Johann had named his daughter Susanna Irene and the tiny girl had twenty-five aunts fussing over her every need. Two of the nurses had lost their babies to disease on the trip home and one of them had immediately become surrogate mother to Susanna removing the need of Katia, Marie, and Elizabeth to share feeding duties. A delegation of all the nurses had insisted it was unseemly for a great lady to nurse her own child, and a reluctant Elizabeth had agreed to the second woman who had lost her child nursing Stephan as well.

Johann had resumed his duties, and while he was still mindful and diligent, the wit and humor was gone. He spent most of his days and all of his nights in seclusion. Elizabeth spent her days unobtrusively pumping the North Americans, especially Peter and Ian, for information on the lands they came from. What the land was like, the people, how good the crops were, what the weather was like. Before the battle, Ian had told Andreas that his country was going to open the interior for settlement to keep the Americans from encroaching on their territory. Although only inhabited by raving bands of nomadic peoples and great herds of wild animals, the land was fertile and surveys had been completed on the best places for settlement. A great railroad was being planned to connect the interior to the more populous areas.

Andreas had arranged for Wiggam to bring out from Kabul a representative from Canada. The man had been very helpful, providing Andreas with some literature on the country, some maps, and letters of introduction to officials in the consulate at Odessa.

One day during the trip to the coast, Ian had been asked to accompany Andreas and Elizabeth on their daily ride outside the main column of troops.

"I wonder if you could clear something up for me, Ian," Andreas said. "You say your country is a dominion, but independent of England, what does this mean?"

"We are not a Republic, like the United States," Ian said. "The Queen is still our head of state and the ultimate final say in government affairs, but we have self-determination. We make and enforce our own laws and elect our own representatives to a House of Parliament, which is responsible for the governance of the country to the betterment of all. The country is broken up into different provinces, which have their own parliaments responsible for local administration of that province."

"Much like our system then," said Andreas. "Do you have local aristocrats as governors?"

"We have a governor general, who is the Queen's direct representative for the whole country, and lieutenant governors for the provinces. While at the moment, they are all British appointed and technically have the power to impose their wills, they would find it very difficult, if not impossible to do so. They are mostly figureheads."

"Tell us about these wild lands you want to inhabit. Are they like the American badlands? Full of robber barons and lawlessness?" Elizabeth said.

"We are forming a national police force," Ian said. "Which I hope to be a part of, to control that kind of thing. By settling the land with farm communities on a regulated basis, the type of things that are going on in the States should be minimized. We have and are perusing good relations with the native peoples, not like the Americans who see them as impediments.

"I have heard from people who have been there," Ian continued, "that the region to the east of the great mountain range that runs down the western edge of the country is not unlike your steppes. It has rolling areas of great plains, grass areas, and forested hills."

That night, snuggled together under their blanket, Elizabeth asked, "Will they allow us to go?"

"We are becoming too powerful to ignore, but not powerful enough to stop them from squashing us if they want to. They will find a way to get rid of us, they always do. If we handle this right, it should not be a problem," Andreas said.

"Are we agreed? This Canada, then?" she asked, reaching for him.

"My lady's wish is my command," he said, responding to her eager touch.

Rudy came to see him the next morning. He and his battalion had accompanied them on the way back. They would be going home and it was faster to go this way than wait for the transport ships to take them up to the North Sea. "Andreas, I wonder if we could impose on you for a week? My lads could use a break before we leave again," he said.

314

"Of course," Andreas replied. "All of our people will be going back to their homes as soon as we return. There will be lots of room."

"Thank you," he said, "and I would like to speak with you at that time on another matter, as well."

"All right, then," Andreas said. "We will be loading first, so I should have all the political nonsense over by the time you and your troops land. If not, I will make sure Ivan or Johann escort you to the villa."

The rest of the day was spent packing everything but the essentials, and as dawn was breaking, the camp was on the move and loading on the waiting British transport ships.

They were unloaded at Odessa harbor quickly; the British commodore in charge of the flotilla promising Andreas the rest of his troops would be in port and unloaded by dark. Military personnel were on hand to shepherd the troopers to their bivouac area, while the field grade officers and their wives were to be billeted in the same hotel they had used on the outbound trip. Andreas had insisted on Ian being a part of the hotel contingent, saying he was his aide and necessary.

When they had arrived at the hotel, Andreas took Ian aside. "I know you have to report in with your people," Andreas said. "Tell them I have not released you from duty with me yet, but should do so by the end of the month. I will be using you as a middleman between them and me. That's all you need to know right now."

"Yes, sir," said Ian.

"Oh, yes. Ask them if I could schedule a meeting with them at some point in the next three days. I will let you know when, as soon as I find out what my schedule is."

"Sir," Ian said, saluting.

No sooner had Andreas and Elizabeth, with nurse, been shown their suite, than the inevitable aide was at the door requesting Andreas's presence to the commander. Andreas, having anticipated it, pulled the thick copy of the report of the campaign he had made for the general out of his saddle bag, tucked it under his arm, kissed Elizabeth, and followed the aide out of the hotel.

"Colonel Andreas Bekenbaum reporting as ordered, sir!" Andreas said to the general's back.

"Yes, yes, sit down," the viscount said, waving a hand at his forehead by way of return salute. "Here, have one of these, you look like you can use one," he said as he handed Andreas a glass of brandy.

"Is this your report?" he asked, taking the thick file from Andreas and tossing it on his desk. He sat down behind the desk, "You didn't really shoot that man as we heard, surely you had him shot, correct?"

"No, sir, I really shot him, on the spot, and reprimanded the major for not doing her duty and protecting her commander better," Andreas said.

"Really, Andreas, discipline is good, but that is surely going too far. The poor woman did the best she could under the circumstance. I would like to meet the young lady in person at her earliest convenience," he said.

"I am afraid that won't be possible, my lord, she is dead," said Andreas.

"My God, man, that was going too far!" an outraged viscount said.

"Oh, I am sorry, sir, you misinterpreted what I said. She was my brother's wife, sir, and a week after the battle, she died in childbirth, sir," Andreas said hastily.

"Oh my, how terrible for him. How is he holding up? I don't think I would survive long if that happened to me."

"He gets a little better every day," Andreas replied. "Life must go on, sir, and he loves his daughter dearly."

"Yes, life is like that sometimes," said the general thoughtfully.

"Fifteen thousand, fifteen thousand," he continued, "everyone is very impressed, Andreas. We knew you would do well, but this is incredible. They were first class troops, too, not tribesmen."

"First class troops, maybe," Andreas said. "Courageous, yes. Ill lead, yes. The man attacked us with no intelligence, no scouting, and using tactics that were obsolete fifty years ago. He used a frontal assault against modern weapons and paid the price for it. Had he used different tactics, this would have been much different and the price we paid would have been a lot higher."

"Yes, but still the glory, the magnificence," the viscount said. "Tomorrow, you will parade and present your battalion before us. We and the people of Odessa need to see the valiant warriors who did such wondrous deeds in our name. Two in the afternoon, I think, with a reception for the field officers at eight. Oh, and before I forget, here is a briefing on what we would like you to undertake next year," he said, handing Andreas a thick packet of papers. The interview was clearly over as an aide opened the office door and motioned for Andreas, the viscount already reading the after action report Andreas had given him.

Andreas slammed the door to the suite behind him and tossed the orders onto a chair.

317

"He wants a show, Liz, a God damned show. Not even five minutes to relax," he blurted out, then stomped back to the door and flung it open leaning into the hallway.

"Get your asses in here, right now," he hollered into the hallway before stalking back into the suite.

"Settle down, my love, you know not to make decisions when you're upset," Elizabeth said with her hand on his shoulder.

All the majors, male and female of his inner court came running into the suite.

With a sneering voice, Andreas said, "The viscount will have a parade, I think, at two, I think, with a reception for field officers at eight, I think. We'll give him a parade, all right. Everyone in field uniforms, with weapons, in route march formation, wagons included. Make it happen."

By noon, everyone was assembled, last-minute adjustments were being completed as Rudy's battalion reached the field. They were in their best uniforms all a glimmer in their shiny brass buttons and helmets. Lances tips gleamed brightly in the sunlight.

"Very pretty," said Andreas to Rudy.

"Making another statement, are we, Colonel?" said Rudy.

"No, not at all, Lieutenant Colonel, the viscount said the people wanted to see the heroes, so we are going to show them the heroes. You go in first; we will follow, wouldn't want to make all those shiny uniforms dirty now, would we?" he replied with a smile. "He wants us there at two, its one thirty now. How much time will you need, ten minutes?"

"Should be enough time, why?"

"I don't want to run you over when we enter the square at two," Andreas said.

Andreas looked down the line at his loosely formed columns of eight. Ian's red jacket the only color in a sea of grey. The only thing polished was the rifle barrels over left shoulders. Female officers were beside their troopers, rifles slung across their backs, any with babies had them in specially designed harnesses against their breasts leaving their arms free to move.

"Battalion will prepare to march at the trot!" shouted Andreas, "March!"

The sound of over two thousand horses trotting down cobble stoned streets was overpowering, as was the cheering the crowds lined up along the path gave them as they passed. Dignitaries were still rushing to their seats as the battalion burst in to governor's palace courtyard, the viscount and his party having just enough time to return the salute of the first eight to pass them. The courtyard was soon filled with the sounds of trotting horses, officers yelling commands, and rattling wagon wheels, as each troop expertly wheeled in to its designated place and came to a halt. Each squadron's commander rode to the center front, and Andreas and Elizabeth walked their horses along the front of the squadrons until they were in the center of the formation.

Then came the shouted reports from, first, sergeants to under officers, then under officers to squadron commanders, then squadron commanders to Andreas.

Andreas presented a hand salute and shouted, "Viscount Odessa, Bears and Eagles all present or accounted for!"

The Viscount returned the salute and rather shakily said, "At ease."

"Battalion, prepare to dismount, dismount," shouted Andreas. The battalion dismounted in unison, holding horses with right hands. "At ease," he shouted again, and the thump of two thousand boots hitting the ground reverberated in the courtyard.

"Men and women of Andreashost and King's Loyal German Battalion," began the Viscount, "we have assembled you here to express our appreciation of the successful completion of your mission. A hazardous mission, which despite facing overwhelming odds, was completed with minimal loss of life or injury. On behalf of Mother Russia, I express our gratitude." He then stood back and a man in a British General Officer's red uniform strode forward.

"Men and women of the combined expeditionary force," he began in English. "On behalf of Her Britannic Majesty Victoria, we wish to congratulate you on your accomplishments and reward you with the following citations.

"Captain Ian McDonald, Canadian First Cavalry Division; Lieutenant Colonel Rudolf von Hoaedle, King's Loyal German Cavalry, you are awarded the Distinguished Service Medal for your actions on the battle field.

"Lieutenant Siegfried Hesselman, King's Loyal German Cavalry, at great personal risk, in the face of great odds, for the rescue of a fellow trooper, you are awarded the Victoria Cross.

"Majors, Ivan Makarov, Katia Makarov, Johann Bekenbaum, Irene Bekenbaum, Patrick Molotov, William Olynick, Peter Adamentzuk, Marie Adamentzuk, you are, by permission of the czar, awarded the Distinguished Conduct Medal.

"Lieutenant Colonel Elizabeth Bekenbaum is awarded the Military Cross. Colonel Andreas Bekenbaum is awarded the Distinguished Service Order.

"The Andreashost is awarded a Distinguished Unit Citation.

"Lieutenant Colonel von Hoaedle and Colonel Bekenbaum are inducted into the Order of Bath and recognized as Knights of the Realm."

The general then took a step back and was replaced by Viscount Asmanov.

"By order of Czar Alexander, all enlisted troopers of Bear Squadron are awarded the Cross of St. George, Fourth Class, all non-commissioned officers of Bear Squadron, the Cross of St. George, Third Class. All enlisted troopers of Eagle Squadron are awarded the Cross of St. George, Second Class, all non-commissioned officers of Eagle squadron, the Cross of St. George, First Class.

"All officers below field grade of Bear Squadron are awarded The Order of St. George, Fourth Class; Field grade officers of Bear Squadron, with the exception of Lieutenant Colonel Elizabeth Bekenbaum and Major Irene Bekenbaum, are awarded the Order of St. George, Third Class.

"All below field grade officers of Eagle Squadron are awarded the Order of St. George, Second Class. Field grade officers of Eagle Squadron and Lieutenant Colonel Bekenbaum and Major Irene Bekenbaum are awarded the Order of St. George, First Class.

"Colonel Andreas Bekenbaum is awarded the Order of St. Alexander Nevsky and by order of Czar Alexander, promoted to Ataman, Andreashost.

"Major, Lieutenant Colonel, and Ataman Bekenbaum, ascend the podium."

The three officers handed the reins of their horses to subordinates and Elizabeth quickly unclipped the harness holding Stephan and handed him over to his nurse. The three officers arranged themselves in order of rank in front of the viscount. He went first to Johann placing the ribbon holding his medal over his neck and kissing him on each cheek. He then handed him an open box holding the same medal.

"This is Irene's, Johann, please accept this medal and my personal condolences."

"Thank you, sir. What about our two killed in action?" Johann asked.

"Their medals will be given to their families, Johann," the viscount replied, moving on to Elizabeth.

"Ilana and I can't express the pride we both have on your accomplishments, Elizabeth," the viscount told Elizabeth after he had hung her medal around her neck.

"Thank you, my lord," she said, her voice just over a whisper.

The viscount first took Andreas's colonels rank shoulder boards off and replaced them with ones that had a single general's star on them. Then, he hung the Order of St. George around his neck, followed by the Order of St. Alexander Nevsky.

"The point of your little demonstration has sunk home, Andreas; for the sake of decorum, please, have the proper uniforms for the reception. Ilana has put a lot of effort into the planning."

"Sir, yes, sir," said Andreas.

The viscount shook hands with the three of them, then took a step back, came to attention, and saluted them. "You can take them back to barracks now, Andreas," he said.

The three officers returned his salute and marched back to their horses, Andreas and Elizabeth mounting theirs. Andreas looked over at Elizabeth and nodded, then she and he separated, going to the heads of their units.

"Battalion, prepare to mount!" Andreas shouted. Waiting until the order had been passed from officer to officer down the line, then he shouted, "Mount!"

"Battalion, in columns of eight will pass in review in parade order. Execute!"

First the Eagles in columns of eight separated by one pace and squadrons by five paces expertly wheeled and trotted by the reviewing stand, followed by the wagons and mounted troopers of the Bears, Elizabeth at their head.

As Andreas was pulling his highly shined boots over his red-striped dress uniform trousers, Elizabeth came out of the bedroom with her maid in tow, putting the final touches on her dress.

"Oh my, the viscount is going to be upset, Liz. He told me dress uniform for tonight; somehow, I don't think what you're wearing qualifies," said Andreas.

She was wearing an extremely low cut, floor-length, dark blue silk dress, ruffled thin straps arranged at mid-arm leaving her neck and arms bare. Her Gräfin sash of office had her Order of St. George pinned to it and around her neck above her Adam's apple was a dark blue ribbon with her bear and rifle pinned to it.

"Why no, Andy, this is the proper uniform to attend a party for a women of my status. I want to be a woman tonight, not an officer. A woman you can be proud of," she said.

Andreas took her right hand in both of his kissed it and said, "If you were a milk maid, I would and always will be proud of you." As always, that was the right answer.

The party was large. Over three hundred people were there, ambassadors and diplomats from many countries, as well as all the local and more than a few of the Moscow aristocracy were in attendance. All wanted to be seen with the new bright stars of the Russian court.

Andreas found himself surrounded by those wanting to curry favor, or simply to be seen with him. Many had opinions on his triumphs and somehow felt they had been a part of it all.

"Lord Bekenbaum," a rotund boyar said. "How is it that you have been able to increase production and returns on your lands in such a dramatic and short time frame? I am envious. I receive nowhere near the returns you are obtaining."

"I ask one tenth of my tenants' production as rent and taxes," Andreas said. "Not the one third that all of you demand. That leaves more for my tenants to improve the lands or their herds and perhaps to make a small profit, which they will in turn spend buying better implements and allowing them more food and better accommodations, which leads to higher productivity."

"Which leads to higher productivity, which leads to more tax money," the boyar said. "I never thought of it like that before."

"If the czar raises your taxes so high that you cannot spend any money on improving your own lot, eventually the tax revenue will go down as your ability to repair or purchase improvements dwindles," Andreas said. "I keep ten percent of what I receive, send thirty percent to Moscow as required, and spend the rest on improving roads and building schools and medical facilities. So far, I have had to ask Moscow for nothing except for the normal military expenses."

"Is ten percent enough?" the man asked.

"My needs are simple, good sir. As are my dear wife's," Andreas said. "We have our own herds and lands that provide us with a generous income. We have helped start a shipping company and a seed cleaning mill. So our income is not dependant on only one source. We are looking at others, but being away from home for almost two years has put our plans somewhat behind schedule."

"That explains it then," a landed baron said. "If you would have been here and been dealing with the peasant riffraff on a daily basis, you would know better. You are young; you will learn."

"Yes, I am young, good sir, and I am always willing to learn," Andreas said. "Please, if you could enlighten me on where I am going wrong?"

"The peasants are only taking advantage of you," the man said. "They know you are young and inexperienced. They hide much of their production from you, then spend what they have on liquor and gambling. They do not respect you for being soft. The Russian peasant will only respect power and fear. You must project more of your power and make your people fear the consequences of your displeasure."

"This is how you manage your lands?" Andreas said.

"Yes, I find it works very well, and when the returns start to fall, I burn a few villages and expel the tenants as an example to the others."

"Too right," a British lord said, catching the tail end of the conversation. "The lazy buggers will take every advantage they can. I am clearing most of my land to pasturage for sheep. I receive a better return on the wool and have less tenants to worry about."

"But what of your grain fields?" Andreas said. "Are you not concerned you will not have enough grain to feed your people?"

"That is not my concern," the British lord said. "Parliament will address that issue. My concern is to maximize my profits and grow my estate."

The Russian and British landowners moved off discussing the various ways they both agreed to maximize profit leaving Andreas with the boyar, alone for the moment.

"That is a short-sighted vision," the boyar said. "Yours is much better I think. Like your vision of warfare, we landowners must change our way of doing things. Already the peasants are complaining. I can't blame them really. We rob them blind, leaving them little to live on, then expect them to fight for us to repel an invader that may be better for them than we are. I think I will try your way on a few villages this year and see how it works."

"If you can read English, you should read the book from Adam Smith, called the *Wealth of Nations*," Andreas said. "It has much to say on how a small change can have a big impact over time."

"The reason your people were asked to come here originally was to show us how to better our production," the man said. "I remember that. Now, your people are outdoing us, even though you started with nothing and those foolish aristocrats are jealous. Instead of doing the same as you are doing, they do the same as they always have and then complain to the czar about your unfair advantages."

"My people did not come here under the same circumstances as the German settlers," Andreas said. "We have no tax breaks and must serve in the army, just as every other Cossack family must. But I understand what you are saying. Already the czar has cut back on many of the agreements that were made with the German settlers. Don't forget, they had to pay back the cost of the land and the cost of resettlement first."

"And still they prosper and do better than our own people," the boyar said. "They took unproductive land, made it productive and profitable, now the lazy Russians cry foul and want it all. No wonder many of them are moving back home or thinking about it."

"Like I said to the Afghan elders," Andreas said. "First make sure your people have enough food to eat and crops to sell, to make life a little easier. Then think about doing other things. Unfortunately, many of the landed class do not think of these things and think it is their right to do what they will, forgetting it is the peasant that is making them their money."

"I think you will go far, young Andreas," the boyar said. "We need more men like you. Alas, I fear we are doomed to have more like this one that approaches. Good evening to you, my lord, and the best to your good lady, as well."

"Ah, see how the tradesmen scurry away from their betters, my lord," the young man in a Life Guards major's uniform with much gild and decorations on it said. He was a little older than Andreas, and his tailored and spotless uniform told of his wealth.

"His kind will never have the breeding to succeed in society, I think; don't you agree, my lord?"

"I would not know," Andreas said.

"Ah, yes, you are new to the landed class," the major said. "Well, I am sure you will find out soon enough about men like those. I am pleased to tell you that I have used my influence with Uncle Alexander and have been given permission to join your next expedition."

"Oh, yes?" Andreas said, narrowing his eyes slightly and looking the man over again.

"Oh, yes. Father has agreed that I be made colonel and is giving me a battalion of conscript infantry to go with the battalion of cavalry I already have at my command. You will be serving under my command, my lord, I hope you don't mind?"

"You have experience?" Andreas said.

"Oh, yes," the major said. "I have been on the staff for many years. The czar also took my recommendation not to send us to Turkey but to Kazakhstan instead. There will be more profit in land for both of us."

"You plan on subduing Kazakhstan with a battalion of conscript infantry and two battalions of cavalry?"

"Oh, no," the major said. "You will be supplying five thousand cavalry, three batteries of artillery, and five thousand infantry."

"Oh, I will be supplying fifteen thousand or so troops, and you will be in command?" Andreas said. "And how long will I have to raise that many troops? I cannot do it in the six months you have given me."

"Oh, your infantry can just be common peasant conscripts, only half of them need weapons," the major said. "I am sure the great Andreas will not have a problem recruiting skilled cavalrymen. In any case, I will not be ready for another year and a half. You have that long to prepare. I have read the account of your battle. I will be issuing you only our normal rifles. Your people used up too much expensive ammunition."

"Well, thank you for your consideration, Major," Andreas said. "I see my dear wife is beckoning me for what I am sure will be a long boring conversation with the viscount's lady."

"Your dear wife is telling me she is becoming tired, my lord Andreas," Ilana said, a twinkle in her eye. "After all, you have just returned from a long and strenuous travel. The viscount has given permission for you all to leave, as you must all be surely tired."

"Thank you, my lady," Andreas said.

"Come, I will escort you and your party to your carriages."

Ian ushered two men into the suite, both men were dressed in business attire, carrying briefcases.

"My lord, I would like to present Mr. Conway, Canadian Consul General and Mr. Patterson of the Canadian Immigration Department. Gentlemen, Earl Bekenbaum of Katherintal."

Andreas walked over and shook the men's hands. "A pleasure, gentlemen, please, come sit, some tea? Elizabeth, we have visitors."

Andreas introduced the two men to Elizabeth and all five sat at the sitting room table, the two servants pouring the tea then withdrawing. After expressing compliments and generalities for a few moments, Andreas got down to business.

"Mr. Conway, Captain McDonald has been invaluable to me. His bravery and courage is a testament to the personality of your

329

countrymen; please, convey to your government my high esteem and praise of this noble officer," Andreas said. "He has also informed me that you have a lot of empty land you would like to have settled, and I believe I can assist you in that area."

"Certainly my lord, what areas would you be interested in and how many settlers would we be talking about?" said Conway. "We have many areas bordering the Great Plains that have very good farming prospects and settlements in place that already have a number of towns and villages in place that would welcome new arrivals." As he spoke, he spread out a map, which depicted an area just to the north of the American border and west of Hudson Bay.

Andreas smiled and shook his head.

"No, I believe we are more interested in the land that borders the eastern slopes of the Rocky Mountains," he said.

"But there is nobody there! It is only inhabited by savages and gangs of illegal American traders. No, no, until we can send in a police force to clean it all up, it is totally unsuitable for settlers of your caliber, my lord," an astonished Conway said.

"I believe I said I could help you out, Mr. Conway. Please, don't let these opulent surroundings and the manner in which we are dressed today mislead you. Elizabeth and I are cattle and horse breeders; farming is but a small part of what we do. We would be coming with two thousand highly trained and disciplined cavalry troopers, complete with families and medical personnel. Most, if not all, of these troopers are educated and many have trades that will be required. We are not pampered European farmers. We are used to the frontier way of life, and this would not be much of a challenge to us."

"But we cannot have troops loyal to a foreign power controlling an area of... What size an area would you require?" said Conway.

"I believe two hundred thousand acres would be sufficient," replied Andreas.

Patterson placed his hand on Conway's arm.

"I believe my lord is a peer and Knight of the Realm? That would mean you are classed as a citizen of Great Britain, which in turn means a citizen of Canada, as well. These troopers hold allegiance to you?" he asked.

"Yes, they are all free men who have freely given their allegiance to me," Andreas said.

"You would be willing to swear allegiance to Queen Victoria and her representatives?" he asked. "That won't cause a problem with you and your present government?"

Andreas and Elizabeth both smiled.

"Not at all," said Elizabeth. "Despite all their honors and titles and their presumption of allegiance, they have neglected to ask us to formally commit. We, all of us, are free men and women and can do or go where and what we want."

Then Patterson smiled, rose, and extended his hand to Andreas, who rose and accepted it.

"Then, my lord and lady, I think we have a deal," he said. "We will go over the final details with you later, but in return for settling and helping to civilize the area, I don't think deeding the land you are asking for in return will be a problem."

"Mr. Conway, a fully trained and veteran battalion, used to the conditions they are likely to face is more than we can dream for. The police force is only a vision and two or three years away from reality. This would go a long way to solving the problems we face."

"How soon could you be ready, my lord?"

"Depending on transportation and arranging transit from the United States," Andreas said, "as soon as January this year or, at the latest, next year. The sooner the better, I think. Elizabeth and I have been planning this for a year already. Captain McDonald and Mr. Remington made up our minds for us, telling us of the lands and people."

"I will begin arrangements for transportation and the land title procedures immediately," said Conway. "We can utilize McDonald as liaison?"

"Agreed," said Andreas and with a final handshake all around, the three men left.

"You know, Andy," said Elizabeth, "I believe they are more excited about this than we are."

The battalion pulled out of Odessa an hour after dawn Thursday morning. Being so close to home and the troops becoming restless after three days off, it was felt the time to go had come. They left in their by now standard travel formation, five hundred Eagles in front and five hundred behind the Bears, who interspersed ranks of two-wheeled supply wagons with their own ranks of mounted troopers. Once again, the streets were lined with cheering crowds of well-wishers as the battalion left the city as fast as it had entered it.

As they began the climb of the last hill before the valley that held the villa, Andreas called the four sub-lieutenants he used as messengers to his side.

"Officers meeting, all officers, officers mess, two hours after dismissal," he ordered. The four men spurred up and down the line spreading the word to squadron commanders, who then had their own messengers spread it to the officers under them.

Andreas pulled Bartholomew to the upwind side of the column and stood looking at the home he had left almost a year ago, spread out in the valley below. Elizabeth drew up beside him, today she had their son in the harness before her. Together, they watched the battalion enter the villa, the inhabitants of which were waving and cheering, wives and sweethearts clutching horses and being grabbed by troopers and placed on the saddles before them. When the last of the troopers had dispersed to handle their horses, Andreas and Elizabeth rode slowly down the hill, headed for his headquarters office. As they dismounted and tied their horses to the hitching post outside, the nurse that cared for Stephan and her husband came by and not heeding Elizabeth's protests, carted him away with them, saying they could have him back in the morning. They took the two horses with them when they left.

Andreas walked into the office he had not used for ten months and looked around, Elizabeth following him in shutting the door behind her.

"Well, I guess I can review some reports for two hours until the meeting," he said.

"I have a better idea," he heard Elizabeth say.

He turned around to see that she had already removed her blouse and was in the process of undoing her pants as her bare back was walking to the room he used as a temporary bedroom. Her trousers hitting the floor, she turned at the waist and crooked

333

her finger at him before sprinting into the bedroom, Andreas in hot pursuit.

Two hours later, the assembled officers sprang to attention as Andreas and Elizabeth entered the room and marched to the front. He motioned them all to sit, and he and Elizabeth stayed standing at ease until the last had sat.

"Tomorrow afternoon, we will hold our awards ceremony," he began. "I will decorate the field grade officers, the field grade officers will decorate their officers, and the officers will decorate their men. If we don't do it that way, we'll be at this for two days, and I am sure that the lot of you want to get busy baby making."

The room erupted in laughter and was just beginning to settle down, when Katia burst out, "And just what were you doing for the last two hours?" she said.

"Why, I'll have you know," replied Elizabeth, "I was riding my stallion, dear sister, just like you were."

The room erupted again with a very red-faced Katia trying to hide behind Ivan.

"Alright, settle down," said a still chuckling Andreas. "I have a proposal I would like you to hear and think about, then tell your men before muster tomorrow.

"I have accepted a commission from the British to pacify and settle one of their territories called Canada. It is a one-way trip. I have promised them two thousand men and families and if possible, I would like it to be you Bears and Eagles. I want to make this perfectly clear, Elizabeth and I are going and anyone else that wants to come will do so voluntarily. I will not force or compel anyone to come that does not want to and will release anyone from their oaths to me if they don't want to join us."

"What will we be doing if we stay," came from a captain in the group.

"I believe that high command has plans to conduct operations against the Ottomans next year. You would be deployed to that region to take a series of fortifications that the czar wants under his control, or you will be going to Kazakhstan on a similar mission to what we are proposing, but with much higher risk," answered Andreas.

"Again, tell your men before parade muster tomorrow. I would like to hear from them one way or another by next Friday. Good evening, everyone. My lady," he said, offering her his arm and as the room sprang to attention, they left the officers mess headed for the main house.

They were intercepted by Stephan's nurse and her husband, an officer in the Eagles, before they reached the house.

"My lord, lady," she said, "we will be coming with you."

"No, dear," said Elizabeth, "you and your husband take your time and think about it. Don't make a hasty decision."

"No, sir," the husband said, "we have been talking about it for months now; most of the officers have, and I am sure most of the men too. We knew you were planning on leaving, just not where. Where you go, my wife and I follow," he said firmly.

"Captain," said Andreas, "the trip is one-way. We go by boat as far as we went to get to Afghanistan, then we go overland as far again. It is, for the most part, uninhabited country. Everything we need, we will have to bring with us. The people that are there do not speak our language. It will be hard."

"My lord, do you think the czar thinks about that when he sends us to Kurdistan or Siberia for the same reasons. Have you ever seen anybody come back from there? No, when we are no longer useful to him or become too powerful, he will send us away and hope we die. At least this way, I have a choice. With the Russians, we will have none," said the man with finality in his voice, and they walked away, Stephan still in the nurse's arms.

The inner circle came into the dining room as a group and arranged themselves around it. When everyone was finally settled, William began to speak in English.

"Why now, my lord? You have all this to lose," he said, gesturing to the room around him. "You have fame, large landholdings, and a fine reputation."

"Elizabeth and I together own eight hundred acres, the rest we hold at the pleasure of the czar. Should we incur his displeasure, or if one of the royal family or their toadies decide they want it, the czar will take it all back. If we stay, next year we will be ordered to attack some very well fortified fortresses. Should we succeed, the next year we will be asked to do something more difficult, until we die or become too famous, then they will ship us off to some other God-forsaken place and be forgotten. The men that serve under me have even less, they depend on me; if I am removed, the next commander will most likely not care for them as I do.

"In America, what you make or build is yours. Here, they can take it away, or have you disgraced or arrested on a whim or killed. We have gone generations, indeed, hundreds of years fighting and killing each other; this time with this country, next time with another against the first. Each of us only want to live and grow and feed our families. Yet every year, the best of us is sent to die, for what? Not some ideal or freedom, but for greed and land for a ruler. When we have a fool for a ruler, like this Nicolas is going to be, we starve or die or both, because of his ill-advised judgments. If you have a ruler like that, you vote him out and get a new one.

"I release all of you from any allegiance no matter what kind that you have or think you owe me. I must do what I think is right for me and my descendants, I will hold no one as I am held."

With that, Andreas got up from the table and left the house.

The group sat in silence for a few moments before the three North Americans looked at each other and rose from the table and silently headed for the door, leaving only family behind.

"He loves all of you almost as much as he loves me," Elizabeth said. "Right now, he is with the only one he feels does not judge him. Who takes him as he is. Sometimes my Andy is so alone, you all think he is so strong, that he needs no one. Right now, he is down with his only friend agonizing over whether he is making the right decision or not. I cannot help him with this." Then Elizabeth also rose and walked to the office room where she and Andreas had spent so many happy moments together. Katia bolted out of the chair and caught her sister.

"Can you do nothing to help him, Lizbet?" she asked.

"No, not this time," Elizabeth said. "You see, Sister, I feel as he does, but I have you and I am not afraid to ask for help."

Andreas was stroking Bartholomew's neck when his ears pricked up and Andreas felt a presence on each side of him.

"You know, I think I'm going to get that horse drunk one day. Maybe he'll tell me all your secrets," said Johann.

Andreas smiled a small smile, then Marie put her arm around him and laid her head on his shoulder.

"We can't know all that God has in store for us, Andy," she said. "I do know that if we stay here my husband and perhaps my son, will be gone for most of their lives and possibly die for people who don't care. We will be coming."

Johann placed his hand on Andreas's shoulder and said, "Brother, you and I have spent the night sharing blankets in blizzards; we have saved each other's lives, been rained on, starved, and spent countless nights on guard or patrolling. You were there for me when I married Irene, and you were there for me when she died. I see now what Papa did and how he agonized over it. When we leave here, we will never come back, never see loved ones or places again. My Susanna deserves better than this; I deserve better than this. I will be coming, Brother." Then, shocking Andreas, he kissed him on the cheek.

"Come, that hay burner has had enough of your attention. Your lovely Liz is waiting. She needs you now."

Andreas put the final signature on the papers before him, stood, and donned his dark blue tunic over his white blouse and pulled it down over his red-striped trousers. As he buckled his sword belt and made sure it was hanging properly, Elizabeth walked out of the small bedroom, making sure her sword would hang properly over the ankle-length, red-striped skirt she wore instead of trousers today.

"At the risk of ruining the fine polish on our boots, I believe walking is preferable today," Andreas said, kissing her. "I wouldn't want you to wrinkle that beautiful skirt."

"Ha," she replied, "you just don't want anyone to see my bare calves but yourself."

338

"And beautiful calves they are, too," he laughed as they walked out onto the porch.

He grabbed Stephan from the nurse and her husband who were waiting on the porch placing him on his right hip. "Not today, Captain, today is your day; please, join your troop mates and enjoy the day."

Andreas steadfastly refused to give his son up to the many offers he received as they made their way to the parade ground, only relinquishing him to his grandmother, who had yet to see him. As his father stood to attention and began to salute him, Andreas pulled him to him and hugged him instead. The two men held each other for some moments before they slapped each other's backs and broke apart.

Andreas kissed his mother on the cheek and gently pried his son from her arms. "He is as much a part of this as we are, Momma," he said.

Elizabeth nodded towards the end of the parade ground where a trooper was waving a small flag to signal them that all was in readiness and the couple with Stephan now on Andreas's left hip climbed up to stand on the small raised podium.

A flurry of orders could be heard and the battalion in columns of eight marched onto the parade ground squadron by squadron, in their blue tunic and red-striped trouser or skirted dress uniforms. Female officers with children, like Andreas, had them hoisted on left hips. As the first row passed the podium, Andreas and Elizabeth saluted and held the salute until the last row had passed them. When they had formed in their squadrons before him and been placed at ease, Andreas began to speak.

"We are here today to honor you for your valor, courage, and sacrifice. None of these watching will know the terror of the thundering hooves approaching you, the roar of the rifles, the stink of the gunpowder. All of us think we know, but none really do, what hell each of us was experiencing as those horses came closer and closer, when they broke through our lines and injured or killed our comrades. We are here to honor you who have come home and those that did not. May God keep you always in His thoughts."

He then called the field grade officers to the podium, personally awarding them their medal, pinning Irene's to Susanna's dress. Elizabeth kissed each officer on both cheeks before handing them a box. In this fashion, each trooper received their award until one private was left. The private, joined by a grey-haired veteran and a middle-aged woman, climbed to the top of the podium. Andreas first pinned the St. George Cross, First Class to the trooper, who moved to stand beside Elizabeth, then hung the Order of St. George, Third Class on first, the mother of the first trooper killed, then on the grandfather of the second. Johann joined the two civilians on the podium, holding Susanna to his chest.

"Attention!" Andreas barked. "Present!" the whole battalion crashed to attention and rendered the hand salute. "Hurrah! Hurrah! Hurrah!" the battalion shouted in unison to the three representatives of their fallen comrades.

Johann approached Elizabeth and handed Susanna to her, then walked to the front of the podium.

"Comrades in arms!" he shouted out. "Last night, you were asked to consider a proposal. You were asked to consider this proposal carefully and to report back here next week with your answer. You have unanimously reported to your officers that you wish to make your decision known now." He paused, looking at the assembled troops squadron by squadron.

"Troopers of the Bears and Eagles, all those in favor of the proposal, take one step forward."

With a resounding crash, two thousand pairs of boots took one step forward. One step that would change theirs and their descendants' lives forever.

The family was gathered around the extended dining room table. Included were Ivan's mother and father.

"I apologize for the abrupt way you learned of this news," said Andreas to the elder Bekenbaum's. "I had hoped that the troops would take the week I gave them to consider the proposal. I would have informed you of our plans in a more suitable way. I have accepted a commission from the British to settle and domesticate one of their colonies called Canada. I will be receiving two hundred fifty thousand acres of deeded land as compensation. This land will be distributed amongst those that accompany us."

"My God," said his father, "that's as big as the whole district of Odessa, and you say it's deeded, not held at the pleasure of some lord? How big is this country?"

"Yes, it's deeded in my name," Andreas said. "The country is almost as big as Russia, and the interior is almost uninhabited steppes. There are perhaps twenty thousand nomadic hunter-gatherers living in small family groups scattered in an large area about one thousand miles from east to west, and perhaps five hundred miles north to south. I am told it is only one third of the country. Most of the population is on the eastern end and is split between the English and an old French colony that the French ceded to the English well before Napoleon. A rugged mountainous area separates the eastern portion from the interior, which is what they call the Great Plains. These run until they reach even higher and more rugged mountains, which stretch from Alaska to Mexico and to the Pacific Ocean. Our lands will be in the foothills and lower slopes of those mountains just up from the United States border."

He went on to explain that Elizabeth's lands and holdings had already been liquidated and his own were in the final phase of being sold. The rents and taxes he was allowed under the Russian agreement were still in force until the end of the year. All of this and including the money he still had left from the bet he had won the year before, would pay all the costs for transporting the people and goods to where they were going to start the overland portion of the journey. Draft horses, livestock, implements, foodstuffs, and lumber to build the transport carts would be purchased locally. Only the Eagles would be allowed one horse each to transport. Baggage would be kept to minimum; wheat and barley seed as well as some shrubbery seed would be taken along.

"Would you want to come along? We have room for you," Andreas asked his father and uncle.

"Thank you, but no," his father said. "We have been discussing going back to Germany, all of us. Most of the younger sons are going with you, the eldest were born here and will most likely stay. For us, there is nothing for us here. Your sister Ingrid's husband has accepted a position with the German government, and they are moving back. Heiner is already running our estates in Cologne. Johann and Marie are leaving with you; there is nothing holding us here," his father told him. "But what of the Russians? Will they let all of you leave?"

"They made me an officer and a noble on a whim," Andreas said. "The only condition was that as long as I held the commission and the title, I owed them certain services. I made no oaths, nor signed any papers. My men are my men, not Russia's men. They swore allegiance to me and are free to cancel that if they wish at the end of each campaign season. They have not. So, no, the Russians cannot hold us. They might try, but they can't afford alienating the rest of the hordes by stopping us by force. We are small, but well known, if they try and squash us now, it will cause problems. No, they will let us go, save them the problem of trying to have us killed for being too popular and a possible threat."

After a push on the arm and a stern look from Marie, Peter cleared his throat and said, "Excuse me, gentlemen. Marie has expressed an interest in meeting my family, I wonder if it would be possible for us to leave early? We could meet up with you later."

"It should not be much of a problem; I am unsure of the distances involved. Perhaps, you could stop by the office Monday morning; we can go over the maps and suggest a rendezvous point," Andreas replied.

Early Monday morning saw Andreas sending Ian to Odessa with some requests for information from his consulate and a request for an audience for Elizabeth and himself with the viscount. As Ian was leaving, William, Patrick, and Peter came in toting a batch of maps. The maps were spread out on the floor of the office. They showed major river routes, road networks, and railroads of the eastern and northern portions of the United States. Andreas listened as the three men discussed the merits and detriments of various routes and methods of getting from the east coast to the interior and up to the Canadian border. The discussion went on for a few hours before a general consensus was reached. They would make land fall at Baltimore, then proceed by rail to Omaha, switching to the Union Pacific Railroad to Fort Laramie, where they would head inland on the Bozeman Trail. Peter and Marie would visit Peter's parents in Minnesota, then link up with them at Fort Laramie. Patrick would go to Texas and meet some

343

of his ex-Confederate friends, buy one thousand head of cattle, and bring them up from Texas to Fort Laramie. William would head to Baltimore, arrange all the transport, purchase farm implements, lumber, livestock, and draft horses.

They would plan to reach Baltimore by the first of April, reaching Fort Laramie by May first, and leaving May fifteenth.

"Now all we need to do is figure out how to get from the head of the Bozeman Trail to where we are going in Canada," William said. "We don't have any details on terrain or land routes. I heard the Piegan Tribe goes into that area as part of their northern range. If things are peaceful enough, we might be able to convince them to show us the way. Things have not been going well between the western tribes and us lately."

"Perhaps, I can help you gentlemen out in that area," came a voice from the door way. Rudy was standing there with an arm full of papers and a big grin on his face. "The British have been exploring and mapping the area for two hundred years and have very good maps. We should be able to find an easy route to our new settlement."

"Our new settlement?" Andreas asked.

"Our battalion's enlistment is up at the end of the year. Technically, even though we are not allowed in Britain itself, we are British Citizens. I, like you Andreas, am a peer. The Canadian government is overjoyed that we expressed an interest in immigrating to Canada and have given us fifty thousand acres of land next to yours, the British are paying for it as part of our pension. They are also going to pay for our transportation from Hamburg to . . . I see it will be Baltimore."

"Can you be there by April first?" Andreas asked. "You have to get from here to Hamburg."

"There are good rail links from Odessa to home," Rudy answered. "We will liquidate anything we have at home and board ship. The trip from Hamburg is shorter than yours, two weeks instead of three. If you would be kind enough to dispense with our horse flesh, we won't have to worry about transportation for them home, then selling them there."

"Vacilly will most likely take the lot of them," said Andreas. "They are good mounts and well trained, they will be an asset to him. I'm planning on taking all the Eagle squadron mounts with us. The rest of the herd will be disposed of. William assures me that there are plentiful mounts for sale in America to rebuild our herds. One thing more, every one speaks English there; how is your troopers' understanding of the language?"

"All of them have an understanding; we have been with the British for a long time."

"Better than us, then. From now on, have your troopers converse with even our German speakers in English. We will be having our English speakers training everyone at least in the basics, most of the Germans have rudimentary English already," Andreas said.

"Many of the native tribes understand French somewhat; they have been trading with the French for years. Do we have any French speakers?" asked William.

"Myself and a few others," said Andreas, "Rudy has a few more."

They spent the next while discussing a number of options for routes into Canada and types of provisions. When a tired and dusty Ian walked into the office and they realized the sun was going down, the discussions came to an end, each man leaving for his supper. Ian followed after handing Andreas two letters, confirming his appointments in Odessa on Wednesday.

345

The town was beginning to fill up with its winter residents from Moscow and more northern cities for their annual escape from the cold winters, and Elizabeth felt she would rather go home than spend a night in the hotel. Putting up with the stares and listening to the rude comments about their heritage while walking down the street was one thing, having to put up with it overnight was too much to ask for. They had opted to wear their normal clothing that day so they could ride to town instead of taking a carriage, so were not wearing the appropriate clothing normally associated with their stations. As they rode up the long drive to the viscount's estate, an open carriage with two immaculately dressed couples riding in it approached them. One of the women made a comment about dirty Cossacks as they passed them, which earned her a menacing look from Andreas; she was about to say something more, when the man opposite hushed her by smiling and saying something to her quietly.

"Good afternoon, Graf and Gräfin Bekenbaum, nice day for a ride," the man said, doffing his hat.

Andreas nodded his head back in return, still glaring at the outspoken woman, who had now turned white, lips trembling in fear.

"It's a good thing my husband has just had his lunch, my dear," Elizabeth said to the woman, "else he may have taken offense to your remark. Cossacks have terrible tempers when they are hungry."

Andreas looked at Elizabeth and the ugly look left his face as they both laughed at the woman's expense, which seemed to unnerve her even more. As they rode to the front entrance of the residence and pulled to a stop, a number of servants descended on them helping them dismount, leading their horses away, and ushering them in to the viscount's and viscountess's presence in the tea room. After a suitable amount of time of pleasantries, the viscount got down to business.

"How is the planning for next year's campaigning going? We are hoping to start a late March departure," the viscount said.

"I am afraid we will be unavailable, my lord," replied Andreas, "we have accepted a commission from the Canadians and will no longer be available for service to Russia."

Ilana became visibly angry and was about to say something to express her outrage, when the viscount put his hand on her arm to calm her down.

"So, you did remember our conversation back on the Austrian border and took advantage of the loop hole I provided for you. My spies have been telling me you were up to something, but not what. You see, my dear, Andreas is a free man; he serves us at his pleasure, not ours. They have given you acceptable terms, I presume? How many of you are leaving and how soon?"

"Yes, my lord," said Andreas, "the terms are very good; clear title to about one hundred and fifty square miles of land and immediate citizenship for all of us. All of the Bears and Eagles and their family members will be coming. More would like to, but they are not in the same position as we are. Everyone has, or is in the final process of disposing of all their assets, and I will be returning to your possession the lands I administer on your behalf at the beginning of January. We should be departing mid-February. You have received the taxes and rents for last year, my lord?"

"Yes, they were double what they were before you took over," answered the viscount. "What did you do differently?"

"I lowered the rents to what they were supposed to be; lowered the taxes to ten percent like they were supposed to be, instead of the thirty they were being charged. I kept twenty percent of that, as I am entitled to, and spent eighty percent of the rest fixing roads and bridges in the district."

"That is what I keep telling all those fools in my other districts, but they are all too greedy to see the big picture," said the viscount. "The rate everyone is going, the working people, who we all rely on, will not have enough left to pay for their necessities, and we will have a big problem on our hands."

The meeting ended on a positive note and the two couples walked arm-in-arm to the estate's entry way.

"What would you have done if my husband had not been so understanding and had you arrested Andreas?" Ilana asked.

"I would have done nothing," Andreas answered with a smile, "four thousand Cossacks would have done my talking for me, not to mention the sixty thousand other troops at my command."

Nodding at the viscount he continued, "A wise man once told me to tread lightly and carry a big stick. It looks like I won't be needing the big stick this time."

Characters

Eagles Bears and Beavers

Regimental motto; determination against all odds

Characters:

Andreas Bekenbaum, Earl and leader of the Cossack host.

Elizabeth Bekenbaum, Andreas's wife, Baroness in her own right and founder of the Host's medical corps.

Johannes Bekenbaum, Andrea's younger brother, member of the inner circle and commander of an eagle squadron.

Stephan Bekenbaum, Andreas's eldest son and heir.

Susan Bekenbaum Anderson, Johannes' eldest daughter

Ingrid Bekenbaum, Stephan's wife, an eagle and a bear.

John Bekenbaum, Andreas's youngest son.

Rudy von Hoeadle, Major of Kings Loyal German Cavalry Regiment and member of Andreas's inner council

Greta von Hoaedle, Rudy's wife

Ivan, Andreas's cousin and brother in law by marriage

Katia, Elizabeth's sister and Ivan's wife

Peter Chimilovich, blood Cossack, US Marine and Andreas's brother in law

Marie, Andreas's sister and Peter's wife

William Olyinick, Major, US Army, first Cavalry and member of Andreas's inner council

Patrick Asminov, US Army, First Cavalry, General in Confederate Army, member of Andreas's inner council

Ian McDonald, Canadian Military officer, liaison to the Cossack group, later superintendent of the North West Mounted Police

Bill Hancock, Texas Cowboy

Bartholomew, Andreas Bekenbaum's horse

Sammy, Wilhelmina Rosenthal, teenaged Texan girl masquerading as a cowboy

Bill Hasendorf, buffalo hunter.

Sergei Chimilovich, Peter's father

Inga Chimilovich, Sergei's wife

Leechang Yu, former body guard and instructor for the Chinese emperor, civil engineer

Chow Yu, Leechang's wife

Edward Stewart, horse wrangler and teacher

Mindy Stewart, his wife

Lionel Anderson, British officer and friend to Stephan Bekenbaum

Sergei Petrovitch Chimilovitch, Peter and Katia's son and Stephan Bekenbaums cousin.

Major Alex Hood, Coldstream Guards, British liaison to the Regiment during the Great War Campaigns

Colonel Edward Makarov, commander of the Eagles, Great War Campaigns.

Christine Bekenbaum, Johannes and Wilhelmina's youngest daughter, first female combat officer of the Regiment.

Tatiana Romanovchuck, (Romanov) last surviving member of the Czars family.

Nicolas Andreas Johnavitch Bekenbaum, Naj, first born son of John and Tatiana

Sandy Chimilovitch, second cousin to Nicolas Bekenbaum

Calvin Motz, Major Calgary Highlanders

Katherine Engelmann, Kat, wife of Nicolas Bekenbam

Ingrid Zimmerman, Major in the regiment

Hans von Bekenbaum, Colonel German Army